King of Sinners

DANIELLE SARAH NOUHA JULLIENNE

KING OF SINNERS
DANIELLE SARAH AND NOUHA JULLIENNE

Editing by Jennifer Innamorati, Night Owl Editing
Proofreading by Stevi Mager-Lightfoot, SML Editorial
Cover design by Crimsons Designs
Formatting by Melissa at To.All.The.Books.I.Love

This book is a work of fiction. All characters, places, incidents, and dialogue were created from the author's imagination. Nothing in this story should be constructed as real. Any similarities between persons living or dead are entirely accidental.

Naya

It's been a month since I left what happened in my past behind. I was looking for a new beginning, a new place to call home. And I found it in Springfield, Tennessee. But the guilt of leaving my sick papa behind, along with the stress of keeping my new veterinary clinic afloat, don't allow me to fully move on.

A new opportunity lands at my doorstep when I'm also offered a job as the new vet at the largest ranch in town. I accept, even though my client, Callan Hudson, is a grumpy and closed-off rancher who knows exactly how to get under my skin. I'm supposed to hate him, but he somehow makes me feel safe, cherished, seen.

When my old life catches up to me, I find myself in danger again, which pushes me more and more into the arms of my new nemesis. Eventually, I have to return to Raleigh, where I'm forced to face the demons of my past, causing me to question everything I thought I knew.

Callan

Being the Founder and President of the *Sinners & Saints*
Motorcycle Club is no small task. I didn't gain the name, *King*
for no reason. I'm ruthless when necessary, but protective of my
people. That aside, all my time and energy go into my ranch,
All Saints. The cowboy life is in my blood, after all.

When my stallion falls ill, I'm tasked with finding a new doctor.
But I never expected the vet to be a small, fiery pain in my ass.
Naya Ohara is a thorn in my side, the source of my frustration,
and everything I never knew I needed.

One day, the President of the Raleigh Riders, our rivals,
reappears fifteen years after an almost deadly encounter. But
what brings him to town so suddenly?

Naya's involvement soon becomes clear, and she's no longer
safe. My instinct to protect her makes me throw caution to the
wind. So, when she leaves, I decide to go after her, putting
myself and my crew at risk.

Trigger Warnings

Graphic violence, physical assault, gun violence, torture, decapitation, kidnapping, mild stalking, mention of parental death, mention of domestic abuse, mention of emotional and verbal abuse, mental health issues, mention of drug addiction/abuse, sexually explicit scenes (nudity, masturbation, mild breath play, mild degradation, impact play, anal play).

Anarchy - Odysseypark
Rise Up & Fight - Traitors to the Crown
Way down We Go - KALEO
Bleeding Out - Chance Pena
Last Resort - Reimagined - Falling In Reverse
ATTN: - Picturesque
I'll Follow You into the Dark (Cover) - Austin Criswell
A Little Bit Happy - TALK
Bleed - Elliot Greer
HEARTBEAT - Isabel LaRosa
BURNING IN DESIRE - Chris Grey
Talk - Hozier
I Feel A Sin Comin' On - Pistol Annies
Lydia - Highly Suspect
Wicked Game - Witchz
Twin flame - Brennan Story
Save a Horse (Ride a Cowboy) - Big & Rich

Kill Bill - SZA
Deli - Ice Spice
Best Friend (feat. Doja Cat) - Saweetie
Bitch Better Have My Money - Rihanna
Low - SZA
WAP (feat. Megan Thee Stallion) - Cardi B
Barbie World (with Aqua) - Nicki Minaj, Ice Spice
Area Codes - Kaliii
Bodak Yellow - Cardi B
Pour It Up - Rihanna
Feeling Myself - Nicki Minaj, Beyoncé
Vegas - Doja Cat
Thot Shit - Megan Thee Stallion
Paint the Town Red - Doja Cat
You Wish - Flyana Boss

Glossary

<u>Italian</u>

Testa di cazzo: Dickhead

Cazzo: Fuck

Stronzo: Motherfucker

Mi hai rotto il cazzo: You're being really fucking annoying.

Minchione: Idiot

Cagacazzi: Pain-in-the-ass

Cristo Santo: For God's sake

Bimba: Little girl

Cuore mio: My heart

Piccola puttanella: Little slut

Puttanella mia: My slut

Principessa: Princess

Mia cara: My darling

Lasciati andare, puttanella: Let it go, slut.

La mia brava piccola puttanella: My good little slut.

Amore: Love

Amore mio: My love

Sei l'amore della mia vita: You are the love of my life.

<u>Japanese</u>

Haru-kun: Sunshine
Watashi mo aitai: I miss you, too.
Nante koto da: What a horrible thing (oh my God)
Ohayo: Good morning
Moushi wake gozaimasen: There is no excuse (I'm sorry).
Iie: No

To everyone who wants to save a horse and ride a cowboy...
...who also rides a motorcycle and leads a gang...
...and unalives people.

Prologue

Fifteen Years Ago

I grab my new leather jacket, slipping it on like a second skin, and catch a glimpse of the back in the mirror across from my bed. I take a minute to really look at the insignia embroidered in the fabric.

'Sinners & Saints' is written in big letters across the top. An angel with large white wings sits right under, her neck exposed and bitten by a snake that hugs her body. The woman is surrounded by lilies and skulls.

It's hauntingly beautiful and carries so much meaning.

There are no saints without sinners.

The guys and I are headed to Hamilton's Tavern for our first gang meeting.

When I was granted leave from the Nashville Devils to start my own motorcycle club, it was hard to find a place that would accept us, but the Hamilton's always made me feel welcomed. In exchange for having access to their bar, we've promised them protection. Now that my parents are gone, Hank and Delilah are the closest thing I have to family.

A burn starts behind my eyes, tears forming, and I close

them. Every time they're shut, I'm back with my *mamma* and *papà*, and it brings me peace for a moment.

I look around my childhood room and all the memories of them. I swallow the lump in my throat and walk out the door.

Forty minutes later, I'm in front of the tavern. Knox is waiting for me outside.

"Took you long enough."

I tuck my helmet under my arm and glare at him. "Let it all out now because this behavior won't be tolerated once we step through those doors."

Knox sneers at me. "You might be the boss in there, but don't forget I can kick your ass out here."

"I'm older and stronger, Knox. We've been through this before."

"Only by two years, and last time I checked, we have the same strength," Knox retorts with a pout.

I snort and walk past him into the bar. "If you'll excuse me, I have actual important business to attend to."

Once inside, I greet Hank and Delilah, who are behind the bar, and grab a Dos Esquis. There are still a few guys missing, so the meeting will start when they arrive.

Knox sees a girl at the counter and immediately heads her way. I know what he's planning, so I shout, "Don't take too long!" He waves me off as he sits next to her.

A few minutes later, someone taps my shoulder and I turn to see him standing there with his new date. "Cal, this is Summer. We're headin' outside for a bit," Knox says with a smug grin.

The girl gives me a timid wave. "Hi."

"Nice to meet you, Summer." I glance at her attire and notice her apron. "Do you work here?"

"Yes, I'm new!" she quips. "I just got off my shift."

That explains why we've never seen her before.

"Well, have fun. Knox, an hour tops."

"Yes, Dad," Knox sing-songs.

A few of the missing gang members roll in. We've only been operating for a short time, so we're still building our crew. Most of the guys are neighborhood kids that Knox and I have known from our childhood. The others were referred to us by their friends.

We have no way to properly vet our members yet, so we're only taking their word for now. *Not very smart, but we need to start somewhere.*

It's almost been an hour since Knox stepped out, so I decide to check on him, grumbling and already preparing how to punish Knox if he delays us. On my way out, I see Rhett, one of my most trusted crew members, and two newcomers approach the entrance.

"Head on in, fellas. We're 'bout to start. I'll be back in a few minutes."

But instead of going inside, they follow me to the parking lot. When I turn around to confront them, they push me to the ground. My shoulder throbs from the direct hit.

"What the fuck are y'all doin'?" I yell, shielding my face from their vicious kicks.

"What makes you think we should take orders from you?" one of them spits.

The other shouts, "We don't need someone new tryin' to run these streets!"

"Rhett, what is goin' on?" I snarl, trying to get off the asphalt and dodge their blows. Thankfully, I have my leather jacket on, which protects my back from getting scratched. My ribs, however, are taking a beating.

I hiss when Rhett's boot connects with the side of my skull. Pain explodes in my head with a blinding whiteness, and black spots appear for a few seconds before I'm able to move again.

Everyone is inside, so I doubt they can hear the commotion, and I can't spot Knox. I call out for him, but there's no response.

"No one's comin' to save you," Rhett states as all three men pull out knives from their waistbands. Confusion swarms in my head, but it's short lived as I'm consumed with dread.

One of them grabs me from behind in a chokehold and drags me farther into the lot, while the two others alternate between holding me down and attempting to slash me with a knife. My survival instinct kicks in and I'm able to knock one in the face with my boot, but Rhett succeeds in piercing the knife through my jacket, opening a deep wound across my ribs.

"This is from Mason," he seethes.

Agony shoots up my body like fire. It makes me dizzy.

Then, they leave me on the ground to die.

Just as darkness is about to close in, I feel a pressure at the side of my throat and hear Knox's muffled voice yelling to someone. "His heartbeat is slowin' by the second. Put him in my truck and take him to the hospital, right now!"

The rest is a blur.

When I finally come to, I hear Knox talking to my old boss, Jesse, the President of the Nashville Devils. Both are standing at the edge of the bed in my hospital room.

"Callan wasn't protected, he trusted those men." Knox lets out a breath, a look of disbelief on his face. "I was headed back into the bar and saw a limp body layin' in a pool of blood. I recognized him right away. I left him alone in the bar for an hour, and came back to him almost fuckin' dead in the parkin' lot." Knox's voice is choked. "A few of the guys had the idea that they could run things better than Callan. It was an unfair attack; three against one, and they were armed with knives."

A jolt of anger runs through my body and realization dawns on me as I recall Rhett's words. "Mason," I croak, my throat dry.

Knox's and Jesse's heads whip toward me. "Fuck, Callan! You're awake."

"Mason," I rasp again.

Knox shoots me a quizzical look. "Mason who?"

Jesse intervenes, his face a look of pure fury as he spits out, "Mason Caldwell. The Raleigh Riders."

I grasp the hospital bed sheets with both hands, quivering with rage.

When the time comes, I will get my revenge. I will end them.

1
Callan

"**G**et on your knees or sit on my cock. Your choice. Make it now or I'll make it for you."

The blonde's breathing becomes ragged as she contemplates her decision, her face a mixture of confusion and arousal.

What I said was crass, but I don't give a shit. She either takes it or leaves it. It's not everyday you get to fuck the president of the Sinners & Saints Motorcycle Club. And if that's what she truly wants, she's got options.

The woman kneels between my legs in the back of my truck, keeping her big, hazed eyes on mine. She looks like a doll.

I motion for her to lift her skirt and she inches it over her hips, exposing her bare ass. My dick twitches.

I crack the window. The glass is getting foggy and it's hot as Hell in this leather jacket. People will probably see and hear us now, but no one will dare interrupt. We're in *my* parking lot, on *my* property, and I own the cops in this town. It's handy to have them on payroll; it keeps things running smoothly.

I put my head back on the headrest as the Barbie-looking girl slides her lips up and down my length. She's taking me like a pro, eager to please. I let out a low growl, the feeling of her mouth around me sending the blood straight to my cock. My chest heaves as my orgasm nears the edge. I gather her blonde locks in my hand and pull her head up, making her wince from the strain. I don't want to come in her mouth.

I'm rough in bed. Most women love it. And it's the case with *what's her face* from her flushed cheeks and the smell of her arousal in the air. I don't even know this girl's name, and I'm about to pound her out. I might be an asshole, but there's no fucking way I'm bringing her back to my place; that's my sacred space, and no woman has crossed that threshold in a long time. And I'm sure as hell not going back to hers. If she wants to have sex with me, it'll have to be in the back of my truck. A quick fuck. *Wham bam, thank you, ma'am.*

I pull a condom out of my back pocket and throw it at Barbie. No raw dogging for me today, or ever. If there's one thing I'm certain of, there aren't any mini Callans running around town.

She tears the wrapper open and holds the piece of rubber between her fingers. I let go of her head as I push my pants down lower, letting her roll the protection on me.

"Ride me. Don't stop until you come. And don't even fuckin' think of kissin' me."

She obeys immediately.

Damn. This feels good, and the perfect distraction I needed from the constant, intrusive thoughts in my brain about work.

I ended up at The Crown for a meeting with my accountant, Henry. The pub was previously owned by a nice couple in their early forties, not much older than I am now. I had been a regular at their bar for a while and got pretty close to them. Weeks after a dreadful altercation in the parking lot in which I was involved, I approached them with a buyout offer—a way to cover the damage, too—and they agreed to sell.

What better way to legitimize my already thriving business? Unlimited beers for me, easy write-offs. The perfect hustle for laundering illegal money.

Henry is the only man I trust to oversee the Sinners & Saints books. He makes sure the cash flow is moving the way it should, and that everything looks above board in case the IRS decides to spring an audit on us. Most importantly, he knows how to keep his fucking mouth shut.

I wish this woman on top of me would keep her mouth shut, too. It feels good, but her drunken moans are distracting.

My accountant spent most of the afternoon giving me a rundown of the different financials for the first six months of the year. Most of it went above my head, especially when he threw around words like "futures" and "derivatives."

I groan as Barbie picks up her movements, her head thrown back as she cries out. I place one hand on her throat while I grip her hip with the other and start to thrust.

So tight.

The gist of the meeting was that S&S is sitting pretty with more gains than losses, and Henry doesn't foresee any budgetary issues.

Good. I've put my sweat, blood, and tears into this club.

I pinch Barbie's nipple as I keep pounding into her, warmth pooling in my groin.

Years ago, when I realized I'd need more money to take care of my mother, I'd ventured out into the city and gone around the bars where bikers would hang out. I was eighteen years old and had thought I was a *man*. I had just recently gotten my motorcycle license, so I felt like a badass.

Turns out, I wasn't. I got chewed up and spat back out by the older gang members, used as an errand boy.

The memory is a reminder of how far I've come.

I pull up in the parking lot of the town's busiest bar with my used Harley Davidson bike I saved up for. The revving of the engine gets the attention of the many bikers posted up on their motorcycles. They're older, scarier, stronger, but I'm sure they'll want fresh meat. Someone who can keep up.

"What do we have here?" one of the men asks.

Another laughs. "Looks like a lamb who doesn't know it's just walked into a lion's den."

I walk up to them, confident. I know I won't be able to defend myself in a fight—there are too many of them—but I need to show them I'm not scared. "That's funny. Comin' from old folk like y'all, I thought you'd appreciate my directness."

The first man who spoke, the leader, I assume, pushes himself off his bike and walks over to me. I cross my arms over my chest, hoping it'll make me look tougher than I feel, as he comes right up to my face. "Say that again, you little fucker."

"I said, y'all are old and could use someone like me." Not exactly my words, but that's what I meant.

The man punches me in the gut and vomit flies out of my mouth on contact. Fuck.

"That's for thinkin' you're hot shit, boy. You wanna act like a man? Then, take a beatin' like one."

He and three other men beat the shit out of me that night, and by the end of it, I could barely stand. I thought I had what it took to be in a gang.

They were still impressed by my tenacity, so they took me in as their little bitch, and I agreed. Anything to help my *mamma*. She needed me to provide for her, so I did what I had to do.

"Turn around," I tell Barbie. I can feel my balls tingling and don't want to see her face as I come.

Eventually, I climbed up the ranks of the Nashville Devils and the president of the motorcycle club, Jesse, became my mentor. I learned a lot about the ins and outs of leading a gang.

Three years later, I created Sinners & Saints. I'm the

current president, and together with my second- and third-in-command, we monitor the daily activities of our crew. But I've been able to take a few steps back when needed to focus on other things. My two henchmen are capable of dealing with the rowdiness of the guys without me.

Barbie starts rubbing her clit in circular motions. "That's it. Make yourself come," I say, my voice strained.

Her pussy tightens around my cock, my words giving her the push she needed.

"Oh my God!" the blonde yells. "Yes, yes, yes!" She spasms around me.

"Fuuuuuuuck," I grunt as my cum spurs out into the condom, my thrusts becoming erratic.

A few minutes later, Barbie heads back inside the bar. I pull out my phone and see a message from Knox Davenport, my best friend and right-hand man.

> Dav: You nasty little fucker. I saw you bangin in the truck.

I let out a scoff. I knew we'd be caught by someone.

"Line up the shots!" Davenport hollers through his cupped hands from the other end of the bar.

I take a sip of my beer. The Dos Esquis goes down smoothly. I always make sure to have my favorite brands in the bar. "Summer, another one of these, please," I ask, gesturing with my drink to the bartender. "And not that shit in a bottle. Get me a glass." Beer always tastes better when it's straight out of the tap.

I glare at Knox. He knows I just came here for the meeting, not to have fucking a party and get drunk. Barbie was a much-needed and appreciated distraction, but now we need to focus.

But once Knox gets going, no one can stop him, not even me. His energy is too contagious, and I'm the only one immune to it. I'm used to his ways by now, having known him since we were young boys when we learned to ride horses together, then bikes as we got older.

Sometimes I want to go back in time, look at the blonde, smiling kid who came up to me that first day of training, and tell him to fuck off. Who approaches a kid who is clearly uninterested in making friends? Knox Davenport, that's who. He ignored my grumpiness and latched on.

But life wouldn't be the same without my brother. We've grown together in life and in business.

Knox hollers again and I wince. I can feel a headache creeping in. I bow my head, rub my temples, and curse through my lips as I watch Summer place little shot glasses on a tray and slide them down the smooth wooden bar top and over to Knox. It's Christmas in July apparently because Knox is giving everyone free drinks like he owns the place.

Summer smirks as she puts the last shot on the counter. She knows I'm not having this bullshit.

"He's gonna make me regret this, isn't he?" I mumble to her. The dumbass is already drunk.

"Yup!" she replies, with a suspicious amount of glee.

"JÄGERBOMBS!" Davenport screams as the patrons of the bar erupt in cheer. It's a fucking shit show and it's not even midnight. The place is packed, and the heat from all the bodies in the building has me wanting to step outside to get some air.

Knox saunters over to me and tucks his blonde hair behind his ears like he's about to lay it on thick. I prepare myself for the rant that's about to come, and I'm contemplating if I should just punch him in the throat or on the nose to save time.

"You need to loosen up, dude. Have some fun," he slurs.

I grunt. *"Cagacazzi." Pain-in-the-ass.* "You're relentless. Both of us can't be drunk tonight, Dav."

Knox rolls his eyes. "No one said you had to get *drunk*." He passes me one of the two shots he's holding, clinks his glass to mine, and says, "Drink up, buttercup."

I sigh in defeat and in laziness. I don't have the energy to argue with a grown man who throws tantrums like a two-year-old when he wants something he can't get.

"Cheers, Blondie," I reply.

He gives me the side-eye right before bringing the glass of Jägerbomb to his lips. "I hate it when you call me Blondie."

I shrug my shoulders. "I know, that's why I do it. I love fuckin' with you. It's the only way I can tolerate your annoyin' ass." Plus, with his long, blonde hair, he looks like he definitely could be in a L'Oréal commercial.

I swallow my drink and my face twists from the burn of the alcohol running down my throat.

"Ah." I exhale as I slam the glass down on the bar. It didn't take much for him to convince me to drink it, but what's the harm in one shot?

"You're messin' up my game by callin' me that bullshit nickname."

A smile creeps on my lips. "What game, Dav? You mean the one where you rely on me to pick up chicks 'cause you know they wouldn't approach you with a ten-foot pole if you weren't with your hot best friend?" I say, smugly.

I might not give a shit about taking women home, but I know I'm a good-looking guy. I'm not short of prospects at all, I just don't care. Most women in Springfield want to get married and have children. The ones who are here in Nashville only want to get with me because they know who I am.

Callan Matteo Hudson. President of the Sinners & Saints Motorcycle Club, owner of many lucrative establishments, including this bar, The Crown Pub.

Knox looks like a deer in headlights after my comment, and I burst out laughing. I'm not the type of person you'll notice or hear in a crowd, I'd rather stay in the shadows, but some things are worth a good chuckle.

I look around. Everyone is engaged in conversation and having a great time. I can hear the music getting louder and laughs filling the air.

Knox shoves my shoulder with a grin. "You're a piece of shit. Wouldn't get a smile out of you if I showed you a video of babies gigglin', but if it's at my expense, you'll gladly roll on the floor laughin'."

"Stop bein' so fuckin' dramatic, Blondie."

"How'd it go with the girl in your truck, anyway?"

I scrunch my nose. "Meh. A fuck is a fuck."

Knox laughs. "You're a heartless prick."

"You're a hopeless romantic," I retort. Knox is a lover boy. Every girl he sleeps with, he ends up getting attached to. Even if she's no good for him. We'll probably be in the bar a month from now drinking over how some chick fucked him over. He never learns his lesson.

As if the universe read my mind...

"One o'clock. I call dibs," Knox says as he tries to look casual by slipping onto the stool next to me. I glance to the other end of the bar and see a brown-haired woman unmistakably giving us 'fuck me' eyes.

I purse my lips. First, I get suckered into a party at my own bar. Now, Knox is forcing me to be his wingman. I refuse to be dragged into his shenanigans, but it's too late. Just as I'm about to tell him to fuck off, the girl is no longer at her seat and is coming straight toward us. *Goddamn it.*

"Hey, cowboy. You were lookin' a bit lonely. Thought I'd keep you company," she purrs to Dav. "Who's your friend?" she asks, taking my hat to put it on her head.

Is she trying to get both of us to leave with her? That's bold.

In my world, if you wear a cowboy's hat, it means you're going home with him, and that's not what I'm looking for tonight. I snatch the hat off her head and she staggers back a little, shocked. I put it on and tip it forward to hide my eyes.

Knox shoots laser beams at me and mouths, "Don't fuck this up for me."

I grunt in response and shoo him away. Luckily, the brunette gives up on me and focuses all her attention on my best friend. Fucking perfect.

She takes his hand and leads him to a back booth for more privacy. *Alright, my work here is done.*

I take the last swig of my beer and head out the back door.

When I'm back in my truck, I open the glove compartment for my cigarette case. The smell of marijuana hits my nose. I take a joint out, put it to my mouth and light it, taking a large inhale of the drug. The smoke goes down my lungs, my body mellowing.

I blow the smoke out the window and close my eyes.

There's nothing waiting for me at home, but I decide to go back to the ranch anyway. So, I put out the joint and place it back in the container.

I've had a long fucking day. Between the pub and the ranch, there are days where I barely make it to bed.

Some of my cattle tore down a part of the fence, so I had to replace it, with no help from my trusted ranch foreman. Tucker had to go home to his pregnant wife, who was having contractions or some shit. I sound bitter, but I'm genuinely happy for him. I just wish it had happened when the fence wasn't broken.

I don't see myself ever settling down and starting a family. There was a time I thought I could have had that—with Alison.

My jaw tightens, and my hands flex open and closed. I shake away those thoughts. I'm not interested anymore.

I've got my ranch, my businesses, and my crew. That's all I need. Nothing more, nothing less.

I bought the All Saints Ranch in Springfield a few years ago, when I decided it was time to sell my family ranch. I made a lot of money through other ventures and decided it was time to upgrade. More space for my people, cattle, and horses. I wanted to have enough acreage to build a horse haven, and that I did.

I pull up to the main residence on my property, nodding as I pass the security guard at the entrance to the long driveway, and park my truck in front of the door.

I kept the porch lights on when I left, so even though it's pitch black outside, the entirety of the house is cast in a warm glow. As I step inside, I hear the sound of Harley and Davidson, my two German shepherds, racing to meet me at the door. What started as a joke to name them after my favorite motorcycle brand ended up sticking, and I couldn't imagine them with any other names.

They round the corner of the hallway, bumping into each other and nearly tipping over the entry table by the door. I reach down, scratching each of them behind the ears.

"Hey boys." I kneel so I'm eye level with them. "What have you two been up to while I was gone?"

Harlo lifts his paws onto my chest and licks my face. I back away and laugh, a warm feeling spreading through my chest. They might be large, herding dogs, but they're loving and affectionate.

The property is completely fenced in and secure, so I let them roam the land; but after the cattle destroyed the barricade, I decided to keep them inside until it's fixed.

I give them each another rub under their muzzles before I rise to my full height and head for the bedroom, both of them trailing on my heels. I kick off my boots and take off the leather jacket that's been keeping me warm all evening.

I can still smell the cheap perfume Barbie had on, clinging to my shirt like a bad memory. I want to take a shower and wash the obnoxious floral smell off my skin.

I take in my reflection in the large mirror of my bathroom. My long hair looks disheveled, and I attempt to run my hand through it to fix it. There are a couple of scratches on the top of my shoulders where Barbie tried to find purchase as she rode me. Those will fade, but the large scar that runs down diagonally from my left pec to the middle of my abdomen won't be fading anytime soon.

I grind my teeth as memories of that night begin to surface. *Not tonight, Callan.*

The hot spray of the shower beats down on my back, removing the tension of the day better than the cumulative time I spent out at the bar. When I get out, I'm less stiff. Not enough to get rid of my stress, apparently. I run a hand through my wet hair before tying it in a loose bun and sighing. *Whiskey. I need whiskey.*

I throw on an old tee and a pair of gray sweatpants and pour myself a glass before tossing the drink back in one swig. The alcohol seeps through my veins, causing a slight numbness in my body.

As much as I want to lie back, relax, and enjoy what's left of the evening, I can't. I'm already planning out what needs to be done tomorrow. Check the sturdiness of the barricade, meet with the Sinners and Saints boys to discuss an incoming shipment, and to top the list, check-in on Ace.

My stallion, Smokin' Ace, seemed a bit off this morning, and I'm worried he might be sick. My usual vet, Dr. Porter, recently retired. He was the nicest old man and loved my animals as much as I did. But he's pushing seventy-five years old and can't come around the farm like he used to.

Being a ranch vet isn't easy, so it's been difficult to find someone who's willing to travel to us weekly and be on call. We've been on the hunt for a new doctor for over a month. Well, Knox has been on the hunt. One of the many joys of being my trusted sidekick. He gets to do all the shit I don't want to do.

At that thought, I pick up my phone and shoot a text to remind him we need to find a new doctor ASAP. I don't expect an answer anytime soon, since I'm sure he's balls deep in the brunette from the bar.

To my surprise, my phone rings.

I don't get the chance to say hello.

"Way to ruin the mood, you dick. I'm tryin' to have fun and you're talkin' 'bout dyin' horses," Knox says, exasperation in his tone. He sounds out of breath.

"*Minchione.*" *Idiot.* "Who checks their phone when they're havin' sex?" I retort.

"Who texts their best friend at ungodly hours of the night talkin' 'bout work? I thought somethin' had happened," he argues.

I can hear shuffling in the background and the hint of a woman's moan.

"Call me tomorrow, jackass. You need to hurry and find me a new vet."

"Unbelievable," Knox says right before hanging up.

A notification pops up; a text from Tucker with an update.

Sabrina had their baby earlier in the afternoon, and he's now the proud father of a girl. The text is accompanied by a couple of photos. One is of a fresh, out of the womb baby, that I assume I'm supposed to think is cute, but really looks more like a little potato with big eyes.

The next photo is of Sabrina holding the baby in a hospital bed, with Tucker sitting on the edge. Both are looking down at the little girl like she just taught them the secrets of the universe.

Something tugs at my chest.

As I scroll through the photos, I'm extremely aware of the silence surrounding me, but to quiet my mind is the challenge. I type out a quick response congratulating the new parents.

I head back to my room, ready for this day to be over, the worries of the day and my headache temporarily washed out.

Today's problems can become tomorrow's for now.

2
Naya

"W atashi mo aitai, papa." *I miss you, too, papa.*
"But it's only been a month!"

I shuffle some papers around on my desk. I can't find the file for my next patient.

My dad sighs. "I know, *Naya chan*, but the place feels empty without you." My face twists at his words, the guilt slowly creeping in. After what happened, I moved in with my father for a few weeks, and we fell into the same routine we'd had when I was a teenager. It was peaceful, like the old days, but I just couldn't stay.

"I still don't understand why you had to run off like that," he adds.

I can't tell him why I left. Not when he's in such a fragile state. My father constantly worries about me, and adding to his stress would only make him sicker.

"I got a job opportunity I couldn't pass up, *papa*. I needed a change." I hate lying to him, but it's necessary until further notice.

"Are you sure it isn't because of your break-up with—"

I let out a frustrated sigh. "*Papa*. I really don't want to talk about him."

I still can't find the stupid file and my patient will arrive at any moment.

"I get it." *He doesn't.* "How are you finding the new town, anyway?"

"Good. Laura and I are still adjusting, but the clinic is well-established and everyone has been nice so far." At that same moment, the front door opens. "Dad, I have to go, someone just came in. I'll call you back later, okay?"

He agrees and I hang up. I look up at the staff room TV monitor that displays the camera footage from the lobby. Mrs. Havilland is here to pick up her cat who is recovering from a surgery he had two days ago. I take a deep inhale and push myself off my chair. Laura stepped out for a minute, so I'm covering the front desk while she's gone.

"Hello, Mrs. Havilland. How are you doing today? Henry will be ready to go in a minute."

She smiles, causing the wrinkles on her face to stand out. "I'm doin' alright, darlin', thanks for askin'. How much do I owe ya today?" she asks, while digging into her purse.

I pull up the fee chart. "It's $800 for the removal of Henry's benign cyst."

She shakes her head in disbelief. "Darn lucky I love this cat so much, 'cause he sure doesn't come cheap."

I chuckle as she inserts her credit card in the machine. "I'm sorry, ma'am. I'm just trying to keep this clinic afloat," I joke.

In reality, as much as this is costing her a large sum, it's not nearly enough to cover the expenses of owning this clinic. When I moved to Springfield to take over Dr. Porter's practice, I knew it would be hard, but I couldn't have anticipated *how* hard it would be.

I don't have enough clients, some having left when he did, claiming they couldn't trust a vet with significantly less experience. This place is barely breaking even, but I love this job so much. Even if I have to scrape to make ends meet, I could never give up. I put up some ads around town advertising my services, and I'm hoping it will drum up some extra business.

"Lucian sure did a good job keepin' this place in business all these years, especially with *those clients* of his."

I know nothing about the people around this town, so Mrs. Havilland's tone grabs my attention. I'm not one to gossip, but if they were patients of this clinic, I feel like I should know... And what better way to pry than with a nosey elderly lady?

"What about those clients?" I ask as innocently as possible.

"Those darn biker boys that run 'round town terrorizin' the folk," she replies with a hint of sarcasm.

My eyes widen. Biker boys? *Not again...* "What do you mean by 'terrorizing the folk'?" My heart rate increases as I try to calm my breathing.

"Oh, sweetie. I'm just kiddin'. They're nice boys. Cute, too. If I weren't so old, I'd try my luck with one of them. Any of them would do." She winks.

"Mrs. Havilland!" I exclaim in fake outrage, my breaths already evening out.

She laughs out loud, and I shake my head with a cackle, deciding to lay the topic to rest for now. None of those 'biker boys' have been in the clinic in the past month, and Laura hasn't mentioned them. So, I'm assuming they also moved on to another vet.

Once the payment is complete, I grab Henry and give him to Mrs. Havilland. When she's gone, I release a pent-up breath and head back to the staff room. She's probably going to be my only client for the day, unless there happens to be an emergency.

I grab my book from where I had left it face down. Minutes later, I'm so caught up in the steamy eighteenth-century romance I'm reading, I don't hear Laura come through the back door and into the room.

"Hello? Earth to Dr. Ohara!" she yells with a smirk. "Reading your porn again?" Her eyebrows wiggle.

I roll my eyes. "It isn't porn. It's a historical romance."

"Tomato, *tomato*," she says as she heads to the fridge to grab a bottle of water. "Same difference. You end up horny as hell in the end regardless. You need to get yourself some real dick."

She's not wrong. It's been a while since I had any action down there, and ten years since I've dated someone new. I've never been great with staying casual. I'd rather not engage in a situation I know won't lead anywhere. I'm the type to get attached, and men these days are always looking for the next fling.

Since breaking up with my ex-boyfriend, I haven't been able to go on any dates. Laura is relentlessly trying to get me on dating apps, but I'd rather lie in cat vomit than go through pictures of shirtless guys holding fish. I don't trust men anymore.

So, it's been me, my vibrator, and some historical rakes. *It is what it is.*

I laugh. "Maybe you should give them a try. It sounds like you're curious. I could introduce you to the Duke of Hastings," I quip.

"Nuh-uh, hunny. I don't need books to get me going when I can just watch the show. And the men in the city are easy pickings. If you ever feel like coming out with me, just say the word. I know you wouldn't have any trouble finding a man to take home," Laura states confidently.

She knows I won't go out, and it's not because I think hooking up is wrong. To each their own. I've just always needed the closer connection that you find in a relationship.

Right at that moment, the phone rings and Laura sets her

water bottle down to answer it. I pick up my book again, eager to return to the scene where the Duke was busy ravishing the viscountess. I read two more pages when she comes waltzing back in with a huge smile on her face.

"You won't believe the call we just got!" she screams. She's so animated, I'm getting excited just by proximity.

She claps her hands. "A man called to inquire if we had any openings to examine a horse on his ranch! He's one of Dr. Porter's patients." Laura knows the tough financial situation the clinic is in, so I understand her enthusiasm. There are tons of ranches in this area, but most of them are probably well established and have long-standing relationships with their vets. Most of them aren't looking for change. If we're able to secure this ranch, it could be the answer to all our problems.

I run to the big filing cabinet where the doctor kept all his files. "What's the name of the ranch?"

"All Saints."

I dig through the drawers. "Bingo!" I grab it and smack it on my desk. We go through the information and both our eyes bulge out of our heads.

"Holy shit, Naya!" Laura exclaims. "This place is huge and used to bring Dr. Porter *a lot* of money. We're set!"

Don't get ahead of yourself, the nagging voice in my head says. My brain refuses to let me get excited. I've always been the type to get hopeful too quickly, only to end up disappointed.

"I told him you'd stop by the day after tomorrow at eleven thirty," Laura says. Her smile now takes up half her face.

Despite my fear that this might be too good to be true, I match her grin. "Okay, that's great."

"That's *great?*" Her excited expression has now shifted to disbelief. "That's all you have to say? This is good news! This ranch could be the clinic's saving grace, and all you have to say is 'that's great'? Can't you at least *pretend* to be happy? All Saints is the biggest ranch in the county." She crosses her arms over her chest and peers at me with a disappointed look.

"How do you even know that?"

"People in small towns talk...*a lot*. I've been getting all the gossip at the front desk. Apparently, some guy bought the ranch a few years ago and turned it into a horse sanctuary," she explains.

I shrug, although my heart races at hearing that the ranch is that big. "Well, I *am* happy, but let's not get our hopes up, okay? It's just one appointment. Let's see how it goes before we celebrate."

I know I'm being a tad pessimistic, but I can't help it. I'd rather have low expectations. I can't handle another failure.

"You're right. I'm sorry," Laura says, her enthusiasm completely dissipated. *Great*, now I feel like a bitch.

"Don't apologize," I reply quickly. "I appreciate how much you care about this clinic. I couldn't run this place without you. Just because I'm hesitant to get excited, doesn't mean you can't be."

She smiles. "I'll be overjoyed for the both of us, then. By the way, did I mention how hot the guy sounded on the phone?" She winks and turns on her heel, back to the front desk. "Enjoy your porn!" she calls over her shoulder as she heads down the hallway.

Before I know it, evening has come and it's time to close. I activate the alarm system right as I step out the front door. It's quiet at this time of day, the other businesses in the plaza all having closed a few hours earlier.

Springfield is a quaint town with not many habitants. I'm used to the hustle and bustle of bigger cities, but I needed somewhere small and quiet where I could start fresh. I moved almost nine hours away, a place where I know no one, have no past, and no memories.

I jump into my old, 1997 Jeep Wrangler and head down the road toward my neighborhood. I chose a small house close to work so I could walk on the likely occasion my car decides to call it quits. Laura moved in close by with her aunt and uncle while she saves up for her own place. I urged her to stay with me, but she didn't want to impose, as if she could ever. I roll my eyes at the thought.

As I make my way down Hertz Road, a truck appears behind me from a side street, high beams on. The harsh light causes me to squint, the glare in my rearview mirror obstructing my vision.

I fidget with the mirror to get it at a good angle, but it's to no avail. I curse under my breath. *For god's sake, are the high beams necessary?*

I move to the right lane to allow the truck to pass me, but it stays behind me the entire drive to my place. My heart starts racing as my hands tighten on the steering wheel, and I look around quickly without focus.

I speed up, and when I turn onto my street, the car finally passes me as I pull into my driveway.

What the hell was that? I cut the engine and stay seated for a couple of minutes to calm down. When Laura and I came here a month ago, everyone back home told us we were crazy for moving to a new state on a whim, with barely any prep. I always dismissed their concern. I'd never had a moment where I worried for my safety...until now.

When I gather myself, I step inside the house, and I'm instantly hit with a sense of peace. It's nothing fancy, a simple place, but it's *mine*. No negative memories are associated with it. I've decorated it just how I like it, and I can now say it's starting to feel like home.

I grab a bottle of wine off the drink cart and pour myself a healthy glass. I need it more than ever today after the slow day at the clinic and the phone call with my father.

I love my dad more than I can put into words, but I worry for him as he gets older. Sometimes, I wonder if I made the right choice by leaving Raleigh. I needed a clean break, but I left behind a key piece of my heart.

Knowing my dad is stuck back home by himself eats away at me. The medical bills from his debilitating condition are draining his retirement money. He will eventually need a full-time nurse to take care of him, but there's no way he could afford it. I sometimes feel selfish for leaving him behind when I could be helping him. He's the first one to say I deserve a good life, but I can't help the way my guilt gnaws at me.

I take a huge sip of wine and sit on the couch, turning on a cheesy romance movie. I try and fail to shut off my mind.

I hope that this week's ranch visit will lead to something more. Lord knows I need it, the clinic needs it, and my dad needs it.

3
Callan

I wake up at five in the morning to the sound of my rooster, Johnny, crowing at the ass crack of dawn.

I let out a low grumble and sit up on my California king-sized bed. It's obnoxious, *I know*. But I'm a big guy, I need space.

The sun is beginning to rise and, from my bedroom, I can see how it casts the land in an orange glow. Living on a ranch with these views makes it easier to wake up this early.

I rise to my feet, ready to start the day.

A couple hours later, I'm in the back field gathering some hay when Knox walks down the path toward me. He stares at me with a grin; I'm shirtless, in jeans, with a western hat on.

"Howdy, cowboy," he teases.

"Easy for you to make fun when you haven't lifted anythin' other than your dick in years." I swipe my hands down my face to wipe away the beads of sweat and cross my arms. "Can I help you, Davenport?"

"You're so grumpy in the mornin'."

"*Mi hai rotto il cazzo*," I retort. *You're being really fucking annoying.*

Knox laughs. "Sorry, I don't speak *Guido*."

I just grunt in response. He's been around me long enough to understand the language or tone at least.

"Have you had your coffee yet?" Knox asks.

"No." *What is he getting at?*

"Ah! That's why you're actin' like an unpleasant prick. Let's go inside."

I put the last bale of hay down. He's right. It's actually recommended not to talk to me until I've had my caffeine fix. So, I follow him into the house.

Shortly after, the house is filled with the aroma of a fresh brew, and I take a sip of my first cup. "Who's this new vet you found?"

"Dr. Ohara. The new vet who took over for Lucian."

"I didn't know he was findin' a replacement."

"Apparently, many of his clients requested one so they wouldn't have to move to a different clinic. He posted a random ad on a job site and someone took the bait."

I take another sip of my coffee. "How long ago?"

"'Bout a month. Some patients still walked out on her, though."

Her? I wonder why I haven't heard of this new vet. Then again, I haven't had to check on my animals since Dr. Porter retired.

"Is she new here?"

"Yes. Lucian told me she moved from out of town. What's with the questions?" Dav asks, a little confused.

"How did we not know that a new girl was comin' into our territory? That's the main answer I'm lookin' for," I bark.

"Girls," Knox says, exaggerating the 's' at the end of the word.

"There's two of 'em?"

"Yup. She brought an assistant."

"What the fuck? Are any of y'all actually doin' your jobs? I should be aware when strangers move into my town."

"Don't worry. I already spoke to the guys and they've gone 'round to check on 'em. No suspicious activity happenin' over there."

I shake my head, my anger surfacing bit by bit. "Davenport, you tell those guys that if they ever forget to report to me again, I'm goin' to sew their fuckin' mouths shut," I grit through my teeth. I need to know the ins and out of my town to make sure no one tries to mess with my territory.

I command the West side of Nashville, too. But with Jackson taking care of things there, I have no worries.

Knox nods his head. "Consider it done, King."

We say our goodbyes and Knox heads to Nashville early to check on our warehouses. Meanwhile, I get back to work.

I don't play favourites with my animals, but I have to admit that Ace has a special place in my heart, whatever is left of it. He was the first animal I bought when I acquired All Saints. I was proud as hell of the new land and bought this gorgeous stallion with the shiniest black hair and thick mane. I love that horse the same way some might love their children. He's been through it all with me.

I do a quick check on the cattle and see nothing to be concerned about. I head over to the fence they destroyed to make sure the barrier is still sturdy enough. The area has been patched up for the time being, but I'm still waiting on an order of wooden planks that match the fence so it can be fixed. Tucker is going to be away for a few weeks, so I'm on my own.

Once I confirm the barricade is still standing and I won't be losing any of my cattle in the immediate future, I complete my rounds of the ranch, then head over to the second stable.

I have two stables on the ranch, one where I typically keep my horses, and a slightly smaller one where I tend to keep individual horses if they look ill, in an effort to isolate them. There was nothing wrong with Ace when I saw him yesterday, it was just a gut feeling after having him for so long. He wasn't eating as fast as normal and seemed tired when I took him out. I brought him over to the second stable just in case he had some sort of illness that could be passed along to the other horses.

My brow furrows when I see I was right to be worried: his nose is running and his eyes are watery. Having grown up around horses, I know how to spot a cold, and while it's not any cause for major concern, he still needs to be assessed. I fill up Ace's water and leave him some soaked hay since I assume his throat is sore.

By the time I'm finished with all my tasks, it's seven in the evening. The sun has begun to set and the heat that has been present all day has lessened. The club meeting is at nine thirty. I make a stop inside my house to let the dogs out, then head over to the stables to check on Ace and the others again. The horses in the main stable all appear to be doing well, none of them seem to have caught any illnesses.

When I check in on my stallion, he looks in the same condition as earlier today, which stalls my fears that he may have a worse viral infection. I'll feel better once the vet confirms everything is okay.

I gently stroke his coat. "Hey there, boy," I say in a hushed voice. "How are you feelin'?"

He lets out a gentle huff against my hand as I pet his snout. I give him one last pat as he bends his head down, nuzzling into my shoulder. I call out to Harlo and Dave and they obediently chase after me.

I pass my pick-up truck and walk straight to the garage where my bikes are lined up. I decide to take my new custom Harley Davidson Road King. When I take a seat and turn on the ignition, I feel the hum of the engine roll through my body as the bright lights from the bike illuminate the driveway.

It's exhilarating and the best part of riding a bike, that initial rumble of the motor shooting adrenaline straight up my spine. It's a fucking drug.

I slip on my riding gloves and kick up the stand. I pull the clutch in, putting the bike into neutral, and press the starter button. The night air whips through my hair, and I feel my shoulders relax, removing the exhaustion from the day. This is when I feel most alive and the most like myself. Riding allows me to clear my mind anytime things get overwhelming at the ranch or when issues pop up with the business, I know I can hop on my bike and hit the road. And for as long as I'm out there, those issues don't exist.

After nine, I'm usually the only one on the road as I reach the town's boundary line to the S&S warehouse. In official terms, the warehouse is a large storage facility for the bar, and while we do use it to store excess stock, it mostly functions as a safe place to hold arms for trade deals and for the motorcycle club to meet. We never conduct actual trades there, the warehouse is a haven for the club, which means the less people are aware of its location, the better.

When I pull up to the building, dozens of bikes are already parked out back. As I get closer, I hear loud voices resonating through the steel walls. Everyone is in high spirits because the shipment we're set to receive next week means big money and further control of the arms trade in the south.

I walk through the doors and clear my throat. "Sorry to break up the party, boys," I yell out so I can be heard above the noise. The chatter ceases as everyone gives me their attention. "I want us coordinated for next week. There can be absolutely zero fuck ups with this shipment. We all should know our rules and if you *don't*, then figure it the fuck out. If this deal doesn't go through as planned because of someone in this club, don't bother comin' back here. Understood?"

It's deadly quiet, you could hear a pin drop. Laying underneath the statement is a clear threat. You don't get to just *leave* the club. It's a known fact. Everyone here is in it for life. The only way out is in a coffin.

"Knox, Jackson and I will be the ones receivin' the shipment at the drop-off location," I say, although this much is obvious. The three of us always handle the big deals. "We'll need some men close by in case shit goes sideways and we need back up; and some will need to stay back here to make sure the warehouse is protected in case anyone on the supplier's side has any bright ideas of tryin' to get the drop on us. I want all our bases covered."

Heads nod across the room, indicating they understand what's expected of them and where they fit into the plan. With that, I grab a beer off the table, take a sip, and raise the bottle in the air. The others raise their own bottles and chatter resumes. Business talk is over and everyone is free to enjoy the night, wherever it takes them.

Knox saunters up to me. "Hate to break it to you, boss, but that meeting could have been an email," he jokes as he brings his drink to his lips. I don't laugh, watching him as I take another sip.

"We need to be ready," I reply dryly. "We can't afford any fuck ups, not this time. This deal will put us in a position to expand into Mississippi."

This is the largest shipment we've had in the club's history. We made contact with a gang in Georgia who has access to government weapons and were all too willing to sell. Sure, it came at a steep price, but we'll make it back and then some. And if this all goes to plan, the value of having European contacts will be priceless. Over the years, I've expanded my network into Eastern Europe and have made many connections with real military forces and militia composed of civilians. I've been waiting for the perfect time to open up importing and exporting with our partners overseas. There's no better time than now.

Jackson walks up to us. "We'll be ready, Cal." He clasps his hands and stretches them out in front of him, causing the rings on his fingers to glint in the overhead lighting. "No need to worry," he confirms, his thick British accent lacing each word.

"Good," I grunt out as I take the last sip of my beer. "I've got enough on my plate to worry 'bout."

Knox gives me a concerned look. "How's Ace doin'?"

I shrug. "He's alright. I'm lookin' forward to gettin' a proper diagnosis, though."

"I'll be there to greet the doctor tomorrow. I know you'll be busy with the cattle and stable."

I can always count on Dav to be there when I need him, without even asking. I guess that's what happens when you've been friends for so long. We're brothers and he knows me better than anyone.

But I guess I'm good at hiding some parts of myself because he doesn't know the burden I carry on my shoulders on a daily basis. I've not had a moment of rest since my pops passed away and there's no end in sight. My stress goes deeper than the ranch and business. *Much* fucking deeper. I'm a pro at not letting others see the strain. I always feel responsible for my people's wellbeing, and make sure they are taken care of, even if that means putting myself on the backburner.

You're a fucking man, Cal. No time for pussy shit, I remind myself.

The remainder of our time is filled with discussions about our plans for the trade. Some of the guys shoot the shit about women and the pussy they're getting. They're being downright foul, but I'm glad they feel comfortable enough to be themselves here. I can't help but laugh at the nonsense I'm hearing.

The door to the lounge area opens and Tucker's head pops out the corner. The guys holler and whistle.

"You made it!" Dav shouts over the guys.

Tucker approaches us at the back of the room where we had a bar installed, and I get up to greet him. We shake hands and I bring him in for a hug. *Why the fuck not? He just had a baby.* He's taken aback for a moment, but leans in willingly. "Congrats, *Daddy Tuck*," I tease.

"Daddy Tuck," Dav shouts while grinding the top of Tucker's head with his knuckles.

I roll my eyes and shove him off the poor guy. "Do you always have to be so fuckin' annoyin'?" I ask Knox and he shrugs in response.

"How's father life treatin' you?" I ask Tucker.

"Oh, it's crazy, man. My heart was already livin' outside my body, my wife bein' my entire world. Now, we both share one in the form of a tiny human. It's surreal. We're over the moon."

I clasp his shoulder and give it a squeeze. I'm happy for my friend, but my chest feels hollow. At that same moment, I realize I might never get to experience that type of love.

4
Naya

"**N**aya! Naya! Naya!" my father calls out to me again and again.

I can hear him, but I can't reach out to help him. Several doors line the endless hallway. I run as the corridor keeps getting longer and longer. I jiggle every doorknob, but they're all locked.

I knock on a door. "Papa? Are you in there?" He doesn't answer and my pounding turns frantic. My heart feels like it will jump out of my throat.

My papa's voice echoes in my mind, more desperate than before. "Naya!"

I feel like I'm in a fucked up carnival fun house. Is this a sick joke?

My name keeps ringing in my head, and I need to get it out. I clutch onto my hair and scream.

I wake up in a panic, cold sweat sticking to my skin. I let out a groan. My nightmares seem to represent the helplessness I feel in real life, not being able to help my dad. It breaks my heart to think I won't be there if anything were to happen to him. I constantly remind myself I'm doing all this to help him, but it doesn't ease my mind.

It's five a.m. I sigh. I've got hours until I have to leave the house. Usually, I open the clinic early, but I don't have any appointments booked this morning and the ranch visit is not until later. Laura will take care of opening the office, and if any emergencies happen, she'll give me a call.

I sit on the recliner by the window and grab my book from the table where I left it last night. I settle into the chair, tossing a blanket over my lap, and begin to read as the sun rises through the glass beside me. This is a rare morning where I get to truly relax.

In the middle of reading *Ravishing The Duke*, I fall asleep. When I wake up, I realize it's already ten a.m. I rush to get ready for the day with my trusted cup of coffee—I never leave the house without having a coffee first—and I just know that today is going to be especially tiring after my short night.

Before backing out of my driveway, I peek through my rearview mirror to make sure I'm alone. Yesterday's incident got me a little paranoid. Though nothing happened, thank God, it made me question if I've been taking my safety for granted.

A flash of broken glass flickers behind my closed eyes. *Blood drips down onto the ground. "Look what you made me do, Sugar."* The memory of *his* voice sends a shiver down my spine.

I breathe in deeply. For the past few weeks, I haven't been able to start my day without taking a second to gather myself. It's a way for me to take one last inhale of all my problems and exhale the bullshit. It grounds me in a sense, and today, I need all the grounding possible. I really need this to lead to a permanent job.

Before hitting the road, I press play on my bad bitch playlist.

As I near the property after a short drive, my heart rate increases wildly. I'm so nervous, and although it's normal for me to have jitters when meeting someone for the first time, there's something about this encounter that feels important. *Duh, your livelihood depends on it.*

From what I can see, this ranch spans over hundreds of acres and my eyes go wide as I approach the gate. The front is lined with mature oak trees and a massive arched gate, the name 'All Saints' written in big, bold letters. The metal is gold, shiny, and so classy.

It's an impressive entrance and it makes me even more anxious. I'm not used to this kind of wealth. I didn't grow up poor and never felt like I was missing a thing. But we didn't have luxury, and *this* is luxury.

My car stops at the front of the barricade where two security guards are posted up near the entryway, one inside a booth and the other walking around with a phone to his ear. Neither of them acknowledge me.

What kind of ranch is this? I've been around farms my entire life, and I've never seen one with a security detail. Something tells me there's more to All Saints than meets the eye.

I press the button on the intercom. "Dr. Ohara, welcome. Drive straight through to the house. I'll meet you there." The man's voice sounds smooth and pleasant, and I wonder if he's the guy Laura was referring to.

My jeep trails down the bumpy, gravel road, also lined by big trees, and as I get closer to the buildings, my mouth parts open. There are two brand-new trucks and an expensive-looking muscle car parked in front of the house. I'm suddenly embarrassed by the dinky, old piece of trash I'm driving. I really hope it doesn't sway them in their decision. I might not have the finest things, but I'm a damn good vet.

Next to the fleet is a mansion. The biggest one I've ever seen. As I pass a roundabout and water fountain made of white stone, I squint to look up at the statue in the bright sunshine. It's a figure of a naked woman with angel wings, a snake climbing up her leg while she stares down at it. She is the embodiment of radiance and power.

As I park the jeep next to a shiny, black pick-up, a man bursts out the door, a smile plastered on his face.

Well, he looks nice.

I look at my reflection in my car mirror quickly and pat down my hair.

The blonde guy hops down the steps to greet me as I open the car door. Within a couple seconds, he's in front of me with his hand out, and I grab onto it as he helps me out of my seat. *Chivalry is not dead, apparently.*

"Thank you," I say, feeling my cheeks flush. I rub the palms of my hand down my jeans to get rid of the moisture. *Get a hold of yourself, woman.*

"I'm Knox Davenport. But everyone calls me Dav," he says with a little wink.

I smile at him, my stomach somehow settling right away. "Hi, I'm Dr. Ohara. Well, my name is Naya," I reply, stuttering.

"Nice to meet you, Dr. Naya Ohara," Knox purrs.

I roll my eyes internally. *Flirt.* "Are you the owner of this property? It's beautiful."

"Nah. King, the bossman, owns the ranch. You'll meet him when we head to the stable." Knox reaches for my supplies in the trunk. He slings the bag over his shoulder at the same time I reach for it and he purses his lips. "I got it, doc."

"Thanks. I'm not used to having help," I say, honestly. I play with the hem of my shirt, embarrassed I let that little bit of information slip out of my mouth.

"You're not from here, are you, Dr. Ohara? Welcome to the South. You better get used to havin' help," he answers with a little chuckle, his southern drawl thick as a brick.

My mouth opens and closes a couple times as I think of something to say. He's right, I'm not from Springfield. But I am from the southeast. City men are different; they're not as endearing, and their southern charm isn't as strong as in these parts.

Knox turns on his heels before I get the chance to respond and walks toward a stable at the back of the house, and I notice a slightly smaller building tucked behind the huge mansion. I don't know who this 'King' is, but he must be filthy rich to own a property like this. Even the barns are bigger than my house. As we get closer to the first one, I hear faint grunting in the distance. *What is that? An animal?*

Dav turns the corner and I follow.

That's when I see *him*.

A tall, shirtless man stands at the back of an old red pick-up. His chiseled chest glistens with sweat and dirt, mid-length hair tied up to keep the strands out of the way. His back is to us as he moves bales of hay, and it gives me a direct view of his defined lines as his muscles strain. His biceps flex as he grabs onto the bundles, bringing my attention to the large veins on his hands and arms. The man has tattoos *everywhere*. I can't help but gawk.

The sound of his grunting resonates louder now that we're in his proximity and travels straight to my core. It sounds *feral*. I grab onto the edge of my shirt and lift it away from my skin to get some air. I tell myself it's because of the July heat, and not the man in front of me.

The massive angel wings on his shoulders look reminiscent of the ones I saw on the statue in the driveway. Before I can explore that thought further, he turns to face us. If I was mesmerized by his back, I'm outright stunned by his front.

Wide shoulders, large chest, cookie-cutter abs. A jagged scar cuts across the center of his abdomen, but somehow the imperfection only adds to his beauty. I've never seen such a godly-looking man. His face is beautiful, his sharp jawline covered by a dark beard. My heart skips a beat, maybe two. The sun shines in his eyes; they resemble pools of honey.

The man looks like he's been carved by the hands of angels. He must be the owner of the ranch.

His gaze lands on me, stealing my breath away. I inhale sharply, trying to steady myself, but it feels as though all the blood has rushed from my head and has congregated in my lower body. I can't tell what he's thinking. I can barely think at all.

I forget that Knox is standing right next to me until he clears his throat. "Callan, this is the new vet."

I startle and stick my hand out. "I'm Doctor—" but I get cut off mid-sentence.

"Absolutely not," the man—*Callan*—growls out, his tone final. He sounds angry even, and I'm confused.

He turns his face away from us, grabs a shirt from the bed of the truck, and hops off. Without saying another word, he marches away, leaving us where we stand. We're both stunned, but Knox lowers his head and shakes it in disapproval. *What the hell is going on?*

"What just happened?" I ask him.

"Don't worry 'bout it, Dr. Ohara. I'll talk to him. Let's just go see the horses," he responds, rubbing his temples.

"What did he mean by 'absolutely not'?" I question again. Then, it clicks. Does he not want to hire me after one look at my appearance? I glance down at my clothes. I may not be wearing designer clothes or shoes, but I still look professional. There's no reason why he shouldn't want to hire me. He doesn't even know me. I'm more than capable of taking care of his animals.

Anger surfaces, my breath getting caught in my chest. When I look back in the direction he stormed off, I see he still hasn't reached the house.

And I do something I never thought I'd do.

I jog after him. No man is allowed to dismiss me by judging my exterior.

Struggling to catch up, I yell, "Hey, you! Stop!"

Knox runs up behind me. "Naya, he didn't mean anythin' by that. He's just grumpy," he explains.

I laugh and it comes out a lot more cynical than I expect. "Grumpy? You mean he's just an asshole."

I keep the same pace up as I approach the big, burly jerk, who has stopped and turned around. "What is your problem? You don't even know my name. I'm highly qualified—"

"I've seen enough. It's a no," Callan says, bluntly, cutting me off yet again. Not only is he a jerk and an asshole, he's also rude. *Great. Chivalry is in fact dead.*

There's no ounce of emotion on his face. The hint of anger I saw minutes ago has vanished. I don't know what I did for him to dislike me this much already.

I growl in frustration. "You're being disrespectful!"

"I don't care. This is my ranch and I don't want you workin' here." The ferocity of his stare penetrates me so deeply that I struggle to formulate words.

"I–I–I don't want to work for—someone like *you*, anyway," I stutter indignantly as my chest heaves.

An amused smirk tugs on his lips. "Is that all you got, little one?"

I gasp, but under my shock, there's a burning intensity from the fire in his eyes. I feel hot, and I don't know if it's because of the man in front of me or the rage boiling in my veins. "Who do you think you are?"

"Not your client, that's for sure," he spits.

I have the urge to flip him off, but I'm a *professional*. So, I take a few deep breaths, ground myself, and put on a tight, *professional* smile. This only seems to amuse him further.

I didn't realize Knox has been standing right next to us the entire time, and when I look at him, he's grinning. *So, this is amusing to him, too. Unbelievable.*

"Don't listen to him, Naya. He's in a bad mood. Come see the horses," he urges me.

"Don't make excuses for him," I say, irritated. I cross my arms and stare Callan in the eyes, not flinching once. He glares back at me and doesn't stand down either.

I don't know how long we stay in a staring contest, but Knox interrupts us. "Cal, just leave us alone, man. I got this."

I look over to where I parked my Jeep and consider making a run for it. But then, I think about my dad and how having the ranch as a client wouldn't solely change my life, but his, too.

Even if it means working for an ass like Callan.

The ass in question grunts before Knox gestures for me to follow him. I let out a sigh and reluctantly head after him back to the barn. When I step through the doors, I'm left stunned.

Even the *animals* live in luxury here.

The barn has huge stalls for the horses, covered loafing sheds, a beautiful tall center aisle, and a cupola on the roof. Everything on this ranch oozes extravagance, and as much as it makes me feel uncomfortable, I can't deny its beauty.

We walk through the stable's beautiful black iron gates and brick floors, until we get to the back door and exit. Knox takes me to a second building, a little smaller than the first one, and I immediately spot a stunning dark stallion resting in the corner of a stall.

I reach out to touch him, but hesitate. "Is he usually jumpy?"

"Callan or the horse?" Knox asks, jokingly.

I burst out laughing and he joins in.

"I'm glad I could break the ice. I could feel the tension

cracklin' and the heat flowin' between you two. It's like lava was about to erupt from your heads."

Shit. I hope he didn't notice how flustered I felt in the moment. "Let's pretend that *never* happened, Knox," I say deadpan.

He chuckles. "Please, call me Dav."

Warmth fills my chest. I barely know this man and he wants me to call him by his nickname. I'm sure he and I could be great friends. I smile. "Fine. Dav, is the *horse* usually jumpy?"

Knox shakes his head. "Nah, he's more of a people person than I am," he says with a joking lilt.

"What's his name?" I get closer to the horse, not wanting to startle him.

"Smokin' Ace. We mostly call him Ace, though."

"Ace," I repeat as I circle the huge stallion.

Up close, I can see that his nose is running and there are definite tears leaking from his eyes, which indicates that his ducts are probably plugged. I carefully place my hand on his throat and wait for him to swallow, and when he does, there's a small, almost imperceptible stutter, which makes me think it's probably sore.

I turn back to look at Dav who is now leaning against a rail at the front of the stall, staring at me as I work.

"Do you, or your boss," another flair of annoyance shoots through me as I think of Callan, "happen to keep a record of his health stats and vitals?"

"Yeah, Lucian kept that information in the main stables. Let me just run back and grab it real quick."

A few minutes later, Dav jogs back, holding a clipboard, and hands it off to me. I look over the stats that were taken while the horse was healthy. Ace is in spectacular condition. I lay the clipboard down on the ground and open my bag of supplies to get ready for the assessment.

I hold my wrist up as I reach out and gently press my fingers against Ace's pulse point, and I start the timer on my watch. He lets out a high-pitched whinny. He's a bit nervous, understandably, as I'm a stranger. I ask Knox to come forward and hold onto his snout to calm him a little and Ace visibly relaxes.

I nod my head as I finish and grab the clipboard to write down what I found. Next, I check the horse's respiration rate, then reach into my bag to grab a thermometer. I layer it with some petroleum jelly before walking toward the horse's hind end with my hand on his body so he's aware of my movements, and I stand out of the way of his back limbs to avoid potentially getting kicked as I lift his tail. Slowly, I slide the thermometer into his rectum, and wait for it to make a beep.

When I pull it out, Knox looks at me like he wants to throw up. I give him an inquisitive stare.

"I've seen a horse's temperature get taken more times than I can count," he explains, letting loose a deep breath. "But the thought of someone shovin' a thermometer up my ass always makes me want to crawl out of my skin. Makes me feel bad for the poor boy," he says, looking at Ace with absolute pity.

I can't help the laugh that comes out of me. Of course, this tall, handsome man would be brought to his knees by the thought of someone sticking an object up his butt. "You know, it's really no big deal," I joke. "I could show you if you'd like."

His eyes widen in shock. He takes five big steps back until he is pressed against the wall. "Not funny, doc."

I continue laughing. If only his boss was this easy to talk to. I wonder if I'll have to be around him all that much if I end up getting this gig. I've been shown around by Knox, so maybe I'll get lucky and only deal with him. I make a mental note to ask him about that. Once I regain my composure, I hit him with the facts.

"Okay, so Ace has a bit of a cold," I explain. "When did the symptoms start?"

"Day before yesterday. Cal noticed he seemed off," he says confidently now, as all talk of rectal insertion has been taken off the table.

"Right," I say, noting this information down in the chart. "I don't see any indication that there's any other severe virus. There's nothing to be too worried about; the cold should clear up in about ten days. Try to keep him away from the other horses until then. But make sure to give him some extra attention. Horses get stressed when they're all alone. We wouldn't want his health to deteriorate."

Knox looks relieved. "Noted." He looks at Ace and pats the stallion's back. "Looks like it's gonna be you and me for a while, stud. Two lonely boys needin' each other's company."

I smile. "I would like to come back next week to check on him," I add as I crouch down to pack my bag.

"Whatever you think is best, doc."

When I stand, Knox is right at my back waiting to help me with my bag. *A girl could get used to this.*

When we get to my Jeep, I take another look at the sprawling mansion. Seriously, how much money does this ranch make? I see a flicker through the window as if someone was there, but when I blink, it's gone. *Has he been watching us?*

"If anything changes with Ace or any of the other horses start looking ill, feel free to give me a call," I say, putting my attention back on Knox.

"About that," he says, his tone more business-like than I've heard at any point today. "How would you feel about takin' the ranch on as a full-time client?"

My mouth opens, but nothing comes out. Butterflies flutter

in my stomach and my breakfast threatens to come up. *This is what you wanted, idiot. Speak!* But then, I remember that having All Saints as a permanent client also means having *Callan* as a permanent client. My eyes flick back to where I swear I just saw him in the window. Knox follows my gaze this time and offers his reassurance.

"Don't worry about him. Seriously, he's just under a lot of stress and you caught him on an off day," he says, clearly trying his best to convince me.

I let out a disbelieving snort. Callan judged me before even getting to know me. That's a clear sign of his personality. The question is, am I willing to let his shitty character stop me from doing what I need to do to survive? The thought of Laura sitting in the office this morning with quite literally no work to do flashes through my mind, along with last night's nightmare. I know the answer.

"Yes, I can take on the ranch as a client," I say. "But on one condition."

Knox gives me an intrigued look.

"I only deal with you when I'm here."

He reaches his palm out to mine and we shake hands. "Deal," he agrees.

5

Callan

"**Y**ou did *WHAT*?" I roar.

"I asked her to take on the ranch as a full-time client," Knox repeats as if I didn't actually hear him the first time. "Look, *Hudson*, I don't know what your issue was back there, but you know we need a vet. I watched her examine Ace. She's good, and he likes her."

When Davenport calls me Hudson, I know he means business. He's either angry or sick of my shit—or both. It's the same when I call him by his full last name. I could care less about how he feels right now, though. There's no fucking way that chick is working on the ranch.

"I don't care how good she is," I say, gritting my teeth. "It's not happenin'."

"Oh, it's happenin'," he says with a smug smile on his face. "And she'll be stoppin' by next week as well."

I turn my back to him and grip the kitchen counter with my hands. I try my hardest not to scream, but God damn it. I take a deep breath through my nose and face him. He's lucky I'm not gifting him with a swift punch to the nose. Dav is like a brother, so I wouldn't hesitate to knock him out for making this decision without consulting me first.

"You don't call the shots 'round here," I say, coldly. "I do." I point to my heaving chest.

A flicker of hurt flashes across his face before it's replaced with a stoic, hardened look. "Sorry, *boss*," he says, the sarcasm and anger thick in his voice now. "I've only been here with you from the start. My bad thinkin' I would have some say."

I run my hand through my hair and take another deep breath. I can count how many times Knox and I have genuinely fought, and I'm not willing to add this to the list. Not when he isn't the real source of my frustration. I don't fully understand why I'm this riled up; my emotions are revving in my body. But...*that woman.* She was *maddening.* One look at her and my composure dissipated on the spot. Despite what Knox says about me not being a people person, I had actually been looking forward to meeting the new doctor. The ranch really does need a reliable vet.

What I hadn't expected was to turn around and be faced with the most beautiful woman I have ever laid my eyes on.

She was flawless, straight out of a cowboy's wet dream. Her skin was smooth and light brown, and she looked both innocent and sinful at the same time. Her brown, curly hair laid around her shoulders, cascading over her perfectly-sized chest. Her tits were snug under the black t-shirt she wore and her nipples protruded from the cotton. I wanted to run my callused thumbs over the perky buds and feel her shudder under my touch. She wore faded, light blue jeans that hugged her curves like a glove. She appeared as an angel, carefully dropped onto my ranch to remind me that I'm no saint.

She looked divine, and smelled it, too. I caught a whiff of her sweet aroma when I walked away in an effort to avoid her seeing just how much my body had reacted to her presence. If she smelled that delectable, I wonder just how good she tastes.

The image of her laying on the barn's floor, legs spread out while I ate her like my last meal, had flashed right before my eyes. If the thought and look of her didn't have me fully hard, her running after me screaming sure did the job. Something about a woman that doesn't just lie back and take shit really gets me going. She has no idea who I am or what I'm capable of, yet she stood up for herself. That is the telltale of a strong woman. There's no way I could tolerate seeing her on the ranch on a regular basis.

"You haven't even looked into her," I say, willing my voice to be calm. "We can't hire someone we know nothin' about."

He glares at me as though this is a weak excuse. He's not wrong. "I've already got Jackson handlin' the background check," he replies simply. "We'll know everythin' before she comes back next week. If anythin' is suspicious, we'll just tell her we found a better fit. Alright?"

It's far from alright, but I don't have any other arguments against this, and the look on his face says he knows it. And I'll be damned if I stand here and admit to my brother that I just don't want to be around a woman who makes me feel as though I'm ten seconds from shooting in my pants like some twelve-year-old prepubescent boy.

I groan in defeat. "Okay."

Four days later, I'm in my office at The Crown, nursing a glass of bourbon, and looking over documents for a new investment property I want to purchase out in Montana. It's taking twice as long as it should. I'm absolutely exhausted, and this is the first time I've sat down all day.

The planks for the broken fence came in, so Knox and I

worked together to get it fixed. Then, I took a few of the horses out for a ride and checked on Ace. He's already looking better in comparison to just a few days ago.

Summer walks into my office. "Heads up, Jeremy was just caught stealin' out of the till."

For fuck's sake. I put my glass down and rub my temples. This is the last thing I want to deal with right now. "Did he think he was smart enough to get away with stealin' from the bar? Sometimes, I really wonder about the pure idiocy of this new generation."

Summer chuckles and steps out. "Not my problem, now!" she yells as she makes her way back behind the bar.

Jeremy is a new waiter I hired a few months ago. He knew exactly who his employer was when he took the job, meaning he knew who he was stealing from. The sloppy way he went about it is more insulting than the meager amount he probably took.

I'm a few steps behind Summer when I see two of my men holding a squirming boy by the arms. He's visibly shaking.

"Where's the money, Jeremy?"

"I didn't take anythin'!"

I'm already over this shit. I let out a large exhale. "Follow me," I order the two guys as I walk back to my office. Jeremy shouts and wriggles in their hold, but they're both stronger than him. I've had enough of his incessant whining, so I whirl around and kick him in the nuts. "Shut the fuck up, Jeremy." A loud oomph comes out of his mouth and he cries out in agony.

As soon as we enter my space, I turn left and walk through another door. The room has a wall covered with monitors and two chairs.

"Sit him down."

Jeremy falls onto a chair, still clutching his groin.

It'll be hard for the boy to continue denying the theft once I pull up the camera footage, where he can clearly be seen pocketing the cash.

"You have two days to bring back double the amount of money you took from the bar, or I'll stop by your family home and collect it myself." My face is passive as I make the threat. Dealing with juvenile shit like this is just a waste of time.

He nods, but doesn't say a word.

"Well, then. You're dismissed." Jeremy scrambles off the chair. "Oh, and Jeremy?"

He turns around. "Yes?"

I send my fist to his face and knock him right in the nose. His head flies back and blood splatters. "You're fired," I say, and he flies out the room.

It's a shame, he'll probably need that money to have his broken nose fixed now, but he'll have to steal from someone else to get that job done. I can't let those who go against me get away with it. If you're going to have the balls to steal from the President of the Sinners & Saints, then you better man the fuck up and take your punishment.

He's lucky that all he got was a broken nose. I was feeling generous today.

As invigorating as it was to remind the boy what the cost of stealing from me truly was, by the time I get back home and let the dogs out, I'm drained.

The sun is just beginning to set when there's a knock at my office door. I look up and see both Jackson and Knox standing in the entryway to the room.

"Hey boss, hope we're not interrupting," Jackson says. He's holding a manila envelope. They're both giving off nervous energy which puts me on edge. I straighten up in my chair and throw back the rest of my drink as I wave them in.

"No, come in. What's goin' on?" I ask, hoping to just cut to the chase.

They both take a seat in the leather upholstered chairs across from my desk.

"Listen, before you get upset," Knox starts, and immediately, I feel a dull throbbing in my head. Whatever this is doesn't sound good. "It's really not a big deal," he assures me.

Famous last words.

"What isn't a big deal?" I press.

Jax shifts in his seat and drops the envelope onto the mahogany desk top. I pick it up and slide out the papers as he begins to speak.

"We ran a background check on Naya Ohara," he says in a dull tone.

Knox opens his mouth to start speaking, but I hold up a hand to stop him. "Let Jax speak, Dav. I already know you're an advocate for Dr. Ohara, no need to beat a dead horse," I say, tossing him a glare.

He shuts his mouth and gives me the finger. I snort.

I turn back to Jackson. "Continue," I say as I begin looking at the papers in front of me again.

"Knox is right, it isn't anything crazy," he pauses. "Just a tad suspicious."

I nod my head for him to keep going.

"She moved here a month ago from Raleigh. She was previously the co-owner of a successful veterinary clinic before she moved to Springfield."

I shrug my shoulders, missing why they felt like this was worth bringing up. "Okay, this isn't groundbreakin' information."

The papers spread out before me highlight basic intel on Dr. Naya Jun Ohara. Twenty-nine years old. Born and raised in North Carolina, went to an all girls private-school where she graduated top of her class. She went on to attend the University of Georgia for veterinary school before moving back to Raleigh to open her own practice with her friend and classmate, Laura Brooks. The rest of the papers go over simple information: awards received through school, clubs she was a part of, volunteer work, etc. From what I can tell, she kept to herself and nothing stands out as being particularly noteworthy. I'm unsure as to why the guys both look so antsy.

"It seems like one day she just closed the clinic. No explanation, no notice. One day she was in Raleigh, five days later she was in Springfield. It's unclear why, though. She has no family or friends here."

This piques my interest. I lean back in my chair, folding my outstretched hands in front me. "So, she's on the run." It's a statement, not a question because if what they're telling me is accurate, which I trust it is, that's the only logical explanation.

"We think so," he says in agreement. "Her father is sick, they seem to be close, and she just *left* him. She has to be running from something for her to leave her entire life behind."

I nod, absorbing the information. "What about her mother? Where does she live?"

"Deceased. She passed away ten years ago. We didn't look into the cause of death, but we can if you want," Jackson replies.

"No," I say, shaking my head. "It doesn't matter. What I want is for you to find out what she's runnin' from. I don't care how long it takes or what lines you have to cross to get the information, just make sure you get it."

Knox, who has been surprisingly quiet throughout the whole exchange, pipes up. "Should I call and tell her not to come back?"

"Oh no, Blondie," I say, tossing him a playful smile. "We'll be keepin' her on until we find out what she's fleein' from. If she truly is on the run from somethin'—or *someone*—they're bound to come lookin' for her here in Springfield—our territory —sooner or later. What we need to know is if they're goin' to be a threat to us. Until that's determined, she stays."

What exactly are you hiding Naya?

Naya

The last month has been a constant flurry of things to do, since I didn't have a lot of time between signing the lease for my new place and taking over the clinic. I did everything at warp speed because I wanted to get out of Raleigh as fast as possible. Doing it this way meant I didn't get a lot of downtime to explore my new surroundings.

I've been to Nashville only a handful of times, but it was always to run errands, so I never got to really experience it; it was always a quick in and out. However, today, I decided to make the best of my Sunday afternoon, grabbed a coffee in Nashville, and explored a bit. It was wonderful and one of the first times I really felt like Tennessee could be *home*, not just some place I'd run to.

I should have known that feeling wouldn't last because as soon as I arrive home, I receive a text from my dad telling me he'd had a bad fall. I feel sick to my stomach.

I immediately call him and he picks up on the first ring. "Hello, *Naya chan*." His normal, raspy baritone comes through the line.

"*Nante koto du, Papa*, are you okay?" I fail to keep the panic out of my voice. I'm already picturing my father on the ground, hurt and with no one to help him. A little sob escapes my lips, but I swallow it down quickly. I can't let him know how much his condition stresses me. He'll never sleep at night.

A deep sigh comes through the line. "I'm fine, Naya. I considered not even telling you, but I figured if you found out somehow, it would have been a bigger issue down the line."

"You thought right," I say, my voice sounding trill in my ears. "What happened?"

"I was coming down the stairs and I missed a step...or two," he admits with reluctance. A gasp comes out of my mouth and he hurriedly continues on. "When I stood up, my ankle was hurting something fierce, so I called a cab and went to urgent care. It's just a sprain; the cost of the visit hurt more than my ankle."

"I'll send you the money tomorrow."

"Now, you listen here, girl, I am your father, and I won't be taking any of your hard-earned money," he says adamantly. Junpei Ohara is nothing if not stubborn.

"Seriously, *Papa*, I'll have a bit more money coming in soon. I've just signed on to be the vet for a local ranch." I still can't believe my luck with keeping All Saints as a client at the clinic. I can feel my heart rate take off just thinking about it. It's clear this couldn't have happened at a better time. Dad needs my help more than ever right now.

When I had gone back to the office that afternoon, Laura had nearly lost her mind with excitement.

"They're keeping us as their clinic?" Laura had asked for the fifth time.

I couldn't help the wide grin on my face and nodded.

"Oh my God! I knew they would!" She had clapped her hands from joy.

"We're going to be okay!" I squealed and we'd locked in an embrace.

Though, once that excitement had waned a bit, she was full of questions about Callan. She was considerably disappointed when I told her that my interaction with him had been limited, and the little I did speak to him was hardly in a professional manner. I'm still furious at the way he stormed off after rejecting me without a second thought. His unpleasant expression when he'd said, "absolutely not." The annoying hitch in his breathing when he'd gotten angry, the dumb sound of his voice barking at me while we argued. I want to growl in frustration just thinking about his stupid face.

I left out how his back muscles had rippled while he worked and the way his tattoos had stood out against his sun-kissed skin.

Snap out of it, Naya. You're on the phone with your injured father for God's sake. I clear my throat to bring myself back to our conversation. "So, yeah, this new ranch is going to help the clinic a lot."

"I'm glad to hear that, *haru-kun*." *Sunshine.* "You've been working so hard these past few months, you deserve every bit of success that you get," he says.

I smile. My father has always been my most ardent supporter. I know he means every word he says. "Thanks, Dad, but I wouldn't have made it this far without you," I reply. "I'll text you when I send the cash. Love you, bye!" I hang up the phone quickly before he can protest.

I leave the kitchen, and move to my bedroom, throwing myself onto the bed.

My mind drifts back to Callan. He was so large, but moved with such ease and fluidity, making it clear he's comfortable with the hard work on the farm. The image of his upper body is permanently etched in my brain.

When he'd turned around and faced me, I couldn't help but stare at the harsh scar across his chest, and I wondered whether it came from an accident on the ranch or some other incident. My mind says it's the latter. The scar had run diagonally from his pectoral muscle down into his six-pack abs and looked jagged, as if whatever had cut him had really snagged. My mind's eye moves lower as I remember the indented lines on either side of his abs that ran down into his jeans. I groan and roll over onto my stomach as I feel my clit begin to pulse with need. *What is wrong with me?*

I have no idea how I'm going to make it through tomorrow's follow-up visit. Chances are I won't even see Callan. When I agreed to take on the ranch, Knox gave me his number, and told me that he lives in the "smaller" house behind Cal's. I didn't get to see that side of the mansion, but if it's anything like the two stables, there's nothing *small* about it. I figure I'll probably be working more closely with him than his boss if last week was any indication.

I strip out of my clothes and head for the shower, needing to wash the day off of me.

When I wake up in the morning, I go through my normal morning routine of grinding my coffee beans and brewing a fresh pot. Instead of allowing myself to be alone with my thoughts, I decide to head to the office and open up early.

I'm seated at my desk reviewing some files when Laura walks in humming. I've left the lights off, so she lets out a yelp when she finds me.

"Why are you here so early?" she exclaims. I look at the clock on the computer. It's an hour before the clinic is supposed to open and before she starts work.

"I could ask you the same question," I reply, trying to sound nonchalant.

She shakes her head, dropping her bag onto the desk. "I couldn't sleep. Figured I'd get ahead on some paperwork. You?"

"Same." She raises a single eyebrow but doesn't ask any more questions. We both sip our respective coffees as she regales me with the events of her weekend, which put my exciting walk around Nashville to shame. By the time our first patient, a bunny with gut stasis, comes in, I know far too much about Laura's Saturday night exploits.

The day passes by quickly. There are more patients today than there have been in a long while. I'm starting to think the clinic may be turning a corner.

I text Knox to confirm that it's still okay for me to stop by the ranch around five p.m. He responds with a thumbs-up, but I almost spit my afternoon coffee when he adds that he needs to head into Nashville, so he won't be able to meet with me. He assures me that security is aware I'm coming and Cal will accompany me around the property.

My heart drops. *Are you fucking kidding me?* I almost text Knox back to give him hell for going against his word so soon, but I refrain from doing so. I'm a grown adult. I can take care of myself and can most definitely handle an overgrown man-child. I was hoping Callan wouldn't be home, or at the very least hidden away so I wouldn't have to see him. But it is what it is.

I'll have to put on my big girl panties and face the grizzly bear head-on.

I shake out my shoulders and remind myself that I didn't spend all those years in school to feel less than by some rich, better-than-everybody cowboy. I'll go in there, do my assessment, and leave. If he tries to cause a fuss, I'll deal with it. If I can handle a sick and aggravated bull, I can handle *him*.

A couple hours later, it's time to close. Before we head into our separate cars, Laura looks over at me and tosses me a wink and a sultry smirk. "Tell the cowboy I said hello."

"I'll pass that right along," I say sarcastically, and hop into my Jeep. I do my usual deep breathing once-over and pep talk before I drive off. I'm going to need all of the positive vibes for where I'm going.

When I pull up to the gate of All Saints, I hit the buzzer to let Callan know I'm here. I hear his low voice saying, "Come on through."

I suck in a deep breath and pull through the compound. I park my car in the same spot as last week, and look up toward the house, expecting to see Callan come out the front door. Instead, he rounds the corner with two large German shepherds at his heels. They're off leash, but he doesn't seem to have any worry about them running away from him.

He's shirtless, once again. *Seriously, dude?* Is he part of some half-nudist colony I don't know about?

His upper body is on display, but I force my eyes to stay away from his broad chest that's glistening with sweat. He's wearing fitted jeans that sit low on his waist, held up by a brown, leather belt with a big buckle, and to top it all off, he's wearing brown cowboy boots.

It's visual porn, and I have to close my eyes and count down to keep my composure intact.

Five, he's a jerk, don't waste your googly eyes on him. *Four*, even if he has the body of a god, don't let it persuade you. You must stay focused. *Three*, the animals. Think of the animals. *Two*, you hate men. I repeat, you hate men. *One*, whatever you do, don't. Make. Eye. Contact.

With that, I puff up my cheeks and let out a huff of air.
You can do this.

I jump out of the car and slap the fakest smile onto my face.

I breathe in, reminding myself that no matter what he thinks, I *am* capable.

7

Callan

"Afternoon, Dr. Ohara," I say, trying to keep my voice steady. And it's damn harder than it should be.

Naya is looking effortlessly gorgeous as she gets out of the wreck she calls a car. Her hair is combed back in a slicked bun, she's wearing a light denim shirt, and underneath, a white tank top that lets me see the clear outline of her breasts.

Her face is bare from any makeup, but her cheeks have a rosy tint. She's *beautiful*. The women I'm used to are done-up Barbie dolls. There's nothing wrong with that, but seeing *her*, fresh-faced, angelic, and innocent-looking makes my dick twitch in my jeans.

The things I would do to her. The way I would taint her innocence. I want to turn her into my personal—

"Good afternoon," she replies, curtly, before looking down to the dogs. "Who do we have here?" She bends down to give them a closer look.

She looks nervous. I suppose that makes sense, given our last interaction. But after taking in the information that Knox and Jackson brought forward the other day, I have no interest in trying to push her away now. *Keep your enemies close and all that.* Calling her my enemy may be a reach, but I do want to know what she's hiding.

"Harley," I say, pointing to the dog on my right, "and Davidson." I look to the one on my left. Naya stretches back up, a sly smile on her lips.

"Someone's a fan of bikes," she notices.

"Somethin' like that," I respond, keeping my voice neutral.

"I'll just take a quick look at Ace and the other horses, and I'll be on my way."

She turns around, and I get a front row view of her delectable ass. I can't stifle the groan that escapes my mouth.

What is wrong with you? Settle the fuck down, cowboy. I need to stop acting like a horse in heat.

Naya faces me and gives me an inquisitive look. I shake my head, willing her to ignore what she just heard, and she does.

I follow after her. "I can take your bag." The least I could do is be nice.

Her brows shoot up. "I'm good, thanks. I definitely don't need *your* help."

The way she says "your" makes my fists ball. She has an issue with me, and it doesn't look like she wants to be here, but can I blame her? I basically told her to fuck off the first time we met. It was a visceral reaction to the way her presence made me feel. And anything that makes me *feel* should stay the fuck away. Even if it's in the form of a fucking goddess.

My eyes narrow. "I should've canceled this appointment."

Naya falters a step or two, visibly offended by what I said. But she gathers herself within a second. "Unless you're a sick horse, I didn't come here for you," she spits.

"Some say I'm not too far off." Right on a silver fucking platter. *This is too easy.*

"Did you just make a reference to your penis?" She's taken aback, but I can hear the slight amusement behind her icy tone.

"Sure did." With no ounce of regret. *Push her away.*

"Men are disgusting," she grumbles under her breath. She begins to fidget on her feet, restless by this conversation.

"Or what? You're gonna leave? Be my guest, Dr. Ohara."

Naya's shoulders roll back and her chest heaves as she tries to collect herself, but it's to no use. Her face reddens, and I'm this close to stepping back before she explodes right on the spot.

Her finger points right at me, her nostrils flaring. "Listen here, *Callan*. I need this stupid agreement between us to work for the sake of my clinic, and I won't allow you to mess it up with your pretentiousness and weird insecurities."

Fuck. Her. "You think I'm fuckin' insecure? Trust me, *little one*. I'm nothin' close to insecure. I just know what I don't want, and that's you on this goddamn ranch." I want to strangle her, yet the way her mouth twitches in anger, almost into a snarl, makes me want to suck on her bottom lip and pull on her hair.

"Don't. Call. Me. That."

I inch closer to her. Her breath catches. *So, I'm not the only one who feels something.* I want to push all her buttons, drive her up the fucking wall. But I've got shit to do, and I need her to check on Ace.

"If you don't like it, then leave," I seethe.

She inches closer. My breathing stops. Fuck.

"No. Now, get out of my way and let me get to work."

She turns on her heels and storms away. I follow her to the stable, having lost this battle.

The forecast called for rain today, and although it's early in the evening, the sky is already covered in clouds. Harlo and Dave are both terrified of thunderstorms; they haven't left my side all afternoon.

When we make it to the horses, I stand back and watch as she begins to work.

"Have you noticed any changes in Ace?" she asks, her tone all business.

"He seems back to normal."

Dav wasn't wrong; she's good and in her element as she checks over the large stallion. I struggle to keep my body still while I observe her maneuver through the stall.

Finally, she finishes the exam and focuses her deep brown eyes on me. "I'd say he'll be back to a hundred percent within a few days."

I nod, but not a word comes out of my mouth. I remind myself to breathe, feeling frustrated at the way my body reacts to her mere presence.

"Let me do a quick check on the other horses to make sure no one else has fallen ill, and then you can move him back to the main stable at the end of the week." There's a tentative smile on her face, she's trying to keep things professional despite our little 'argument' and what I know she must have felt earlier.

No longer trusting my voice, I simply nod again, grabbing her bag off the floor as I head over to the other building.

I can't see her face, but her body language tells me she's disoriented. Probably because I'm helping her after our bickering match. I may be an asshole sometimes—okay, a lot of the time—but my *mamma* didn't raise me not to have manners.

"You don't have to do that," Naya says, briskly.

"Deal with it," I retort, letting my southern accent really drawl out.

She relents. "Thank you."

The rain that was threatening to fall finally makes an appearance as I feel the first rain drop hit my face. We both look up to the darkening sky at the same time. Sensing a downpour on its way, the dogs run toward the house at full speed to seek refuge under the wrap-around porch. We both continue to walk in silence as the sky drizzles. The air begins to cool, but the tension between us feels like a portable heater keeping me warm.

She's behind me and, even though there are a couple feet between us, I can sense her presence as if she's standing right next to me. I'm tempted to leave her in the stables by herself, as I'm more than confident she doesn't need an audience, but my pride refuses to let me go. I won't run and hide from any woman, no matter what reactions she brings out of me. Especially not on my own property.

Once we make it inside the larger barn, we turn to face each other.

"Cat got your tongue?" she asks, her tone too curt for a tease, but I know she's trying to break the tension. It's in the air, thicker than a bowl of oatmeal. But this is my chance to reclaim my manhood. If I can revert into being my asshole-self, maybe the pull I feel toward her will break, and I can go back to swearing off all women.

"I just have nothin' to say. I'm here to make sure you're doin' your job."

Naya's face crumples. *Oh, fuck.* If she was a kettle of boiling water, she'd be exploding with steam right about now. I'm not scared of anyone, but seeing her like this, I almost want to curl into myself.

They always say, the smaller the woman, the feistier she is.

Naya lowers her chin to her chest and looks up at me through her piercing eyes. She inches forward and hisses, right above a whisper, "Fuck you, Callan."

That'll do it. The opposite of what I'm trying to accomplish.

Her threat goes straight to my cock and it springs to life. At this point, I don't even care if she sees. Her fists are balled on each side of her body and she glares at me with such viciousness in her eyes, I want to devour her whole.

No one *ever* threatens me. No one dares talk shit to me. Everyone knows who I am, what I do to people who disrespect me.

Except her.

It's a fucking turn on, and I'm *so* hungry for her.

But I'll be damned if I let her know a fraction of how she makes me feel. First off, she's not here for me, she's here for the horses. Second, I'm not sure she can be trusted, given that Jax still hasn't been able to figure out what she's running away from. Third, she looks like the relationship type. I won't be able to give her what she wants.

If I fuck her and things go south, I'll lose a good doctor, and I may even feel guilty for hurting her. Like I said, I might be an asshole, but I know the difference between right and wrong.

I hold her stare a moment longer before exiting the stable without looking back.

How can a woman I don't even know waltz into my life and create pure chaos? There is turmoil inside me, and I don't know how to fix it or get rid of it.

I cut down the gravel path that leads to the main house. I notice a green Ford F-150 driving slowly—too slow to just be casually passing by—down the main road, past the gate.

I see a dark brown-haired man, with a cigarette hanging out of his mouth, in the driver's seat before he speeds off. Even from this distance, I know exactly who I'm looking at.

Mason Caldwell, President of the Raleigh Riders. The bane of my existence.

The simple sight of him springs my fury to life. What the fuck is he doing here?

I call my guards and ask them to keep a close eye on the gate and around the property. "I want all the security footage from the past hour. And if that motherfucker tries anythin' funny, find him and bring him to me," I say through gritted teeth.

Our clubs don't typically cross paths, as the *Royal Douche Canoes* deal in drugs out in Raleigh. So, there's no reason for Mason to be here. Lately though, I've heard rumblings of him wanting to expand his territory out to Tennessee, which is fucking ballsy if you ask me, especially given our history.

I've not stepped foot on his territory in the fifteen years since the altercation.

If he's in Springfield, he's definitely plotting something, and I need to nip it in the bud *now*.

Minutes later, I receive the footage from the cameras around the estate. I open up the feeds on my computer and see Mason circle around the ranch a few times in his truck.

When I zoom in, I notice he's alone, but there's a semi-automatic rifle on the seat next to him. I crack my fingers together, anger quickening my blood, as I watch my enemy scan my property.

I want to fucking kill him.

He's so close, I can taste the sweet revenge on my tongue. I've waited years to get my hands on him, and I just might get the opportunity now that he's in town.

I ring Dav's phone, but he doesn't pick-up, so I shoot him a text to call me back ASAP. I walk in circles around the main floor.

My rival driving right in front of my house is a clear intimidation tactic. If he wants a turf war, he'll have to make the first move. I have no interest in playing his games.

I pour myself a glass of whiskey from the mini bar, hoping it'll calm me down enough to gather my thoughts.

My phone rings as I chug the liquid courage. It's Knox.

"Mason is here," I state as soon as I pick up, poison lacing my tone.

"What the fuck do you mean?" Knox snarls.

"I just watched him drive by the ranch. He's plannin' somethin', Knox. We need to get to him first."

I hear shuffling on the phone and faint voices in the background. "I'm at the warehouse with some of the guys. I'll get them to do a drive 'round Springfield. What are the orders, boss?"

"If you find him, detain him. But don't kill him."

"Clear. Bring him to you alive...or barely. What about any others?"

"The more the merrier. It's time they all get to meet the King."

"Got it. Otherwise, how are things goin' back at the ranch?"

I hesitate. What was bothering me before seeing Mason comes back to the forefront of my mind in a rush. "I can't do it."

"Do what?" Dav asks, confusion in his voice.

"Her. I can't do *her*."

There's a pause before Knox's chuckle turns into a belly laugh. "What is up with you, bro? She's just a vet. She ain't here to torture you. I've never seen you this wound up before."

How do I make my best friend, my brother, understand that I can't have Naya working on the ranch without telling him it's because I can't fucking control my impulses around her. He would never judge me, but I'm not ready to tell him how messed up I feel already. My heart wants to come out of my mouth at the thought of admitting she might have reignited what I've worked so hard to keep inside for years. *No feelings, no attachment, no pain.*

So, I do what I know best, I deflect.

"She's a good vet, but she needs to go, Knox," I say, determination in my voice.

He sighs into the phone. "We still don't know what she's runnin' from. I thought you wanted to keep her close." I know he's trying to get me to see reason, but I'm so far past that. My mind is buzzing, and all I can think about is how she needs to go before she messes everything up.

"I've changed my mind."

8
Naya

fter checking on the horses—they all seem to be healthy and strong—I head to the main house to tell Callan that I'm ready to leave. Once I near the door, I stop in my tracks when I hear his voice, talking to someone.

"I've changed my mind. And at this point I don't even care. She's a charity case, and I can't have her workin' on the ranch. End of story."

I cringe, hurt and anger churning inside me.

I spin on my heels and trip on my way down the porch, a curse escaping my mouth. *Shit.* I hope he didn't hear that. I back away slowly and the door swings open.

Callan is standing at the entrance, his shocked expression morphing into something unreadable. Mine is flushed, not from embarrassment, but in pure fury.

He just called me a fucking *charity case.*

My chest is heaving and I see he's doing his best to keep his eyes trained on my face despite the way the raindrops have made my white shirt cling to my skin. *Pervert.*

We gaze into each other's eyes for what feels like hours, both refusing to break contact. We look like two animals about to pounce, ready to rip the other to shreds.

And right now, I'm not sure if he wants to hurt me, or tear my clothes off and *then* hurt me.

I break the silence, but my eyes don't leave his face. "I'll have my assistant send you the bill for today's visit." I'm eager to get out of the rain that is now starting to come down harder, and away from him.

Callan's attention is no longer on my face.

"Callan, are you listening to me?"

He takes a step back into the house. "Yes, ma'am. The bill will be sent tomorrow and Ace can go back in with the other horses in a few days. Got it."

"Alright. If anything comes up, Knox has my number. Have *him* give me a call. Otherwise, there's no need for me to be back for a while." My insides are screaming at me to confront him about what he said, but this jerk isn't worth my time.

I run to my car as the rain begins to pelt down. I try to start the engine, but it keeps turning over. I smack my steering wheel hard, frustrated that the car is struggling to turn on.

I let out a sigh. I notice Callan watching me through the window but he's the last person I want help from. I grab my phone to text Laura and don't realize that the ass has walked up to my car door. I jump and press my hand to my heart.

I roll the window down. "Can I help you?"

"I was just 'bout to ask you the same question," he scoffs. "This old thing givin' you trouble?"

Flames ignite in my eyes. Does he realize insulting my car probably isn't the best way to offer his assistance?

"Oh, I'm sorry," I say in the most insincere, sweet voice I've ever spoken. "Is my car ruining the aesthetic of your driveway? I wouldn't want you to suffer any more than you already have by me being a *charity case.*" I smile, but there's nothing warm about it.

Callan's face drops.

I hate him for his attempt at being a gentleman when he just insulted me. I already felt like I didn't fit in this type of environment, and now I'm just angry at myself for not listening to my gut. I should've run for it when I had the chance. I'm not meant to be here, but I let Laura and Knox convince me otherwise. *Arghhhhh.*

At least he has the decency to look remorseful, although it's more likely he's upset he got caught.

"Look, if your car is givin' you trouble, why don't you come on in?" He points over to the house where he left the door open, soft, inviting light pouring out, but I still shake my head.

"No, thanks." I place my hand on the wind-up crank with the intent to roll up the window. I'm ready for this conversation to end. "I'm good. Someone will pick me up." *Not exactly true, but whatever.* I hope he gets the point and leaves me alone.

Laura still hasn't responded. I curse the Heavens for having the worst timing. I pinch the bridge of my nose, a headache creeping in and only getting worse. Why did my beater decide to call it quits here and now?

Callan narrows his eyes. "Okay, then you can wait for them *inside* the house."

Now, he's the one who sounds impatient, and I can't tell if it's because I refused his invitation to come in or because his umbrella is starting to blow in the wind and he's getting wet. If he thinks I'm going to sit in his house and sip tea after what I just heard him say about me, he's got the wrong idea. I was willing to overlook his shitty attitude, but this crossed a whole other line.

"I'm good," I repeat.

Clearly tired of my rejection, Callan lets out a frustrated sigh, plants his hand on the roof of the car, and leans in close. His scent envelopes me, deep and woodsy, with just a hint of tobacco. It's heady, and I fight the urge to move closer and take a deep sniff.

"Listen, Dr. Ohara," he starts, his voice gruff and low. "I won't say it again. It's stormin', and I ain't lettin' you sit in the car."

I scoff and open my mouth to tell him he doesn't *let* me do anything. I'm a grown-ass woman. I do what I want. But he doesn't take a breath.

"Get. In. The. House. Now."

If I thought his voice was deep before, it's sunken to the pits of Hell now. His stare holds an unwavering intensity as he waits for me to get out of the car. The anger in his eyes is an indication that, if I refuse one more time, he's going to rip the door off the hinges and drag me inside. *Why does that sound like a good alternative? Lord, help me.* I break the intense eye contact to look at my phone: no new text notifications. I let out a groan and hit the steering wheel again.

"Fine," I relent, because at this point, I don't know when Laura will get here and, and if I'm honest, I don't really want to sit in my car for hours. I also may be just a tad curious about what the inside of Callan's house looks like. I'll go in, try to get a hold of my friend again, and wait at the entrance. No playing nice.

He steps back as I open the door and extends the umbrella so it can shelter me from the rain. I would rather be soaked than be this close to Callan, so I try to sidestep him, but I bump right into his body, his hardened crotch coming flush to my backside.

We both freeze. *Fuck.* I feel the metal rod, now growing by the second, right against my ass. My breaths stutter and catch in my chest as I try to steady myself. But I'm not the only one struggling to keep my composure. His breathing matches mine, our inhales and exhales in sync.

At his towering height, his chin reaches the top of my head, so he tilts it forward, his mouth grazing my ear. Slowly, he lets out some air, and I shudder at the feeling against my skin.

I need to get away from him. *Now.*

I run toward the house and enter.

I'm stunned. I don't know what I was expecting, but it wasn't this. His home is stunning. It's a modern farmhouse, light, open, and decorated beautifully, making me wonder if a woman once lived here. If the house looks big from the outside, it's even larger from where I stand in the foyer, and I find myself feeling a tad overwhelmed.

You don't belong here, a voice in my head reminds me. I dig my fingers into my palm. Callan said so himself by calling me a charity case.

I look to the left and my jaw drops at the sight of the most gorgeous kitchen I have ever seen in my life. It's all white, with light gray granite countertops and a massive island with shiplap siding. This room alone is the size of my entire home.

"Do you like to cook?" I hear a deep chuckle of amusement behind me. I realize Callan is closer than I thought when I feel his body heat warming my back, which reminds me where I am. I mentally chastise myself for being caught admiring his house.

"On occasion," I reply, casually. Although, in all honesty, I *love* to cook. I find the process of preparing a dish from scratch to be peaceful and satisfying.

The grunt he lets out in response indicates he doesn't quite buy my feigned nonchalance, but he doesn't push it any further. "Would you like somethin' to drink?"

I consider saying no, but I still don't know when Laura will get back to me, so I might be here for a little while. I also need to take off the edge of this stressful situation. "I'll have a glass of wine if you're offering."

"White or red?" He seems happy to be playing host. His mood swings are giving me whiplash.

"White, please," I say, while I pretend this isn't an extremely uncomfortable position I've now found myself in. If I drink red wine, I'll feel hotter than I already do, and my skin is burning the hell up.

"You can go to the livin' room. I'll meet you there."

He heads through the kitchen to another room connected to it, where I assume he keeps his alcohol. *Must be nice to have money.* I walk to the living room and my phone buzzes with a text notification. *Thank God!*

Except, it's not Laura.

> Mason: Hey sugar. I've been trying to get a hold of you…

My heart sinks, an unpleasant shiver running up my spine. I don't know what's going on, but *he's* been calling me sporadically for the last two weeks. Sometimes, he leaves messages asking to call him back, which I never do. Other times, he'll text me to demand I respond, which I will not do under any circumstance.

It's been weeks—though it had ended long before that for me—more than enough time for him to lick his rejection wounds and move on. We don't have anything further to say to each other, and I'm not going to indulge him every time he wants a chat.

I tuck my phone back into my pocket and look around, feeling like the walls are closing in on me despite the obnoxious size of the living room.

Suddenly, a hint of dread seizes me. *What the hell am I doing here?* I can't sit on Callan's couch and watch TV like we're best buddies. I need to find a way out of here as soon as possible. I'll just call a cab.

As if my thoughts have summoned him, Callan appears from the hall holding a glass of wine and a glass of amber liquid, neat, for himself.

"Sit," he orders. A command, not a request. I take the glass, down half of it while eyeing him, and instead of sitting down, I walk to the French doors that face out onto a field. I can't even see where the property line is from here, and I'm shocked at just how much land he has. If I squint, I can see a house farther down with its own separate garage, where I assume Knox lives. Just as I had assumed, it's not small by any means. It's smaller than the main house, but still way larger than mine.

My phone rings. I place my glass down on the coffee table and pull it out to hopefully see Laura calling to say she's on her way, but it's *him* again. I grip my phone and silence the call. It rings once more. He never does this. He usually rings or texts me once, never multiple times in a row.

Callan must notice my reaction because he stands up from where he was sitting on the sofa and walks over to me.

"Is your ride on the way?" His tone almost sounds worried. My breath catches in my lungs. Between the wine and him standing so close, I feel warm all over.

"Yes," I say as I attempt to put some space between us. My phone rings again. I don't even bother looking as I silence it. At this point, I know it's my ex-boyfriend. *Why is he doing this now of all times?*

Callan looks at me questioningly. "Well, someone is tryin' to reach you, sweetheart." His voice is a low purr in my ear, and I feel it straight down to my toes. I have to remind myself to breathe. I might die of suffocation if I stay around this man any longer.

"It's no one." I don't understand why he cares about who's calling me, and I don't know why I'm being so secretive about it. Callan takes one step forward, and I back up flush against the glass door. He stares down at me and my phone rings once more. *Damn it.*

I lift it up to stop the ringer, but this time, Callan grabs my wrist. My eyes go from Callan's hand, to his face, back to my wrist, and I'm in utter shock.

"Mason? Mason who?" Callan hisses, his grip tightening.

"Mason Caldwell! Not that it's any of your business. What the fuck do you think you're—"

He looks at the contact name and his face flashes with utter rage. "No. Better question," he silences me. "Why the *fuck* is Mason Caldwell callin' your phone?"

I freeze and stare at him, my eyes wide. "Do you know Mason?"

I try to snatch my arm back, but his grip is too tight to shake off. He crowds in closer to me. I seriously can't breathe, I need space.

"I asked *you* a question," he snarls. I can feel the warmth of his breath on my cheek and another rush of heat flows through my body.

I use my last two working brain cells to formulate a response. " I don't know."

This isn't the answer he was looking for, there's rage in his eyes as he mockingly repeats my words back to me. "'*I don't know?*' Really, sweetheart? Is that the best you've got?"

What is he even talking about? *God, why is it so hot in here?*

"He's my ex!" I snap, louder than intended. I'm so overwhelmed right now. There's way too much going on. My car broke down, I don't want to be here, I desperately need a shower, Mason is harassing me, and Callan is being so unpredictable. I can't deal with the hot and cold. I hate him for the way he makes me feel. I'm so furious, I could charge him like a bull, yet I'm so aroused that I could combust at any moment.

He drops my hand, and I watch as multiple emotions flash

across his face. I expect him to back up and finally give me some room, but he moves closer instead. There's no longer any space between us. My mind urges me to push him away, but my body begs me to lean into him. I rest my head back against the window and shut my eyes. How has this gotten so out of hand?

"If he thinks he can get to me by sendin' you, tell him to try again," Callan threatens. His booming voice reverberates along the glass and I snap my eyes open. I'm sick of being treated like a puppy who just pissed on their owner's brand new carpet.

I reach my hand out and shove him away. "I don't know what the fuck you're talking about, Callan!" I shout in his face. It feels good to finally let out some of the pent-up anger toward him. I'm tired of trying to be the bigger person. "I don't know why you think he would "send me," but I'm no one's puppet. Next time you get in my face like that, I swear I'll make you choke on your own balls."

"I don't appreciate bein' lied to."

"And I don't appreciate being accused. Now, back the hell up."

He snarls. "You don't get to tell me what to do. My house, my rules. And I want fuckin' answers, Naya."

He doesn't budge from where he stands. His shoulders are drawn back, his chest is up, his right fist is curled at his side. He looks like a pure predator ready to attack his prey, and instead of cowering, I challenge him and match his stance. *How dare he treat me like a child?* I fight to ignore every ounce of attraction I feel toward him, but my body betrays me over and over again. I can't, *shouldn't* want him. My mind is against it, I hate him. He's an asshole.

But the rest of me didn't get the memo.

"I didn't even want to come inside in the first place," I argue. "Who do you think you are? I have no idea what happened between you and Mason, and if I'm being honest, I don't want to know. Keep me out of it! I've already had enough with one psycho, I don't need another one in my life. So, let me go, Callan, or I swear I'll—"

As if my words spark some sort of fire in him, Callan places his left forearm against the glass and inches his face to mine until the tip of our noses touch. "Or you'll *what?*" he snaps in a low, grating voice. "I don't think you'll do anythin', sweetheart." I try to speak, but his right hand comes up to my throat and he clutches on to it, applying enough pressure to stunt my breath. I let out a small croak, but he doesn't let go. "Shut the hell up, Naya."

Then, he steals my breath away by doing the one thing I've wanted and despised in equal measure.

He kisses me.

9
Callan

All of my restraint snaps like a cord pulled too tight. One minute I see Mason's name on her phone and I'm demanding answers, the next my mouth is claiming Naya's. And Heaven help me, she tastes even better than I could imagine. I hear a desperate sound, and I'm shocked when I realize it's coming from me. She drives me wild.

This woman angers me to the point of no return, but the incredible amount of pure, unadulterated attraction I feel toward her has broken the dam. She doesn't back away from a challenge and doesn't make anything easy for me; which is something I lack in my life. Everyone around me cowers and shrinks in fear, but Naya doesn't. She's a fucking queen in the making.

I push away from her mouth for a fraction of a second to catch my breath, and when I stare into her eyes, my emotions and hunger are mirrored back. I attack her lips once more with fervor. I taste her top lip, nibble on the bottom one, running my tongue across it to tease her, and her mouth slightly opens. An invitation to take it further, so I swipe my tongue against hers.

The current of electricity that travels through my body is nothing I've ever experienced before. It shoots straight down to my aching cock, which hardens so much, it's almost painful. It strains against my zipper and begs to be let out, but it's not the right time. Instead, I move my arm that was leaning against the glass and wrap it around Naya's hip to bring her body flush to mine. It's not a soft, gentle tug.

She moans into my mouth at the feel of my hard front and relaxes into my hold. There are so many things going through my mind at the moment. What is she hiding? What are her intentions? But none of that matters now that I've tasted her. It's a mixture of sweet and minty, with a hint of cinnamon. I don't want to ever consume anyone else.

Naya's clothes are still wet and clinging to her body from the rain. Her white tank top is now see-through, and I can see she's wearing one of those padless, lacey bras, her hard nipples protruding through the fabric.

Fuck me.

I just want to reach over and pinch each one between my fingers until she pleads for me to stop, and then lick and suck them gently to soothe the sting. Neither of us stops the kiss, and it gets more and more intense as the seconds tick by. My fingers snake into her hair and I pull her head back hard, causing her to moan into my mouth for the second time.

If that sinful sound is any indication to what she sounds like during sex, I'm fucking done for.

Her hands travel under my shirt, up my chest, and across my scar, and goosebumps erupt all over my skin. I growl at the contact. No one has touched me like this since Alison, and that was a lifetime ago. This feels different. I'm ready to come in my jeans and we've done nothing more than kiss.

Naya lifts one of her legs up around my waist, and I take it as an opportunity to lift her up by the ass, without letting go of her lips. I press her back against the glass door a little harder than expected, but she doesn't seem to mind. *God. She must like it rough.*

Her phone rings for the fifth time, and I grunt in frustration. Through her lips, I ask, "What the fuck does he want?"

"I really don't know," she replies as she presses kisses to my mouth. "He's been calling me on and off for the last couple weeks, and I never answer. He doesn't usually harass me like this."

"Answer the call," I order. I catch her bottom lip in-between my teeth.

She pulls back from my face, eyes wide. "No! Are you crazy?"

"I am. Answer the phone, Naya."

I set her down and she blinks, before looking for her phone that has ended up somewhere on the floor at some point in-between our argument and makeout session. When she finds it, it's still going off. She tentatively brings it up to her ear and answers. "Hello?"

I mouth to her to put it on speaker, but she shakes her head. I glower at her. My sweet, little doctor is a brat.

I take a step toward her and she sighs in defeat, putting the phone on speaker.

"Where the hell are you, Naya? Why have you been ignoring my calls?" Mason's cringey voice asks. My cock softens at the sound. This is the quickest I've ever been turned off.

Why the fuck is he still talking to her like this if they're broken up? Frustration begins to boil inside of me, and I start pacing around the living room. I might not understand how I feel about Naya, but my instinct is to protect her from that piece of shit.

I cross my arms at my chest as I wait for her to respond. She looks away from me, takes a breath. "Mason, I'm at work. You know, that thing you never wanted me to do?" Her tone is laced with venom, despite the way she's started trembling. *So, he was controlling.*

"Naya, I know you're not working."

"What do you want, Mason?"

The line goes silent for a moment. Then, it dawns on me. Mason passed by the estate earlier. I assumed it was because of me and his expansion plans, but no. It has to do with *her*, which explains why he started calling her nonstop. He saw that she was here, on his rival's property. He probably thinks there's something between us, so the fucker got jealous and started harassing her. I wonder if she knows he's in town. From the way she's acting, I assume she doesn't. *Is that douchebag stalking her?*

"If you don't need anything, I'm hanging up, Mase." *Mase.* I scoff and roll my eyes.

"We need to talk. I miss you," Mason replies, his tone now soft. I want to fucking puke and punch him in the face at the same time. He's lucky the boys never found him earlier. If I ever get my hands on that guy, he's going to regret living.

Naya sighs into the phone. "Stop calling me. Bye, Mason." She hangs up. She looks up at me right away. "That was the most uncomfortable conversation ever."

I nod. I don't want to spook her or say much until I get to the bottom of what's going on between them, but tonight's not the night for a round of interrogation. It's getting late, she's been working all day, and I don't believe anyone is coming to get her.

"Look, I know you don't really want to be here, but there's a storm outside. Your friend isn't comin.' I would take you home myself, but it's too dangerous to drive."

Naya checks her phone and her shoulders drop at the obvious lack of text messages. A part of me is disappointed at her reaction. We didn't start off right, but I was hoping the kiss had eased the tension between us. Turns out, she still hates my guts.

"How 'bout we get you up to one of the guest bedrooms. They all have adjoinin' bathrooms, so you'll be able to shower and relax. I'll give you some clothes to wear," I add.

She seems to debate the idea for a few moments, then exhales. "Sure."

I turn around and lead her to the staircase.

"You didn't tell me how you know Mason." Her voice comes out shaky.

"Let's leave it for now, you need rest." I don't think I'd be able to talk about that asshole right now without exploding. She doesn't say anything else, which I take as acquiescence.

Once upstairs, I show her to the guest room at the end of the hall.

"Wow," Naya mutters from behind me once I open the door. The way she's been reacting to my home is cute as hell. She doesn't seem to come from money, not that it would ever be an issue for me. Besides, I didn't grow up wealthy either. I worked hard to make this life for myself.

"A bedroom fit for a queen," I say.

Her lips tip up at the corners, the first genuine smile of the night. "If this guest bedroom is fit for a queen, I can't imagine what your bedroom looks like." The words aren't even out of her mouth before she shrinks into herself. Her cheeks turn bright red and she covers her mouth with her hand. I fight the urge to answer with something witty and crass, I don't want to embarrass her further. She looks fucking adorable right now.

"It's fit for a *king*," I say, my smile wide. She flushes even more and looks away.

I show her where the towels and toiletries are in the bathroom, how to adjust the thermostat, and where the extra pillows and blankets are. I excuse myself for a few minutes to get her a change of clothes.

When I step back into the room, Naya is on the edge of the bed, playing with her nails.

I inch closer. I want to lay her down, climb on top of her, and kiss her until she can't breathe. I'm hardening in my jeans at the mere thought, but I don't know where we stand. Was the kiss a one-time thing? *I sure fucking hope not.*

She's your new vet. Keep it in your pants, Cal.

"Here are some of my lounge clothes. I tried to find a pair of joggers with a drawstring, so you can pull it tight enough. There's also a large t-shirt and a pair of socks in the pile."

Naya doesn't answer and simply nods. So, I set the items down next to her and walk out of the room, deciding to give her space.

As I click the door shut, I hear the water turn on. I let out a groan.

Naya is one wall apart from me, naked and wet, and I'm out here, desperate and on fire. I go to my room, rip my clothes off, and step into my shower. I let the blazing hot stream fall on my back as I brace myself against the wall and fist my cock.

There's only one thing that comes to mind as I attempt to jerk my problems away.

Dr. Naya fucking Ohara. My biggest problem of them all.

10

Naya

I close the bathroom door and turn the shower on, letting it heat up while I stare at myself in the mirror.

All I had to do was check the horses and leave.

I failed at the leaving part.

I'm supposed to hate Callan, but now we're playing house in his huge mansion. I feel so small compared to everything here, including him. And not in a cute way—in a pathetic way.

My fingers subconsciously reach for my mouth, and I rub my lips, remembering the way his teeth pulled on them. The way his tongue danced with mine. The sounds of satisfaction that vibrated against my mouth. The taste of *him*.

I groan and step under the rainfall shower. I've only seen these on TV, but I'm not surprised since this is one of the fanciest bathrooms I've ever seen. And it's a guest one. Callan's space must be mind-blowing. I'm tempted to take a peek, but I wouldn't dare venture to his side of the house at this hour. It might give him the wrong idea.

When I made a comment about his room earlier, I didn't mean for the words to come out as they did. I could tell he wanted to respond with a witty remark, but I was happy he decided to spare me. I couldn't have dealt with the way my body might've reacted then. I can't even deal with it now and he's not here.

As I begin to wash myself, my nipples harden into tight buds. Before I can stop myself, I reach my left hand up and give my right nipple a pinch. A moan slips out of my mouth before I can catch it. I shouldn't be doing this here, especially not in his house and while he's present. What if he hears me or even worse, walks in on me? I would be horrified and never recover. Even though what happened in his living room gave me more than enough material to get off to.

God help me. I can't do this anymore.

I have to relieve myself of this self-inflicted torture. If I forbid myself from coming any longer, I might combust into a million tiny pieces. Nothing will compare to the real deal—I make that thought immediately disappear back to where it came from.

You hate him, he's a dick. He's your client. You cannot sleep with him, I repeat to myself over and over. I just need to release this tension, and everything will go back to normal. I'm sure of it.

I grab the sprayer, aiming the jet against my hand, and adjust the temperature until it's the perfect warmth. I guide the head directly against my throbbing center. The feeling makes my knees buckle and shoots a wave of pleasure up my body. The glass around me fogs and the shower fills with steam. The heat, combined with the intensity of the stream on my clit, sends me to another dimension. I can hardly breathe, the rise and fall of my chest growing faster by the second.

I close my eyes and hum at the thought of the man who drives me crazy. Sure, the thought of *him* had gotten me a little —*a lot*—hot and bothered, but this need has nothing to do with him. It has simply been a little while. *Keep telling yourself that, Naya.* I grit my teeth and attempt to get him out of my head.

Another moan slips out, this one louder. *Oh god,* I can feel myself getting wetter, and it has absolutely nothing to do with the water hitting me with force. I reach my left hand out on the shower door in an effort to ground myself. I'm tumbling over the edge.

My inner muscles begin to clench, and I bite my lip as I throw my head back, squeezing my eyes shut as the orgasm overtakes me. Waves of pleasure crest around me, and I get a flash of luscious brown hair and a tattooed upper body. *Callan.*

When I'm done washing myself, I dry off and put on one of the many moisturizers lining the shelf. The bathroom is stocked with expensive skincare products and toiletries that put mine to shame. Each item seems carefully picked out. There's no way Callan is responsible. He must've had a woman buy all of these. Or maybe they belonged to someone and he kept them here.

Why do I care?

Who he sleeps with is none of my business. He doesn't belong to me, and he never will. We had a moment of weakness, emotions were flying high, and the tension needed to break. That kiss was a means to an end; now I can go back to hating him and he can continue being a raging dick.

After what I heard him say on the phone, I don't think I'll be working here much longer, anyway.

I glance at the clothes he left for me on the bed and the unbalanced part of my brain urges me to take a quick sniff. They smell exactly like him, as though laundry detergent couldn't even remove his deep woodsy scent. I throw the oversized shirt over my bare chest and pull on the joggers. I'm a tad embarrassed to be going commando in his pants, but I didn't pack for today's situation.

Note to self, always keep a change of clothes in the car. Just in case.

I tighten the drawstrings and head to bed.

I'm suddenly overwhelmed with thoughts of what happened downstairs. The way Callan raised his voice at me when he saw Mason calling. How do they even know each other? From what I gathered, it doesn't seem like they have a good relationship. They might even hate each other. I'm curious to know what happened, but I'd rather stay out of it.

I still don't understand why it even mattered to Callan. The way he gripped my throat, pulling me in for a kiss that felt like a brand on my lips. It wasn't slow and timid like so many of my past first kisses. No, this was hot and dominating. It was as if he wanted to lay claim not only to my body, but to my soul.

As I lie down, I play back the sounds he made in my head. I try to think of something else, *anything else*, but it's no use. I feel slick between my legs and let out a low moan. I'm already halfway there just thinking about our tongues tangled together.

Fuck it, round two. I wiggle the joggers down my thighs and kick them off the sheets. I spread my legs and reach down to where I'm aching. I gently slide my digits up and down my soaking pussy. I press my finger against my throbbing center and a gasp escapes my mouth as some of the tension releases. I imagine his rough calloused hand rubbing circles on my clit, and I throw my other palm over my mouth to stifle the groan that wants to come out. I move quicker and another surge of liquid heat flows out of me.

It's not enough.

I think once more about how he kissed me, not like someone fragile, but as a woman who could handle being dominated.

I thrust two fingers inside my opening, not holding back as I picture how he would do it. I feel close as I grind on my hand, pressing the heel of my palm firmly against my clit and pushing my hips up for even more friction. I urge myself to the edge as I guide myself to my climax.

I might never get to experience Callan, so I'll take what I can get. Right now, I hear his voice in my ears, his breath on my skin, his body wrapped around mine. I'm pumping at a speed I didn't know I could move. My orgasm surfaces quickly, but hard. I grab a pillow and stuff it over my face, biting down hard as I explode all over my fingers. My whole body goes limp and I breathe through the sensation.

I just came on Callan's guest bed.

I don't even have the energy to feel ashamed. I'm exhausted and can still hear the thunder and rain outside. I turn to my side and finally let sleep claim me.

I'm exhausted and so ready for the weekend. If this is what it's like to complete the requirements for veterinary school, what will it be like when I move to Georgia?

I keep an iron-tight grip on the steering wheel through the rain that's coming down a bucket a drop as I drive off campus. Lightning brightens the ominous night sky and every boom of thunder seems to shake the car. I contemplate if I should stop and pickup food for dinner. Dad is working the night shift at the hospital today, so he won't be home when I arrive, and mom...

Well, I doubt she bothered to cook anything.

I try my hardest not to hold anger toward my mother. It's not her fault; addiction is a hell of a disease.

The house is completely dark when I pull up. I sigh, grabbing my backpack from the passenger seat, and I go inside. I call out to mom, but get no response.

A shiver creeps up my spine. Something doesn't feel right.

But I shake off that thought. She probably went out to see her dealer.

Thunder rolls outside, making me jump. I can't remember the last time we had a storm this bad.

As I step into the kitchen, a strike of lightning flashes and briefly illuminates the room. Confusion and dread consume me; I swear I saw something lying on the ground.

I flip the switch, and my soul exits my body as I take in the sight before my eyes. Mom. She's lying unconscious on the floor with a makeshift tourniquet tied around her arm and a needle just out of reach.

I let out a blood curdling scream.

"No, no, no," I cry out as I run over to her. "Mom! Oh God, oh God."

I can't seem to move fast enough. My body is shaking uncontrollably. I feel like I'm going to be sick. I reach out to check her pulse. She's cold.

"Mom, no," I sob. The air gets sucked out of my lungs and I struggle to take a breath. I'm hyperventilating.

I pull out my phone to call 911. The operator gives me instructions on how to perform CPR and reassures me the paramedics are on their way. I do my best to listen to the steps despite the exigent buzzing in my ears. My head feels like it will explode at any moment. I do the compressions and try to blow air into my mom's lungs, but in my heart of hearts, I know there's no saving her.

She's gone.

I stop and bring her head into my lap. I gently stroke her hair as tears pour down my cheeks. This is the last time I'll ever hold my mother.

I startle awake. I touch my cheeks, wet with tears, and turn my head to see Callan leaning up against the bed frame, pulling me against his body in an embrace. I should be rattled that he's in the room, but I'm just relieved to not be alone. In the back of my mind, I know this isn't right, but I don't have the energy to fight it. I lean into his warm embrace and breathe in his intoxicating scent.

"Shhh," he coos, as he gently rocks me back and forth. A small sob escapes me. "You're okay, sweetheart. It was just a nightmare."

I shake my head. He doesn't get it. It wasn't just a dream, that was real. A memory I try my hardest not to think about but always seems to resurface when a thunderstorm strikes.

I back away just enough to look at him. It's dark, his features sharp with only the moonlight pouring in from the window. I'm struck by how handsome he is. I search his eyes, wondering why he's even here. Although, as he holds me tightly in his arms, I don't really care what the reason is.

My panic subsides and my heartbeat slows. I reach up to touch his cheek, feeling the scratch of his facial hair against my palm. He lets out a pained sound, his eyes a clear giveaway that he's doing his best to hold himself back.

But I don't want him to, I want him *unleashed*.

I need the distraction from my racing mind.

So, I stretch out farther and let my fingers run through his hair. I grasp onto the long strands and bring his lips down onto mine.

11

Callan

I woke to screams coming from the other side of the hallway. For a moment, I was confused as to what could be making that noise at this time of the night.

Then, I remembered. *Naya.*

I shot out of bed, reached into my nightstand, and grabbed my gun. I have firearms hidden in multiple places around the house in case I need to defend myself. With the shouts and hollers I heard, I was hoping not to find an intruder lurking the halls.

I quickly moved down the long corridor. I quietly entered the guest bedroom, my back against the door, and my glock loaded and ready to shoot.

Instead, I found Naya, still asleep, thrashing in bed. She let out a piercing scream. Something in my chest tightened.

I raced over to the other side of the bed and layed the gun on the nightstand. I tried to wake her as I sat down. Tears stained her cheeks, and I wondered what she could be dreaming about that would lead her to cry in her sleep.

"What happened to you, Naya?" I whispered softly. I didn't want to scare her, so I shifted slightly as I reached to hold her tightly. She began to wake up and her eyes snapped open.

She was covered in a cold sweat, her hands shaking, and I could almost see her heart pounding out of her chest.

Naya quickly glanced around the room and a look of confusion crossed her face until she saw me. I'm thankful she didn't fight me. I'm probably not her ideal candidate to receive comfort from, but I knew I had to be here. I heard a small sob escape her lips and I tried my best to soothe her.

She started to pull away, and I worried for a moment that she'd come to her senses and would tell me to get out of the room.

Instead, she reached up and touched my cheek, and I felt a spark shoot through me. I let out a groan of desperation. Slowly, but surely, she guided my mouth down to hers and kissed me.

God, she's the most intriguing woman I've ever met, not afraid to put me in my place. Ever since the first day she waltzed into my ranch, I've struggled to convince myself that I don't want her. If she doesn't want me and I can't have her, I'm going to soak in every moment I can get.

Only in my boxers, I rely on the bed sheets to cover the large erection I'm now sporting. Naya lets out a soft moan, and I take the opportunity to sweep my tongue in her mouth.

It hasn't even been twenty-four hours since I last kissed her, but it feels like I've waited a lifetime to get another taste. Her grip on my hair tightens, and I growl as I bask in the slight sting that accompanies the sweet taste of her kiss. She pulls back and her chest heaves in the moonlight as she tries to catch her breath.

"Callan." She says my name as if it's a prayer, a benediction. A hope of things to come, and I'll be damned if I don't oblige. The sound of my name rolling off her lips snaps the thin thread of control I had left.

"Naya," I respond, my tone just as reverent.

I tear myself out of our embrace so abruptly she falls onto

her back. A small yelp escapes her, but I silence her with my mouth as I roll on top of her body. Our tongues tangle as our kiss goes from soft to hard and desperate. I have to fight the urge to explode in my pants when she begins to suck on my tongue. *Holy fuck.*

I move away from her again and she responds with a whine of protest. The cry turns into a moan when I trail kisses down her jaw. I stop right between her neck and shoulder, and inhale my way up her throat to her ear, before nibbling on her lobe. Her smell is intoxicating, a drug I never want to be sober from.

My hand wanders underneath her shirt and, *hallelujah,* her bra is gone. I pinch one nipple and she lets out the most delicious mewl. I move to the next one and I'm rewarded with the same cry. Music to my fucking ears. I want to hear every single noise she can make by the end of this.

"Sweetheart, I could listen to you make that sound all night," I murmur, my voice husky with desire. "I need this shirt to go."

I shift back and she doesn't hesitate to peel off her top so quickly *The Flash* would be proud. When she's removed her clothes, I realize what I hadn't noticed before. Not only is she not wearing a bra, she also isn't wearing underwear. *She's trying to kill me.*

Cause of death: fatal arousal.

"What are you doin' to me, Naya?" I ask, my voice barely a whisper.

I press a kiss on her lips before bringing my attention back to her breasts. I pinch her left nipple again, harder this time, then bring my mouth down to suck it. My tongue laps on and around the pebbled bud and the feeling on my tongue elicits a groan from me. Her nipples are so fucking perfect, I could spend an entire day playing with her tits. She moans desperately and shamelessly. *I love it.*

She arches her back up to push more of her breast into my mouth, and I open wider, wishing I could devour her whole. When I switch sides, she snakes her fingers into my long hair and shoves my head down hard.

"So eager, darlin'," I hum, my mouth still around her breast. My warm breath sends shivers across her body and goosebumps erupt all over her skin. I bite her nipple and she squeals, making my cock pulse in my briefs. *That's what you get for being a brat.*

I crawl up her body and place myself between her legs. I press my crotch against her with only the material of my boxers separating us. She's soaking, and I can feel how wet she is through the fabric. The pulsing of her pussy against me feels like a heartbeat against my cock. I kiss her like a man starved as I rock against her faster and faster.

"*Callan*," she cries out, gasping for air. "God, I'm so close already."

Her words spur me on, and I thrust against her even harder. I'm close too, but tonight isn't about me. Naya needs me. She needs *this*. So, I stop myself. I'm painfully hard, but I need to focus on her pleasure only. She realizes I'm no longer moving and throws her head back in frustration.

"Sweetheart, I need to feel you comin' around my fingers. I want to feel just how tight you are," I whisper in her ear and the whimper that follows confirms she wants this just as much as I do. "Is that alright?"

She nods her head eagerly.

"No, Naya, use your words."

"Yes," she replies, her voice strained as she tries to maintain control. "Yes. Touch me."

I plant a kiss on her lips while my fingers trail down her chest and stomach. My callused hands against her soft skin are like a match made in Heaven. When I reach her center, I feel a strong heat, her core hot like a volcano. She's so fucking ready for me.

"You don't have to beg, darlin,' but I won't be mad if you say please," I tease.

"Please, Callan."

I tease her opening, then slip two fingers into her pussy with force and she gasps.

"You're so fuckin' wet." I slip my digits in and out in a steady rhythm. "*God*, Naya. You're makin' a mess. Is all of this for me?"

Her wetness is leaking down my hand and there's a dampened stain right under her ass. I glance down at my body where I've made a mess of my own. There's a small round precum spot right where the tip of my dick rests in my briefs. I groan and tuck my cock up; it feels like a bomb ready to detonate. I want to taste Naya's pussy and cover my face with her juices, then I want to shove my dick so far up into her she cries and pleads for me to stop.

Naya lets out a high-pitched cry. When her muscles begin to grip tightly around my fingers, my cock twitches at the thought of what it would feel like to really be inside of her.

A crack of thunder echoes through the room and I watch her flinch. *Was her dream caused by the storm?* I have the overwhelming need to remind her she's safe with me, even though I'm not fully convinced that's true.

Keeping up the pace, I pump my fingers into her. I grab her face with my other hand and harshly kiss her lips. "Focus on me." My hoarse voice is barely recognizable to my own ears.

I curl my fingers inside her, pushing down gently on her lower stomach, my eyes still trained on her face. Her moans get louder, her breaths turn harsher, and she is right on the edge of losing control. *All because of me.*

"Let it go, sweetheart. Come for me."

The waves crash against her at my words, and I watch as she has the most beautiful orgasm I've ever seen. Her eyes squeeze shut and her head moves side to side as though it's too much as her walls clamp around my fingers.

"Atta girl," I say, satisfied despite the aching bulge in my underwear.

Once she has come down from the high, and only then, do I remove my fingers from inside her. I shove both into my mouth.

Naya tastes like Heaven, a meal designed to turn me into a glutton. I kiss her once more, swirling my tongue in her mouth so she can see just how good she tastes.

I move away and she reaches out to grab my arm.

"But—" she utters, looking at my cock that's standing at attention right in her view.

I shake my head. "Not tonight." This time was all about pleasing her, anything to get her mind off whatever plagued her dreams.

I palm my aching cock. As much as this pains me, it's not about me.

But there *will* be other nights.

<h1 style="text-align:center">12
Naya</h1>

Oh my God. What the hell have I done?

I've just had the best orgasm of my life at the hands of a man I've sworn to hate. A man who called me a *charity case*. My heart is palpitating, my breaths are still ragged from the intensity of my climax. I groan in embarrassment.

I watch as he walks out of my room with the biggest, raging hard-on I've ever seen.

Not tonight, he said.

Not ever, I should've replied.

It was a moment of weakness. But this push and pull between us has to end at some point. I've been trying to convince myself he's the most selfish jerk of all time, but then he barges in, a knight in shining armor, to save the day.

Whenever nightmares of my mother's death have plagued my dreams in the past, I was always alone to face the backlash and would end up having a sleepless night. Callan didn't soothe me in a conventional way—*making me beg for an orgasm*—but it did help to some extent. For the first time, I'm not scared. Even though I can't stand him, or accept the fact that maybe I don't actually hate him, knowing he's here soothes my broken heart.

But tomorrow, things will go back to normal. I'll call Knox and tell him they'll need to find a new vet. I need the money, but to what extent am I willing to suffer for it? This anguish might be self-inflicted, but I refuse to get entangled with yet another egotistical, rich guy who thinks he's better than everyone. I've had enough with my ex-boyfriend for a lifetime. And the fact that they know each other doesn't put me at ease. I have so many questions, yet I don't have the courage to hear the answers. Mason broke my trust, toyed with my emotions, manipulated me. I never want to have another man's filthy hands on me. And by filthy, I mean up-to-no-good.

I pick up my phone from where it's sitting next to Callan's gun. *See? No good.*

There are five text notifications and two missed calls from Laura. She apologized and asked if I got a ride. She had a family emergency in Knoxville and had to drive there and back in the storm. Although it's late, I text her back, letting her know I'm stuck at All Saints and that I could use a ride in the morning. I immediately get a response back.

> Laura: Omg... you're IN his house???

I groan. I can't believe she's still up. I don't want to have this discussion right now.

> Me: Can you pick me up in the morning?

> Laura: Of course, I'll be there first thing. I'll bring coffee. We have a lot to talk about!

I put my phone down, let out a pent up breath of air, and stare at the ceiling. I bring my hands to my face and rub my eyes a few times to make sure I'm here and this isn't an extension of my dream. The wet spot on the sheet reminds me that none of this was made-up, no matter how much I want it to be. I roll over to the other side of the bed, doing my best to calm my mind and fall asleep.

I wake to my phone buzzing on the nightstand. I squint, seeing it's already bright out. I reach over and pick up.

"Hello?" I say, groggily.

"Hey!" Laura's voice is way too chipper at this hour in the morning. "I'm here. Well, I'm at the gate, but security won't let me through until Callan gives them the okay, and he's not answering the buzzer."

I let out a grumble. He's probably not up yet. I'm still naked under his sheets. Goddamn it. I don't know where my clothes are, and I need another shower. I can either walk down that long-ass driveway and meet Laura at the gate, or I can wake Callan up and have him buzz her in.

I make the decision in two seconds flat, jumping out of bed and pulling on my now dry clothes from yesterday. I look around for my underwear, even checking under the bed, but it's nowhere to be found.

"Damn it!" I say to myself, giving up my search. I notice my reflection in the mirror; my hair looks like a bird's nest. I try to run my fingers through it, but there isn't much I can do. I just pray Laura doesn't ask about it.

I tiptoe down the stairs, but every step I take sounds ridiculously loud. When I get to the front door, one of his dogs—Harley, I think—crooks his head to one side at me. I close my eyes, hoping he doesn't bark. Thankfully, the universe is looking out for me because he turns around and heads back to the living room. The little Houdini act I'm trying to pull isn't worth his time.

Once I'm outside, I take a deep inhale of the fresh morning air. Out here, I can pretend that last night didn't happen. I walk over to my Jeep, grab my bag, and begin my walk down the long driveway.

This may indeed be my most embarrassing walk of shame to date.

Security gives me a nod and opens the gate just enough to let me slip out. I wonder what this must look like to them. Laura answers that question for me when she lets out the biggest squeal as soon as I open the car door.

"Oh my God!!!" Her loud voice, two octaves higher than normal, makes me wince. "Did you sleep with him?"

"We aren't talking about this." I try my best to keep my voice neutral as flashes of last night blaze through my mind. The way he spoke to me, *God*, I could come just thinking about it.

Stop it. I chastise myself.

"Oh, we're talking about it," Laura replies, unadulterated joy in her voice. She hands me my coffee cup and pulls out of the driveway. "What's he like in bed? I hear those ranchers are a good lay. Did you do it in the stables?"

Laura blurts out question after question, without taking a single breath. This woman is relentless.

I pinch the bridge of my nose. I should have just walked home.

"I didn't sleep with him," I sigh, although I know that, if things had gotten that far, there's no way I would have stopped him. "We just kissed...amongst other things."

There's no *just* about it, though. The kisses we shared lit me up inside. An untamable fire is blazing under my skin. I can still feel his lips on mine, his breath on my skin. A shiver breaks across my body.

The shriek Laura lets out almost pierces my eardrums. "WHAT OTHER THINGS?" she screams. I burst out laughing as I cover my ears.

"Laura, you're two seconds away from detonating. I don't know how safe I am in this car anymore," I joke. "Long story short, we argued, we kissed, and we left it at that. Later on, I had a bad dream and he came to my room. One thing led to the next and...he ended up fingering me," I admit, quietly. My face heats up as color rises to my cheeks.

Laura's mouth opens up wider than a gaping fish. "What does this mean? What happens now?"

"I don't know, but it doesn't matter." I do my best to sound authoritative. "I'm dropping them as a client."

Laura lets out a little gasp. "We need them, Naya," she argues. Her eyes are on the road, but I can tell from her voice that she isn't happy.

"We'll be fine," I reply quickly, having already rehearsed this speech in my mind multiple times since I decided that All Saints needed to go. "We'll just put up more advertisements, let people know we work with large and small animals. Another ranch will come around," I explain and realize I'm attempting to convince myself more than I am her.

She doesn't say a word. I can count on one hand the amount of times I've seen my friend genuinely at a loss for words, so I know she's not thrilled about what I'm saying, but it has to be done. There's no way I'm ever seeing Callan again.

"Anyway, enough about that. Is everything okay with you? What happened last night?"

Laura's shoulders drop as she lets out a pent-up breath. "Yes. My uncle was out fishing with a friend and suffered a minor heart attack. He was rushed to the local hospital, so my aunt and I had to meet him there. He's recovering well, though." My chest tightens. I know how much she cares for them.

I grab her hand in mine. "I know things are a little coocoo on my end, but you know I'm here for you, right? Whatever you need."

Laura nods and gives me a smile. "Thank you, Naya."

Right then, my phone buzzes and I see a message I assume is from Callan. My heart races and my palms start sweating. Something tells me he won't take too kindly to the fact I slipped out without even saying goodbye. It was a cold move, even more so for me. I've never done that before.

I open the text.

> Unknown: No goodbye?

I was right, it's Callan. It's not in my nature to be so insensitive, but I can't think straight when it comes to him. I can't let him get to my head, even if it means doing something this harsh. He opened his home to me, comforted me when I had a nightmare, gave me a mind-blowing orgasm, and I repaid him by leaving unannounced. *I'm a terrible person.* I can't think of the right words to say, so I settle on thanking him for his hospitality.

> Naya: Thanks for letting me crash last night.

Three little dots immediately appear at the bottom of the screen, but disappear as fast as they showed up. I hold my breath, expecting him to rip me apart, but after five minutes of radio silence, I realize no response is coming. *Okay, I deserve that.*

Laura drives me back home and waits for me while I take a

quick shower and change before heading to the office. I can tell she's still upset about letting the ranch go, but she'll get over it. I want to hug her for caring so much about the clinic. Laura has proven to be the most caring person I've ever met. I'm so thankful she agreed to uproot her life to come with me to Springfield on such short notice. She's been my biggest supporter and has given me the strength to not give up even when it feels like the world is against me.

On the drive to work, I text Knox, too much of a coward to phone him.

> Me: I won't be able to take on All Saints after all.

> Knox: Why not?

> Me: The clinic is too swamped at the moment.

The lie stings twice as much knowing we're the exact opposite of swamped.

> Knox: I understand. Thanks for takin the time to examine the horses yesterday.

Humph, he took that much better than I was expecting him to. I let out a sigh.

We pull into the plaza's parking lot, and I take a second to think about the predicament I'm in. I lost a very good business opportunity because I can't control my own impulses. My car is dead and still parked at the All Saints Ranch. My ex has somehow weaseled his way back into my life.

And *Callan*. The burly, grumpy rancher who has left a mark in my head and on my body. I bury my head into my hands and let out a loud growl. I completely forget about

Laura's existence until she rests her palm on my thigh and gives it a little squeeze. I look up at her and she offers me a sad yet hopeful smile. I return it, glad she's still on my side.

She motions her head toward the clinic's door. "Ready to make today our bitch?"

I giggle. Our bad bitch mantra. Laura always knows how to make me feel better. "Let's do it," I reply.

Hours later, I'm stuck in the staff room analyzing the advertising budget for the clinic, and I wonder how we're going to be able to fund more ads. It initially sounded like a great idea when I was trying to prove my point to Laura, but it might not be doable at all. I'm out of options. I can't take out a loan at the bank, I've exhausted my funds, and my dad definitely doesn't have extra money laying around.

I hear the front door bell jingle, indicating someone has walked in. I look at the clock. Our next patient shouldn't be in for another hour. We don't normally get many walk-ins, maybe someone has come in with an emergency.

I grab the remote and turn on the CCTV footage, but what I see makes my jaw drop to the floor.

Standing at the front desk, talking to Laura, is Callan.

And he looks furious.

13
Callan

I sit in my office, staring at my phone for the tenth time since this morning.

Letting her *crash*? Is that what she calls what happened last night? I'm not so old-fashioned that I believe a hookup is supposed to mean anything special. Hell, there's a trail of women in Nashville who will tell you I never gave them a second look afterward.

But I know it was more with Naya.

The way she moaned my name. The way she begged for it. I know we aren't anywhere close to done. If she wants to run away, fine. *I love the chase.*

I may not have let her suck me off last night, but I'm no saint. And I'm certainly not a martyr. As I left her room, I grabbed her lacey little thong off the floor and headed back to my room with an iron rod in my pants. I have never craved a woman so badly. I wanted to sink into Naya's sweet pussy when I felt her coming around my fingers. I *needed* release. The second I closed the door to my room, I pulled my boxers down and got on the bed. I lifted the undergarment to my nose and took a deep inhale, moaning out in ecstasy.

She smelled just as sweet as she tasted on my fingers. In the back of my mind, I know this behavior might not be normal, but she brings out something primal in me. I'd wrapped the soft material around my hand and began stroking my cock already wet with precum. I rubbed it slowly at first, picturing how it would feel to have her mouth on me. How I would make her beg for air as I shoved myself deeper down her throat. I could just picture how sexy she would look with her mouth full, saliva leaking down her chin, and tears running down her cheeks, making her eyes glisten.

My thoughts are interrupted when Dav barges into my office, Harlo and Dave in tow. If I didn't know any better, I'd think they were his dogs because of how obsessed they are with him.

"When did you get here?" I question. I didn't even hear him enter.

"A few minutes ago." Dav doesn't sound pleased. I can't figure out what the hell he could be mad about so early in the morning, but I've got bigger things on my mind. Like what Naya's punishment is going to be for leaving. "I got a text from Naya," he adds.

This catches my attention.

"What did you do, Hudson?" His voice is sharp. I don't have to question if he's pissed now, I know he is.

"What did she say?" I shoot right back.

"Apparently, the clinic is suddenly too 'swamped.'" He gestures quotation marks. "And she is no longer able to take on the ranch as a client."

My brows furrow. I turn my back to him and settle deeper into my seat, wondering how I could have read everything so wrong. I try to put the pieces together by thinking back to last night and walking through the events that occurred, but nothing makes sense.

Earlier this morning, dread had churned in my body when

I noticed she was nowhere in sight. The bed was made up, her clothes gone. I barged down the stairs, hoping to find her in the kitchen sipping on a mug of coffee. But of course not. Naya Ohara would just up and leave without a word after what happened. *Without saying goodbye.* The thought fills me with an emotion I can't place. Anger? A sense of abandonment? Last time someone left me without any final words, my heart got so broken I vowed to never love again.

"Her car is still parked outside." Dav continues. "Did she stay the night? Did you *sleep* with her, man? Tell me you didn't fuck this up."

"I didn't sleep with her." Venom tingeing every word I speak. "But even if I had, it would be none of your fuckin' business," I seethe.

My heart is beating out of my chest as I try to absorb what has happened in the last twenty-four hours.

"Like hell it ain't my business," he retorts. The anger in his voice matches mine. "She was a good doc. We needed her here. You could've fucked any bimbo at The Crown, but she's the one you chose?"

I keep myself still. Refusing to even move an inch because God knows if I do, I'll probably walk over to Knox and put his head right through a cabinet. I take a quick inhale, which doesn't help shit, before I respond, "Her car broke down. It was stormin', so she stayed in the guest bedroom. And I simply comforted her after a nightmare. That's all."

He looks like he believes that as much as he would believe me if I told him Ace started shitting cotton candy. "Well, you better get her back." He cuts me one last dirty look before turning on his heels and heading to the door.

A few hours later, I'm in Naya's Jeep outside of her office. I'm fuming.

Angry at her for how she left, mad at Dav for putting this on me, and pissed that I have to convince her to come back to the ranch when she shouldn't have dropped us in the first place. I wanted her to leave, knowing I wouldn't be able to control myself around her or focus on anything but her, yet now that she left, I've changed my mind. *No one said I was logical.*

When I walk into the building, I'm greeted by a young woman at the front desk. She looks to be in her late twenties with long blonde hair tied up in a ponytail and a friendly smile on her face. I see her do a double take as I walk in.

"Hi there! How can I help you?"

"I need to speak with Dr. Ohara," I reply.

The smile on her face dissipates as she realizes my visit likely has nothing to do with a sick animal.

"Oh, um," she stutters over her words. "I think she may be in the back. Can I ask what this is about?"

"I just need to discuss business with her." I'm trying to keep my temper at bay, but my patience is quickly seeping out. I'm about to walk to that back room and fetch her myself if this receptionist doesn't get moving.

She opens her mouth to respond when I hear light footsteps coming from down the hall. We both turn toward the sound and there *she* is, standing at the entrance of the waiting room.

"Callan, what are you doing here?" Naya asks by way of greeting.

"Callan?" the receptionist whispers, talking to herself. I see a flutter of recognition in her eyes as she looks at me once more before turning her gaze back to Naya. Clearly, someone has been talking about me. Did Naya tell her what happened last night?

"I think I'm going to take my lunch break early," the assistant says.

Naya pins her with a deadly stare. "It's ten a.m, Laura..."

"Well, a coffee break, then," *Laura* replies. "I really want to try the new café that opened down the road." She grabs her purse and is out the door before Naya can raise another argument.

Once Laura's gone, it's so quiet in the room, you could hear a pin drop. I refuse to break the silence.

"Seriously, Callan," Naya exhales, finally breaking the silence. "What are you doing here?" Her voice sounds defeated..

"You know," I say, ignoring her question. "If a man has you beggin' to come at night, the least you can do is say goodbye in the mornin'." My voice is filled with more bitterness than I intended.

Her cheeks turn the most delicious shade of pink, and I fight the urge to cross the distance between us and push her against the wall. Everything about this woman drives me wild.

"That's what you came here to say? Okay, fine. *Goodbye,* Callan." Naya's tone is final. It's adorable that she thinks she can dismiss me so easily. She turns around to walk back down the hall and this time, I act.

Before she can even take a full step, I'm in front of her. In an effort to get away, she backs up right against the wall. I rest my hands on either side of her face, trapping her, and she gasps. I look down at her chest and see that it's heaving. I want to put my mouth on hers and steal the air from her lungs, making her need me to breathe. From here, I can smell her sweet, yet spicy scent. I have to force myself to focus on what it is I want to say.

"We aren't done here, darlin'," I say, my voice too low, revealing the unquenchable need to take her right here, right now. "You aren't leavin' the ranch. I won't allow it."

"Why not? If I remember correctly, you *wanted* me to leave," she says. Her tone is indignant, yet her eyes are glazed. I feel a sense of satisfaction that she's just as affected by me as I am by her. I release her from the cage I have her in, confident she won't try to make an escape. Even if she attempts to run, she won't get too far.

"Well, as much as it pains me to admit, sweetheart..." I notice she bites her lip at the term of endearment, and I wonder if she's thinking about how I called her the same while I watched her come. "We need you. There isn't another vet available and on call in Springfield," I continue.

"I'm sure you could find someone," Naya says, her eyes going to the floor, and I know I've got her. She may not like me, but she loves her work, and the thought of the animals not having a reliable doctor will eat away at her.

"We can't. These animals need the best care, and that's you. At least stay on 'til we can find someone else."

Naya looks to the door where her employee slipped out minutes ago. I bet she wishes she wasn't alone with me right now.

"Fine, just until you find someone else," she agrees, but her arms are crossed. She's not happy about this, but I couldn't care less.

She's staying, whether she likes it or not.

I take another step back. No way in hell am I looking for anyone else, but whatever makes her agree to come back. "Alright, I'm glad that's settled."

I walk out the clinic, leaving her as still as a statue.

"What the fuck do you mean this is all of it?" I bark at the men, looking down at the supply of guns that have arrived from Georgia. If I had to guess, about twenty-five percent of the delivery is missing. We're five cases short. It's not a detrimental amount, not enough is missing where I wouldn't make my money back, but it pisses me off all the same.

"We agreed on fifteen containers. I paid for fifteen, not ten," I say, letting my voice boom out in the abandoned depot where we're doing our first trade with Beridze's gang. The guy I'm dealing with is a lackey at best and looks terrified that I might knock his teeth out. Honestly, he's right to worry. I'm three seconds away from having my way with his face.

"My boss got orders from your men to bring some of the guns over to Raleigh," he mumbles, his voice quivering. How did a kid like him even get into this business? He clearly doesn't have the stomach for it. He doesn't look older than twenty years old.

"Why the fuck would I want my guns shipped to—" I stop midsentence. I only know one person in Raleigh who would want to fuck up my dealings. *Mason.* I grit my teeth, Jackson and Knox are on either side of me and they seem to have made the same connection I just did. I turn around and kick an empty beer bottle laying on the ground. When I turn back to the young man, my face is stone and my voice ice cold.

"What's your name, kid?" I ask as I circle around him slowly. Knox and Jax lay their hands on their weapons. I'm not going to hurt him, but I want to scare him enough to never step foot here again. Aleksandre better have a hell of a reason to send part of my shipment to another fucking state without speaking to me.

The boy's shaking in his pants when his reply comes out in stutters. "M–my name i–is Nino, sir."

"Nino." I let his name roll off my tongue. I approach him carefully and pull out a shank from my black, leather combat boot. I rest it against his neck. Aleksandre is an idiot for sending this kid here by himself.

"Tell your boss I expect the rest of my order here by next week, and if he wants to continue doin' business in the U.S., he better fuckin' verify who he's dealin' with. I didn't request anythin' to be shipped to Raleigh."

The boy backs away slowly. "I'll let him know, sir." He spins on his heels and runs along with the two drivers he came with. Once we're alone, Jackson is the first to speak.

"You think it was the Raleigh Riders?" His eyes reflect the same anger I'm sure is in mine. Where I tend to lash out and voice my fury, Jackson is all cool rage. You can barely tell when the emotion is going through him. He keeps it coiled tight, but when he finally lets it go, he could make even the largest man cower. Silent but lethal. That's why he's my main enforcer.

It's clear as day that Mason and his gang of idiots are responsible for this, who else would send our guns to Raleigh? This has nothing to do with the arms trade; I don't think he's looking to crack into our business. Even though he's been trying to relentlessly bring drugs into my territory, this was just posturing, a pathetic dick measuring contest. He wants to challenge the Sinners & Saints, angling for a turf war. It's been a long time coming, but I think seeing Naya on my property triggered him into action. If it's war he wants, then it's war he'll get.

"I know it was," I reply. "He's also Naya's ex." The dual looks of shock on Knox and Jackson's faces tells me they weren't expecting to hear that. I figure I might as well drop the big bomb on them at the same time.

"Hold on. She was dating the president of the RR? Does she know about S&S?" Jax asks.

I shake my head. "I don't think so. When I confronted her about it, she seemed to be confused by how I knew him. I think he's part of the reason she left Raleigh."

"So, he wants her back?" asks Jackson. I can see his brain churning in an attempt to put the pieces together.

"He wants a lot of things," I say with a low chuckle. "But he can't have any of them. I think it's time we remind 'em exactly who the Sinners & Saints are."

14

Naya

"I need a vacation," I mumble to myself as I lock up the doors to the clinic. In the time I've been here, I've only taken one day to myself. But in the past few days, more has happened to me than in the last several weeks. My brain is fried and my body is exhausted.

After Callan left this afternoon, I dropped to the floor, knees close to my chest, and buried my face between my legs. As much as I want to stay away, my body screams at me to sink into his arms and never come out for air. Last night, I felt safe for the first time in ages. In all of the years I spent with Mason, I never once felt that secure. This realization upsets me more than the way I feel toward Callan.

Laura had walked back in minutes later with three coffees and found me sitting against the wall. She had rushed over to me, concern riddled all over her face.

"What the hell happened, Naya?"

I groaned. "Callan," was the only word I managed to say.

"What did he do? Do I have to throw elbows? I swear to God, Naya, I will break down his stupid golden gates, march right up to his burly ass, and beat it mercilessly," she threatened.

There wasn't an ounce of humor in her voice or on her face.

She was dead serious. I burst out laughing and threw my arms around her neck, causing her to stumble backwards. We both fell to the floor and she joined in on the laughter. We stayed like that for a while, staring at the ceiling.

"You're crazy, Laura. I love you, but we don't need to hurt him."

"He wanted to convince me to come back to the ranch," I added with a sigh.

"And?" Her voice was riddled with excitement.

"I said yes."

Laura squealed and clapped her hands together.

"That's great news!" she exclaimed, but suddenly went silent and turned to face me. "Wait. You were so dead set on not going back this morning. What made you change your mind? Was he *that* good last night?" She wiggled her brows.

I laughed. "Wipe that look off your face. This has nothing to do with his skilled fingers. We agreed it would be until he finds a new vet." I internally cussed her out for reminding me about his talent. I swore I could still feel the aftershocks of my orgasm, all at the mercy of his hands. I couldn't imagine what it would be like with something else...

Laura rolled her eyes. "Sure."

I smacked her shoulder. "Hey! He said so himself."

I decided to change the topic, not wanting to think about Callan anymore.

"Is the third coffee for him?"

"Yup. I wasn't sure if he would still be here when I got back. But it's yours now, you clearly need it more." Laura chuckled.

She wasn't wrong. I needed all the caffeine I could get my hands on.

We finally made a move to get off the floor, Laura first, and she extended her arm to help me up.

"By the way, I ought to fire you for pulling that stunt earlier. Leaving me alone with him like that?"

Laura faked a look of outrage and brought her hand up to her mouth. "How dare you! I helped you save the clinic. If I hadn't left, you probably would've stood your ground and not accepted his offer to go back. So, you're welcome," she said with a cheeky smirk.

I rolled my eyes. "Get back to work," I had ordered, and went back to the staff room to continue going over the marketing budget, with a little less stress than before.

I finish locking up the office and input the alarm code. I ended up letting Laura leave early, given we had no afternoon clients booked and she was up most of the night driving. I was planning on walking the fifteen minutes it takes to get home, but I'm stunned when I turn to the parking lot and see my Jeep waiting for me. *Huh?*

I left my car at Callan's house this morning, how did it end up here?

He must've brought it with him when he dropped by earlier. I'm irritated that he had the nerve to fix my car without asking me first. It's a grand gesture, I admit, but it only makes me feel more belittled. He already thinks I'm a charity case, and this just proves it even more. I can take care of myself.

I huff all the way to my Jeep. On the windshield, I find a note.

Text me for your keys.

Argh. I crumple the little piece of paper and pull out my phone. If this was a way to get me to talk to him, he's slier than I thought.

Me: Location please.

Callan: Hi to you too.

Me: Don't be a smartass. Where are my keys?

Callan: "Thank you for fixing my car Callan."

Callan: "I don't know what I'd do without you Callan."

Callan: My pleasure sweetheart.

I stare down at my phone while the messages come through and I want to launch it right at his face.

Me: Are you done treating me like a charity case?

The three dots appear and stop a few times before his response comes in.

Callan: You're not a charity case…

Me: Where are my keys?

Callan: Naya.

Me: What Callan?

Callan: I'm sorry for sayin that. I was stressed. I didn't mean it.

I'm stunned. He actually *apologized?*

Callan: The keys are hidden in the front left tire.

Me: Thank you. For fixing my car. But don't do it again.

No response comes through. I throw my phone on the seat and grunt. This man brings out such anger in me, it can't be good for my health. I realize I must have come off as an ungrateful bitch, but he started it.

Only people you care about can elicit these types of feelings, my mind whispers.

"Shut up," I snap back.

I'm losing my mind.

15

Callan

My plan to retaliate against Mason is set in motion. I always have things mapped out. As the President, I have to be on top of things. I didn't end up here for no reason. It's years of being calculated and foreseeing what bullshit I may have to deal with.

Mason, as moronic as he may be, knew I wouldn't take his messing with my business on my back. If he wants to take money from me, I'll take money from *him*. It's that simple.

An eye for an eye. That's how things operate in our world.

I called Bentley, an old friend of mine out in Raleigh. He's not a patched member of S&S and more of a lone wolf, but he's helped us move weapons through the Carolinas on more than one occasion. I got him to confirm the location of one of the labs where Mason has his drugs produced. He must have sensed something was going down as he didn't ask a single question and got the information quickly. The less he knows, the better for all of us.

When I hang up the phone, I look at Jax. "Bent confirmed the address. He's sendin' it over to you."

He nods, knowing what he needs to do. As long as this day has felt for me, it's going to be an even longer night for Jackson.

145

He and a couple other S&S members will be riding up to Raleigh tonight.

By tomorrow morning, that lab will be nothing more than ash.

The Raleigh Riders have multiple drug facilities across their city. They're heavily guarded and the guys will have to be meticulous with how they approach the situation. The one we decided to hit is the main workshop where they cook meth and cut most of their drugs. All of their shipments go through there and get distributed across the other hideouts.

The plan is to raid the house in the early morning hours and disrupt their morning delivery. They usually move the drugs just as the sun rises in USPS postal trucks. Each one carries over a hundred disguised packages. We'll intercept one of the vans before it sets off, overthrow the driver en route, and steal it. There's no way we're driving the drugs back to Nashville, so the guys will dispose of the truck before they get back. Jax and a few others will deal with the lab itself.

"How many guards are we expecting?" Jax asks.

"Bentley said the house has three points of entry. The front, back, and a side door that leads straight down to the lab. Your best bet is to use the patio entry and head to the basement from the inside. Apparently, the main and side entrances are heavily guarded."

Jax chuckles and it's a rare sound. "Don't worry about me, boss."

Over the years, Jackson has been able to plant informants across Mason's operation. I don't know how he did it, but the man is efficient, and if he doesn't get what he wants, he leaves destruction in his path.

I smack him on the shoulder. "I know I can count on you, brother. Are you all set with weapons?" I ask.

Knox cuts in. "I loaded 'em up with handguns, rifles, and

silencers. Oh, and explosives," he says with a smirk. Knox's favorite.

Jackson nods. "Thanks, Dav. I'm rounding up the troops. We're leaving in an hour," he confirms.

"Keep us posted," I say, and we part ways. It'll be a long drive for them, but they should arrive in time to mess up their morning delivery.

That ought to remind Mason what it means to mess with us, and if it drives the Raleigh Riders off our land and back up to North Carolina, so be it. The goal is to get them the fuck out of Tennesse, stat.

16

Naya

It's been almost two months since I agreed to stay at All Saints as their vet. Despite Ace having almost fully recovered at that point, Callan and Knox still asked me to come to the ranch for regular checkups, before I eventually found out that one of the other horses wasn't feeling very well. The two burly ranchers were obviously worried that something was making their animals ill, so I started coming to the ranch every week.

I'm not too worried since animals can often get colds and other minor illnesses, but I'm also happy to keep an eye on them. Nothing makes me happier than being around animals. I've also started checking on their cattle and the small rabbit run. And since then, they've also decided to add two small pigs named Bert and Ernie. They're small, spotted white and brown, and cute as hell. I spend most of my time cuddling them.

Before I knew it, weeks and weeks had passed.

Sitting on the ground in the pig's barn, I replay every conversation with Callan, and they've been more frustrating than the last.

On my first day back at the ranch, I had requested that our relationship remain strictly platonic.

"We need to keep things professional," I tell Callan as we walk to the stables. Something flashes over his face, but it's there and gone before I can understand what it is.

"I never wanted it to be anythin' more," he retorts with a shrug.

My body tenses, and I almost stop walking. Liar. "Good. I'm glad we're on the same page. So, we forget what happened the other night."

"Already forgotten." He tips his hat and turns around. "I'll see you around, darlin'."

And that was it.

Callan has been respectful of my wishes, though he's become grumpier than before, and I didn't think that was possible. He's downright unpleasant to be around, so I've tried to avoid him at all costs.

However, not a day goes by where I don't think back to the moment we shared, the memory forever ingrained in my mind.

But I can't let myself be deterred by my attraction to him.

The purpose of this deal is to keep the clinic afloat and help my dad with his medical bills. I left Raleigh to build my own life, away from any distractions, and not to get entangled in a situation that could do more harm than good.

The minimal interactions that we've had have been solely related to the farm animals and their care. Sometimes, Knox comes out to the stables to keep me company, which seems to only annoy Callan. We've become close over the past weeks. Knox gets a good kick out of it and Callan has caught us giggling on multiple occasions. He'd grumble past without a word to either of us every time.

Today, I'm doing my routine check on the cattle when I see Knox waving at me from a distance. He joins me in the pasture and we fall into a comfortable conversation as he tells me what's been going on between him and his new girlfriend,

Joanna. Callan drives by in the old, red pickup truck and glares at us.

"What's his problem now?" I ask Knox.

He just laughs and shakes his head. "Beats me. But he's been in a shittier mood lately. I wonder why," he says, sarcastically.

I shove his shoulder and roll my eyes. "I've got nothing to do with the rod stuck up his ass!"

"Not a lot of people can get under King's skin, but you, my friend, seem to be great at it," Knox retorts.

I scoff. "Why do you call him King?" This is the second time I've heard Knox call him by that name, but Callan has never asked me to address him that way.

"We all do," he replies, casually. "He earned the name the same day he gained his scar."

I noticed the scar on his torso the first day I saw him, but I still don't know how he got it. "What happened?"

Knox looks around as if to make sure that no one will hear him and lowers his voice. "That's not my story to tell, short stuff. But it wasn't pretty."

I look back at Callan loading the bed of the truck with hay and he catches my eye. I wave at him, but he narrows his eyes in return and turns away abruptly.

I groan in frustration and march off in the opposite direction. Knox opens his mouth to stop me, but decides against it after I give him a death glare. He chuckles, and I curse the day I decided to come back to work at this ranch.

A few hours later, I turn onto my street. It's been a long day, and I just want to take a shower and curl up on the couch. When I reach my driveway, I realize my front porch light is on.

That's weird. I swear I turned it off before leaving this morning.

A sense of dread fills me. Something is wrong. I squint my eyes to get a good look at the front door and notice the torn mesh screen.

Shit. Could an animal have tried getting in while I was gone? That seems highly unlikely and also doesn't explain the light.

I reach for the glove compartment and search for anything I can use as a weapon. I rifle through piles of tissue, random pieces of paper, and old headphones. *Bingo.* A rusty screwdriver. I grab it, leaving my things in the car, and head to the front door.

I tiptoe up the few steps to the porch and they creek under my feet. I halt. If someone is in there, I hope they didn't hear the noise.

As I approach the door, I see it's cracked open. I can feel my heart pounding as I brace myself to enter my home, careful to not make a sound.

I push the door open. My breathing turns erratic as I look around in a panic. Most of my furniture has been tipped over, drawers and cupboards have been opened and emptied, papers scattered all over my kitchen island. My heart sinks. Someone was in here, and they were looking for something. What exactly? I don't know. I have nothing to hide.

I stand frozen in the hallway, not sure what to do, as fear seizes control of my body. I brace both hands on the wall and lower my head to my chest. It feels tight and my head is already aching.

I thought things were going well for me. I managed to

escape an abusive situation, settle into a new hometown, and successfully run my own vet clinic. In a few hours, my life has just been turned upside down and a familiar fear comes back to haunt me. *How did today go so off the rails?*

For a moment, I forget there is a possibility the intruder could still be in the house. When the thought occurs to me, I dart back outside as quietly as possible and jump back in my car, locking the doors.

Shit, shit, shit. What should I do?

I clutch my phone in one hand, my keys in the other. I'm so distraught, I don't know whether I should start the car and drive away, or call the cops and wait.

My instinct tells me to run, but I'd rather stay and get to the bottom of who did this.

I debate calling Laura, but what could she possibly do? I also don't want to drag her into a dangerous situation. I could stay at her place tonight, but there's no point in her coming here.

My mind drifts to Callan. I'm sure he'd come to my rescue in a heartbeat, but I refuse to be at his mercy. I don't want to owe him anything. He's done enough favors for me already.

I settle on the next best thing: Knox.

I put the phone to my ear and it rings twice before he picks up. "Hey, sweetness," he drawls. I want to roll my eyes at his flirty greeting, but my heartbeat is too loud in my ears for me to concentrate on anything.

"Knox," I mumble, my voice shaky.

He senses the panic in my tone. "What's wrong, Naya?"

"I got home after work and found my porch light turned on and the mesh door torn. I went in and saw—"

He cuts me off right away. "You what?"

I take a deep breath in and continue. "I walked into the house and the entire place was ransacked. There were things everywhere, my belongings were scattered all over," I explain, tears now welling in my eyes. A drop rolls down my cheek and I sniffle. My emotions are catching up to me, and I'm struggling to keep it together.

I hear some rustling on the line and a door closes. "Where are you now?" Knox asks.

"I'm locked in my car in my driveway."

"Drive away, park on the street, and wait. Don't you dare go back in there, and don't get out of the car. I won't be long."

I hang up the phone and do as he says. I park my Jeep a few houses down, still in view of my house, and wait.

17
Callan

I'm burnt out and ready for a stiff drink, a hot shower, and my bed. Instead, I have to herd the cattle over to the next pasture. I curse out loud. I walk around to the back of the house to find Harlo and Dave lying in the grass next to their kennel. I whistle at them and they come running.

When I get inside, I can't even make it up the stairs to my room and collapse on the couch.

My unplanned nap gets brutally interrupted by the loud noise of my door closing shut. It slams with so much force the windows rattle. I startle out of my sleep in a panic until I realize it's Knox's obnoxious ass marching down the hallway.

Why the hell did I agree to let him stay on the ranch? I groan and roll myself off the sofa. The dogs fell asleep next to me on the floor, but got up and went to Knox as soon as they heard him.

I don't even have time to give him hell for barging in the way he did before he snaps at me.

"Where the fuck is your phone, bro?"

I look at him, dumbfounded. *My phone?* "It's on the kitchen counter, why?" I ask, confused.

"I've been callin' you non-stop for the past ten minutes."

"I was asleep, Knox, as you can clearly see. What's gotten up your ass?"

"It's Naya," he says, and he doesn't even get to continue before my mind starts reeling and my heart rate increases. *What is it with hearing her name that gets me all worked up like this?*

"She called. Her house got broken into and she went *inside,* by herself."

My first thought is whether or not she's okay. I can't explain this impulse that comes over me to protect her first and ask questions later.

"She's fine, Callan," Knox confirms. He must see the panic in my eyes.

The second thought is why the fuck did she call Knox and not me? Does she like him? Is there something he's not telling me?

No. I shake that idea out of my head. I must be losing it to be jealous of my brother. He wouldn't involve himself with her knowing what happened between us.

"I told her to drive away and wait in the car," Knox continues, but I don't let him finish. I bolt to the foyer, grab my keys off the mantle, slip on the first pair of boots I see, and I'm out the door before he can say another word.

I hop in my pickup truck and lower the backrest of the passenger side of the car. Behind the seat, I find two Glock 19s, a semi-automatic rifle, and a pump-action Remington Model 12. Whoever decided to mess with Naya has it coming. They better pray I don't find them still in the house, but if they are, they certainly won't be returning home. I open the middle compartment and grab a dagger.

I drive off, almost running right through the gates before they have a chance to open, and race toward Naya's house. I break at least five road laws, but I don't give a shit. My girl needs me. I scoff. *My girl?*

When I pull into her street, I spot her Jeep parked two houses down. The car is turned off and it's pitch black inside. Atta girl. *Never seen nor recognized.*

I drive up to it slowly and park behind her. When I exit my truck, I see Naya fiddling with her phone before her flashlight turns on. She beams it right in my face, making me squint from the brightness. She rolls down her window and glares at me.

"What are you doing here, Callan?" She looks both surprised and angry to see me. I'm starting to get sick of her shit. I'm here to help and she's acting as if I'm the one who just ransacked her house.

"I'm here because your house got broken into, and whether or not you want to acknowledge it, it's not safe for you to be here right now. So, enough with the catty bullshit. At some point, you'll have to accept that I'm in your life. And if I were you, I'd make peace with it sooner rather than later," I spit. I march back to my pickup and grab the shotgun, cocking it as soon as it's in my hands.

Naya's mouth is agape but she doesn't utter another word. *Good.* She needs to learn she's not getting rid of me. I don't know when I began feeling this duty toward her, but I'm tired of fighting it. And now that she's in danger, the urge to protect her is even stronger.

I turn to face her. "Stay in the car, Naya, or I swear to God you'll regret it." She sinks in her seat, but the fire in her eyes doesn't fully extinguish. She wants to argue, I can tell, but she's holding back.

I continue walking down the street and around the perimeter of the house to make sure there's no threat.

When the coast is clear, I enter using the front door.

There's shit *everywhere.* There's no one in sight, but I keep my rifle close. I find the stairs and make my way up, checking every room. When I get to Naya's bedroom, I see her dresser has also been ransacked. Her clothes are all over the floor. I bend down to pick up a pile and two small articles of clothing fall out. Her thongs.

Great. Just the thing I wanted to see right while searching her house for an intruder. The urge to shove one in my pocket for later is strong, but I refrain. It's been torturous having her around while keeping things *platonic.* I groan before moving on.

Nothing of value seems to have been taken. All of her electronics are in place and her jewelry is still on her dresser. I open the closet and, on the floor behind the hanging clothes, lies a small safe that has remained untouched. Who would want to break into a house and leave empty-handed?

Mason, that's who.

Of course. It's the only logical option. He shows up out of the blue, steals from me, and threatens Naya's safety. He probably came here in search of something, or someone, he couldn't find. He deserves to be punished for this.

I run back downstairs and out the door to find Naya still sitting in her car. "Is everything okay?" she asks. Worry fills her expression. I need to get her out of here ASAP.

"Uh-huh. There's no one inside, but whoever did this was lookin' for somethin'. Any idea what that could be?"

She narrows her gaze on me, and I can see her mind reeling. "No. I barely have anything important other than jewelry and my clinic's paperwork. I don't know why I was targeted."

"Let's head back inside. Pack some of your things. You can't stay here, it's not safe."

"What? No, it's fine. If the coast is clear, I doubt the intruder would come back twice in the same night."

Is she serious? "Naya. Your house was broken into. You're not stayin' here. Period," I bark.

"Callan. You don't tell me what to do, alright? It's my house, and I want to sleep in my bed tonight."

"I have a perfectly comfortable bed waitin' for you at my place. Let's go." She is the most stubborn woman I've ever met.

"I'm not going back to yours," she says, shaking her head.

"The hell you aren't. Get out of the car, Naya."

"I'll stay at Laura's place tonight, then."

"Someone was inside your house while you weren't home, which means they've probably been keepin' up with your movements. If you go to Laura's house, you risk takin' the threat right to her doorstep. Be smart about this, Naya. Go pack your things and come with me."

She still doesn't budge, so I continue my argument. "I have 'round the clock security, a-state-of-the-art alarm system, and two guard dogs. Hell, if you don't want to be in the same house as me, I'll stay at Knox's for the night." At this point, I'll try anything to get her to agree.

A little smirk creeps on her lips and she crosses her arms. "I'll stay at Knox's house, then."

"No fucking way, woman," I seethe with a growl. All of my buttons have been pushed, and I snap. I reach into the car through the cracked window, pull up the manual lock, and open the door. Naya's face shows a mixture of shock and confusion. She has no idea what's coming.

I wrap my arms around her waist and hoist her out of the seat, throwing her over my shoulder. Naya screams at me to let her go, but I ignore her pleas as she squirms in my hold, her fists hitting my back feel like tiny flutters. *Cute.*

Having her ass so close to my face is hardening my cock.

"Good luck tryin' to get down, *bimba*," I shoot and that seems to anger her even more.

"Callan, put me down! This isn't funny," she yells while flailing her legs like a fish out of water.

I let out a loud chuckle. "We're goin' inside to pack an overnight bag and then we're gettin' the hell out of here. You're stayin' with me on the ranch for at least a week."

I cross the road with Naya hanging on my back like a sack of potatoes, and when we get inside, I immediately take her upstairs and throw her on the bed. Her body bounces off the mattress and she lets out a gasp while clutching onto her chest. "You're a neanderthal!" she shouts.

"Usually, throwin' you on the bed like a rag doll would result in other things. Unfortunately for you, this is a serious situation and we need to leave. Now, for the last time, pack your bag, Naya."

Finally understanding I won't give up, she throws items into a duffle bag she grabs from the closet, grumbling the entire time. When she's done, she stands with her hands on her hips, watching me with a fierce intensity.

For a moment, I consider I may have truly met my match in this woman from North Carolina. I hold her stare, unwavering.

"Are you goin' to be a good girl and walk back to my truck, or do you need me to throw you over my shoulder again?"

Naya doesn't reply, but grabs her bag and walks around me to the door. I follow closely behind all the way to the truck.

"Leave your Jeep here. I'll have one of my guys search it for a tracker." She seems to do a double take at my words, but reality sinks in and she nods. I know Mason, he's a crazy motherfucker. I wouldn't put it past him to bug her car and phone.

I glance at her in the passenger seat as we head back down the road to All Saints. She looks tense, her jaw is clenched, and she's looking out the window, her arms crossed against her body.

"Listen, Naya," I say, trying to keep my voice level as I

focus back on the road. "Believe it or not, I'm not the bad guy in this situation. I'm just tryin' to help."

"Oh, no." Her voice drips with sarcasm. "You're definitely not the bad guy, *Callan.* You pulled me away from my home, without any consideration for what I wanted when I didn't even call *you!*"

I'm not going to lie, the last bit stings. I'm still wondering why the hell she didn't call me, but now doesn't seem like the appropriate time to start that line of questioning. Instead, I decide to finally give it to her straight.

I sigh. "Naya, despite what you think of me, I'm actin' in your best interest. I didn't mention this before because I wasn't sure what it meant or if it mattered, but Mason passed by the ranch the second time you came by."

She whips her head around to face me. An emotion I can't quite place is on her face. Shock? She doesn't say a word, so I continue. "When I saw him, I figured he was just tryin' to antagonize me. We've had a long-standin' rivalry, so I equated it to that. There was no reason to tell you at all, but then I saw him callin' you. When you told me 'bout the connection you two had, I wondered if his drive-by was a coincidence, or if he was keepin' tabs on you. After today, I'm confident it's the latter. He messed with one of my business deals and broke into your home in an attempt to threaten you."

The silence in the car is deafening, and I wish for the millionth time since I've met Naya that I could read her mind.

Finally, she speaks, her voice is smaller than I've ever heard it before as the reality of what I've said sinks in.

"Mason is in Springfield?"

18

Naya

y mind is working in slow motion, trying to catch up and process what Callan just told me.

"Mason is here?" I ask Callan again. "And you think he's the one who had my house broken into?"

He gives a quick nod of his head. I wish I sounded stronger, unfazed in this moment, but if what he's telling me is the truth, then Mason wasted no time finding me. He warned me that I could never leave him, and I laughed in his face. I thought I was safe moving nine hours away. Now, he's here. *Oh God.*

My skin crawls, wondering how long he's been watching me and how often. Has he sat outside of my home, a place where I'd started to feel safe? Outside of my clinic?

I've been so oblivious and confident that I wouldn't be at risk this far away, but I should've seen it coming. Mason would never let me go so easily.

"I know everything about you, Sugar," Mason whispers in *my ear, his voice sending a feeling of dread down my spine.*

"I wish I could say the same about you, Mason." This makes him chuckle.

"You know everything you need to know."

"It's not enough," I argue.

"I'm more than enough for you; you'll never find something

165

better," he says, while cupping me between the legs. The innuendo makes me want to throw up.

I thought I loved Mason, but I was beginning to see his true colors. At this moment, I wish I were blind. And anywhere but here.

"Let me go, Mase." I shove his hand away.

"Never. You'll never get rid of me."

Those words suddenly come back to me, and my whole body shudders. Of course he'd look for me.

My brain finally catches up to something else that Callan mentioned. Mason messed with Callan's business? I know what my ex-boyfriend's dealings were, and to think that Callan may be involved in the same dirty business makes me want to be sick. Another reason why I can't allow myself to fall for him.

The rest of the drive is quiet.

As much as I wish I wouldn't react this way, I instantly feel more relaxed as we pass security at the gate of All Saints. Callan jumps out of the truck and slips on a black, leather jacket. *Sinners & Saints* is marked across the upper back, with *Springfield* written at the bottom. In the center is a picture of an angel, similar to the statue at the front of the ranch. She's stunning, wings spread out wide, her neck tilted to the side, with two puncture wounds from the snake coiled around her body. Flowers and skulls fill the space around her. For a moment, I'm mesmerized by this insignia that is both terrifying and beautiful in equal measure. Callan turns around to look back at me, and I snap out of my daze.

"You want me to carry you again, sweetheart?" He's got a smirk on his face that says he would absolutely do it.

I let out a huff and get out of the truck. When we step inside his mansion, he lays my bag down at the base of the stairs and heads over to the living room. I follow him without saying a word. I wish I could think of something to say, but I'm in shock over everything that has been revealed tonight.

He turns to me, his face is like stone, but his eyes are somehow soft. I can tell he's genuinely worried about me.

"Can I get you a drink or somethin' to eat?" he offers, and I'm hit with the sense of familiarity from having been in this very same place a couple months ago when my car broke down and I got stuck during a thunderstorm.

I haven't eaten yet. I'd been planning to cook something at home. After the night I've had, a drink sounds more than necessary. "Yes to both."

He nods, seemingly happy I'm not putting up a fight for once. "What can I get you? Same wine as last time?"

"No." I shake my head. "Something stronger, please."

A few minutes later, he's back with two glasses of an amber liquid with large ice cubes. When I raise the drink to my lips, I realize it's bourbon. The unique 'sweet like vanilla, spicy like clove, and smokey like a pipe' scent hits my nose instantly. I take a swig. It's smooth, with a slight sweetness to it, and the burn that runs down my throat is just what I needed. I let out a content sigh.

Callan observes me as I take another sip before glancing down the hall.

"Alright, I'll get dinner started." He looks like he's not sure what to do with himself, and I wonder if he cooks often. "How do you feel about steaks?"

"Sounds good to me," I reply, my voice still not sounding like my own. "Do you need me to help with anything?"

He shakes his head and gestures for me to sit on the couch. "Relax, make yourself comfortable. I'll let you know when it's done."

He exits the living area and heads to the kitchen. I look around the familiar space and wonder how I've found myself in this position again. It feels like just yesterday, I was standing in this very room, staring out the window right before Callan kissed me. The memory of his lips still linger on mine. I don't think I'll ever forget our first kiss. It was rough, full of tension and anger, yet soft, a promise of more to come. His goal was to shut me up, but the magic he left in his trail will forever haunt me.

I sip on my drink and, for a moment, I forget that the problems I tried so desperately to leave in Raleigh have followed me straight to Springfield. I can't even begin to think about how to manage the situation I'm in.

The delicious aroma coming from the hallway distracts my spiraling thoughts. I get up and head over to investigate the scent. When I walk into the kitchen, Callan is putting the steaks onto plates that already have sides of rice and vegetables.

"I'm impressed."

He smirks as he places a plate on the island, and I pull out the counter stool in front of it and take a seat. A few seconds later, he's sitting beside me and I'm struck by how normal this feels. I quickly remind myself I was brought here against my will and my mood shifts.

He smiles up at me, a full smile with straight, white teeth, and I swear my heart stops. "A man has to know how to cook for himself, Naya."

I'm surprised. I was able to come to the conclusion that Callan was a self-sufficient man, but I assumed he'd have a personal chef cooking for him. He definitely could afford it.

Now that I'm aware of Callan's involvement with Mason, I'm compelled to think he deals drugs. *That would explain how a small town Tennessee rancher is living the life of luxury.* How else can you justify his wealth? The thought that I let someone like that touch me makes my stomach roil, and I lay down my fork.

"You alright?" he asks.

"What do you do, Callan?" I decide it's best to just be direct.

He drops my gaze. "Well, as you know, I own this ranch and the animals take up most of my time. Workin' the land is a large amount of effort, but Dav is a great help. I own a bar out in Nashville, too."

"Bullshit," I spit. I've spent the last decade of my life being lied to by a man I trusted. I'm not about to be lied to by a man I barely know.

He narrows his eyes. "What the fuck did you just say, sweetheart?"

I glare at him dead in the eyes and repeat myself. "I said *bullshit!*" I yell, and he seems surprised by my outburst, but I am so *tired*. I'm exhausted from the lies. There's no way Callan is just a simple, albeit grumpy, rancher, and I feel stupid for thinking that was ever the case.

"I was with Mason for years and he's no rancher. You said he messed up one of your business deals, and there's no way that had anything to do with All Saints," I huff. "If you're part of a drug ring, you may as well come clean. I don't want to have anything to do with someone like him again."

Callan throws his head back and laughter booms around the kitchen while I scowl and fight the urge to slap his stupid face.

When he stops, he looks at me, no trace of humor left in his eyes. "Naya," he says, his voice low and menacing. I feel a shiver move down my spine. "Never, and I need you to really listen to me, *never*, ever compare me to Mason Caldwell again. Understood?"

I swallow, feeling like a small child being chastised. The way he talks to me is maddening, but a sick part of my brain enjoys fighting with him.

"We don't deal drugs," Callan continues. His tone is measured, as if he's calculating every word he says to make sure I understand. "Mason wants to bring 'em onto our territory, but as long as I'm breathin', that won't happen. He can bet money on that," he seethes, and his anger seems to have shifted to my ex.

I don't miss that he said *we* instead of just referring to himself. "'We' being the Sinners & Saints?" I ask, innocently.

He looks surprised for about a half a second before he schools his expression once again. "What makes you say that?"

"I'm not an idiot," I say calmly, although nothing inside of me feels peaceful right now. "I read the back of your jacket and put two and two together."

He picks up his glass and shoots what's remaining of it straight down his throat. I watch the column of his neck move as he gulps down the liquid, and I feel a pulse in my lower body. *Focus, Naya.*

"You got me," he replies, a deep throaty sound leaving his mouth. "Let's just say we don't see eye to eye with the Raleigh Riders."

I nod, only mildly relieved that I haven't found myself back in another situation with a drug dealer. "So, if it's not drugs, what do you deal with in your 'business'?" I ask, placing air quotes around the word because whatever it is, it sure as hell isn't legitimate.

His voice is sharp as a razorblade when he responds, "That ain't for you to worry about."

I'm about to argue that, as he just dragged me onto his property, it is exactly for me to worry about, when Knox comes bounding in. He doesn't seem surprised to see me seated at the island, so I assume he had anticipated his boss bringing me here.

"Hey, doc," he says in a light voice. "Nice to see you again."

I narrow my eyes at him. "I called *you*, Dav. Not him." I point to Callan, who's watching our interaction with a look of both intrigue and wariness.

"I had to tell him," Knox responds with a shrug of his shoulders. "Besides, you're always welcome to come back to my place if you don't want to stay here." He throws me a dirty smirk and winks. I hear Callan growl. *Interesting*.

"Yeah," I say with my best flirtatious voice. "I'd love that. Could you help me with my bag?" I begin to get off the chair, but Callan grabs my forearm so tightly, it feels like a vice.

"You're stayin' here." There's no mistaking the dominance in his tone, and I feel a rush of heat move through me. Knox, however, just laughs and raises his hands in mock surrender.

"I'll leave my porch light on for you, darlin'," he whispers. "Ya know, just in case you wanna sneak out once this guy is asleep."

I let out a choked laugh, my attention fixed on where Callan's hand has still not released my arm.

"Is there a reason you're here, Davenport? Or did you come just to piss me off?"

Knox smiles like absolutely nothing in the world could knock him off kilter. "Nah, I actually wanted to talk to you."

Callan nods, stands up, and finally lets go of my arm. "Outside," he orders Knox.

With that, they both march out the door, and I'm left in the kitchen, wondering what the hell I've got myself into.

19

Callan

"So, you got her to come..." Dav pauses. "Here, I mean." He laughs at his own joke, but I'm not in the mood. "You looked real domestic in there."

"What do you want, Knox?"

His expression turns grim. "Just got a call from Summer. Looks like there's trouble at the pub."

"What's goin' on?" I ask, rubbing my temples, eyes closed. *I can't catch a break.*

"There are some guys there that don't belong on our turf. I'm goin' to check it out with some of the crew."

"Bikers?"

"Seems like it. I have a feelin' it's the Raleigh Riders."

I clench my fists. "They're gettin' bolder by the day. Take care of it, Dav. I can't leave her here."

I start pacing around my porch. I hate not being able to deal with these things myself, but I refuse to leave Naya alone. What if she runs off again? If Mason has informants in town, she's not safe anywhere but here, with me.

"Alright. I'll see you tomorrow, then."

As he ambles down the stairs, he gives me a parting look over his shoulder. "By the way, I think she could be good for you, Cal."

I watch him walk away, feeling a tightness in my chest. I take a deep breath of the night air, then turn and open the door. When I walk into the kitchen, I find Naya washing dishes from dinner.

"You don't have to do that," I say as I head over to her. "You've had a long night. Go relax."

"No," she replies stubbornly. I'm beginning to think she'll say no to just about anything I say to get a rise out of me. "You did the cooking, so I'll clean up. It's only fair."

"Fine, at least let me dry," I shoot back at her as I grab a dish towel. We stand side by side in silence as we do the dishes together, and I think back to Knox saying we looked *domestic*. I don't do 'domestic', at least not in a long while.I wonder what's happening to me, when Naya's voice interrupts my thoughts.

"So, about what happened between us two months ago..." She looks at me to make sure I'm listening. I dip my head, indicating she should continue, but now my mind drifts back to that night, the way she felt, how she sounded, and damn it, my cock is semi-hard.

"I just want to be clear. If I do spend some time here, that won't be happening again."

I let out a snort. "Okay," is my only reply. We agreed to keep things platonic while she worked on the ranch, but the fact that she's brought it up clearly means she still thinks about it.

"I'm not joking, Callan. That was clearly a mistake on both our ends. I needed a distraction and we did something we probably shouldn't have. It can't happen again," Naya repeats.

I narrow my eyes at her as I dry my hands. I move to the side so that I'm directly behind her, my hands on either side of her body, holding the counter. I press myself against her back firmly. My hardened cock pokes at her ass through my jeans as I push into her further, causing her to lean over the sink. She doesn't say anything, but the darkness outside and the light in the kitchen has turned the window into a mirror, and I can see her close her eyes and bite her lip. I bring my head down to whisper into her ear.

"Sweetheart, do you know what one of my jobs is on the ranch?" I'm so close to her, I brush the tip of her ear with my lips. I nip at the lobe ever-so-slightly. She attempts to muffle a whimper, but I hear it, loud and clear.

Naya says nothing and simply shakes her head. I smirk, knowing I've got her right where I want her. She can tell me it was a mistake all she wants, but I know the truth. She can deny it until she's blue in the face, but if she didn't want this, she wouldn't let me get this close.

"My job is to break horses. I'm gentle with 'em. I gain their trust 'til they're eventually ready for me to ride," I whisper as I thrust my crotch against her backside once more. "I've broken some of the most stubborn horses you'll ever come across. So, believe me when I say...you. Will. Break."

Still trapped between my arms and the counter, she turns to face me. Her lips are so close, I could kiss her with just the smallest shift in position. Her eyes are focused on mine, and I can see how at war she is with herself. Caught between her stubborn pride and lust.

I press myself against her front this time and my dick is even harder than it was. Seeing her beautiful face and knowing how much I affect her is a turn on like no other. I dust my lips against hers and she lets out a small moan.

I step back.

"There *will* be a next time, Naya," I say as I head for the hallway. "But when that time comes, you'll have to beg for it."

I leave her dazed and panting in the kitchen as I head for my room. I press my hand against my cock, which is now at full attention in my pants, but there's no relief to be found. I don't think my body will ever catch a break until I'm sliding deep into Naya.

I feel restless as I pace in circles around my bed. It's too early for me to sleep. I need to ride. I send a quick text to the guards, asking them to keep an eye on the house. Naya will be safe here, nobody gets through security without permission from either of us, but better safe than sorry. Especially where Mason is involved. I wasn't going to leave her alone tonight, but I'm way too wound up to be around Naya right now.

When I get to the main floor, I head into the living room. Naya is sprawled out on the couch watching a movie. When she hears me enter, she jumps up into a seated position and casts me a glare.

"As you were," I say, trying to keep my voice light, but I'm mesmerized at the sight of her looking so at home here. "I'm goin' out for a ride. My guards are on the property if you need somethin'."

"I don't need babysitters," she answers, her tone surly.

I run my hand through my hair and take in a deep breath.

"No one said anythin' about babysitters. I just need to let off some steam, and I want to make sure you're safe, alright?" I realize the mistake in my words almost immediately as a wicked smirk plants itself on her face.

"Get yourself a little wound up, cowboy?" Naya laughs, and damn if the sound doesn't light me up a little bit.

"Nothin' a bike and some night air can't fix," I reply, coolly. The smile on her face says she knows I need a different type of *ride*, but since I told her I was going to make her beg for it, I can't just approach her and fuck her senseless on the couch. She giggles softly as I make my way to the door and it takes everything in me not to march right back and stick my dick in her mouth.

I hop on the first bike lined up in the garage and head out

into the night. Immediately, I feel a boost of serotonin and some of the tension rolls off me, disappearing like the road dust I'm leaving in my wake.

I kick up the speed. I have no plan for where I'm going, I just know this is what my spirit needs. Thirty minutes later, I'm outside The Crown. It was the only place I could think of. I'll have a quick drink here and go back home. *Home.* Right now, Naya is probably getting ready for bed. I groan.

Fuck, if a ride can't even get her off of my mind, then this is going to be a week from Hell.

I hop off the bike and head inside. I head straight to the counter and sit on a stool at the end. I don't notice anything out of the ordinary, and I can't pinpoint the men that Knox was referring to. I don't even see him. My brows draw together in concern as I look around the room.

Summer is busy working the bar, but she sees me and gives me a smile and a quick wave before coming over.

"What can I get ya, boss? The usual?" she asks as she opens a bottle of beer and slides it down the bar to a waiting customer.

I nod. She grabs a frosted glass and pours me a beer. I take a sip and let the chill run through my body. I'm halfway to feeling relaxed when I feel a palm touch my shoulder.

"Howdy, cowboy," says the owner of the hand that is now creeping toward my neck.

I turn my head and...*son of a bitch*, it's Barbie. I should have recognized that overpowering perfume before I even saw her face. She extends her other hand out to grab my drink, taking a sip. Annoyance flares through me.

"What do you say we get out of here," the blonde whispers in my ear. Her breath is warm and smells heavily like beer. I not-so-gently remove her hand from my shoulder.

"No thanks." I don't even bother to look at her as I turn her down.

This doesn't stop her, though. "Aw, come on," she whines. "Last time was great. Let me do that for you again. I'll let you fuck me in the bathroom."

She winks at me and runs the hand that had been on my shoulder up the inside of my thigh, before lightly running it over my cock. *A cock that doesn't get hard...what the fuck is that about?* The sensation feels nice, but it's as though my dick hasn't gotten the memo that it's being touched.

I would be more concerned if I hadn't just been hard forty minutes ago.

Naya. She's done this to me.

Weeks ago, I would have taken up Barbie's offer and fucked her in the bathroom. Sure, she reeks of desperation, but sex is sex. Now? I'm repulsed. I tasted Naya on my fingers once, and now she's the only one I want.

"Touch me again and you'll never be welcomed back here again, understand?" My voice is low and menacing. Normally, I wouldn't be this brash, but since the woman refuses to take the damn hint, here we are. She nods, just slightly, her eyes wide as her hand slinks back from my leg. "Good. Now, please get the fuck away from me. Your perfume is givin' me a headache."

She doesn't say a word as she gets up and moves to the other side of the bar. I stay where I am, sipping my beer.

Minutes later, Knox emerges from the back with some of our crew and two men I'm assuming are the bikers who've come on our territory. I straighten, take one last sip of my drink and move off my stool.

"Knox. Who do we have here?"

"These two guys thought it would be funny to show up to your bar and scope out the scene. Had to have a little talk with 'em in the back." Dav cracks his knuckles and my eyes shift to the men. I notice the black eye on one of them. I laugh inwardly. I can always count on Knox to take care of business discreetly.

"Thanks for stoppin' by, boys, but y'all can see yourselves out."

The guy with the black eye speaks up. "We weren't tryin' to cause any trouble, we just wanted a drink like everyone else," he responds with attitude.

"That wasn't a suggestion, it was an order," I state.

Knox cuts in. "Looks like one black eye wasn't enough. How 'bout we head back there and see what else I can do."

I'm not one to turn down violence, but I have no intention of cleaning up Knox's bloody mess all night. I have someone to go home to. Someone who plagues my thoughts.

I'm so utterly fucked.

"I'll do ya one better. If y'all think you're so tough, how 'bout you prove it. Two on two. Race down 12th Avenue East and back. Don't get caught by the cops, don't hurt anyone, and if you're back here before us, we won't torture y'all into tellin' us who *really* sent you here."

Knox gives me a nod of approval. We both know they won't win.

"Deal," says the other guy.

We walk out of the bar and prepare our bikes. Summer sends one of the waitresses out to start the race. The girl stands between us and our rivals, and counts down. When she gives us the signal, we rev our engines and speed down the road.

Dav and I end up at the front and we look at each other, grinning like there's nothing between us and the open road. I can feel the cool, humid air hitting my neck. The vibrations roll through me and it's the most powerful feeling. The bike moves underneath me like it's part of me.

I glance back and see the guys tailing us closely. I still have no doubt we'll win, but it seems like we have some competition.

Knox looks back, too, then moves away and decelerates to meet the other guy, getting as close to him as possible. This throws the man off as he begins to swerve, momentarily losing control of his bike and almost hitting his friend. It causes enough of a distraction to slow them down, and Knox catches up to me again.

We continue racing down the street until we hit the end and turn back. The guys have yet to reach us, so we're winning by a longshot. We pass them on the way back, and I salute them. They only have a few seconds to catch up or else they might not leave the pub alive. Regardless of if they win, they won't get off so easily. I'll still beat the information out of them. I need to know if Mason sent them.

Dav and I reach the Crown and the guys pull up behind us moments later. I don't waste any time hopping off my bike and shoving one of the twats to the ground. Knox apprehends the other guy before he can run off. We drag them to the back door of the pub and to the stairs leading to the underground space.

The door unlocks once it recognizes my face in the identification detector.

We throw them to the ground and tie their legs and wrists.

The men holler at us to let them go, but I have no time to waste. "Tell me who sent you and we'll all be out of here quickly."

"Psht. In a body bag for them maybe," Knox scoffs.

"Give us what we need and you might get to leave alive."

"With one or two missin' limbs," Knox adds with a grin. The guy is relentless and bloodthirsty tonight.

"Dav, shut the fuck up," I snap.

"Fine, fine."

"Who sent you?" I ask again, giving them one last chance to answer before I let Dav have his way with them.

"No one! Nobody!" they both exclaim at the same time, and I laugh.

"How stupid do I look, motherfuckers?" I whip out the gun tucked in the waistband of my pants and shove it in Thing One's mouth. "Again. Tell. Me. Who. Sent. You. Or I will shoot you down the throat and expose your entire brain all over this floor."

He struggles to respond with the weapon in his mouth, but I don't take it out. "Please! *Please*, don't shoot me," he mumbles. I pull out the gun and hit him with the grip, knocking some of his teeth out. He screams out in agony.

"Let's try this again." I grab Thing Two by the hair and lift his head off the floor, putting my gun against his throat. I remove the safety and the sound causes the guys to shake in terror.

"No, no! Don't shoot him. That's my little brother, please!" Thing One yells through his bleeding mouth, the words barely comprehensible due to his missing teeth.

"Then, tell me who sent you and I won't kill him."

He finally complies. "Mason. It's Mason."

That's what I thought. I turn to look at Knox, but there's no surprise on his face. We both knew it would be him, but we couldn't act without a confession.

I get up, leaving the guys on the floor and give the gun to Knox. "Have fun," I say, and he grins back at me.

It's time for me to go back to the ranch.

20

Naya

I throw myself back onto Callan's couch as soon as he closes the door behind him. I sigh and look up at the cathedral-like ceiling of his living room. I bring my hands up to my chest and squeeze, a desperate attempt to get rid of the feelings I have in my heart. Warning signs are written all over this situation, but our actions tell a different story. I grunt into my palms as I swipe them down my face. I can't believe I agreed to keep working here and thought I could somehow avoid Callan for the rest of my life.

Growing up, I was a control freak. I always needed things to go according to plan, or else it would send me into a spiral. Whenever I would really lose it, my dad would hold me and gently stroke my hair. "Haru-kun, *man makes plans and God laughs*," he'd murmur. I don't know if it's God, but someone sure as hell is laughing at me out there because *this* is not going the way I had planned.

"It's my job to break the horses. I've broken some of the most stubborn horses you'll ever come across, so believe me when I say...You. Will. Break."

I hear Callan's voice in my mind as clearly as if he were standing right in front of me, and another rush of heat flows through my body. It was almost embarrassing how much I

183

wanted him at that moment, and feeling how desperate he was almost tipped me over the edge.

"There will *be a next time, Naya. But when that time comes, you'll have to beg for it..."* Like hell, I *never* beg.

Unable to focus on the television any longer, I shut it off. When I stand, Harlo and Dave follow me. My heart squeezes as I see how close they've gotten to me, but I squash the feeling. *They're Callan's dogs, not yours. Don't get attached.*

Since he's out, this is a good opportunity to do a little snooping. After all the things he said—and didn't say—tonight, I was able to figure out that he is part of a gang. *Sinners & Saints.* From the way he spoke, I guess he isn't just part of it, he leads it.

I don't know how I keep finding myself with these types of people. When I met Mason, I was in the thick of my 'bad boy' phase. He intrigued me enough to ignore one too many red flags. He came into my life, swept me off my feet, took care of me, and spoiled me, but hid his true identity for years.

I vowed to never again involve myself with someone who lived that kind of life. I wanted *normal.* So, who would have thought that the rancher who might save my practice would be another gang president? Callan says they don't deal in drugs, but he refuses to tell me what it is they actually do. Of course, my mind leaps to the worst-case scenario. What if they're sex traffickers? Or worse? A cold shiver runs down my spine at the things I heard happen among other gangs when I was with Mason. I'm just easy prey at this point.

But I'm not convinced that's it with Sinners & Saints. It may be my own downfall, but I do trust Callan and Knox to keep me safe.

I walk down the hall and enter what must be his home office. It looks amazing, and I'm not even surprised. There's a large wooden desk in the center of the room and two brown leather chairs in front of it. Off to the side, there's a beautiful upholstered couch, a coffee table that matches the desk, placed only a few steps away from a woodburning fireplace.

Bookshelves line the walls behind the desk, and I approach them, curious to know what a man like Callan reads. I snort. *Classics*, of course. A tattered copy of *Jane Eyre* stands out to me, and when I open it, I find that the binding is loose. This book must have been read hundreds of times. I place it back on the shelf and continue looking around the room.

What's notably absent are pictures. Where many would have photographs lining the walls of their study or on their desks, Callan keeps his office devoid of any personal effects at all.

My curiosity gets the best of me as I near the desk. I need to know what he deals in. I give a tug on one of the drawers, but it's locked. I try the next one, locked again. I shake the last drawer a little too hard and grunt. Not surprising, someone like him wouldn't just leave incriminating papers laying around.

I exit the room and continue down the corridor, and I find myself in an open wing of the house. It's so different in comparison to the rest of the modern farmhouse look. The walls are painted a navy blue, a wet bar in the corner. *I guess this is where he makes the drinks.* I can't believe that one man lives in a place like this by himself.

There's a slight smell of tobacco in the room. I wonder if he smokes cigars. I head back the way I came, Harlo and Dave still at my heels. I check the time. Callan's already been gone over an hour, but from the look on his face when he left, I think it'll be a long night.

I pass my bedroom—I need to stop thinking about it as *my* anything—and keep walking down the long hallway to where his room is located. The door is slightly ajar. As I let myself in, I can't help the gasp that comes out of my mouth.

If I thought the rest of his house was luxurious, it's got nothing on this room. *Fit for a king,* indeed.

I look over my shoulder, feeling as though I'm about to get caught, before I step farther inside. I stare at the ridiculously large, too-big-for-one-man bed right against the wall. If he were to have a foursome, each person would have enough space to move around freely. I resist the urge to jump on it.

I walk over to his closet and my jaw drops. This must be some kind of sick joke. Whatever it is that *Sinners & Saints* does must be a huge moneymaker. His closet is the size of the guest bedroom, if not larger. Three walls are lined with built-in clothing racks, and between each one are floor-to-ceiling panels for folded items and shoes. I didn't think average people had closets like this, but then again, Callan is anything but *average.* I walk out feeling embarrassed that I let him into my home today. I wonder what he must have thought when he saw where I live. I know I'm not a charity case, but I feel a bit like one at this moment.

There is a chair in the corner topped with some folded clothes. I can't resist the urge and grab the first item in the pile, bring it to my nose, and inhale deeply. It's a smokey, musky, and warm smell—evocative of the woods.

That's when I hear a cough from the other end of the room.

No. No. No. My body freezes. After what feels like an eternity, I think that maybe, just maybe, I made the sound up.

Slowly, I turn around. Callan is leaning against the wall with his arms folded across his chest, a smug smile on his face. I drop the shirt like a hot potato as my gaze meets his.

"Already fixin' to beg, sweetheart?" His tone, low and rough, makes my whole body shiver.

My face is burning, and I curse myself for getting caught. Curiosity really did kill the cat.

I lift my head, hoping I'm the portrait of cool confidence.

"I see nothing here worth begging for." I keep my voice indifferent, as if I hadn't just spent the last ten minutes gawking at his entire room and sniffing his fucking clothing.

He pushes off the wall and prowls toward me. "Is that so?"

The intensity of his gaze is almost too much, and I find myself staring over his shoulder just to avoid looking into his eyes.

He stops about two feet away from me and I chance a look at his face again. *Big mistake.* I can see unparalleled need and restraint in his eyes, and it causes a tingly feeling low in my body. But if he thinks I'm going to *beg*, he's greatly mistaken.

"Go to bed, Naya," he says, his voice deep and commanding, and I want to say no just to see how he would react. Instead, I slip past him and walk out the door.

When I get to the safety of my room, I close the door and slide down, sitting on the floor.

I don't know how much longer I can stay here without losing my mind.

I wake up in a daze. I swipe my hands across my face as if it will remove the tinge of embarrassment that I still feel from last night.

I look at the time and notice I have an hour and half until work. I crack open my door, but there's no sound. I creep down the stairs. I'm in desperate need of coffee, so I'm extremely frustrated when I get to the kitchen and see that his coffee maker looks like something that requires a degree in engineering to use it.

Okay, no coffee for now.

I look around his kitchen and feel a little rumble in my stomach. If I can't have coffee, then I'll make breakfast. A part of me hopes the smell of food will lure Callan out of bed so that I don't have to go knocking on his door. My cheeks flush. Not going anywhere near his room after the sniffing incident.

I open the fridge and find it stocked, as if he just bought groceries. I try to picture Callan strolling the aisles of a supermarket, but I just can't do it. The thought of his big, muscular frame pushing a small cart incites a little giggle. I'd love to watch him do mundane adult tasks.

I take out five eggs and some vegetables, and get started on an omelet. The yummy scent invades the kitchen and makes me even hungrier. As I'm about to slice some bread, Callan walks through the door, with Harlo and Dave right behind him. When they spot me, they run over, nudging my legs with their heads. They catch me off guard, and I laugh as they poke me for attention until I bend down to pet them.

When I finally look up, Callan's standing tall next to the counter, and I notice he's shirtless, wearing only a pair of sweatpants. His hair is slightly disheveled, as if someone has been running their hands through it. *God, is that how he walks around? The women of Springfield must not be able to get anything done, ever.*

"Mornin'." I feel his stare burning into me as I resume placing food onto two plates and slicing the loaf. "You didn't have to do that." His voice sounds gruff, half-asleep, and I get goosebumps at the thought of him whispering in my ear with that low rumble first thing in the morning in bed, while he brings his hand to—

"I know, but you made dinner last night, so making breakfast seemed like the right thing to do," I interrupt my own thoughts and pop the bread into the toaster oven. "I hope you like eggs."

Callan nods in confirmation, and I put a plate in front of him. He looks hesitant, as if unsure if the food is safe to consume.

"I promise I didn't poison it." I hold my right hand against my heart with a smirk. "Scout's honor."

He lets out a low chuckle and takes a bite of his meal. "Thank you, darlin'."

"I would have made coffee, too," I say, eyeing the machine. "But your coffee maker looks like it was developed by NASA."

He shakes his head with a smile. "It was a gift from Knox. It's a little over the top, but it makes the best cup of joe in Tennessee. I'll show you."

He's already eaten his entire omelet and I haven't even started mine. "Do you want this?" I ask, pointing at the food on my plate. "I can make another one."

"Nah, I'm good. I need you to eat, anyway. No croakin' on my watch," he teases as he heads over to the coffee maker.

I savor every bite of my food as I watch the shirtless God in front of me make coffee. I feel content when he's around, stunned at how easy this whole morning feels, and last night's embarrassment almost forgotten. With Callan, it's always easy, which is what makes this whole ordeal even more complicated. I want to hate him, he's constantly getting under my skin, but a big part of me wants to relish in him, and in the sense of security he brings me. I grew up being a caregiver and my job even consists of caring for living things. I've never been able to escape it, but with him, it's different. He's the one to take care of me and it feels right.

As he's about to pour the coffee into a mug, I interrupt him. "Actually, could I get that coffee to go? I need to get to the office. I can ask Knox for a ride if you're busy," I say, trying to keep my request casual.

The muscles in his back tense. "I'll take you," he grunts. "I'll just grab a shirt and we'll head out."

I'm almost tempted to tell him not to bother. It seems sinful to cover that body up, but I keep my mouth shut as I watch him amble up the stairs.

When Callan drops me off some time later, for a moment, I hope Laura isn't in the office and I'll escape her questioning. But the second I walk through the door, I'm met with a piercing squeal.

I nearly drop my coffee.

"Please, please, please tell me that was Callan," she exclaims before I can even put my bag down.

"Down, girl," I sigh. "It's not what it looks like."

"Well, from over here, it definitely 'looked like' you were getting out of Callan's truck. So, you better spill the beans," she retorts.

"Okay, fine. Yes, he gave me a ride. But only because my house got broken into last night and I had no other option."

"WHAT?" Laura shrieks. "Are you serious? Why didn't you call me?"

"I was going to, but I didn't want to burden you. There's nothing we could have done. I texted Knox and he sent Callan to my rescue. *This* was not my doing." I make my way to the back room to rest my things.

Laura follows me into the staff room. "Naya, you could've at least texted me! You could have come over."

I shake my head. "I thought of that, but Callan pointed out that it wasn't safe to bring the threat to your doorstep and, as much as it pains me to say this, I actually agreed with him. I'm staying at the ranch for the next week until things calm down." I don't know how we're going to survive a whole week.

Laura scoffs out loud and crosses her arm. "A week, huh?" She lifts a brow.

"Yes, Laura. A week," I confirm with an eye roll. I know exactly what she's thinking, and there's no way. I'm not staying there for more than seven days, and I'm not sleeping with him. Matter of fact, I'm going to try my hardest to avoid him, just like I've done for the past two months. I'll just get Laura to take me to my car, that way I won't have to bother Callan for rides, and I'll work late nights and have dinner here. I'll only go back to the ranch to sleep. *Easy Peasy.*

Laura backs out of the breakroom laughing.

I continue to my office and turn on my computer to go through my emails when my phone vibrates in my lab coat. I pull it out and click on the text notification. I immediately feel critters crawling up my skin.

> Mason: We need to talk.

I don't bother replying. As I've told him many times, I have nothing left to say and there's absolutely nothing for us to talk about. And after that little show he put on last time, there's no reason for me to indulge him. If what Callan said last night is true, Mason could be behind the break-in.

My phone buzzes again.

> Mason: Come on sugar. Give me a chance to explain.

My entire body shudders at the sight of the nickname he used to call me when we were together. At the time, I thought it was cute. When we kissed the first time, he said, "Sweet like sugar." And it stuck. Now, I want to gag and hurl. I might be sweet like sugar, but I'm hard as ice. And if you hurt me once, I'll kill you twice.

The clinic just opened its doors and I have an appointment in a few minutes, so I don't have time to bother with this. I chug my coffee, slip my phone back into my pocket, and walk out to the front to greet Rexford, a labradoodle, for his annual check-up and shots. My pocket vibrates for the third time this morning, but I ignore it.

Thirty minutes later, I come out of the exam room followed by my new friend Rex and his owner, a nice middle-aged man. We approach the front desk and I notice that Laura is on the phone. Her face is blank and pale.

"Um, yeah. Could you please hold, sir?" she says to the man on the other end.

I whisper to her. "Is everything okay, Lau?"

She gives me a brisk nod. "Uh-huh." Then, proceeds to ring up the bill for our patient. Once they're out of the door, she whips her head toward me.

"Naya, it's your ex-boyfriend." She points nervously toward the phone.

My heart sinks in my chest. *Mason?*

"Mason?" I ask out loud.

"Affirmative."

What the fuck? *What the fuck.* What the fuck!

"How did he get the clinic's number?" I whisper-shout. I'm panicking.

I start shaking out my hands and breathing in and out slowly to regain my composure, but nothing is helping. I'm only working myself up more and Mason is still on hold. I can see the red light blinking.

"Naya, everything will be okay. Just breathe. I'll just tell him you're not here," Laura says in an attempt to calm me down.

"No! You don't understand. We can't just get *rid* of Mason. Now that he knows where I work, he won't stop," I cry. Tears fall from my eyes and I wipe them away with shaky fingers.

"I don't care. You're not speaking to him in this state,

Naya!" Laura argues. She grabs the phone, puts it to her ear, and takes a deep breath before speaking.

"Hi! Thanks for your patience. My apologies for the long wait. I had a queue of patients to take care of. Who did you say you were looking for?" she asks with a slight accent in an attempt to mask her own voice. Mason and Laura barely interacted when we were together but I'm sure he'd be able to recognize her.

I can't hear what he's saying on the other end, but whatever it is causes Laura to grimace. I can clearly picture his face and demeanor, and I know he'll be losing patience, and fast.

"Sorry, there's no Naya here. But can I get you in touch with one of the other vets in the clinic?" There aren't any other doctors here, so I really hope he lets this go and hangs up. My anxiety has not decreased at all. I'm lightheaded and weak.

Thankfully, Mason declines the offer and Laura hangs up. I feel my phone buzz again. *Shit.*

"He's texted me twice already. This has to be him again," I explain.

I pull out the device and see that I have two unread messages from Mason.

Mason: Please answer me sugar.

Mason: You won't be able to avoid me for long Naya. You belong to me.

The last one was sent right as he ended the call with Laura. The phone slips out of my hand, and the last thing I hear before I pass out is Laura screaming my name.

My eyes flutter open and I'm met with harsh ceiling lights. I hiss in pain before closing them again. My head is throbbing and the brightness of the room isn't helping. What the hell happened? I try to bring my hands up to shield my face from the glare, but my arms fail to listen to my brain's command. It feels like my whole body has gone limp.

I turn my head to the side and slowly open my eyelids again. I see a countertop with medical supplies and realize I'm in one of my exam rooms. I hear shuffling next to me and a soft voice.

"Naya? Honey. It's Laura."

I try to speak, but my mouth is so dry. "Water," I manage to croak. She passes me a glass with a straw and I want to kiss her for this. I won't have to sit up to drink. I sip the whole cup in less than ten seconds.

"I'm going to help you up now, okay?" she asks, her voice still soft. I nod and she comes over to grab onto me. I feel another arm hold me. I jerk away and come face to face with Callan.

I internally scream at the sight of him. *Why is he everywhere?*

I get up too fast and blood rushes straight to my head. I cry out but Callan catches me before I'm able to fall over. "Take it easy, sweetheart. You already fainted once," he says. His tone is half concerned, half angry, and I don't know if the latter is at me.

I'm so disoriented. "What happened?"

"When you saw Mason's last texts, you just passed out," Laura explains. "I had to catch you before your head smashed onto the floor. I didn't know what to do, so I called Callan," she continues, and I see the silent apology in her eyes. We'd been doing just fine taking care of ourselves before these cowboys entered our lives. Now, they're on speed dial whenever we're in distress. *So much for girl power.*

"How did I get up here?" I'm currently laying on an exam bed, and I know Laura couldn't have lifted my dead weight.

"That's where I come in, darlin'," Callan quips from the side, and I want to smack the smug look off his face. I make a sudden move again, and I'm reminded that my body is still too weak.

"Show me the messages, Naya," he orders. *This again?*

"Why?"

"I want to see what that piece of shit said to you," he says, the anger is back in his eyes. Not wanting to get into another battle over my phone, I reach into my pocket, but it's not there. *Oh, that's right.* I remember it falling out of my hands before I blacked out.

"Oh, yes, I have your phone. You dropped it. Here you go." Laura hands him the phone as I throw her a death stare. She's really testing this thing between Callan and me.

He goes through the messages and his face contorts with rage. Whatever happened between him and Mason must've been a big deal. There's no way he's this upset because of what Mason said to me.

"I'm takin' you back to the ranch until I've figured things out with Mason," Callan states.

"I'm already staying for the week," I say, confused.

"You're not leavin' until it's safe."

"What do you mean?"

"I mean you're not leavin' the property until I make sure Mason is no longer a threat. However long it takes. You're not leavin' my sight. And that means no work for a while."

I throw my head back in a humorless laugh and hop off the bed, my energy fully restored from the sheer amount of outrage coursing through my body. I knew he was too good to be true.

He's just another alpha male that wants to control me. Mason didn't want me to work and now Callan is implying I should stay in *his* house until things are safe?

"Are you kidding me right now? You want me to shut down the clinic and stay in your stupid mansion like Rapunzel until *you* decide it's safe for me to come out?" I scoff and it turns into a hysterical laugh. "You've got me fucked up, Callan."

I don't realize I'm in his space until he latches onto my neck with his big tattooed hand and drags me against the wall. Laura gasps from the side. "Watch your fuckin' tone, Naya," he seethes into my ear. "You might think you have the right to lash out at me, but you don't understand who I truly am, sweetheart. I'm on *your* side, and the quicker you realize it, the less trouble we're gonna have."

I scratch at his skin to remove his grasp on my throat, but it's to no avail. He squeezes harder and when I peek to the side, I see Laura slowly backing out of the room. *Traitor.*

"I don't care. I'm not closing the clinic!" I yell. I'm not letting him take away the one thing I care about.

"Fine," he barks. "But you're gettin' dropped off and picked up every day, and I'll have one of my members stationed at the clinic while you and Laura are here. If you need to go anywhere, you take 'em with you. Understood?"

I don't have the energy or the breath to complain. "Fine," I rasp. "Now, let me go!"

He unhooks his fingers from around my neck, and I rub the sensitive skin. He's right to say I don't know who he is, and that thought bothers me. If he wants me to play house, then he has to let me into his life to some extent.

"For the record, I would *never* in my life try to control you. Everythin' I'm doin' is to keep you safe. Whether you agree with my ways or not, doesn't change that fact." He walks toward the door, leaving me standing against the wall. "I told

Laura to clear the rest of your day. Let's go." And with that, he exits the exam room.

I should be appalled by his actions, his bossiness. Instead, I'm shamefully turned on. *What is wrong with me?*

Several seconds later, after I've gathered myself the best way I could, I follow Callan out and spot him at the front desk talking to Laura. I catch the end of their conversation.

"You have both our numbers, so if you notice anythin' out of the ordinary, give us a call right away. Knox is outside, and he'll make sure you get home safely. I'll have someone guard your place all night. If you're uncomfortable or worried at any point, let him know and he'll bring you to the ranch. Got it?"

Laura nods enthusiastically. "Yes, got it!" I roll my eyes. Of course she's soaking this in.

We all leave the clinic, closing early for the day, and I hug Laura goodbye before she gets into her car and drives off, followed by Knox. I give him a wave and a small smile as he starts his bike.

I hop into Callan's truck and we head to All Saints.

21
Callan

Naya fucking Ohara.

She frustrates me to the point of no return, but I still can't get enough of her.

This woman is able to effortlessly boil the blood in my veins. And at the same damn time, that blood rushes to the tip of my dick, and I end up with a hard on every time I'm around her. I'll have to see a doctor soon if this doesn't stop.

I know exactly what could appease this problem, but I refuse to give in. Little miss 'always has an attitude' needs to be taught a lesson. If there's one thing my *mamma* taught me, it's chivalry and hospitality. And Naya wouldn't be able to see those qualities coming if they hit her in the face.

I understand I have an unconventional way of dealing with certain situations, but I'm a rancher, a biker. We're rough, gritty, and don't take no for an answer. She'll have to learn to accept my ways one way or another because I'm not letting her out of my sight until Mason is no longer a problem. I don't know why I'm so compelled to take care of her. I haven't cared about a woman to this extent since my mother and Alison. But Naya needs me. Even though she'd never admit it.

Our drive starts out quietly, with Naya looking outside while I think of the next move. Now that Mason has made it clear he's targeting her, we need to step it up a few notches. I have to meet with the guys today, and I don't want to leave her alone at the ranch in this state. So, she'll have to tag along.

Jackson should be almost back from Raleigh by now, so I give him a call. The phone rings on the bluetooth in the car and it startles Naya out of her daze. She quickly glances at me before turning back to face the window.

Jax picks up a couple seconds later, his voice loud through the speakers.

"Callan," he states in his calm, monotone voice. He's always so cordial and proper. *Brits.*

"Jackson. How did everythin' go?"

"Mission accomplished," he confirms. I knew he would deliver. This man does no wrong.

"Good. How long 'til you're back in town?"

"We're about thirty minutes out," he replies. Perfect. That gives enough time for us to get downtown.

"Meet me at The Crown. Let everyone know I'm callin' a last-minute assembly."

"You got it, boss," Jackson says before hanging up.

The last bit of my conversation must have caught Naya's attention. "Where are we going? I thought we were heading back to All Saints?"

"We'll end up at the ranch, but we're makin' a stop in Nash-ville first," I reply without taking my gaze off the road. I can see Naya eyeing me from my peripherals, but I can't gauge what she's feeling. "Is that cool?" I ask her.

She straightens in her seat. "Yeah, I guess. I have nowhere else to be, anyway. What's The Crown?"

"It's the bar I own in Nashville."

"And who's Jackson?"

I chuckle. "Are we playin' a game of twenty questions?" Though, I'd do anything to keep this woman talking.

I see her shrug from the corner of my eye, and I glance at her.

"Just curious," Naya responds, an amused glint in her eyes.

"Jax is my second oldest friend. He acts as my sergeant-at-arms and road captain. He upholds all the laws and rules of the club. He makes sure that all the committee orders are carried out as fast as possible and keeps the peace while on a run." I don't normally have to explain these things to people, as most of the business in the motorcycle club is private. But Naya has a genuine interest in what I do, so I indulge in her curiosity. And for some reason, I want to tell her the truth. I want her to know more about me.

She nods her head as I speak, and I can tell the information is soaking in. Her expression is wary, but not scared.

"So, he kills people?"

That incites a genuine laugh out of me. She's not wrong. Out of everyone in the club, Jax has the most blood on his hands. He's never minded bloodshed.

When Knox and I first found him in the alley of a bar in downtown Nashville, he had been badly abused. He had barely had any clothes left on his body and his face was battered. We happened to notice him hiding behind a garbage bin on a drunken night out when Dav and I went to take a piss.

When we asked what had happened to him, his only response had been, "You should see the other guy." His thick British accent surprised us. What was someone from the UK doing all the way in Nashville alone? From then on, we took him under our wing. And to this day, we still don't know his last name. There are many things he still keeps hidden, but we've given up on pressing him for information on his past. He needed structure and an outlet to cope with his many demons, and we gave him just that.

Jax is like a brother to us now, but we don't mess with him. Everyone knows not to fuck with him.

"Not quite," I respond, hesitating to tell Naya the truth. I'm not sure where she stands on the violence scale.

"Be honest, Callan. I don't want any secrets. If I'm going to live under your roof, I need to know these things. I refuse to be kept in the dark again," she argues. Kept in the dark *again*. It seems like Mason really did a number on her.

I sigh. "Okay, darlin', but what we do ain't for the faint of heart," I explain, giving her one more chance to back out, but she doesn't and urges me with a nod of her head.

"Fine. Jackson has killed people. People unworthy of bein' alive."

"And what makes you all decide who's worthy or unworthy *to live*, Callan? Last time I checked, you weren't *God*," she fires back.

I scoff. "Sweetheart, in my line of work, I see a lot of fucked up shit. Trust me, some people deserve to die." I grit my teeth before I notice she's turned somber at that.

I decide to try and lighten the mood. "And last time I checked, *you* were the one who called me God first," I say, hoping the little reminder of me pounding her pussy with my hands will smack the sassiness right out of her, as well as distract her.

It does. Naya gasps and shakes her head, her cheeks going bright red.

"I can't believe you just said that!" she yelps.

"I sure did. Next time you wanna be smart with me, think 'bout what I can do to you."

"You're a dick," she mutters as she hides her face in her hands. *Checkmate.*

I chuckle again and continue. "Anyway, Jax isn't the only one with blood on his hands. We gotta do what we gotta do to survive. It's a dog-eat-dog world out there," I continue. She doesn't seem bothered about my admission, which makes sense given her ex is also in a gang, but deep down, I still hope this doesn't change her opinion of me.

"Thanks for the honesty," she says after a few moments of silence.

"Does it bother you?" I can't help myself from asking.

"Not really. I mean, I've been around violence before, so it's nothing new. It doesn't change the way I view you, if that's what you're asking," she adds as if she could read my mind.

I simply nod, relieved.

"So, you're the president, I assume? And Jackson is your sergeant and road captain. Where does that leave Knox?"

"Yes, I'm the Founder and President of the Sinners & Saints Motorcycle Club," I state proudly because, *hell*, I worked hard to make it here. "And Knox is my right-hand man and vice-president. He assumes all of my duties when I can't be bothered or if I have to be absent." Which has been more often than not, lately. With the ranch keeping me busy, Dav has been stepping up as my replacement. He's a lifesaver.

We pull into The Crown's empty parking lot. It's only three p.m., so the bar isn't open yet.

I park my truck and turn to face Naya. She seems thoughtful, as if she hasn't noticed we've stopped. She doesn't seem scared or upset, to my relief.

"Are you alright?"

Naya startles before looking at me, her eyes locking with mine. She nods.

"I want you to know that I'm *nothin'* like Mason. I will never hurt you or try to control you. And I lead my business very differently, even if that might be hard to believe. Mason will never touch you again. I'll make sure of it, darlin'."

Naya stays silent, her gaze seeming to search mine for something.

After a few moments, she nods again, and I hop out, rushing to her side to help her out. I gesture for her to lead the way and she walks to the entrance of the pub.

As soon as we step in, the loud chatter ceases and everyone turns to look at us. I roll my eyes. It's as if they've never seen a woman before. I have to admit, it's not usual for me to bring someone to these meetings, but this is an important one, and I want them to know who Naya is.

I also want to make sure they know not to fucking touch her, or someone might lose their fingers.

Naya halts in her steps and I walk right into her. She's probably intimidated by the large group of thirsty bikers gawking right at her. I rest my hands on her shoulders.

"It's alright, sweetheart. Daddy's got you," I whisper against her ear and give her a little squeeze, urging her to walk. It takes her a couple seconds to react, making me smirk, and I swear I can feel the heat of her body through my palms. My goal to distract her worked. But seeing her reaction, I might have to keep that in my arsenal for later.

"Nothin' to see here, fellas," I shout. "Keep goin' 'bout your business 'til I'm ready to start."

The men go back to their conversations as I lead Naya to the bar. She still seems flustered by what I said. I love seeing her wilt.

"Hiya, boss!" Summer quips. "Who's this beautiful lady?"

Naya seems to relax and smiles, extending her hand. "Hi, I'm Naya."

Summer shakes her hand and gives her a wide grin. "I'm Summer. Can I get y'all anythin'?"

I take the usual and Naya settles on a blackberry mojito. Summer looks like the happiest person in the world. She doesn't get to make intricate drinks often, given the bar is usually filled with beer drinkers.

Once we've both got our cups in hand, I whistle to get everyone's attention. I look around the crowd but still can't see any signs of Jax or Dav anywhere.

"Has anyone seen Beavis and Butthead?" I yell, and the crowd erupts in laughter.

Tucker pokes his head up and replies, "They went out back for a smoke, King."

"Good to see you, Tuck. Glad you could make it out," I say as I salute him. He's still on paternity leave, but tries to come to some of our meetings when he can.

Right on time, my partners walk in through the back door. Knox smirks when he sees Naya at my side.

"Alright, now that everyone is here, listen up. This fine young woman standin' next to me is Dr. Naya Ohara. She's an extra special guest stayin' with me at the ranch. I've offered her protection, which means all of you are responsible for her, too."

Everyone nods their heads in agreement.

"I brought Naya here today because she's been targeted by her ex-boyfriend, Mason Caldwell." The men explode in furious chatter. "Settle down, boys," I yell over the noise. "She found herself in an unfavorable situation with him and had to leave town," I explain, looking at Naya to confirm if it's okay for me to continue. She nods, and I squeeze her hand.

"Mason has found her again, and is now in our territory. Y'all know how long the Raleigh Riders have been tryin' to bring drugs to Nashville and Springfield. How long they've been tryin' to destroy our trade. And now he's targetin' Naya. We never allowed them to succeed then, and we won't now. Not ever." The men let out a cheer and I raise my hands.

I glance over at Naya and see she has a surprised yet smug look on her face. If only Mason knew that his beloved was standing right next to his enemy. He's alive, but he'd still roll around in his grave.

"Two months ago, some of you rode up to Raleigh to perform a hit on one of Mason's labs and intercept one of their trucks. Apparently, that wasn't enough to keep them away." Knox and Jackson approach us and stand right next to me.

"Now that the first step in our plan is complete, we have to escalate the second part. We're runnin' outta time. Mason knows that Naya is now affiliated with us and won't stop 'til he's destroyed us and her. But we won't allow it."

Over my dead fucking body will I let him take her from me.

"So, I want everyone on high alert. Make sure all of our deliveries are extra guarded. If there are two people usually stationed at pick-ups and drop-offs, I want fuckin' six men there instead. All shipments will be received by Knox, Jax, and myself. No one steals from us again. I'll be sendin' some men to Raleigh 'til things have calmed down. Jackson will be in touch with the chosen ones. You see someone suspicious, detain them and take them to the warehouse for questionin'. We *will* destroy the Raleigh Riders."

I look down at Naya again, and her face shows a mixture of emotions I can't pinpoint. She's not angry, upset, or sad. She's not scared, traumatized, or confused. Determination blazes in her eyes.

"If you spot Mason, do anythin' necessary to catch him. But I'm gonna make one thing clear: bring him to me *alive*. His death will be caused by no one other than me. Understood?" I seethe. Everyone shouts their agreement. "Good. Thank y'all for comin' on such short notice. You're dismissed." Then, I look at Naya and smirk. "Sweetheart, finish your drink. It's time to take you home."

22
Naya

In all the years with Mason, not once did he ever deem me worthy of being aware of his club's activities. At the time, I thought he was protecting me, but now, I see it for what it was. He didn't value me enough to involve me. I was only ever his "play thing," a trophy to sit pretty.

I didn't fully understand what Callan's men had done to Mason's lab, but from the whoops and hollers, I knew it was probably damaging enough to piss him off.

I've never been a vengeful person, and I don't usually hold grudges, but now that Mason's here and threatening me, I can't wait for him to get a taste of his own medicine.

Callan let his walls down as he answered my questions earlier, confirming my suspicions that he was in fact the President of Sinners & Saints. I know it should make me wary, but I'm more intrigued than ever.

"It's alright, sweetheart. Daddy's got you."

I can still hear his words in my head. His voice was smooth and warm like whiskey, and my body instantly reacted. A room full of bikers watched me as I tried to resist the urge to dry hump their leader against the wall.

And the way Callan led his club, with such control and grace, was mesmerizing. I found myself feeling grateful for the opportunity to see him like that. He was relaxed and comfortable in his role, and you could clearly see how much his men respect him and his opinions.

I couldn't tear my eyes away from him, failing to convince my lady parts to stop pulsing at double-time. The effect Callan has on me is ridiculous. He either makes me spitting mad or horny as hell, and I can't seem to reconcile the two.

I need to put some space between us before I detonate from even the slightest touch.

I jump out of the truck when it stops, not giving Callan time to open my door again. I don't know what I'll do if he gets that close.

I walk behind him as we enter the house, and I'm thrown by how at ease I feel in the familiar space. We're both quiet as we enter, and I don't really know what to say to soothe this tension.

"I hope that wasn't too much for you?" Callan asks, quietly.

That's not how I feel at all, but I'm thankful he read my silence during the ride as a sign of being overwhelmed about what took place at the bar instead of me wanting to jump his bones.

"No," I reply, my voice coming out strangled. I clear my throat and try again. "No, I'm happy you let me be a part of that."

I don't think I can properly convey how much it means to me that he didn't just tuck me away and hide who he truly is. He makes me believe I'm strong enough to handle the truth, no matter what it is.

I wait to hear the pitter patter of Harlo and Dave, but the sound never comes. "Where are the dogs?" I question, all the while wondering when I became so attached to the two shepherds.

He stays silent for a moment, as if listening for a trace of them before he responds. "Knox must have let 'em out earlier. We let them roam the land. It's barricaded, so they're fine. I'll bring 'em back in after my shower."

I nod, but now images of Callan's body soaped up as hot water pounds his skin flood my mind.

"Can I get you anythin' before I go up?" He seems completely oblivious to the thoughts consuming my brain.

I shake my head. "I think I'll have a glass of wine, but I can get it myself."

He smirks, and I remember he never showed me where the bar was. I found it while snooping around yesterday.

"Gave yourself the grand tour yesterday, I see?" he mocks, and I'm relieved he doesn't seem upset about it.

I ignore his question and roll my eyes. "You were going to have a shower," I remind him. A wicked look flashes across his face, before he holds his hands up in mock surrender and walks away. Once he's out of sight, I walk down the corridor to the bar and pour myself a *large* glass of wine.

I shouldn't be having this much alcohol right now, but it feels necessary with how my body is reacting to Callan this evening. *Anything to remove the edge.* I grab my book from my purse and settle onto the couch.

About forty minutes later, I hear the familiar sound of the dogs' paws hitting the floor as they run to me. I pet and praise them for being such good boys, before I look up to find their owner staring at me from the doorway. I hadn't even heard him come down.

He's wearing dark wash jeans, and I force my eyes away from his crotch where I can see a very sizable imprint. I take another sip of wine, hoping it will help with my suddenly parched throat.

The plain, black T-shirt he's wearing clings to his skin. It should be illegal for a top to fit *that* well. His hair is damp and hangs loose. I could analyze this man for hours. My gaze reaches up and the small grin on his face says he's noticed my perusal.

"Feel free to borrow any books you'd like from my study," he says, glancing at the one I left on the coffee table.

I snort. "I think I'll pass."

He strides over to pick up my book before I have time to object.

"Why? Is nothin' I have as good as..." He pauses to read the title, and I suddenly wish the floor would swallow me whole. "Ravishing the Duke?"

There's a twinkle in his eyes as he turns the book over to read the synopsis aloud. "After his father's sudden death, George finds himself the new Duke of Marlborough and in need of a wife—"

I jump up from the couch and attempt to grab the book out of his hand, but he raises it above his head and out of my reach.

I try to retrieve it as he keeps reading, but I stumble backwards. I reach out and grab his shirt to stabilize myself. I can feel his body heat through my palms, and it's like an electric shock to my system. I stare up at his face, and I'm met with the same look I received last night in his bedroom before he told me to leave. Desire is plainly written across his face. My heart races as he lowers his hand and drops the book back down on the coffee table.

"Tell me, Naya." His voice is wicked and sultry. I move closer to his warm chest, even though I can hear him clearly. "What is it that you like to read about?"

I know it's a trick question. He leans in, barely an inch of space between us now.

"Don't be shy, sweetheart," he drawls. "I may just indulge you in your fantasies."

I let out a ragged breath. *To Hell with it.* I close the distance between us, or I at least attempt to, because when I try to kiss him, he steps back with a satisfied smile.

He makes a sound of disapproval. "You'll have to beg for it first." It's a demand, not a request. I want to scream out in frustration. How can I be both turned on and frustrated at once?

"Are you kidding me?" I know he wants this just as much as I do. I can see it on his face and through his body language.

He moves past me to sit on the couch and looks at me blandly. "I'm a thirty-six year old man, Naya," he says, his voice completely controlled. "Do I look like I have time to play games? Beg."

I stand in stunned silence as I watch Callan make himself comfortable on the couch. The need between my legs is too great and my body pleads with me to give him what he wants. But I don't cower so easily.

"No."

His pupils dilate as he stares right into mine. He wasn't expecting me to push back. *You're not the only one who can act tough, big guy.*

His eyebrow lifts, his lips curving into a sly smirk. "Is that so?"

I cross my arms against my chest, my legs slightly spread apart, ready for battle. Though my face may show defiance, my insides are bubbling with anticipation. Still, I don't let it affect my stance.

I nod. "I'm not begging."

Callan lets out a little chuckle and lifts his back off the couch to sit on the edge. I can't predict his next move, but the look on his face is a clear giveaway he's got something in mind. His hand reaches for his belt buckle and unclips it, the clicking sound traveling straight to my core.

My breathing instantly speeds up. Callan doesn't take his

eyes off me for a second as he grabs onto the metal and pulls the belt out of the loops of his jeans in one swift movement.

He stands up and walks toward me, a lion stalking its prey.

Once he reaches me, he bends down to run his lips along my ear and down my neck, making me gasp for air. "The things I wanna do to you, *amore*."

Just as I'm about to lean into him, he circles around me, the act almost threatening.

My whole body shivers in anticipation.

Callan sits back down and leans back against the backrest, wrapping the leather around his hand. "Beg, Naya."

Oh, God. I'm melting faster than an iceberg. I've never been this turned on in my life. It's beyond frustrating. I want to rip him to shreds, and curse the day I met him.

I hate that he has this much control over my body. But I can't fight it.

I finally give in. "Fine." My voice is laced with bitterness and desperation. "Please."

I can't believe I just let out that word. *Pathetic.* I should just turn around and go upstairs to save myself this humiliation.

"You can do better than that, sweetheart," he taunts. I glare at him. "Put some emotion in it. I wanna hear how badly you want me."

He's staring at me with pure desire in his eyes as he readjusts his position on the sofa, his legs spread wide. From where I stand, I can see that he's hard, and it sends a rush of heat between my legs. My underwear is soaked.

"Please, Callan," I say, letting him hear the lust in my voice. "Kiss me. Touch me. I want you."

He plays with his belt, and I squeeze my thighs together. *Is he planning on using it on me?* He places it down next to him, and I sigh a little in relief and disappointment.

"How bad do you want me, Naya?" His sexy smirk widens. "Let me hear it, darlin'."

He's pushing me to a point I've never been before. I *never* beg for a man's attention—not like I've had much of it, anyway. I'm not opposed to the idea. I'm just taken aback by my strong reaction to it. He's opening me up to sexual preferences I didn't know I had, and I want to enjoy each and every one. *With him.*

I shift on my feet, not able to keep it together any longer. "So bad, Callan. *Please,*" I whine.

I'm surprised at how easily the words fall from my lips. I expect him to get up and come to me, but he doesn't.

"Then, crawl to me," he growls and, before I know it, I'm on my knees.

Alarm bells are going off in my mind. I should get up and go to my room, but a deeper part of me wants to know what comes next.

I begin to move forward on all fours. Never once do his eyes drift away from mine. When I reach him, he doesn't say a word and continues to watch me. He raises one eyebrow, as if I should know what to do next. I know what he wants, and I cave once more.

"Please." My voice is strangled as I beg.

He leans forward and brings his hand to my chin, swiping a thumb across my lips. Shivers erupt across my whole body. I hear a loud, desperate moan, and I startle when I realize the noise came from me.

"You're such a good girl, sweetheart," Callan breathes out, the words like a gentle caress against my face. A solid pulse builds in the space between my legs.

He moves away once more and it takes every last bit of restraint for me to stay put, not wanting to lose contact with his hand.

Callan nods his head down toward his crotch. "Suck my cock."

My skin flushes and I want to rip my clothes off, I'm so hot.

He really does look like a *king* from down here, studying me with a heated gaze to see what my next move will be.

I don't think twice. I reach out and rub him through his jeans. A hiss releases from his mouth and I smile. He may think he has me right where he wants me, but *I'm* still in control. There's nothing more powerful than a woman in charge of a man's pleasure. As much as I am at his mercy, he's at mine.

His eyes move from my face to my hands, and then back up again. He's trying to maintain an unaffected facade, but his mask is slipping. *I'm doing this to him.*

My mind cheers. I love watching Callan unravel in front of me. I tug at the waist of his unbuttoned and unzipped jeans, and he lifts his hips just enough so I can pull them down with his boxers in one swoop. His cock springs free, and I can see a bead of precum just waiting for me to taste.

I give him one quick stroke with my hand, letting my thumb graze the tip, and I swipe the bead of liquid. I look him dead in the eyes as I stick my finger in my mouth and give it a gentle suck. It's slightly salty, yet sweet, and one-hundred-percent Callan.

He shudders at the sight and his cock twitches in response, but he keeps his hands at his sides. His breaths are heavy as I bring my mouth close to the base of his dick and lick up the underside of the shaft before bringing him into my mouth.

The second I put my lips around him, he lets out a pained groan.

"God, Naya." It's his turn to sound strangled. "Just like that, sweetheart. Don't stop. I don't wanna feel you comin' up for air, do you hear me?"

The request is ridiculous. The man is *huge* and I'm already struggling. Regardless, I hum in response, and I'm met with a loud, "Oh, fuck!"

With one hand bracing myself on his strong thigh and the other holding onto his length, I bring my head up and down in a quick yet steady pace, moaning as I taste his flavor on my tongue.

"Fuck yes, Naya, this is better than I could've imagined." he breathes out, every word going straight to my throbbing center. His pleasure is making me wet beyond belief. "You take me so well. I've been wantin' to fuck that sassy little mouth of yours so bad."

I lift my head, desperate for a breather, and I whisper my response, "Do it."

If he wants sassy, he'll get it.

Callan narrows his eyes at me as I lower my mouth back onto his cock. "One," is all he says, and I wonder if I heard him correctly.

He grabs the base of my neck, pulls me down farther onto him, and thrusts into my throat inch by inch, as if gauging just how much I can take. I move my head, meeting his every stroke, and when I let out a groan, his hands slink into my hair, gripping me in place.

"Keep makin' that sound, and I won't be able to last, baby."

The thought of making him break so easily makes me move faster as I attempt to get more of him in my mouth. A trail of saliva trickles down my chin. Tears fill my eyes and have started rolling down my cheeks. I must look like a mess, with mascara stains all over my face.

I come up for air a second time, and I maintain eye contact with him. He stares into the depths of my eyes and says, "You're fuckin' beautiful like this, Naya." My heart skips a few beats, and I blush as I break contact.

He reaches for my jaw and lifts my head. "Open your mouth," he orders.

I part my lips without a second thought. Our gazes lock as he hovers above me, letting a trickle of spit fall into my mouth. My eyes widen in shock, but my arousal increases tenfold.

Callan grasps onto the nape of my neck and brings my mouth back down onto him. "Two," he mutters, and I glance up at him, confused. What could he possibly be counting?

Right at that moment, he thrusts hard into my mouth. More tears leave my eyes as I try to gasp for breath, but there's no room. He withdraws just a bit and pushes back in, causing me to choke again.

"You have no idea how good this feels," he grumbles.

I watch his chest rise and fall. My lips are so sensitive right now, every stroke against them a direct hit to my clit. The pressure building inside me is so intense, I could come from this alone.

He continues to fuck my mouth, and I move my hand down to press against my center, eager to feel some form of relief. But he reaches out and grabs my arm.

"Don't you dare. I'll be the only one touchin' you tonight, do you understand?"

I pull back to respond, "I need—"

"I know what you need, Naya," he grinds out. "But what I need *you* to do is finish what you started so I can come in that pretty mouth of yours."

Callan's words spur me into action as I once again begin to suck his cock. He mumbles, "Three."

He pounds my mouth ruthlessly. I love it. This time, I don't come up for air, and I heave as he hits the back of my throat. I cup his balls, tipping him over the edge.

"Oh, fuck!" he exclaims. "Oh God, you're so good, baby. I'm gonna come."

His cock twitches in my mouth as he shoots his load down my throat. I swallow every last drop and moan in satisfaction.

I give him a few more rubs with my hand as he winds down from his orgasm. He lets out small whimpers as I continue suckling on his tip. Each sound fills me with so much need, it's almost unbearable.

When he's finished, he grasps my hair and lifts my head. I stand and bend over to kiss him. He explores my mouth as if he will never get enough, but when I begin to pull away, he tugs me back onto his lap, making me yelp. He flips me so that I'm laying on my stomach over his knees.

"Four."

23
Callan

Holy fuck.

Naya sucking my cock was not what I expected it to be. It was so much *better*.

Her warm, wet mouth wrapped around me like silk. Her soft, plump lips turned the most delectable shade of red as they went up and down my shaft. Her smooth tongue felt unbelievable as it lapped around my tip. *I came undone.*

I've never climaxed so hard from a blowjob. If I were any other guy, I'd be spent for the night. But it just made me want her even more.

But not before I punish her for her sassy mouth and coming up for air when I told her not to. Naya is a brat, so she's going to be treated like one until she turns to putty in my hands. I wouldn't have her any other way, though; the challenge turns me on.

There's nothing fun about a woman who submits without a little push and pull. She's *exactly* what I need.

Naya has no idea what's about to happen, and the thought brings a rush of excitement to my body. She lets out a harsh breath as she attempts to turn around and face me, but I growl and pin her down. I grab onto her wrists and bring them to her back, cuffing her in my hands. "Don't move."

"What are you doing?" she exhales, her speech stunted with my knees digging into her stomach.

"Teachin' you a lesson."

Her head snaps up. "What?" she asks, puzzled.

"You heard me, sweetheart. I'm 'bout to show you the consequences of havin' an attitude. Your lips are so sinful they almost made me forget how much I've been wantin' to punish you, but you ain't gettin' off that easily."

Naya squirms and tries to escape my hold, but I push her down. "Callan, this isn't funny!" she shrieks.

Her body language gives off fear, yes, but there's something else that motivates me to continue. My soft cock begins to twitch and threatens to come back to life.

Here we go. I knew it wouldn't take long to be ready for another round.

"I'm not laughin', darlin'," I whisper in her ear. "Now, hold still while daddy punishes you for bein' a bad girl." Her body shudders, but she stops squirming.

I place kisses down her spine and feel her relax in my hold. "Atta girl," I praise in-between each peck. Her body heat is blistering like the sun. She's ready.

I reach for my belt, wrap the brown leather around my fist, and hold onto the buckle. "Stay put, baby. The more you try to wiggle that sweet ass of yours away, the more I'll make this hurt."

I push down her leggings and find a stringy, red lace thong outlining her perky, round ass. I grunt at the sight.

"Fuck, Naya. Look at you. Did you wear this little thing just for me?" I pull on the triangle of her thong, the snap making her flinch. A little moan escapes her lips, giving me a small taste of how she reacts to pain. I knew she'd love it.

"Callan?" she whimpers, having caught onto what I'm planning.

I let out a low chuckle, but this is going to ruin me as much as it'll ruin her. Having Naya at my mercy and trusting me so willingly not only sends a jolt to my dick, but to my heart, and I don't know if I can handle that.

It's all happening so fast, turning into something I don't quite understand, but I can't put an end to it now. Naya might infuriate me to no end, but I'd rather deal with her sass than not have her at all. I'm surprised I was able to withhold myself from her this long, especially after a taste of what it would feel to be inside her tight pussy two months ago.

There's no way I'll be able to stop this time around.

I finally let go of her wrists with my other hand and her arms fall across my legs. I place my palm on her ass and caress her cheeks. "I can't wait to see your golden skin turn red," I murmur and watch in fascination as goosebumps erupt all over her.

I turn Naya's face to me. "Breathe, baby. If you need me to stop, say 'lilies.'" She nods, her stomach rising and falling against my legs, not even questioning why I decided to use that word.

I lift the belt and swing. *Thwack.* "One," I say. She yelps, and I rub where the belt connected to her skin. "For each break you took while suckin' my cock." She's already quivering, and I've barely started.

I want her to be a pile of mush by the time I'm done.

Thwack. "Two."

The leather hits her ass and her whole body jerks as she screams. "Callan! Please," she begs, but I don't let it stop me. She deserves this, and she knows it.

"You got this, sweetheart. You're doin' so well." Her butt cheek is reddening by the second, and a sense of satisfaction invades me. I place my palm on it and she hisses from the sting.

Once the punishment is over, I'm going to worship every last crevice of Naya's body.

I raise the belt and strike her again. *Thwack.* "Three."

This time, her body reacts, but not a sound slips out of her mouth. I slide my fingers into her hair and lift her head up. Her already stained face is streaked with tears.

I bring her lips to mine and kiss her with rigor. "Such a good fuckin' girl. Can you give me one more, Naya?" I ask, but I know the answer. She can take it.

She nods, and it's all I need to give her the last, hard blow.

Thwack. Naya yells, anguish lacing her voice. She's in pain, but she hasn't complained once. She goes limp, her body a wilted flower spread on top of me. A thin layer of sweat covers her skin and her breathing is ragged. Her ass now has an imprint of the belt, and small bubbles of blood appear under her skin.

My cock is now harder than a metal rod. Precum leaks from the tip. I want to be buried so deep inside her, I'll have to be dug out. "Four. That one was for runnin' your mouth and givin' me attitude."

This ought to teach her not to go against my word. But if she does it again, I won't hesitate to punish her over and over. I rub her ass once more before I let my hand slide between her cheeks and her thong. She quivers as my fingers graze her tight hole before I land on the sweet spot.

Oh fuck.

"You're so fuckin' wet, Princess. Did my little punishment turn you on?" I ask, my voice husky. As much as I enjoyed what just happened, she did, too. Her pussy is dripping. She groans out a response while I rub between her folds. Her clit is already swollen and throbbing. If I keep stimulating the same spot, I'll get an orgasm out of her in no time. But I want her first one of the night to be from my tongue.

I circle around the little bud until she shivers, then I stop. "I have to fuckin' taste you." I want to lick every ounce of her arousal and watch her gush in and around my mouth.

I grab her by the waist, flip her over my shoulder, and carry her to my bedroom, leaving my jeans and briefs on the floor.

"Callan, put me down!" she protests.

I don't dignify her request with a response, and smack her ass. Clearly, the belt couldn't rid her of all her brattiness.

I throw her onto the large bed. She looks shocked as her small body bounces off the mattress and she eyes me with wariness, something flashing in her eyes.

Just then, I realize her gaze has fallen to the scar along my torso, and I stiffen.

"How did you get that s—"

"Now's not the time, darlin'. I ain't done with you yet."

And even then, it won't be enough to satisfy my craving. My cock twitches in anticipation.

I tug at her ankles to bring her to the edge and split her legs apart, eliciting a little cry from her. Her red thong is soaked and a darker shade now. I pull the fabric to the side, spread her folds and—

Holy shit.

"Princess, you have the prettiest fuckin' cunt I've ever seen," I say in a low rumble.

She lifts herself up on her elbows but avoids direct eye contact, looking embarrassed and attempting to shut her legs. I put my arm between them.

"Don't you ever hide from me." And that's an order she doesn't even bother disobeying. Her eyes snap to mine before her knees fall open and she lowers herself to the bed.

I tear her flimsy underwear away and, in a matter of seconds, my mouth is on her pussy. Naya gasps, her back arching at the same time as I lick her from her entrance to the top in one go.

"You taste like Heaven. I'll never get enough."

When I reach her clit, I circle my tongue around it, catch it between my lips, and suck. Naya screams out loud, "Oh my God!"

I keep going, alternating between licking and sucking, only stopping to fuck her entrance with my tongue. Her body thrashes as she lets out the most delectable sounds I've ever heard.

I can't stop myself from grabbing onto my cock, already hard again. I jerk it vigorously as I consume Naya with an insatiable hunger. She tastes so fucking good, and I want to bottle it up for later. *Or I could just do this again.* I'm addicted; doing this a thousand times a day still wouldn't be enough.

"*Fuck*, Callan. It feels too good," she grunts out.

"Give it to me, Naya. I want you to explode on my tongue." I let go of my shaft to tease her entrance with two fingers. She whimpers just as I shove them inside of her. I curl the digits up and begin to motion forward. Her moans escalate, louder and louder. Her breaths are harsh and her body flails.

"Let it go. *Now*, Princess," I bark, and that's enough to open the floodgates. I continue to finger and eat her pussy until she screams, her orgasm hitting her like a tidal wave. I slow down to give her the opportunity to catch her breath.

When her twitching subsides, I slide out my fingers and give her one last kiss on her clit.

I climb over her to get a better view of her flushed and satisfied face.

"Callan," she tries to speak, but I put a finger to her mouth, prying it open with my thumb and sticking it in. She sucks it, making me groan.

I need more.

"I'm gonna fuck you now, darlin'. I'll start off slow to give you a chance to adjust. I wanna feel your pussy stretch around me. And once I'm buried to the hilt, I'm gonna pound into you so hard, you'll have to beg me to stop. But not 'til I get two more orgasms out of you. Only then, will I allow myself to come. Are you ready, Princess?" I ask her. She nods around my finger.

I remove my thumb from her mouth, and it makes a popping noise. I use her saliva to coat her bottom lip before I bend down and catch it between my teeth. I could spend an eternity making out with this woman. Naya moans into the kiss as I shove my tongue inside. She meets mine with hers and we greedily devour each other.

My heart feels like it'll jump out of my chest. *What the fuck is she doing to me?*

I break off and place myself between her legs. My hard cock connects with her clit, eliciting the most delicious sound from her, and it takes everything in me not to shove it in without a condom. *Reckless*, I know.

Right at this moment, an image of Naya pregnant with my baby flashes across my mind. Something in my chest twists. I shake the thought out of my head for now before reaching into my nightstand to grab a condom. I rip the wrapper with my teeth and slip it on my dick while Naya watches me. She bites her lips.

"Like what you see, darlin'? I ask her, and she nods eagerly.

"Good," I respond. I tap the tip of my dick against her clit once more before I line myself up with her entrance.

Naya fumbles to take off my shirt and I yank it over my head. I do the same with her top, leaving her in a matching red lace bra.

I curse under my breath. "Shit, I can't wait to get my hands on those tits."

Slowly but surely, I push my cock inside, inch by inch, and

she hisses. A low, pained grunt escapes me. "Fuckkkkkkkk."
Her pussy feels so good, I have to stop for a second to control
myself. Naya shuts her lids. I let her, but not without a cost.

In one quick movement, I thrust and bury myself deep
inside her. Her eyes fly open wide as she screams. "Callan!
Fuck. *Oh my God.* It's too much," she complains.

"You will take it, Naya," I seethe. "Eyes on me at all times,"
I command.

"Yes, *King Callan*," she mocks, and I can't believe what I
heard.

The nickname shoots a wave of pleasure down my spine, all
the way to the tip of my dick, and it feels like a blow to the gut.
If I move by even an inch, I might explode.

*And did she really give me attitude after I just punished her
for her bratty mouth?*

But my brain can't focus on anything other than what she
called me. I've gathered enough of my bearings to start moving
again, so I pull out almost all the way and drive back in with
force. Naya shouts.

"Say that again," I order. She looks at me confused, so I
come out again and ram inside her pussy. She yelps. "Say. It.
Again. Naya," I threaten. I pick up the pace and fuck her hard,
stealing the air from her lungs on each thrust.

"King Callan!" she yells, breathless.

I lower myself to her chest and blow warm air onto her
neck, making her shiver. I bite down hard.

"Who does this pussy belong to?" I ask as I plunge into her
over and over.

"King Callan," she mutters, unable to say a full sentence
without stuttering.

"That's right, Princess. It's *mine*."

I hook my arms under her back and shove a pillow right

under to elevate her off the bed. Her moans change in volume and tone, so I know I'm hitting exactly where I've aimed.

I place my hand on her lower abdomen and apply the right amount of pressure. I feel a gush of wetness as Naya's pussy constricts around my cock.

"Yes! *Yes*, Callan. Right there. Please don't stop," she manages to say.

"Your wish is my command. Come for me, baby."

And she does, so wildly that tears rush out of her eyes and her screams turn silent.

I catch her quiet moans with my mouth and kiss her through her climax. I don't know how I'm holding it together at this point. My dick craves release. But not yet.

"You're givin' me another one."

Naya begins to cry out, but I don't give her a chance to complain.

I flip her on her knees. "Face down, ass up," I instruct. She obeys and lowers her head to the pillow. "If it's too much, bite down on the cushion. If you can't handle it anymore, tap my leg. Understood?"

She mumbles something and I bend down, face-to-face with her ass, before shoving my tongue right into her tight hole. She squeals and tries to hurry away, but I keep a strong grasp on her thighs.

I lick in and around the opening enough to get her used to the feeling, and I can tell the moment she starts to enjoy it. "I'm comin' for this hole, too," I promise.

Then, I lower my head and suck on her clit with purpose, to make sure she's wet and ready for orgasm number two.

When I'm satisfied, I lift myself up and dive back in mercilessly with my cock. Naya clenches her walls around me, the feeling bringing me another step closer to losing control. "If you keep squeezin' your pussy like that, I won't make it, baby," I say, my voice thick with lust.

But she doesn't stop. She's testing me.

I fuck her hard and she directs her shouts into the pillow, biting down whenever I go too deep. "It's too much," she manages to croak, but I ignore her. I won't let up until she gives me what I want. Her pleasure.

"Come for me again and I'll stop."

Naya lets out a frustrated growl and bangs her fist on the bed. She's so fucking adorable when she's mad. I stop pounding her for a moment and she takes long, labored breaths.

I'm tearing her apart and loving every second of it.

I pull out and she whips her head around to look at me. "I thought you said one more—"

Right before she can finish the sentence, I give her one strong pump. Her body almost goes flying forward, but I hold on tight to her hips. She shouts.

"Your pussy was made for me, Naya. Do you hear me?" I pull on her hair and jerk her head and body back to my chest. "Say it," I growl into her ear.

"It was made for you," she rasps. I let go of her head and she falls back onto the bed.

"Now, come for me," I bark. I'm dying for my own release.

Like the good girl she is, she lets herself go, her insides pulsing against me. She's close.

"You can do it," I encourage just as she falls apart. The sweet melody of her moans rings through my ears.

"*Oh my God.* I'm coming," she says, and I take that as my cue to come with her.

I give her a few more strong and steady strokes as I empty my load into the condom, my whole body shuddering.

Naya melts into the mattress and I fall on top of her, no sound in the room other than our intertwined breaths. I roll off to the side, burying her in my arms, her backside flush to my front. The aftershocks of her orgasms are still hitting her, and I hold her tight.

At that moment, I know that I'll never be able to let go of this woman.

Naya gets up to leave, but I grab her by the waist.

"Where the fuck do you think you're goin', Naya?" I growl in her ear as I pull her flush against me.

"To my room?" she responds, but it comes out as more of a question.

"This *is* your room, sweetheart," I whisper, nipping at her ear. "If you think I'm spendin' another night without your tight body right next to me, you're severely mistaken."

A small smile finds its way onto Naya's face, and I know that whatever it is I'm feeling, she is, too.

24
Naya

Morning comes and I'm still buried in Callan's arms.

As I stir, an ache pulses between my legs. I didn't think it was possible to come as hard as I did last night, but here I am, lying boneless and naked next to him. I knew he would be good in bed, but nothing could have prepared me for what I experienced. The dirty words he spoke as he fucked me mercilessly, ruthlessly. Never treating me like someone fragile.

I loved every minute of it.

Watching him come undone unleashed something in me I hadn't even known existed.

Light beams through the cracked open curtains, and I look down at Callan. His big, chiseled frame wraps around me so perfectly. His body, built to perfection and full of ink, is a sight for sore eyes. I let my eyes roam his chest and stop on the scar. My fingers itch to feel the ragged skin. I can't help but wonder how he got this injury, hoping that he will tell me the story one day. But the healed mark only makes him more special and beautiful.

The sun is just beginning to rise when I gently lift his arm off my waist, doing my best not to wake him. I hold my breath when I accidentally jostle his body, but he groans and turns around, bringing me with him, and I end up straddling him.

When I look down, Callan's million-dollar smile beams right up at me. "Mornin', sweetheart." And just like that, everything that was in my mind vanishes as my entire body and brain turn to mush.

I brace myself on his hard chest. "Good morning, King," I respond, a teasing glint in my eyes.

I can't seem to think straight lately... Callan has ruined me for anyone else; nothing and no one will ever make me feel this good again. How could I ever settle for anyone else?

Callan said my pussy was made for him, but it feels like he was made for *me*.

The thought hits me so suddenly, it scares me. I can't remember the last time I felt like this about someone. Maybe in the early years with Mason, but by the time the relationship ended, any romantic notion I had about us had been squashed.

There's no denying that the relationship between Callan and me has changed, but I'm not sure what it means.

Callan must realize I've zoned out. "Penny for your thoughts?"

I giggle. "I'm just thinking about last night." The feelings rush back to me, straight to my core, and my cheeks flush a little.

"Yeah, Princess? If you already need a refresher, I'm more than happy to oblige," he responds as he reaches up to plant a kiss on my lips. I melt into his embrace, but I'm surprised when he pulls away.

"I want to take you somewhere," he says, with a mischievous smile.

Excitement bubbles in my chest. "Give me ten minutes to get ready!"

I meet Callan at the back door and he leads me to the stables. "We're goin' for a horse ride today."

"Really?" I exclaim with glee. I've ridden horses before, but it's been such a long time, and I can't wait to experience it again. "Where are we going?"

"It's a surprise."

We each pick a horse, with Callan mounting Ace, and me choosing a brown mare. "Hello, beautiful," I say to her as I pat her snout. She chuffs in response, and I chuckle.

We exit the barn and head through a meadow. We ride next to each other in comfortable silence, passing trees and fields, the sun already beating down on us. I glance over at Callan a few times, and he looks so at peace. He turns and catches me gawking, then gives me a grin. A quiet contentment spreads through me.

Once we reach our destination, Callan helps me off my horse and leads me to a secluded area, where I notice a blanket and other items waiting for us on the grassy ground.

"What is all this?" I ask, barely able to conceal my delight.

"A picnic for two," Callan says proudly. "I asked Knox to set this up for us."

I didn't even notice him texting Knox, but gratitude wells up inside me. "When did you have time?"

"We always find time for what we want, darlin'." I cover my mouth to hide my grin.

When we settle onto the quilt, Callan opens up a little basket filled with breakfast goodies. "Wow, Knox really outdid himself," I say, with a chuckle.

"He's really a lover boy at heart," Callan replies.

"And how about you? Are you a romantic?"

Callan's body tenses a little and he runs a hand through his hair. "Not anymore." He looks away for a moment. "I used to be with my ex, Alison. But all of my efforts went down the drain when she left me."

"What happened?" I ask.

"She couldn't see herself settlin' down with me, claimin' that the life of a MC President was too dangerous. She wanted a normal, mundane life with kids and a white picket fence. But she knew I couldn't fit into that mold." Callan breathes in for a heartbeat and lets out a puff of air. "I spent three years buildin' my life around Alison, only for her to leave me high and dry. I woke up one mornin' to her gone."

I'm hit with a realization. "Is that why you were upset that I left without saying goodbye?"

Callan shrugs. "Somethin' like that, I guess."

I put my hand on his shoulder, positioning myself on top of him. I kiss him gently, exploring his mouth, and he does the same. I moan as our tongues tangle. Callan moves his lips along my jaw and, when he reaches the column of my neck, he continues kissing down, taking little bites and then licking over the areas to ease the sting.

"I never would have left like that if I had known," I respond, sincerely.

He rolls me onto my back and reaches the top of my breasts with his mouth. My breaths become harsh and desperate.

"I won't let it happen again, *cuore mio.*"

He places soft suckling kisses all around my chest, moving my top before taking my nipple into his mouth. I cry out and see stars as he flicks his tongue over the sensitive bud. I tangle my fingers in his long hair to hold his head tightly against me.

Callan yanks himself onto his knees and my whole body jerks. "Stay on your back and put both of your hands above your head, Princess," he orders.

I'm hypnotized by the deep sound of his voice and follow his command without a second thought.

He places a knee on either side of my body and I watch as he takes his belt off and loops it through the buckle, creating a circle. He pushes my wrists together and slides the loop over my wrists, tightening it.

I know I shouldn't like being restrained like this, but I do. I trust Callan, and know he would never truly hurt me.

I'm so wet. I'm sure I'm soaking the blanket below me, but I can't bring myself to care.

"Don't move your arms," he warns, and I'm tempted to disobey just to see what would happen.

"Good girl," he teases as he moves his head to my breast again, taking my nipple back into his mouth.

I let out a moan. He sucks and bites, the sensation so overwhelming that I wonder if I could seriously come from this alone.

"I could suck on these beautiful tits forever." Callan's voice is a low purr that sends electric bolts to my clit. "This body is mine, every last inch of it. Isn't that right, Naya?"

I nod, unable to form a rational thought, much less a sentence.

"Use your words," he growls. "I wanna hear you say it."

I suck in some air and release it. "My body is yours, Callan."

He moves back up, kissing the opposite side of my neck and peppering it with stinging bites. I thrust my hips up, desperate for relief and unable to reach down to touch myself. He notices my movements, smiles, and places his thigh between my legs, allowing me the delicious friction I seek.

"That's it, Princess," he groans. "Use me to make yourself come."

I move faster, humping his leg like I'm in heat.

"Oh God, Callan," I whimper. "I'm so—"

He halts my words with a searing kiss and breaks off, looking into my eyes.

"I know, sweetheart," he drawls. "I know." He pinches my nipple between his thumb and forefinger. I'm barely conscious of my actions. My hips thrust at a fast pace, and he presses his thigh against me even harder. Before I know it, I'm coming again.

"Fuck, Callan!" The space between my thighs is still pulsing when he moves his head down, lifts my skirt and panties to the side and licks me as if he's a man starved and I'm his last meal.

He pulls my clit into his mouth, and I plead. "Callan, I can't. It's too sensitive." My body feels overworked from last night's orgasms.

"You're capable of so much more than you know. Last night was proof." The smirk on his face is playful, but the tone of his voice is serious. "I'll tell you when you've had enough. Now, say it again, Naya. Who's the King of this pussy?"

I moan at his filthy words. "You are," I say desperately.

"I'm what?" he rasps.

"The King of this pussy." I throw my head back in disbelief at the words coming out of my mouth.

"Then, let the King feast." Those are the last words he says before his head is back between my legs and his tongue is lapping at my core. He rotates between fucking me with his tongue and sucking on my clit with ruthless abandon. I've never met a man who does this so well.

It's too much. Every stroke is exactly where I need him. I'm so sensitive, but he's applying just the right amount of pressure. I furiously thrust against his face and he lets out a low hum of satisfaction, his tongue still inside me, and I feel the vibrations everywhere.

"Oh my God, Callan, I—" I've never felt like this before. I want to come so badly, I'm desperate.

Callan moves his lips back to my clit and sucks harder, slipping two fingers inside of me, and my scream could wake the dead. A rush of liquid leaves my body.

He keeps sucking, and I finally come.

I cry out. My arms are still above my head and my back has fully arched off the blanket, knocking the basket and food sideways.

I can feel how wet the fabric is under me, and I'm embarrassed at the mess I've made. When he raises his head, the wonder in his eyes tells me there's nothing to be worried about.

"Fuck, baby," he croons. "You're so sexy. I want you to come on my face like that everyday."

Callan's face is dripping wet and his words make me giggle. He kisses me again, and I can taste myself all over his mouth.

He reaches up and undoes the belt to release my hands. My fingers tingle as the blood flows through them again.

He helps me sit up and I'm hit with a gentle breeze, reminding me that we're outside. My face flushes at the thought of someone hearing us.

I take a quick glance around, and Callan notices my movements. "Don't worry, sweetheart. It's just you and me...and the horses," he says with a smirk, as if reading my mind. I tap him playfully on the shoulder and attempt to stand, but my legs are two sticks of jello and my knees buckle. Callan laughs and whisks me up in his arms, carrying me over to my horse.

I look up at him, questioning how this tough-looking, grumpy man could be so tender and caring.

"What's on your mind?" Callan asks.

I drop my gaze. "Nothing," I reply, quietly.

"Nothin'?" He raises an eyebrow. I shake my head and he doesn't push me.

He places me on my horse, his hands lingering on my hips a moment too long, before he climbs back on Ace. He nods his head forward. "Come with me. I wanna show you somethin'."

Callan leads us through the south field of the ranch. We dismount, and after several minutes of walking in silence, he opens a small gate in a barricade.

"Callan, this is beautiful," I gasp, stunned.

A field of white lilies stretches as far as the eye can see. My heart tugs, and I smile wide as I take in my surroundings. He holds my hand and gently leads me over to a bench not too far from where we are.

Once we're seated, Callan finds his voice. "This field means a lot to me." He keeps his eyes trained out on the field of flowers, his voice turning solemn. "My mother was the first generation of her family to be born in the United States."

I hold my breath, hoping he'll continue. After a brief pause, he does.

"Her parents met my father's family when they moved to Tennessee. They were one of the few families that were actually welcomin' to newcomers at the time, and they became close friends. My grandparents joined 'em for holidays and, in turn, my *nonna* and *nonno* let 'em join in on the Italian holidays they celebrated."

"When my parents were born, they grew up together as best friends and eventually became more. Both their parents were thrilled. They used to joke that they had no other option but to fall in love." Callan smiles and I can't tear my gaze away from the sight. "But it wasn't forced. It was fate. I'd never seen two people who loved each other more."

He glances at me. I'm watching him intently, and give him a slight nod, hoping he'll keep opening up.

"Did you know that Italy's national flower is a white lily?" I shake my head. "They were my mom's favorite. Every year on her birthday, my dad would have a vase full of white lilies waitin' on the kitchen table and, without fail, my mom would swoon and thank him as if it was the first time she'd ever received them."

Callan pauses for a moment and catches his breath. I squeeze his hand in encouragement.

"When I lost 'em both, I didn't think I'd be able to cope. They taught me so much, like how to work hard, be a man, and how to embrace my different cultures. When my *mamma* passed away, several years after my pops, I had a hard time partin' with our family ranch; it had been with the Hudsons for generations. You'd think I was an idiot for sellin' generational property, but it was time. When I bought All Saints, I had this field planted with white lilies. It seemed like an appropriate tribute to 'em both."

He stares at the flowers, a nostalgic expression on his face.

"I love comin' out here whenever I need a quiet moment to think things through."

"This is a beautiful tribute," I murmur, my voice soft. "Thank you for sharing this with me."

My heart swells in my chest at what he did for his parents. I'm just sad they can't be here to see it. It's beautiful, heavenly.

"Anytime, *mia cara*." He holds my gaze for a moment before clearing his throat. "We should probably head back to the main house. Time to get you to work."

I pinch myself multiple times on the walk and ride back. *Is this man real?*

As he spoke, I was in awe of the flowers and of the man who planted them. He shows the whole world his tough exterior, and I can't help but feel honored that he brought me to a place he clearly treasures, showing me a different, softer side of himself.

I peek at Callan out of the corner of my eye. He's unusually quiet, but I understand. It's hard talking about loved ones who have passed. I get emotional every time I even think about my mother.

I get angry, too, but that's a different story.

I appreciate him for opening up to me and allowing me to learn more about him, and I wish we had more time to talk. It's almost alarming how at ease Callan makes me feel. We started off on the wrong foot, and I'm still wary about our budding relationship, but I can't deny my feelings anymore. The more time we spend together, the more I want to uncover every part of him. The good and the bad. Let him uncover parts of me.

I don't know what the next several days are going to look like, but I still have to make sure not to get too attached. With Mason, I let my guard down too soon and allowed him to take charge, losing myself.

I don't want to repeat the same mistake with Callan. If I can stay grounded and keep my head on my shoulders, it should be fine.

I look up at Callan and stare at his profile. It's perfect. Strong forehead, narrow and slightly pointed nose, full lips, and a chiseled jaw. Now that I think about it, I never stood a chance. Not only is he proving to be a great guy, he's gorgeous, too. *Crap.*

When we reach the back of the house, Harlo and Dave come running from their dog houses and almost trample me to the ground. I bend down and let them slobber me with kisses, and I let out a giggle. Callan stands above me with a cute smile on his face.

"Your dogs might go missing by the end of the week," I joke.

"Oh, really? How come?" he responds, amused, and taking his turn to show them some love.

"I'll take them home with me when I leave," I reply with a huge grin. "I can't pick a favorite, so they're both coming."

His face instantly turns to stone and my smile dissipates. I didn't realize he was sensitive about his dogs.

"I'm sorry. I was just trying to be funny," I explain, but he cuts me off.

"Go inside and get ready for work. I'll wait for you downstairs. Don't take your time," he says as he charges toward the stables with the horses. He walks by me so fast, air knocks me in the face, and I stay frozen in the same spot.

What just happened? Why did he get so angry?

He's such a caveman.

And, just like that, the lovely truce we had ends.

I march toward the house and stroll right past Knox in the kitchen. I don't acknowledge his greeting and go straight to the bathroom in the guest bedroom to take a shower.

To Hell with Callan's demands. He's not my boss.

I shrug his shirt off with force and throw it across the room. The rest of my clothes follow. I step in the shower, not even waiting for the water to heat, and I hiss when the freezing stream touches my skin. *God damnit.*

I'm still flustered by Callan's response to my joke. I teased him, and instead of laughing, he reverted back to his alphahole ways.

Good. This is a great reminder that I should keep hating him.

I scrub my body quickly and forcefully, while cursing myself for even softening toward Callan.

Just then, the bathroom door swings open, and I let out a loud shriek. Callan is in the doorway, glaring at me as if I've just done something wrong. My immediate reaction is to cover myself—very poorly, I might add. There's not much you can hide with two hands when you're naked.

"What the hell are you doin' in here?" he asks, fury lacing his voice.

I scoff. "What does it look like I'm doing, Callan? I should ask you the same question."

"Why are you in this bathroom?"

Are you kidding me? "What's the problem with this bathroom? Please, enlighten me."

"It's not mine," he seethes.

"What's the difference?" I exclaim. "Can we have this conversation when I'm done?" *God.* This man is infuriating.

"I walked into my room expectin' to see you there, but you weren't, so I came to ask you why you're showerin' in here instead of over there." He animatedly points in the direction of his room.

"Again, a conversation we could've had *after* my shower, Callan. Now, get out. I'm naked!" I yell.

He crosses his arms and leans on the doorframe, a smirk appearing on his lips. "It didn't seem to be a problem last night. Or this mornin'. I've seen it all, Naya. I've done it all, too."

The urge to chuck shampoo bottles at his head is strong, but I refrain from doing so and making myself look like a crazy person when *he's* the lunatic here. "This is different!" I argue.

He rolls his eyes. "Next time, shower in my bathroom. This is no longer your room. Capisce?"

"Fine, Callan. Just get out," I say, with a defeated sigh. He turns on his heels and steps out of the bathroom.

I growl in frustration.

When we arrive at the clinic, I don't see Laura's car anywhere. I'm hoping she's okay. Callan said someone would watch her house.

"She's fine, Naya," Callan says, interjecting my thoughts as if he could hear them.

I let out a breath of relief. "Who's stationed at her house?"

"Veronica. She's one of our best trained bodyguards."

My head whips toward him. "There are women who work for you?" I ask, surprised.

He narrows his eyes at me as if my question is ridiculous. "Yes, we have quite a few, actually."

I ponder his answer for a few moments. Mason never had any women in his crew. He claimed it was too dangerous for them. At the time, I thought he was being protective, but now, I see it for what it is: he's a sexist pig. Sometimes, when I look back on my relationship with him, I wish I could kick myself. So many obvious red flags that I willingly ignored because I thought what we had was special.

"Thanks for the ride." I hop out of the truck.

"I'll be back this evening," Callan says in response.

"You know, we could just pick up my car this afternoon so that you don't have to keep driving me around and have to *wait* for me."

Or not. If looks could kill, the one Callan is giving me right now would do the job.

"Close the door, Naya." I do as he says, choosing to let him win this battle, for now.

When I reach the door to the clinic, I turn and glance over my shoulder. Callan is staring at me through the windshield. When he catches my eyes, he makes a 'shooing' motion with his hand to let me know he won't be moving until I'm safely through the doors. I let out a sigh and walk inside. *What has my life become?*

I flick on the lights and head to the back to drop off my bag. The room is silent, and my first appointment isn't for another couple of hours.

Ten minutes later, I hear Laura enter, belting out "Hell on Heels" by the Pistol Annies. When she sees me, she cuts her rendition short.

"*OhmyGod!*" she squeals. "YOU HAD SEX!"

My mouth falls open. I took a shower before work and changed my clothes. Nothing about me screams "*I just had sex.*"

"What?" It's a lame reply, but I've got nothing else.

"Don't 'what' me, missy," Laura scolds. "I know when someone has just gotten laid, and you just had the night of your life. I can see it. Your aura is so much lighter."

"My aura?"

"Yep," she says, popping the 'P.' "And right now, it's screaming, 'I let a cowboy plough my field all night.' How was it? I bet it was good."

Good doesn't even begin to cover it. I didn't know sex could feel like that until last night.

"It was insane," I say, giving into her. My friend screams, and the pure excitement she radiates makes me laugh.

"I want every dirty detail." Laura grabs my hand as she sits at the table. "If you leave anything out, I'll never forgive you."

I spend a good while regaling Laura with last night's 'sexscapade.' She only interjects with the occasional "oh my God" and "holy shit." And when I've filled her in, she finally closes her gaping mouth.

"Babe," she says with laughter in her voice, "you're *so* fucked."

I drop my head into my hands because, *damn it*, she's right.

25

Callan

When I'm sure Naya is safe inside the clinic, I pull out of the parking lot, nodding as I pass Victor, who's on guard duty today. Once on the road, I get a call from Jackson, his voice booming through the blue-tooth speakers.

"Morning, Cal." He sounds tired as shit.

"Hey, brother. You sound exhausted. Why don't you take a day off? Don't want you collapsin' on me," I say, with a chuckle.

"No, it's alright," he replies. "Can you pass by mine? I'm taking Winnie for a walk, but I need to show you something." Winnie is Jackson's dog. It's a cute name for a one-hundred-and-forty pound rottweiler, but I suppose Jackson likes the irony.

"I'm stoppin' by The Crown to help Summer move some inventory, then I can swing by your place after. We need to have a chat, anyway." We need to move onto the next step of bringing Mason's business down.

"Sounds good. Call me when you're on your way."

"Will do."

I spend thirty minutes helping Summer move crates of liquor that got dropped off early in the morning. Most owners would delegate such small tasks to other workers, but I like being as involved in The Crown as possible, and helping out the staff with stuff like this ensures that my workers respect me. It also allows me to have a finger on the pulse of everything that happens here. Owners who act like they're too high and mighty to do grunt work usually are the last to know when their business is about to sink.

When I finish up at the bar, I call Jackson to let him know I'm on my way. Fifteen minutes later, I pull up to security at the front gate, and the guard gives me access up to Jackson's high-rise penthouse.

It's nice, though not the kind of place I'd like to live in. I need fresh air and open land surrounding me, but this apartment suits Jax perfectly. It's sleek, modern, with accents of dark-stained wood all around.

When I get out of the elevator, Winnie runs toward me, and I pat her behind the ears. She's so well trained, making Harlo and Dave look like troublesome puppies. She's a sweet dog, despite the misconception people have about rottweilers, but she can also attack on command. Jackson has a code word he can use with her, but he's never told us what it is.

A light whistle floats through the air, and Winnie abandons me, running to stand next to her owner.

"Good girl." Jackson pats her gently, then turns his gaze to me.

"What's goin' on with the Raleigh Riders?" I ask, skipping any unnecessary small talk.

"From what I've heard, the wanker is pissed that we got to him."

"I bet he is," I snort. Hopefully that sends him back to Raleigh for the time being.

Jackson walks over to his bar cart and pours two glasses of whiskey, sliding one across the countertop to me. It's barely noon and, unlike me, Jax isn't the biggest fan of whiskey, so I know that whatever he's about to tell me isn't going to be good news.

"That bad?" I ask as I watch him take a sip of the amber liquid.

"Oi, not great," he says, grimly. "Our main warehouse was almost seized by the feds. Someone leaked information about one of our incoming shipments, and the guys were followed. They noticed they were being tailed when it was too late."

"Fuck," I say, running a hand through my hair. "Who snitched?"

"None of ours. There's only one other person who comes to mind."

"Mason. Retaliation for the attack on this lab."

"Yup."

"*Stronzo*," I seethe. *Motherfucker.* Thankfully, we've got most feds on our payroll, so following us was probably just standard protocol. Although, if they find anything actually incriminating, they wouldn't be able to 'look the other way' for long. "Did they take anythin'?"

"Nah. It was just routine. But he's trying to get to us," Jackson replies.

I exhaled in relief, before another worry came to mind. "And what about Naya?"

"I asked around and found out she dated Mason for about ten years, almost right until she moved to Springfield. Word on the street is he was controlling, but no one knows what happened between them. Mason is keeping that shit close to the vest, but whatever it was threw him into a weeks-long rage."

I'm hearing Jackson's words, but my brain is in slow motion. Men like Mason don't behave rationally when they're angry. Did he hurt her? I'll tear his limbs if he ever so much as lifted a hand against her.

"Let's just say I was able to convince one of his men to

talk," Jackson keeps going, a twisted smile on his face as he recounts what went down. I'm not sure how much more I want to hear, but I need to know what I'm up against. "If she thinks it's over, it's sure as hell not on his end. He's got men stationed here in Springfield for the explicit purpose of watching her."

He reaches for a folder and shows me a few pictures of men I don't recognise posted around town, a few outside outside All Saints. He then grabs his phone and pulls up some security footage showing the same men outside Naya's house and clinic.

My knuckles turn white as I grip the edge of the counter. "Fuck."

"We need to be careful. She's a liability at this point, Callan—"

I hold my hand up and cut him off before he can say something that would make me want to lower him into an early grave.

"She's no liability," I spit. "She's under S&S protection now. Do you understand?"

He doesn't speak, just nods. He knows better than to argue with me when I'm like this.

"I want every single one of Mason's men found and brought to me."

"Shouldn't be hard; his men are dumber than rocks." It sounds like a joke, but Jackson's face is stone cold. "Do you want them gone?"

"No." I shake my head. "Keep 'em alive 'til I can talk to 'em myself. We'll send 'em back to their leader, but don't worry, I'll let you have your fun before."

This brings a genuine smile to Jackson's face as he slams his drink back. "Consider it done."

On my drive home, I feel on edge.

I refuse to ever view Naya as a liability. When I look at her, I see hope of a future. Something I've never believed in. I don't know her full story, but I can tell she's been through the ringer, and I want to make sure she knows I'll never hurt her. It's not easy for people like us to feel safe.

Mason has clearly put a lot more thought into what he's doing than I initially gave him credit for. Rage courses through me when I think about how he's been slowly infiltrating my territory without my knowledge.

I have no doubt Jax will be able to find whoever is stalking Naya around Springfield. I call Knox to give him an update, but I also want to talk this through with my brother.

Knox picks up on the second ring.

"Cal," he says by way of greeting. He's out of breath and his voice sounds off, almost like he's been running. "What's up?"

At the same time, I hear a soft moan in the background and I cringe, pulling the phone away from my ear. *You have got to be kidding me.*

"*Testa di cazzo.*" *Dickhead.* "Please tell me you didn't pick up the phone in the middle of fuckin' your girl *again*."

"I didn't pick up the phone in the middle of fuckin' my girl *again*," he repeats back to me in a mocking tone. However, the woman he's with is very vocal and lets out a loud 'yes' that I can hear clear as day.

"I'll call you back later," I offer, unable to believe the shit I have to deal with.

"I'm still on the property," he replies. "I'll do you one better and stop by when we're done."

"This is S&S business, so come *alone*," I emphasize. Last thing I need is for some chick to come traipsing into my home.

"Got it." He hangs up.

Twenty minutes later, I walk into my kitchen, surprised to find Knox sipping on a mug of coffee, jeans hanging low on his waist and button-down shirt undone.

I grunt at his presence. "Done already?"

"Hi to you, too, you grumpy son of a bitch."

"Somethin' wrong with the coffee at your place?"

Knox chuckles, unphased by my directness. "My coffee maker broke, and there's no way I'm goin' without caffeine. Joanna kept me up *all* night and mornin'."

"Joanna?" I question.

"Brunette from the bar." *Ah, yes. Barbie's friend.*

"Ah, she has a name," I say, trying to tamp down my sarcasm.

"Yeah." He tosses me a warning glare, and I wonder how much they've seen of each other since that first night.

It doesn't surprise me. Knox is a good man, honorable, and tends to devote himself to one woman at a time. The problem is, he doesn't know how to pick them. I've watched my brother get fucked over more times than I can count by women who only want to know what it's like to be with a member of Sinners & Saints.

I don't want to say anything negative to him right now, but I don't have high hopes for his future with Joanna if Barbie is the kind of company she keeps.

"She says you really fucked up with her friend," he continues, in a clear attempt to steer the conversation away from himself.

"Her friend didn't know how to take a hint. I wasn't interested," I reply, taking the bait.

Knox looks absently out the window and nods before facing me.

"Has nothin' to do with Naya, right?" He already knows the truth, and I don't see the point in lying. I want everyone to know exactly who Dr. Ohara belongs to.

"It has *everythin'* to do with Naya." I cut right to the chase as I walk over to the coffee maker.

He pats me on the back with a smile on his face. "I'm happy for you," he says, sounding genuine. "A little concerned for her, but happy for you."

I roll my eyes. "Does Joanna think you're funny?"

He shrugs his shoulders. "I'm not tryin' to make her laugh, I'm tryin' to make her come." He wiggles his eyebrows.

"Right," I say, blandly.

Knox laughs. "So, what did you call me over for?"

"Mason's got more men in Springfield." I see red at the thought. "I don't know how many. Jax showed me some video footage, and at least a few are stationed here to keep tabs on Naya. He wants her back."

I see shock flash through Knox's eyes, followed by a flicker of anger. He has a soft spot for Naya, and the idea of anyone trying to hurt her or put her in danger is just as enraging to him as it is to me.

"Jax is already on it," I supply, hoping to tamp down on my second's impulse to fly off the handle.

The muscle in his jaw ticks as he nods and runs his hand through his hair. "So, what are we doin' in the meantime?"

At this moment, I feel extremely thankful to have a brother I know will always be in my corner. He's willing to fight just as hard for Naya as I am.

"Naya will remain under S&S protection as planned. She'll stay here until further notice. So, I want security at the gate doubled. I'll be installin' a top-of-the-line security system at her house, which I'll need your help with." In no universe where I exist will she be moving back to that house anytime soon, but this will give me a heads up if Mason gets any smart ideas about trying to break in again. If he sends one of his goons there, I'll get notified.

"Whatever you need," he replies, clasping his hand on my shoulder. "I've got you, brother."

We spend the rest of the day working together. I think he's worried that I'll lose it and hunt Mason down if I'm left alone. He's not wrong.

I order Naya's new security system, which will be ready for me to install tomorrow. I'm acquainted with the CEO of one of the largest and best security companies in the south, so he'll make sure I have everything I need in a timely manner. By this time tomorrow, Naya's house will have around the clock security with cameras both inside and out.

The rage that has been simmering all afternoon begins to boil over.

"Let's race." Dav's voice breaks me out of my spiraling thoughts. He's studying me, an earnest and concerned expression on his face. I know he just wants to get me out of my head, and I'm thankful as fuck. He stands to his full height. "It's been a while since I've kicked your ass."

"In your dreams." I shove him with my shoulder as I walk past him. "I've got to be back in time to pick up Naya, though."

He chuckles. "She's got you whipped, huh?"

I glare at him and he raises his hands in mock surrender. "Learn to take a joke, Cal."

"I will, once you learn how to make one."

With that, I head to the garage and hear him jogging behind me. I pick a bike and hop on. He does the same, then we're off.

We spend the next couple hours racing each other through

the dirt roads of Springfield, all the way to the small town of Paris, and back.

I win, obviously. Although, Dav insists that he let me.

I chuckle. We both know that's bullshit, but the ride really did help clear my head. I'm still angry as fuck at what's happening with Mason, but I know that we've got it handled. Naya is safe and Jax has everything under control.

"I'm goin' to get Naya," I inform Knox as we exit the garage. "If anythin' suspicious happens 'round here, let me know."

He says goodbye before heading down the path toward his place, and I jump into my truck.

I spend the whole drive to the clinic wondering how the hell I'm going to tell Naya that her crazy ex-boyfriend is having her stalked.

26

Naya

A week later

It's been seven days since I moved into Callan's house, and we've fallen into some sort of routine. I wake up, get ready for work, and he drives me to the clinic, since he insists that it's the safest option at the moment. I work myself tired all day, Callan picks me up, then I spend the evening pretending that the sexual tension between us doesn't exist.

I can't lie, Callan has been an excellent host, but I miss my home, my bed, and my things. When he strong-armed me into staying here after the break-in, I couldn't disagree that it was for the best. Who knew to what extent Mason would've gone to find me?

And when I found out he had people watching me, it only solidified my decision to stay.

At the ranch, I'm safe, even though my guardian is a little less than tolerable. I constantly juggle between thoughts of wanting to strangle him and the urge to kiss him. *I need to get out of here.*

I walk into the kitchen after dinner and find him standing at the counter on the phone to someone. As I turn to leave, he holds his finger up and mouths "stay." I grab a bottle of sparkling water from the fridge and sit at the island.

"Tell Summer to close up early. The streets aren't safe tonight. I've got most of the crew circlin' the city, but I don't want her leavin' too late," he orders the person on the phone. He checks the time on his watch. "It's already nine, and I need confirmation that the shipment has arrived at the warehouse. Tell Jax to call me when he gets there." He says goodbye and hangs up the phone.

My mouth has somehow opened during his conversation. I'll never get over how bossy he looks when he conducts business. It's night and day from the grumpy rancher I first met. I guess it takes someone who can buckle up and lay down the law when necessary to keep a business afloat, and Callan is the definition of domineering.

"You can pick your jaw off the counter now," he teases. I close my mouth and glare at him.

"I need to talk to you," I state, ignoring his smug expression.

"Shoot, darlin'."

"I want to go home." His face immediately drops and he prepares to protest, but I don't let him speak. "It's been a week, Callan, and I want to go back." I cross my arms over my chest and settle deeper onto the bar stool. I'm getting ready for a fight.

He lets out a harsh breath and braces his arms on the counter, lowering himself to my level, and looks at me straight in the eyes. "It's not safe now that Mason's men are in Springfield. Why do you need to go back now?"

The intensity of his stare makes me nervous. I shift in my seat and take a big gulp. "I just want my things."

His brow lifts. "I can have 'em brought here."

I scoff. "I miss my bed," I counter.

"I didn't realize mine was uncomfortable."

My eyes grow wide. "Callan!" I argue. "I just want to be in my home. In my own room."

"What's wrong with my house?" he questions as he inches himself closer from across the counter. My breath hitches, and I'm close to losing any form of control I've maintained so far.

"It's not mine," I whisper.

"It's not safe for you out there yet," Callan retorts, his breath tickling my cheek. *Shit.*

"Will it ever be? Just let me go. You can station someone at my house and at the clinic, and I'll be back almost every day to check on the animals," I try to reason with him.

He looks at me intently, then abruptly lifts himself from the counter and smirks. "Fine. I'll take you after work tomorrow. But tonight, you stay in my house and in *my* bed, Naya."

He turns around and stomps out of the kitchen, leaving me speechless in my seat.

When Callan takes me back to my place the next day, he's a lot calmer than I had anticipated. I was expecting him to fight me tooth and nail, but instead, he just told me that a man named Myers would be stationed outside of my home and to let him know of any of my movements. Callan also reminded me that he would be back to drive me to work in the morning. I wanted to argue, but the look on his face shut me up before I could get any words out. I relented; if the cost of sleeping in my own bed at night is being chauffeured to and from work, I'll deal.

Once I enter the house and flick on the lights, Callan pulls out of the driveway, and I'm confronted with the mess that was left behind from the break-in. I groan. I had completely forgotten about the state my home was in. *So much for the relaxing night I had planned.*

I drop my bag on the floor and start cleaning. Every room is in disarray, but nothing appears to have been stolen. Callan was right. This was clearly an attempt to intimidate me, and if Mason really was behind it, it wouldn't surprise me in the slightest.

When I enter my bedroom, a shiver runs down my spine as I consider what might have happened if I had been in the house when the intruder arrived. I take a deep breath and try to calm my nerves as I look around the space where I found comfort for a short while, but now feels eerie and cold.

All of my belongings litter the floor, and drawers have been pulled out and thrown aside. I squeeze my eyes shut, trying to calm my breathing, and when I open them again, my gaze falls to a shoe box on the floor. It's been tossed onto its side, all of the contents spilled out.

I immediately recognize it and my body freezes in place.

When I decided to move to Springfield, *Papa* gave me a box filled with mementos of my mother, mostly pictures, that I could remember her by. He never told me what to do with it, and I had been far too nervous to open it at first, unsure what I would find. I tucked the box into the farthest corner of my bedroom closet and swore I would open it one day when I was ready. Up until today, I had forgotten about its existence.

I kneel down on the ground beside it, looking at the items that have spilled out. I raise a bottle of perfume to my nose and inhale. Emotion clogs my throat as my mother's signature scent wraps itself around me and unleashes memories of her I have spent years trying to forget. All this time later, I still can't help but feel like she chose drugs over our family for the majority of my life. She tried rehab multiple times, but was never able to stay clean for more than three months.

The periods of time when she was sober, though, were beautiful. Trips to the beach or to the park, movie nights, and giggling as I tried to put her makeup on and smeared lipstick all over her cheek.

I hold tight to those memories and wonder what it would be like if life was always like that.

Lying next to the bottle is a diamond necklace and her wedding band. Two pieces of jewelry she never went without, and further proof that whoever came into my home wasn't looking to steal anything of worth. *Then what were they looking for?* A small, terrified voice in my brain tells me that I already know the answer. *Me.* But I tuck away the thought, refusing to let panic take over.

The remainder of the box is filled with pictures of me and her together, most from when I was young. A few are of her and Dad, with some of the three of us, and I find myself longingly wishing that those good days had lasted longer.

I place the box back upright to tuck away the items, when I notice a few white envelopes still inside. I move the pictures aside and reach in to grasp them. Each envelope is sealed, with my name marked on the front. I bring them to my chest as sadness overwhelms me. I would recognize my mother's handwriting anywhere, and I wonder why my dad never mentioned there were letters addressed to me in here.

I open the first one and begin to read. Right away, the date jumps out at me. This was written during one of her many stints in rehab. I would have been around fifteen at the time.

My Dearest Naya,
It's been exactly two weeks and three days since I had to leave you again. Every single day I have been here, I've tried to write this letter, but I

can't seem to get the words out. This is the first time you are fully aware of the circumstances that led me here. The look of disappointment in your eyes as I got in the car with your father broke my heart. I want you to know that I'm doing my best for you. It may not seem like it, but I'm trying.

It's hard, and your father doesn't make things any easier. Like clockwork, everytime I get out, he brings those men around again. A part of me thinks he prefers me high so that he has an easy excuse to treat me like shit all the time. He throws it in my face and says that if I wanted to resist, I would, but what kind of man brings dealers into the home of his recovering wife?

If you're disappointed in me, it's nothing compared to the disappointment I feel toward myself for having let you down once again. I say all of this to you in the hopes that you will one day understand not everything and everyone are as they seem. I will try to do better for you because you deserve me at my best.

All my love, sweet girl,
Mom

A tear slides down my cheek and lands on the letter before I drop it as though the paper is on fire. I had no idea she'd written to me while she was away. Why would my *papa* hide them? And what did she mean when she said "he brought those men around again"? No part of me wants to believe that my father would purposefully cause harm to my mother—*to our family*. But if what she said was true, then he aided her addiction.

I open the next letter and read it, then the next. All were written during different rehab stays. Although they're addressed to me, they read more like journal entries. Each one finds my mother expressing similar sentiments: that she wants to get better, but for whatever reason, she can't because of Dad. She keeps things vague, never outright saying what his involvement was, but by the time I've finished reading all of the letters, I know that my father played a significant role in the illness she suffered.

I grip the letters in my palm, crumpling them in the process. The sadness I felt just moments ago has now turned to anger. I need to get to the bottom of this right away.

I pull out my phone and dial my father's number. It rings a few times before going to voicemail. I let out a growl of frustration and launch my phone across the room. Why had I thought coming back here would be peaceful?

Air. I need air.

I stand up, walk toward the window, and crack it open, taking a deep inhale. I feel better for a second, but my breathing becomes shallow again as my mind begins to race.

I have to get out of here.

I go to where I tossed my phone, pick it up, and dial Laura's number. She picks up on the first ring. I've never been more thankful for my phone addict friend.

"Hey, Naya," she answers.

"Laura," my voice trembles, I can barely speak.

"Are you okay?" Her sunny disposition turns worried.

"No. Can you pick me up?"

I hear the sound of keys jangling and a door slams in the background. "I'm on my way, babe."

In a daze, I walk to the front door, grab my purse, and sit on my porch steps to wait for her. The night air helps loosen the tight sensation in my chest, but doesn't help calm my racing thoughts.

When Laura pulls into my driveway fifteen minutes later, I waste no time hopping into her car.

"What's wrong?" she inquires, concern etched on her face.

I shake my head, not yet ready to talk about what I've found. "Drinks first, talk after."

"Yes ma'am," she replies as she reverses out onto the street.

There's a man, Myers, I assume, parked in a truck right outside my driveway. When he sees Laura's car pulling out, he exits his vehicle. He looks both flustered and upset at my departure, but I don't have the patience to deal with Callan or his men right now. I've told him a thousand times that I don't need a babysitter, and I mean it.

So, I just smile and wave as we leave Myers looking dumbfounded on the street.

Laura asks me where I want to go, and it takes me a minute to come up with an answer. I don't know many places in Nashville. "To The Crown Pub."

She raises a brow. "Are you sure?"

"Yeah. If Callan is so worried about my safety, then we'll go to his bar."

When we enter the pub, it's loud and packed. I recognize Summer and she waves at me. I smile at her and tug at Laura toward the bar. We need shots, ASAP.

"Hey girl, so good seein' ya! Where's the boss?" Summer asks, looking around for Callan.

"Here's not here. It's just me and my best friend, Laura." I point to her standing next to me and she extends her hand to Summer.

"Nice to meet you," Laura says with a smile.

"I'm Summer. Nice to meet you, too. What can I get you girls?"

Laura and I look at each other with a grin and say, "Shots!" in unison.

Summer giggles. "I've got just the thing for y'all. It's one of Knox's favorites." She turns around to grab the bottle, and when she faces us again, we all chant, "JÄGERBOMBS!"

This is definitely my choice of cure for my troubles tonight.

27

Callan

"What do you mean you don't know where they're goin'?" I shout into the phone, anger lacing my tone.

Myers clears his throat, unsure of what to say next. "She hopped into a car with her friend and just left," he explains.

"Well, keep fuckin' followin' her, Myers. What are you callin' me for?" *Is he for real?* He had one fucking job. "Call me when you figure out where she's goin'," I bark at him.

"Yes, boss," he replies, and I hang up.

I run a hand over my face and sigh. This woman doesn't listen. I asked one thing of her and she couldn't even respect that. I've been trying my best to juggle all my responsibilities and Naya is an added stress. One I don't want to get rid of anytime soon, but I'm going to gray prematurely if she keeps this up.

I turn my focus back on the paperwork Henry left me, financial forms to fill out and payroll to sign for the bar and warehouse. Just as I finish the pile, my phone rings.

"And?" I ask Myers by way of greeting.

"She's at The Crown," he replies.

Huh? Why would she go there? I hang up on Myers and

send her a message, my jaw clenched so tight, it's almost painful.

Me: Where are you?

A few minutes later, a response comes in.

Naya: Im safee dont woorryyy.

Me: Have you been drinkin? I'll decide whether you're in danger or not. Why did you leave without takin Myers with you?

Naya: I tlod you I dont neerd a babysitttner.

I throw my phone down on my desk, exasperated. She's impossible.

Me: Do I need to remind you who calls the shots sweetheart?

Naya: I can handel myslef Callan.

Me: Apparently not if you're out without protection right now. Are you drunk?

Naya: Wat if I am? What r ya gonna do bout it???

Me: Fuck around and find out Naya.

Three dots appear and disappear, but no message comes through. She's really testing me.

Nothing bad will happen to her while she's at the bar. I know the guys will make sure of it, and Myers will stand guard, but I'm angry she risked being tailed on the way there. Does she not realize the severity of the situation she's in? Her behavior is reckless, and even more so if she's drinking.

I need to put an end to this.

I find my leather jacket and slip it on as I proceed to get into my matte black 1967 Camaro, a sweet ride. Especially when I need to get somewhere fast.

It takes me no more than thirty minutes to pull into the parking lot of The Crown, and I rush inside. The music is loud, and the chatter even louder. I glance around to find Naya, and I spot her head of curly hair among a group of men, clinking her bottle of beer against each of theirs. Her skin looks flushed and she's wobbling on her legs.

Jesus Christ. She's wasted. My fists clench as I watch the scene unfold in front of me. Who the fuck are those men and why are they surrounding her? I stand in the same spot and observe. I nod to Summer as she greets me but turn my attention back to Naya. Summer notices what I'm looking at, her mouth stretching downwards as she scuttles away to avoid my oncoming wrath.

One of my crew members approaches me. "King! Glad to have you here," he exclaims.

"Not now, Stuart," I bark, making him flinch and retreat.

Finally, Naya turns and sees me. She narrows her eyes as she watches what must be an obvious internal jealousy fit. Then, she shakes her head and focuses back on her conversation. My mouth opens in shock, then clenches shut.

She laughs at something one of the guys says and he puts his rancher cap on her head before squeezing her shoulder. He leans in close, whispering something in her ear, and I watch as his hand drifts down to graze the top of her breast before she pulls away. I see red. I'm overcome with the urge to rip off his arm as he continues speaking to her, his nose tucked behind her ear, although her expression has turned irritated now.

I stalk over to them and grab the man by the collar of his shirt, throwing him to the side, and he falls to the floor. His friends scurry away as I bare my teeth at him.

I yank the hat off Naya's head, making her gasp. "Callan!' she shrieks, but I ignore her.

I chuck the cap at the guy, not caring that I look like an absolute savage right now. "Touch her again and you die," I seethe. My chest heaves, pure rage consuming me.

Naya touches my arm but I yank it away. She flinches, which manages to almost make me snap out of my furious haze.

I keep glaring at the man, while he cowers in fear. No one intervenes; this is my bar and I can do whatever I want. "Get the fuck out, *now*, and never come back here if you want to stay alive." The guy scurries off the floor and zooms out the door, his friends in tow.

I turn to Naya, Laura next to her, disbelief and worry across their faces.

"Laura, go home. Myers will follow you," I say, calmly.

She doesn't argue and hugs an unmoving Naya. "I'll talk to you tomorrow, babes," she whispers to her. *At least one of them listens to me.*

"You." I point to the small, feisty woman in front of me. "Go to my office," I order. She doesn't move.

"Now, Naya." I've had enough of her defiance. Something must be wrong for her to be acting like this; it's unlike her to get this intoxicated. But I know exactly what she needs right now. I grab onto her arm and drag her to the back.

"Callan! You're such a caveman. Let me go!" she yelps.

"How drunk are you?" I ask her, irritated.

"Not much after that display of yours. It sobered me right up! So, thanks for that," she spits.

When we get to the office, I input the code to unlock it and throw her inside. She stumbles on her feet, and I close the door. It's a small space, so she has nowhere to go.

I walk toward her and she backs up slowly, watching my every move. She reaches a dead end when I corner her at my desk and her ass hits the tabletop, but I don't stop. "Callan," she mumbles, her voice squeaky and trembling.

"Not as easy to defy me when you're cornered, is it, little mouse?" I mock, my voice low, as I palm her neck. "Tell me. What happens when you go against my word, Naya?"

She licks her lips as I inch my face closer to hers. "Answer me."

Her usual scent invades my senses, with a faint smell of licorice. Her inhales become more shallow, as if I'm stealing her breath away. But she's the one who steals mine and does so every time I'm in her presence. I crave her closeness, I want to be buried inside her, I want to be consumed by her. I need to know her secrets, what keeps her up at night, her inner demons, so I can slay them away and keep her safe.

Whenever her lips touch mine, every logical thought disappears and it's just us.

Naya struggles to reply. I part her legs to stand between them. She looks down, her eyes widening. She clasps her hands around my wrist to attempt to remove it from her neck, but it makes me squeeze harder. "I'm still waitin'," I say.

"I get punished," she croaks.

I loosen my hold a touch and she gasps to catch her breath, but I don't relent. I grip her throat again. "Good girl. Do you like gettin' punished, Naya?" I ask as I slink my free hand down her body, between her legs, and underneath her skirt.

She nods eagerly, and I push two fingers in her slick folds. "Such a needy *piccola puttanella* for me." A small whimper escapes her lips. Just as she's about to adjust to my thick fingers in her pussy, I retract them.

I find her clit and pinch it. She cries out, her voice strangled. Her eyes start to droop as I take all the air from her lungs. I loosen my grip just a tad and she inhales once more.

"Are you goin' to disobey me again, *principessa?*" She shakes her head, her eyes wide. She looks scared, but her arousal says otherwise. She enjoys pain, and I enjoy making it hurt.

But not as much as I enjoy taking care of her, being with her, getting to know more about her.

I spread her legs more and free my cock out of my pants, giving her pussy a firm slap with the tip. "I don't believe you. You piss me off on purpose, don't you?" I rub her folds to spread her wetness all over and shove myself inside without warning. She chokes on an inhale at the force of my thrust.

I put both hands around her neck and prepare to pound into her. "This is goin' to hurt, sweetheart, but I promise it'll feel good in the end. And when you're close to losin' consciousness, I'll bring you right back," I assure her. "Tap out if you want to, but I suggest you take what I give you, like a good little slut. You deserve it for bein' a little flirt with those men."

I begin to fuck her at a ruthless pace, choking her out until she can't make a sound. Her eyes drift shut, but she fights to stay awake. "Come on, *bimba.* Stay with me," I urge her, her slickness all over my cock, down her thighs, and on the desk. I want to lick it all up, but not before she gives me an orgasm.

I bend forward to kiss her mouth. A jolt passes through my chest at the feel of her lips on mine.

I continue thrusting into her relentlessly, and I sense her body reaching a climax. Her walls tighten around my cock and her chest movements become erratic. I squeeze her neck a touch more and her eyes roll back. She's close.

"*Lasciati andare, puttanella,*" *Let it go, slut,* I say, the italian words rough with need. And that does it. She comes hard all over my dick, and I take it as my cue to release my seed inside her. All of the feelings floating inside of me seem to burst out with my orgasm.

I can't believe just how much I care about this strong, feisty, and fierce woman.

When we've both come down from the high, I remove my hands from around her throat and she lies back on the desk.

I pull out and drop to my knees, her pussy glistening with our cum. She lifts her head and looks at me with questioning eyes. She's barely been able to get words out this entire time. *Good.* It'll teach her to disobey me again.

We lock gazes. "Open wide and don't close your mouth 'til I tell you to," I command and she does what I say. I inch my face to her slick folds, covering her entrance with my lips. I suck, taking in our combined juices in my mouth, and get up to hover over her again.

I spit in her mouth and push her jaw shut. "Can you taste that, *amore mio?*"

She nods, a low moan escaping her, making my dick twitch again.

"Take it as a reminder that I'm the *only one* who gets to touch you. You're mine," I growl into her ear as goosebumps erupt all over her body.

I help her off the desk and she fixes her skirt. "Go to the washroom to freshen up, then I'm takin' you home."

Naya bows her head and walks out of the office without saying a word, which puzzles me. Usually, she has more to say than I care to hear. She seems a little off tonight, even the drinking is out of the ordinary. Her behavior is worrisome and tightens something in my chest. But I won't press her tonight. I think I've proved my point.

I wait for her at the entrance of the ladies' washroom, and she comes out a few minutes later. "Ready to go?"

"Yes," she replies, her voice a whisper.

We leave through the back door to avoid the throng of people in the bar, and I help her into the passenger seat of my Camaro. I turn the engine on and it revs loudly. I back out of the parking lot and head toward Naya's house.

The steady vibrations of the car almost lull her to sleep, but as we turn into her neighborhood, she opens her eyes and glances out the window. Her posture straightens and she rubs her palms on her thighs, taking a deep breath. I'm not sure she notices what she's doing, but it's a clear indication of distress.

"Is everything okay, sweetheart?" I ask her.

Naya startles out of her daze and shakes her head as if to rid of the thoughts. "Umm, yes. I'm fine." But I'm not convinced. I fight the urge to demand what's wrong. It stings a little that she doesn't feel like sharing with me, but again, I won't push her tonight. So, I let it go.

I park in her driveway and, as she begins to get out of the car, I grab her arm and pull her back inside, crushing my lips to hers. She tenses at the initial touch, but melts into my hold almost right away.

"I'm here for you. Have a good night, *principessa*."

She gives me a small smile that doesn't reach her eyes and heads inside the house, without looking back.

When the door closes and the light turns on, I pull out my phone, unlock it, and open the security app I downloaded when Naya's home security system was installed. There's something that she's not telling me. Her behavior was off and I want to find out what's bothering her. The screen loads and four different camera angles appear: front door/hallway, back-door/kitchen, upstairs hallway, and her bedroom. I've got almost her entire house covered with cameras, and she has no idea.

A little detail I may have forgotten to mention.

I watch her kick off her heels and walk to the kitchen to grab a snack. Her movements seem automatic as she walks upstairs and into her bedroom. I click on that feed and it expands to full screen. The room is still a mess, the only one in the house she seems to have left untouched. As soon as she enters, she sits on the bed and reaches for a shoebox, removes the lid, and picks up a letter.

I zoom in and notice tears rolling down her cheeks. *What's happening to you, Naya?* I want to barge into the house and comfort her, but I refrain. She puts the piece of paper back in the box and swipes the drops off her face.

I watch her intently for a few moments as she starts to remove her clothing, before I close the camera feed. *God, she's beautiful,* even when her face is tearstained and sad. I drive away before she can notice that I'm still in her driveway.

When I get home, all I can think about is if Naya is okay. I feel like we've somewhat turned a corner recently. Not just because of the sex, but how connected we are when we're together. I wish she would confide in me and let me help her.

I can't remember the last time I felt the urge to protect someone the way I do with her.

The pained look on her face has me wondering if there's more to her past than just a shitty ex-boyfriend.

28
Naya

My head is pounding. I crack open my eyes, but the light makes the pain worse.

Shit. How much did I drink?

I squeeze my eyelids shut. All of the memories from last night come rushing back at once: my mother's letters; The Crown with Laura; and the look on Callan's face when he found me.

The brutal and unrestrained way he fucked me against his desk.

I loved every minute of it.

He brought me to the edge of unconsciousness, only to pull me back, as if he understood just what my body needed at that moment: a brief break from my spiraling mind.

Of course, that couldn't last forever.

When I bring myself to a seated position and examine the state of my room, I'm reminded of everything that led me to the bar. A groan escapes me. I want to be anywhere but here, yet I feel too sick to move. I pick up my phone from beside me on the bed and check my calendar. One appointment is scheduled for the day and it's a routine check-up. Since I opened the clinic, I have never once taken a sick day, but today might just be the exception.

I phone Laura, putting the call on speaker. I don't even have the strength to lift the device to my ear.

Instead of answering in her normal cheery way, she practically whimpers, "Hello?"

"I'm thinking of closing the clinic today," I say, skipping the pleasantries. I feel as miserable as she sounds right now.

"Thank God," she moans. "I don't think I can get out of bed today."

"Me neither." I slide down onto my back, no longer able to be upright. "Can you call Mrs. Coleridge and reschedule her appointment?"

"On it."

"Thanks, Lau." I pause as I remember how she came to my rescue yesterday without a second thought. "For everything."

"Of course, whenever you need me," she whispers through the line. " Now, let me make this call so I can sleep for the next twenty-four hours."

I chuckle as we hang up. Alone with my thoughts once more, I contemplate what to do about the letters I found. *Papa* hasn't called me back yet, which is concerning. I've always been a daddy's girl, and the thought that he could somehow be involved in Mom's drug addiction makes me feel like my world is crashing down around me. If it's true, I don't know how I'll ever forgive him.

I dial his number once again, and this time, he picks up. He sounds off. "*Ohayo*," *Good morning*, he answers. "Why are you calling so early? Shouldn't you be getting ready for work?"

I ignore his questions, ready to ask my own. "*Ohayo, papa*. I called you yesterday. Is everything alright?"

"I was asleep," he grunts. "I'm not as young as I used to be. I needed an early night." I don't know if it's the tone of his voice or what my mother said in her letters, but I struggle to believe him. "What's going on?" he asks.

"I read Mom's letters," I reply, not having the energy to beat around the bush. I want to know why he hid them from me.

"Letters?" He sounds confused, and I wonder if it's possible that he didn't know.

"She wrote to me while she was in rehab."

There's a pause on the line before he speaks again. "I didn't know about that, Naya. She used that box to store photos. When she passed, I put her jewelry in there and tucked it away. What...what did they say? Did she mention me?"

That last question strikes me as odd, and I suddenly feel protective over my mother's words.

"It was mostly about her time at the rehab center." *A half truth.* "What are your plans for the weekend, Dad? I was thinking of coming home for a visit." The words exit my mouth before I have time to think, but this is no longer a conversation I want to have over the phone. I need to look him in the eye when I demand answers.

"I'm never too busy for you," he replies, softly. "I miss having you around."

Just then, the doorbell rings and my head protests the loud sound. I force myself out of bed and pad over to the window. I squint in the bright light and see Callan's truck parked on the driveway.

Damn it. I forgot to tell him I didn't need a ride to work this morning.

"I've got to go, *Papa*, but I'll see you soon."

I hang up and head to the front door. When I open it, Callan is leaning against the doorframe, holding a Sonic Drive-In bag in his hand, and looking completely at ease. Warmth blooms in my chest at the sight of his smile before I bat it away. *It must be the hangover.*

He trails his eyes down my body, and I flush under his gaze.

I'm still dressed in my skimpy silk pajamas and I almost want to cover up, which is ridiculous considering I can still feel where his hands gripped my throat as he pounded into me last night. At the memory, a pulse begins between my legs and a shiver runs down my spine.

"Thought you might need some hangover food," he says, holding up the grease-stained bag.

"Thanks," I reply, moving aside so he can enter. "I meant to call you. I'm not working today. No ride necessary."

A smirk plays on his lips. "I know."

"You know?" I ask as he sets the food down on my kitchen table.

"Well, I assumed, with the state you were in last night."

Right. I sit and watch him take the food out of the bag. My mouth waters; I skipped dinner last night, so I could use a real meal. He places a wrapped-up breakfast sandwich down on the table and the smell invades my nostrils. I'm *so* hungry. That pesky warm and mushy feeling returns to my chest with a vengeance.

I take a bite and he joins me at the table but doesn't eat anything himself.

"I won't need a ride for the next few days, actually," I say, with my mouth half-full. "I'm going to visit my dad."

He narrows his eyes at me. "Like hell you are."

My hands tighten around my sandwich. The warmth diffuses like smoke. I'm tired of his shit. Does he seriously think he can control every aspect of my life forever?

"I wasn't asking for permission. I am going," I spit.

"Then, I'm comin' with you."

This draws a laugh out of me. "No, you're not. Don't be ridiculous." I don't want him to meet my *papa*—at least not yet. Especially not under these circumstances.

"It's not safe for you to travel that distance alone, Naya."

I don't know whether it's the relentless throbbing in my head or the stress of having to confront my father soon, but his words make me see red. I snap.

"When will it be safe, Callan?" I exclaim. "How long do you expect me to live like this? Despite what you may think, I'm a big girl. I can take care of myself. I don't need you marching in here to tell me when I can and cannot visit my own father!"

"Take care of yourself?" he asks the question as if the concept disgusts him. "Ever since your house got ransacked, you've been under my protection. *I'm* the one who took care of you. You're lucky I even give a shit, Naya, or who knows what would've happened. You're bein' childish, and your reckless-ness will get you killed!" Callan snarls.

I gasp and my hand flies to my chest. "You motherfucker! I never asked you to protect me," I hiss. How dare he call me childish? My emotions are all over the place. The last thing I wanted was to end up entangled with another man as control-ling as my ex.

While Callan's attentiveness sends flutters to my heart, the way he speaks to me sometimes makes me want to reach out and punch him.

"You cried yourself to sleep last night. You expect me to believe that all is well and you don't need me?"

"This isn't a debate—" I start before I process his words. I narrow my eyes at him. "How do you know I cried myself to sleep last night?"

He leans back in his chair, his jaw locking as he holds my gaze but doesn't answer.

"*God damn it,* Callan. Answer me!"

"It doesn't matter how. Everythin' I do is to keep you safe," he responds, dismissively.

Bullshit. "Have you been watching me?" Deep down, I already know the answer.

"You couldn't have possibly thought I wouldn't have had security cameras installed in your house after the break-in."

Cameras. My heart starts racing a mile a minute and I feel like I can't breathe. No wonder he didn't put up a fight when I asked to come home. He's been playing Big Brother from the moment I stepped back into my house.

I stand so quickly, my chair topples over. "Where are they? Tell me where every camera is, Callan, or so help me God, I'll—"

"You'll what, Princess?" he says, his voice calm. It only serves to fuel my rage. I can't believe the audacity of the man before me. "There's one for each exit point, the livin' areas, your hall, and bedroom." There isn't an inch of remorse in his voice as he explains this huge invasion of privacy.

"Are you kidding me?" I squeal, shocked by his admission. He seems unphased by my reaction, and I can't believe he's not taking me seriously.

I'm breathless with rage. "Get out." My voice is a low whisper, but I know he heard me.

When he doesn't move, I reach over the table and slam my hands against his chest. Callan doesn't even flinch.

"I said get *the fuck* out of my house right now, Callan! Or I'll call the cops." I don't remove my hands, and his eyes travel from where they're placed to lock with mine. My anger morphs for a moment as I feel his heartbeat increase, matching mine, my breaths coming out in short pants.

"I don't think that would do you any good," he replies as he rises to his feet. He towers over me, causing me to lean back on the dinner table. "The sheriff and I have an understandin' of sorts," he continues, with a smug smirk.

Of course. He has law enforcement bending to his will. How do I always seem to find myself with these types of men?

My anger resurfaces, and I try to push him away, to no avail. His face is now a mere inch away from mine, our heavy breathing intertwined.

"I said get out," I repeat, the words coming out weak and breathless.

Callan doesn't let up. "I can leave," he says. "But I don't think that's what you truly want." His lips brush mine and goosebumps erupt all over my body. Callan grasps my wrists and pins my arms above my head, and on instinct, my back arches, my breasts now crushed on his chest, and I feel my nipples hardening. *My body is such a traitor.*

His nose trails up my neck as he inhales my scent and my body shudders in response.

He releases me, leaving me on the table, and I immediately feel the loss of his body heat as I stay there, unmoving. He walks to the door, and I hear the hinges creak as he opens it. "Don't do anythin' stupid, Naya."

I jump up and watch from the window as he hops back into his truck and pulls out of my driveway. I'm so angry, yet I can't ignore the incessant ache between my legs.

I spent far too many years stuck in a relationship with a man who wanted to control my every move, so I shouldn't react this way toward him. But my body has other intentions.

Regardless, if Callan thinks he's going to get away with the same behavior, he better think again. I race back up to my bedroom and run to the closet, pull out a duffle bag, and start throwing clothes into it. I have no idea how often Callan checks these cameras, but if I want to leave without him following me, then I've got to go now.

As soon as I finish packing, I run out the backdoor to my Jeep. I never park it out back, but one of Callan's men must have moved it after the break-in, making it easy for me to get into my car without his henchman realizing I've left.

Once on the road, I call Laura and tell her that I need to make an emergency trip to Raleigh.

With my schedule cleared for the week, I leave all thoughts of Callan behind and focus on what I'm going to say to my dad when I see him.

It's been four and a half hours since I left Springfield and there's no Camaro chasing me down the highway. So, I assume Callan hasn't noticed that I'm gone.

I still can't believe he had the nerve to install cameras in my home without telling me. *Fuck him.* My grip on the steering wheel tightens as I think of the unapologetic way he behaved this morning, as if I was a child who wouldn't see reason.

A few minutes after I've crossed the state line from Tennessee to North Carolina, a black Escalade I pass on the shoulder of the road pulls in behind me. I look in my rearview mirror and see a white man with a black beanie and a thick beard. I don't think twice and continue my journey back home.

After a while, the driver starts tailing me and my heartbeat accelerates. I can no longer see their front bumper in the mirror before I switch lanes. I grip the steering wheel with my sweaty palms, anticipating his next move. But he doesn't follow.

Panic sets in anyway, and I start to think of ways to get off the road. I glance at my dashboard and notice that I'm low on gas. Coincidentally, I pass a sign that indicates there's a gas station at the next exit. There's no way the SUV will follow me off the highway.

You're just being paranoid, Naya.

A couple of miles later, I pull into the gas station and go to fill my car. I take in my surroundings and see no one in sight. I sigh in relief. For a minute, I thought that Callan was right, but it was just a false alarm. I can do this on my own.

I walk into the store to pay for the fuel and grab a few snacks for the road.

On my way out, I bump into someone and some of my items fall to the ground.

"Sorry." I bend down to pick them up and, when I rise to my full height, my eyes zero in on the black beanie and full beard from before. I stagger back, but the man wraps his arms around my waist, places his palm on my mouth, and drags me to the Escalade. I try to scream, but the sound is muffled by the pressure of his hand. My heart pounds against my ribcage and I can barely breathe.

A course of adrenaline flows through my body as I flail my legs in an attempt to escape, but the stranger holds me in a death grip. My heel connects with his shin and he yelps in pain, letting out a slew of curse words.

"Stop fighting it, you'll only make things worse," my assailant says, his voice murky to my ears.

There's no one else around, so my cries for help go unnoticed. I glance back inside the store and the cashier is no longer at his post. *Fuck,* I'm screwed.

I stop my thrashing to conserve energy. Who knows how long I'll be held hostage? I'm consumed with fear, but adrenaline keeps me afloat.

The first thought that comes to my mind is Callan. *Shit, Callan.*

He's going to freak out when he finds out I've been taken, and I won't hear the end of it. I can't believe he was right all along.

Mason must be behind this kidnapping, and I curse myself for being so naive. After ten years together, I was ready to give him the benefit of the doubt. I never thought he would hurt me again. But I was wrong, and I should've known better.

I'm thrown into the back of the SUV. My kidnapper ties a piece of fabric around my mouth and eyes, and zip ties my wrists together. I try to speak through the gag, but I choke on my spittle. My body shakes with fear. Everything is happening so fast.

He shuts the door and hops into the driver's seat. I hear him dial a number and someone picks up.

"I've got the girl." I narrow in on the kidnapper's voice. "I'm bringing her to the boss. I should be there in a few hours."

Although I've never seen this man before, I know he must be referring to Mason. And the thought terrifies me. What does he want with me?

His voice rings in my ear: *I'll decide when we're over, Sugar.* I heave.

At the start of our relationship, Mason treated me like royalty. He was there for me after my mom passed, and supported me through veterinary school. Sure, he was a bit rough around the edges, but he always made me feel safe.

However, the second I graduated and work began to take over my life, his entire demeanor changed. Suddenly, he wasn't attentive and sweet; he was angry *all* the time. He complained that I worked too much and, when I was home, I could never do anything right where he was concerned.

He began calling me names and insinuated that I thought I was too good for him. He took every opportunity to belittle me and still, I made excuses for him. I chalked it up to his own insecurities, but the longer I stayed, the more controlling he got. I wasn't allowed to go out with my friends or visit my dad. I had to stay close so he could keep his watchful gaze on me.

The only place of solace I had was the clinic where I worked. The final straw was when he tried to take that away from me, too.

One night, Mason accused me of sleeping with another doctor who worked in my office. It was ridiculous, and I told him as much, but he didn't care about anything I had to say. He insisted that I quit, but I refused.

The next morning, when I got in my car to go to work, it wouldn't start. Turns out, Mason had taken it upon himself to remove a spark plug in the middle of the night so that I couldn't leave. I called a cab to take me to work, heart hammering, unsure what the consequences would be.

When I got home later that evening, he had been drunk and in a rage. It was the first time I had felt genuine fear toward him, and I knew I needed to get out of there *for good.*

"Where the fuck have you been?" Mason asks, his words slurred.

"At work." I avoid his gaze as I walk toward the bedroom. He follows close behind, but stays quiet, like a predator preparing to pounce. He stands silently in the doorway and watches me pack a bag. But when I try to exit the room, he snatches it out of my hand.

"Where do you think you're going?" The intensity in his eyes terrifies me. My fight or flight response kicks in. I just need to get out of there. I duck under his arm and try to run down the hall to the front door.

I don't make it far before his hand reaches out and grabs me. My skin crawls from his touch. He throws me against the wall so hard that picture frames fall and glass shatters on the ground. Pain radiates all over my back.

I'm stunned. Never once has Mason laid a hand on me, but he is not himself.

Or maybe he is, and he's just letting the mask completely slip away tonight.

"Mason, let me go!" I yell.

"Don't be ridiculous, doll." His voice is so calm, yet his eyes swirl with fury. "You're not leaving me, Naya."

He's so close to me, I can detect the stench of beer as his warm breath touches my face. I hold back my urge to retch.

"Mason, just let me go," I whisper. I wish I could be stronger, more confident, but I'm terrified.

"I'll kill you before I let you leave me, doll," he growls.

My breath hitches and I attempt to step around him, but I'm swiftly punished for the action. His large hand comes at my face in full force, knocking me to the ground. A piece of shattered glass sticks into my palm and I watch as blood begins to glisten and drip from the cut, my shock almost drowning out the pain. My face stings where he has slapped me, and I try to hold back my tears. Still, one slips down my cheek as I wonder how I have found myself in this terrible situation.

"See what you made me do, Sugar," Mason grunts as he stares down at me. I hate him. I look at my surroundings and try to determine how to escape.

And then, I see it. A large shard of glass just within reach. Quickly, before his inebriated mind can figure out what I'm doing, I jab it into his thigh.

He lets out a howl of pain, and I take the opportunity to sprint to the exit. I grab his car keys off the hook by the door and continue to run. I hear him call after me, but I don't stop.

Not until I'm locked in the safety of his truck, which I drive to my papa's.

How could I have been so oblivious? Mason was never going to let me go. Tears threaten to spill from my eyes, but I hold them back.

I will not let this man, Mason, or anyone see me break.

29
Callan

A cool breeze blows against my face as I ride Ace to the back of the ranch. He's back in full health since recovering from his minor illness and seems even stronger than before.

The ground rushes by me, and the only sound is the pounding of Ace's hooves as he gallops on the grass. I wrap my hands firmly around the handle and let myself be soothed by the ride, strands of hair whipping my face.

We enter a familiar tree-covered stretch of land and I bring him down to a trot. It's been a while since I've come out here, but shooting is my favorite way to blow off steam.

This morning's conversation with Naya left my blood boiling.

Over my dead body will she be going back to Raleigh.

When I got back to All Saints, I knew a ride on my favorite stallion would help ease the tension. As soon as I got comfortable in the middle of the saddle seat, I gave Ace a few gentle strokes. "It's just you and me today, bud," I'd said as I rubbed at the base of his mane, relief flooding me as Ace huffed, his energy almost back to what it was months ago.

We approach a shaded area and I dismount, leaving my stallion tied to the tree, then walk over to the crate where Dav disposes of his empty beer bottles. The man drinks more beer than anyone reasonably should, but it comes in handy for days like this.

I grab a handful and walk several feet away to a few tables we'd set up for target practice. I line the bottles in a neat row and walk back to the other end.

I pull a gun out of the waistband of my jeans and a sense of peace washes over me as the weight of the cool metal rests in my palm. My heartbeat slows and my breathing eases.

Sinners & Saints deal in the finest weaponry, which means I have top-of-the-line guns at my disposal. I load the one in my hand with ammunition, then raise it up to eye level, gripping it with both hands. Taking a deep breath, I ground myself before lining up the first shot and pulling the trigger. A loud crack reverberates through the forest as the bullet connects with the glass bottle, shattering it. My body absorbs the recoil, but it does nothing to slow me down as I immediately shoot once more.

One after the other, the beer bottles shatter and, with each glass broken, I feel myself calming down.

For whatever reason, Naya is worried about her father. Tensions were high this morning, but I'm sure I can get her to see reason when I speak to her again. If she has to go, I'll join her and make sure she remains safe.

I walk back up to the tables, laying the gun down and reaching for my phone. I pull up Naya's home security system. Sure, it may be an invasion of her privacy, but with someone like Mason gunning after her, that's the least of my concerns. As I open each surveillance feed, my mind swarms with confusion. I can't find her in the house. I check each camera again, but she's nowhere to be found.

Without a moment's hesitation, I call her, but it goes straight to voicemail. I clench my phone, my hand shaking.

I call Myers next, wondering why he would fail to inform me that Naya had left the premises.

"Where is she?" I spit as soon as he picks up.

"Naya?" Myers asks, sounding puzzled.

I grit my teeth. "Yes. Who the fuck else would I be talkin' about?"

"She's still inside. There hasn't been any movement since you left."

I slam my hand down on the table, narrowly avoiding a shard from a broken bottle. The calm I felt just moments ago has already begun to dissipate. There's no way he's *this* inept.

"I checked the cameras, she's not in the house," I snarl.

"Are you sure?" He sounds doubtful.

It's possible that Naya could have felt better and decided to open the clinic for the afternoon, but how did she leave without Myers seeing her? A niggling voice in the back of my mind causes me to question if she would have run off to North Carolina to see her father, but I push the thought away. She wouldn't be so reckless with her safety. Would she?

"Get your ass to the ranch. Right now. I'll be waitin' at the southern edge of the property," I tell Myers before hanging up.

I call Knox and ask him to run down to the clinic and check if it's open.

And then, I wait.

Myers hops out of his truck and removes his baseball cap, unveiling shaggy brown hair. The man looks nervous, and he should be.

"Boss," he says by way of greeting, his head lowered to avoid my gaze.

I skip the pleasantries altogether. Not very often do I have to reprimand one of my men. Most of the time, they're on top of their shit. However, lately, Myers has been pushing my buttons.

"Did I make a mistake when I brought you in, Myers?"

He meets my eyes, but doesn't utter a word. *Smart.*

"I've put you in charge of Naya's protection twice, and both times ended with you not knowin' where she was!" He shrinks as my anger builds. "I gave you one damn job and you failed. Give me one good reason why I shouldn't banish you from the club." A clear threat. The only way out is in a coffin.

He eyes the gun in my hand and gulps. "I'm sorry, King," he pleads. "I don't know how she got out. I didn't see a thing!"

I creep closer to him, right up to his face. I'm sure he can see the rage in my eyes, just as I see the terror in his. "That right there is the problem."

I circle around him and press the barrel into his back, causing him to jerk forward slightly. I can't help but chuckle at his fear. I move the gun away and continue walking until I'm face-to-face with him again.

"I need to know that I can trust you," I say, keeping my voice low. "When I ask you to do somethin', I need to know that it'll be done right. Is that understood?"

"Yes, sir," he replies as he bobs his head up and down.

"Okay, then get outta here."

Shock flickers across his face. I'm sure he was expecting a harsher punishment.

Before he enters his truck, I call out to him. When he turns around, I unload a single bullet into his right foot. *Bullseye.*

He lets out howl as he collapses to the ground, screaming obscenities. I can already see blood staining his white shoes, and his face has turned red as he tries to breathe through the pain.

I turn my back to him, eager to get Ace back to the stables and figure out what's going on with Naya. As I pass Myers on my horse, he's still clutching his foot on the ground. "I don't wanna see you 'round the club 'til that's healed."

Every vein in his neck stands at attention as he nods. Satisfied, I ride away.

Instead of heading to my house, I stomp all the way to Dav's, eager to hear about his visit to the clinic. I step onto his dark, wooden porch and immediately pound on his door.

"Open up, Blondie."

I hear footsteps approaching before Knox swings the door open. "Fuck you," he spits, turning around to walk back to where he came from.

I grin and follow him inside. I have a one-track mind and I need to know if he saw Naya. "What happened at the clinic? Was Naya there?"

We step into the kitchen and he grabs an open pack of jerky, sticking one into his mouth as he replies. "Nothin' happened. It was closed when I got there."

My heartbeat slows as I process what he just said. If Naya's not home and not at the clinic, there's only one other option. I pull out my phone and call Laura.

"Hello," she croaks, and I hear rustling on the other end.

"Laura, it's Callan. Is Naya with you?"

I hear a sudden movement and sense hesitation on the line before her response comes out. "No..."

"No? Then, where is she? And don't try to bullshit me, Laura."

She clears her throat. "Um... I don't know where she is... right now."

"Laura," I growl, losing all patience. "What do you mean 'right now'? Where did she go?" A cloud of worry hovers over my head as my stomach ties in knots.

Laura sighs in defeat. "Fine. She left to visit her father a few hours ago. I haven't spoken to her since she left. Are we done here now?"

I scoff at her attitude. *Women.*

I hang up the phone and turn to look at Knox, who has been quietly watching me. "We're goin' to Raleigh."

Naya

The moving vehicle stops, and I'm immediately thrown out into the arms of someone I recognize all too well, even with a blindfold. The familiar smell, body, and grip. This is my worst nightmare.

Bile rises up my throat.

"Hey, Sugar," Mason drawls, and I almost throw up at the sound of his voice. He's never going to let me go now that he has me back. I don't speak. I couldn't even if I had anything to say with my mouth still gagged.

"Did you think your new boyfriend was gonna keep you away from me, Naya? I told you, it's over when I say we're over. Now that you've seen what's out there, how dangerous it is, you'll appreciate what you had with me even more."

Is he well? I was unhappy, sheltered, and controlled. Mason is delusional, even more than I was during our time together. If he thinks I'm going back to him willingly, he's sorely mistaken. The ounce of freedom I've had has solidified my need to be away from him. And *this* is a great reminder.

He grabs me by the bicep and thrusts my body forward, urging me to walk. He leads me through a door and what I assume is a hallway. The slaps of our shoes on the floor echo around us; the entire building seems to be made of concrete.

I hear the ding of an elevator. *Shit.* He must be taking me to his warehouse. I begin to shake. Nothing good will come out of this. I can't even signal Laura, Callan, or Dav for help. My ears fill with my silent cries, but I hold them in with all my might.

When the elevator doors open, Mason pushes me inside, and I bounce off another person I didn't realize was with us. I squeal through my gag and the person steadies me. I shake them off, disgusted, and Mason laughs.

"Better make friends here if you want to get out unscathed, Sugar."

I start to protest, but only muffled noises come out of my mouth. He unties the fabric around my head, and I roll my jaw a couple times to get used to the feeling. "Don't call me that," I seethe.

"You never had an issue with it when we were together."

"And now, we're not."

I feel him shift closer and he cups my jaw, letting his thumb trace my bottom lip. I open my mouth and bite down on it hard. He howls in pain. "You bitch!"

"Fuck you, Mason! Let me go," I say as I struggle against my restraints.

I can't see him with my eyes covered, but his presence invades the small elevator, and when we get to the bottom, he pushes me out, making me fall to the floor. The faint crack of my skull hitting the concrete sends a roaring pain through my body, and has my heart racing and body shaking.

Mason steps over me and wraps my hair around his fist, pulling me down across whatever room we're in. I yell out at him to stop, as my legs flail out in protest.

"You can scream until you lose your voice, Naya. No one is going to help you here."

I'm trying so hard to stay calm, but Mason isn't the type to make empty threats. "Why am I here?" I cry out. "Why are you doing this?"

He chuckles. "He took what was mine, and now he's gonna pay for it."

I don't understand what he means. Is he talking about Callan? "I don't know what you're talking about! Callan didn't 'take' me. We're not even together, Mason."

"Oh, so moving into his fucking ranch means nothing?" His voice rises as each word comes out of his mouth. "What a whore you've become." He's angry, and the more he gets angry, the more aggressive he becomes.

"I was there for a week because *you* ransacked my house, and he's the only one who cared enough to help me!"

Mason lets go of my head and it bounces off the floor. I hiss at the contact. At this rate, there's no way I'm getting out of here in one piece.

"I sent my guys to find you. I didn't tell them to trash your house, Naya." As if this tidbit of information makes anything better. Why would he send his men to find me? Was he too scared of being seen by Callan and his crew?

"Too pussy to come for me yourself?"

Mason doesn't like that. He bends over, rips my blindfold off, and smacks me across the face at the same time. I gasp and tears well in my eyes.

"I'm not scared of anyone or anything, especially *him*. So, I'd suggest you keep your pretty little mouth shut, *sweetheart*, before I shove something familiar into it. I missed hearing you gag."

Hearing him call me sweetheart sends a shiver down my spine.

Only one other person has called me that. I wish he were here. I wish I had listened to him.

"You're disgusting, Mason. I want nothing to do with you."

He lifts me off the floor and sits me down on a chair. "You have no choice, Sugar."

I feel a sharp poke on the side of my neck and my eyes drift shut as darkness surrounds me.

The sound of gunshots snaps me back to consciousness, but I struggle to open my eyes. My lids try to blink against the harsh, bright light of the room that I'm held in. I don't know how long I've been out, but it must've been a while for me to feel this hazy. My head sways from side to side, and I'm thankful my body is attached to a chair because I wouldn't be able to hold myself up.

I finally find the willpower to open my eyes and wince at the sharp pain in my head. *What the hell did Mason give me?* My thoughts are interrupted as I hear more loud popping noises and shouts coming from outside. I try to make out the voices, but I'm not able to shake this woozy feeling.

Sweat drips from my brow as panic starts to seize me. Are those people looking for me? I'm already in the hands of a maniac. I don't want to be taken by another.

But what if it's Callan? Impossible. He doesn't even know I've been taken. If he's noticed I'm gone, he most likely assumed I went to visit my father and decided to let my stubborn ass go.

I jerk my arms in an attempt to loosen the ropes holding my wrists and the chair jostles a bit. I will myself to stay calm, my heart feeling like it's a mere second away from exploding out of my chest. I take deep breaths in and out.

The sounds are getting closer and the voices are becoming clearer.

I thrust my butt forward, inching the chair to the other side of the room. It's big and mostly empty, the ceiling high, with no windows and a shattered table on one side. When I get to a safe enough distance away from the door in case anyone barges in, but still close enough to hear better through the thin walls, my heart skips as I realize who the voices belong to.

Callan and Knox. *How did they find me?*

I yell at the top of my lungs, hoping they will hear me over the cracking noises. The entire basement is made of concrete, so the echo of the gunshots is intense and starting to hurt my ears. I shut my eyes tight and continue screaming, "CALLAN! KNOX! I'm here! Please!"

After a few seconds, the commotion stops and the silence is deafening.

Shit. Shit. Shit. What if they're hurt? My lips quiver as I hold back my cries. I have to stay strong.

Instead of calling for help again, I stay quiet and try to wriggle my way out of the chair. The cotton rope digs into my wrists, and I wince in pain. My skin is getting raw from the friction, but I have to find a way out of here. No one has entered the room since the fighting stopped. I can't help but wonder why Mason hasn't barged in yet, but by the sound of what happened out there, he either ran away or didn't make it out alive. I hope it's the latter.

I take a moment to study the area to look for possible access points and notice a small window on the right side of the room. It's too high for me to reach, even with a chair. I curse internally and continue to twist and turn in my seat. The more I squirm, the more anxious I become. I begin to spiral and muffle a frustrated scream.

What if I can't get out? What if Callan and Knox are

injured and I can't help them? If everyone's dead, who will get me out?

I look down and notice that a piece of rope has come undone around my ankle, but I can't grab it with my hands. My other leg is still attached to the chair. I lean forward as much as possible, and when most of my weight is on the tip of my feet, I lift the back legs and slam them down. Nothing happens, so I do it again and again, until I hear a faint crack. Despite my panic, I feel a smile widening with a glimmer of hope. I might have a chance.

I continue breaking the chair and let out a growl as I slam down for what I hope is the last time. Thankfully, the back legs break on impact and I fall sideways. I land on my right shoulder and pain shoots up my neck. I'm going to pay for this.

I shuffle on the floor, now able to move my legs more. After a few minutes of wiggling, my foot finally becomes free and I can't help the squeal that escapes my mouth. I maneuver my way up and hop to the concrete wall, banging the chair on it multiple times until it breaks. I shake the rope off my wrists and untie my left foot.

A noise stops me in my tracks. I listen carefully and hear what I assume are footsteps outside the room, but they're light. Then, like earlier, the noise just stops. I grab a broken chair leg and hold it up like a baseball bat.

It's time to greet these motherfuckers properly.

31

Callan

Knox breaks at least fifty traffic laws as he speeds down the highway toward Raleigh.

If Naya left hours ago, she's likely already crossed over into North Carolina. Meaning she's now in Mason's territory and no longer safe. I have no time to waste searching for her, so I shoot Jax a quick message.

> Me: I need you to hack into a phone.

> Jackson: Easy. What do you need?

> Me: Naya's location. Now.

My jaw clenches with tension as I await his response. I won't be able to relax until I know exactly where she is.

> Jackson: I'll have it done in 10.

I release a deep breath and close my eyes for a moment. I'm thankful that I have people I can count on.

I've never felt anything like this before: true fear. The thought that Naya may be in danger has my pulse racing, and I don't know what to do. I've tried calling her, but it goes to voicemail each time, and with each unanswered call, the uneasy feeling in my chest only grows stronger.

Naya entered my life unexpectedly, and although she raises my blood pressure all the time, I can't picture my life without her. She came onto my ranch, cared for the animals, won over my best friend, and stole my heart as well.

True to his word, less than ten minutes later, Jackson sends me a link. I click on it and a map opens with a blinking red dot I assume is Naya's location. I show Knox the screen so he knows to pull off at the next exit.

Fifteen minutes later, we pull up to a gas station. I hop out of the truck before he even gets the chance to put the car in park, and I scour the area to find any signs of Naya. I see her Jeep, but she isn't around. I force myself to breathe. She's probably just inside paying or in the bathroom.

Yet, a nagging voice in my mind tells me that if she left hours ago, like Laura said, she should have been well past this rest stop. I curse out loud and glance up to the sky, running my hands through my hair. Knox gets out of the car and joins me next to Naya's car.

He puts a hand on my shoulder. "We'll find her, Cal. No one messes with the Sinners & Saints. And no one takes what's ours."

What's mine.

I instruct Dav to check her car while I look for her inside. When I enter the small store, there's not a soul to be found. I walk to the front and ring the little, metal bell on the counter. The two seconds it takes for a worker to come out of the back feels like an eternity, and I'm about to jump the barrier and go find someone myself. Soon, I'm faced with a scrawny kid that looks as though he's just gone through puberty.

The boy watches me anxiously, eyeing my leather jacket

and the tattoos peaking out, as well as the gun in my waistband. "What's your pump number?"

"I'm not buyin' gas. I'm searchin' for someone." I pull up a picture of Naya on my phone and show him the screen. Instantly, the boy scowls.

"She was here," he responds, sounding annoyed. "I don't know where she went, but she left her car. If you find her, tell her that she has until 10 p.m. to pick it up or it's getting towed."

I feel my heart drop down to my boots. *This cannot be happening.*

"Did she leave with someone?" I ask, hoping that the child in front of me has more information. No such luck, though.

The little shit just shrugs his shoulders and runs his hand through his mop of curly hair. "I don't know. She paid for her gas, and I went into the back room. When I came back out to stock the shelves, she was gone, but her car was still there."

Just as he finishes speaking, Knox marches in, his face like stone, and I know that whatever he's about to tell me isn't going to be good news.

"I found these." He holds up Naya's phone and keys in his hand. "Outside of the Jeep."

I look back at the boy working the till. "I need to see your security tapes."

He begins to object. "We aren't allowed to show security footage to—"

His words stop when I grab him by the front of his collared shirt, forcing him to lean over the counter and look me dead in my eyes. "I wasn't askin' for permission. We both know you can't stop me. So, I suggest you let me back there right now before I'm forced to end your day with an emergency room visit."

I release his shirt and he looks as if he's about to shit himself, but when he stands up straight, he swings open the little gate to the front and steps aside. *Smart.* "Security footage is in that room." He points to a closed, unmarked door off to the right, his arm trembling.

I clap him on the shoulder and walk toward the door with Dav following right behind me. Just as I suspected, the "security" is pathetic. Two computer monitors sit on top of a table, one shows footage of inside the store and the other of the fuel area. I focus on the latter, rewinding the tapes.

After going back a few hours, I find just what I was afraid of. My jaw tenses as I watch Naya being shoved into the back of an SUV by a man dressed head to toe in black. He's wearing a baseball cap, his head down, clearly aware of the positioning of the cameras.

Naya struggles and attempts to fight his hold, but it's no use, and I watch helplessly as she is thrown into the back of the car. Her assailant jumps into the passenger seat and the vehicle speeds off. The plates on the car have been removed, so I can't even trace it. I bring my fist down on the table, causing the monitors to shake, and turn to face Knox. His face is contorted with rage, and although we weren't able to see the face of the man who took Naya, we both know who's responsible for this.

Mason. That fucker is going to pay for touching what's mine.

Some hours later, we arrive at our third location. Jackson gave us a list of all of Mason's hideouts and warehouses, so we'll keep searching each one until we find where he took Naya. The first two were empty, apart from a few men we quickly disposed of.

But this warehouse is bigger—one of Mason's main trade points—and I can already see some movement near one of the entrances. Something told me it would be the right place.

Knox parks the truck about a mile away and we exit the vehicle, heading to the bed to retrieve our weapons. I lift the tonneau cover and expose the arsenal of rifles and guns we brought with us. Dav grabs a Glock 19 and shoves it into the waistband of his pants, then a rifle. I do the same and we both slip on our ski masks. Mason isn't that stupid; he knows I'll come for Naya, but I don't want to alert him before I see that she's alive.

My phone vibrates in my back pocket.

Jackson: 2 minutes.

Good. Our backup will be here soon.

"The boys will be here in two minutes. I'll take the south entrance to the right, you go to the back and try the basement door." Knox nods and we hear the sound of bikes getting closer.

After briefing them on the situation, we buckle up and start our approach. My heart thuds in my chest as I think of the many possibilities. *What if she's not here? What if she's hurt? Dead?* A sense of dread invades me. I won't sleep until Mason and every single member in his club are dead, innocent or not.

Two men are guarding the south door. I creep up on them as their backs are turned, and I knock one on the head with the heel of my rifle. He lets out a yelp and his hands fly up to the wound. The other guy turns around and opens his mouth to shout, but I hit him in the face with the same weapon before he's able to alert any others of the intrusion. Blood sprays out of his mouth and onto my shirt as he drops to the ground, clutching his face in agony.

I quickly grab both men by the collars and drag them

toward the concrete wall of the building, leaving trails of blood. They attempt to fight their way out of my hold, but I'm too consumed with rage and overpower them easily. I place them back-to-back and pull out a long piece of rolled wire from my vest. The men notice the cable in my hands and cry out weakly. I hit them again.

"Shut the fuck up before I make this even more painful," I whisper-shout.

I tie the wire around both their necks into a knot, and position myself in front of them. With one foot stable on the ground, I place the other on the concrete wall between them. And I pull.

The men's necks squeeze together as they make gurgling noises, gasping for air. One of them tries to claw at his neck to loosen the wire, and the other flails his legs.

"Where is the girl?" I ask, still pulling the cord. I need to get answers.

They both speak up at the same time, but I can't understand a thing.

I slightly loosen my hold on them and the one to the left spits out, "Fuck you. We're not telling you shit." He spits his bloody saliva onto my face. *Hell no.*

Knowing I won't get anything from them, I continue to pull on the cable until I hear their last choked breaths. I've already spent too much time with these fuckers.

I run to the door. A fingerprint lock. *Shit.*

I look back at the men on the ground. There's no way I'm lifting a lifeless body. I reach down to my ankles and lift my pant leg, pulling out a concealed knife. In one swift movement, I slam the blade down on one of the guys's thumbs and hear the bones cracking. The finger detaches and I pick it up and put it against the padlock. It scans the prints and goes green. I walk in and consider ditching the thumb, but I'm sure to run into more locked doors, so I stuff it in my back pocket.

I walk through a long hallway and pull out my phone.

Me: Coast is clear at the south entrance.

Knox: Got in from the back. How many?

Me: Two. You?

Knox: Same.

I put my phone back in my pocket and focus on getting through swiftly. My heart pounds as I step through the many doors on my way, but the rooms seem to be unused. With every empty room, my pulse increases. All I can think about is what could go wrong and how disastrous the consequences would be.

When I get to the end of the hall, there are stairs leading to the basement. My guys are on the other side of the building, but I don't want to waste any time and go down alone. I hear voices, so I pull out my gun and hold it in front of me. When I hit the last step, three men turn to face me in the hallway, confused. One of them draws his weapon with a shout and the others follow suit. Distracted by my presence, they don't hear Knox and the guys approach from the other side.

I try my best to gesture to Knox which guy to take out first without being noticed. Thankfully, we can read each other with ease and he aims at the one standing to my right while I turn my gun to the man in the middle. My henchmen scatter to look for other threats. I give a slight nod of my head before gunshots ring in the air.

Dav's bullet hits his guy in the head and the man falls over instantly, dead.

Mine was able to move out of the way, so I just got his

shoulder, still making him drop his gun. I run to pick it up, but the third guy shoots at me.

I manage to dodge the bullet by a fraction of a second. *Fuck.* That was close.

If I plan on saving Naya, I need to get out of here alive.

Knox jumps in front of me and pulls the trigger, hitting the motherfucker straight in the chest. He falls over and my best friend aims at the other guy, shooting him in the middle of the forehead.

"Thank me later," Knox says, and I knock him on the head with my elbow. He yelps and rubs his skull, cursing under his breath.

"Open your hand."

Dav looks at me with a bemused expression on his face, but extends his palm to me. I reach into my back pocket and pull out the severed thumb, placing it in his hand.

"A gift for your troubles," I taunt, and Knox jumps back, dropping the finger to the floor.

"What the fuck, bro?"

I chuckle. "Use it to open the doors, dumbass."

"You're sick in the head, you know?"

"I know," I respond, walking further into the basement. "We have to get serious, now. Naya has to be somewhere here. Otherwise, Mason wouldn't have this many men guardin' the place when there seems to be no drugs here."

I hear a faint knocking sound, but I can't quite pinpoint where it's coming from. I follow the noise until I reach a locked door. Dav opens his mouth to speak, but I motion for him to be quiet. He stands next to me and we listen. It sounds like someone is banging something on the floor or wall. The guys confirmed there was no one else in the building, so it has to be *her.* My chest fills with hope.

I nudge Knox's shoulder and nod toward the thumb in his

pocket. He looks confused for a few seconds, but catches on and grimaces. He pulls it out and unlocks the door. Not wanting to scare Naya, I push it open slowly and poke my head through the opening.

"Naya? Are you—" *Thwack.* Severe pain shoots through my head and I hiss. Whoever was in the room is attacking me with a wooden stick, and a familiar voice is shouting at me to leave them alone.

"Motherfucker!" *Thwack.* "Get away from me!" Thwack.

"Woah, woah, woah! Calm down, short stuff," Knox says as he pushes his way into the room, grabbing Naya by the waist and pulling her away. She shouts profanities at him, too, until realization dawns on her.

"Dav?" she asks, disoriented.

"Yes. And the person you're hittin' is Callan," he responds, chuckling.

"Oh my God!" she calls out.

I rub the back of my head in an attempt to soothe the ache, and Naya wriggles her body out of Knox's hold and runs to me. "I'm so sorry, Callan! I thought you were one of the guys coming back for me."

I pull off my ski mask and wince as it passes over my bruised skull.

"Hey, sweetheart," I say, with a relieved smile and shaky laughter. I cup Naya's face in my palms and look her over. She's hurt, but alive. I let out a huge breath, pulling her into my chest and she buries her face in my shirt. Sobs escape her, and I hold her tightly, rocking her back and forth.

"I'm here now, Princess. No one is ever goin' to hurt you again."

It might be a promise to Naya, but it's a threat to everyone who's ever posed a danger to her.

32

Naya

oodsy, smokey, and rich.

The smell of comfort.

Callan's arms envelop me and all the emotions I've been keeping inside burst out, as I allow myself to cry into his chest. He feels safe.

"I didn't think you'd find me," I sob, soaking his t-shirt with my tears.

"I'll always find you, Princess."

I cry even harder, not believing that Callan is here.

Knox interrupts us. "Get a fuckin' room, you losers."

Callan punches him in the shoulder. "We aren't even doin' anythin', jackass."

Dav rolls his eyes and walks out of the room, but before he disappears out of sight, he says, "I'm glad you're okay, Naya, but *don't* take your time, you two. Mason will realize soon enough that his men aren't respondin' anymore."

At that, my body tenses and Callan squeezes me. "You don't have to worry 'bout him, sweetheart. I'll take care of Mason. But we need to get outta here."

I nod and follow his lead.

We join Knox in the hallway and he calls the other men that came with them.

"Extraction is complete. We're ready to head outside," he says.

He keeps referring to me as the 'extraction,' and I'm slightly offended that he's comparing me to an object. "You can call me by my name, you know?" I snap.

"You are Callan's, which makes you his property. Hence the extraction."

My mouth opens in shock. "His property? I am no one's property!"

Knox laughs at my outburst.

"Leave her alone, Davenport. She's been through enough today," Callan intervenes. "But he's not wrong; you are mine, Naya."

"Screw you both!"

"I could flick you away with my two fingers, *shorty*. Don't get your knickers in a twist," Knox says, humor in his tone.

I'm happy to have been rescued, but I could do without Dav being here. Given the circumstances, I'm a lot calmer than expected, and I'm not sure that's normal behavior for someone who's just been kidnapped by their crazy ex. But somehow, being with Callan and Knox gives me a weird sense of comfort on the inside, even though my world seems to be crashing on the outside. So, I hang on to that sliver of calmness for the moment. I can't risk breaking down now.

As we exit the premises, we hear vehicles approaching from a distance. I still, my respiration shallow as I try to settle myself. The Sinners & Saints men surround me and we scurry toward the back of the building, where someone is waiting for us in Knox's truck. Callan hoists me up into the car and hops in right behind me, with Knox in the passenger seat. I don't recognize the driver, but he must be a Sinner & Saint if he's with us.

I stare out the window, recognizing the scenery as we drive through the streets of Raleigh. I've only been gone for a short period, but it feels like I was here just yesterday. No amount of time away from this city will wipe away the memories. My pulse races as I struggle to control my quivering palms. Callan's hand falls onto my lap and he gently squeezes my thigh.

"Are you okay, darlin'?" he asks, just above a whisper.

"I will be." *Hopefully.*

"Let me be there for you, Naya. I'd like to take care of you, if you'll let me."

I'm so overwhelmed with emotions right now, I want to burst into tears again. I've never had anyone offer to take care of me. I'm always the caregiver, which is in my nature, but Callan opening his home and himself to me is more than I could've asked for. I don't feel like I deserve this.

Callan has been there for me in every way since I've met him. He might be a rude, burly, and grumpy rancher, but he's mine.

And this is when I realize that I'm falling for him. Or have fallen for him already.

"Okay," I answer, simply.

He smiles so big it warms my heart. "Good. Let's get you cleaned up. Where do you want to go?

"I have somewhere in mind."

I give Callan the details and he pulls out his phone, dialing a number on speakerphone.

The man answers, his thick British accent beaming through the line. "*Ello*, King."

"Jackson. We left Mason's warehouse with Naya, but we're not comin' back to Springfield tonight. Make sure to keep an eye on things and let me know if you hear anythin' 'bout Mason's whereabouts."

"Be careful, Boss."

"Always am," Callan replies and Knox scoffs from the front seat, earning a flick on his ear from Callan.

These two.

Thirty minutes later, we near the outskirts of Raleigh. The car turns onto a street that I recognize all too well.

My chest grows tight. I've spent my entire childhood here. I have many memories in this neighborhood. Some good, but many of them bad. A lump gathers in my throat, and I try to swallow it down.

When the truck pulls into my father's driveway, reality hits me and nerves invade my body. *Shit.* I wrap my arms around myself, shifting my weight on the seat.

"What's wrong, sweetheart?" Callan asks me. I don't know how he noticed my shift in behavior. Apparently, I can't hide anything from him. The aftershocks of what happened today begin to set in, and I regret my decision to come here. Maybe I'm not ready to face my father yet.

No, Naya. This is what you were coming to Raleigh for in the first place. *Get a grip.*

I take a deep breath. "There's a lot you don't know, and this visit probably won't be a good one. I'm nervous."

"I thought you had a great relationship with your dad."

I look around the car, hesitating to answer in front of Knox and the other guy. I trust Knox, but I don't know if I want to air my dirty laundry to him just yet. Callan, once again, notices my dilemma and asks them to get out of the car.

"I'm sorry. I just didn't feel comfortable..." I bow my head down and he lifts it by my chin.

"Look at me. I'm goin' to stop you right there. Never apologize for your feelin's 'round me. I'll always give you what you need, Naya."

"Thank you," I whisper, not knowing what else to say. My face flushes and butterflies erupt in my stomach. The feelings in my heart are growing by the second. Even if I wanted to reprimand myself for falling too soon, Callan is doing a great job ridding me of those thoughts. How can he be so perfect?

"You don't have to tell me anythin' right now. I can stay outside and wait while you talk to your father."

I shake my head. "I need you next to me. My *papa* will probably freak out when he sees me, so I'll need some support." I look disheveled, my cheeks are tearstained, and my clothes are filthy.

"Does he know about me?" Callan asks.

"No, but he's about to find out." I swallow, unable to wet my parched throat. My dad has never been a hard ass when it comes to my boyfriends, so I'm not worried that he won't like Callan, but springing it on him together with everything else might have the opposite effect.

Callan grins. "Let's do this, then."

We walk up the short steps to my childhood home, and I hesitate to ring the doorbell.

"You got this," he reassures me. With him by my side, I feel invincible.

I press the ringer, and I hear my *papa*'s faint voice. "Just a minute!"

I shake out my hands and take deep breaths in an attempt to calm my nerves, and Callan rubs my back to soothe me. A few minutes later, my dad opens the door and exclaims, "Naya! What happened to you?" His face twists from surprise to concern in a matter of seconds.

Callan had tried to remove some of the dried blood on my

temple, his jaw locked the whole time, but I guess my face still doesn't look great.

"And who's this?" he asks, bringing his worried gaze to Callan.

"*Papa*. I think we both have things to explain."

My father nods and moves out of the doorframe to let us in.

Callan looks around, taking in the decor and various photos on the wall. I grew up in this house and it hasn't changed much, so nothing is new to me, but it must be a lot to take in for him, given that I haven't seen many pictures at the ranch. There are photos of my family, my mom and dad. Memories of holidays and trips we'd taken. After my mom died, I stopped looking at them. It was too painful.

"Sit," my father instructs us as we enter the living room, but before sitting down, Callan reaches his hand out. "Let me introduce myself, Mr. Ohara. I'm Callan."

My dad shakes his hand. "I'm Junpei. Nice to meet you."

"We need to talk," I cut into their introductions. When my father's eyes connect with mine, neither of us moves a muscle. I can hear my own heartbeat and my *papa*'s nervous breaths.

I'm unsure if I'm ready to have this conversation, but I could've died tonight and never gotten the opportunity to learn the truth. So, I cut to the chase. "We need to talk about the letters I found."

His expression becomes unreadable. He sits on the couch across from us, gesturing again for Callan and me to do the same.

"What did they say?" There's a quiver in his voice, which tells me he knows more than he's leading on to.

Am I about to accuse my father, the only stable parental figure I had throughout my life, of causing harm to my mother? I glance at Callan and his gaze is focused on me, filled with reassurance. He takes my hand in his and gives it a squeeze.

I can do this.

"That she wanted to get sober." *Papa* scoffs at this, but I continue. "But that everytime she tried to, you pushed her back into using and brought dealers into the house."

Another emotion flashes over his face, but this time, it's clear as day: *guilt.*

He breaks eye contact and looks down at his joint fingers. I squeeze Callan's hand hard before I realize what I'm doing and drop it like a hot potato, muttering an apology under my breath. He grabs my hand back and intertwines his fingers. A sign that he's still with me.

"*Papa,* tell me the truth."

Without looking up, my dad takes a deep breath. "When you were a kid, we struggled financially. When your mom and I got married, she never worked, by choice. I had a good job that could support us both, but when she got pregnant and you came into the world, the extra costs of having a child and the increasing inflation were making it hard to stay afloat."

He stops and meets my gaze, a mix of emotions flitting through his eyes. I nod for him to continue. I need to know.

"A coworker of mine knew that money was tight and had heard about an underground poker club that was accepting new members. I had never gambled with high stakes before, but at the time, it looked like the only way to make quick money.

"We weren't paying our bills on time, our credit card debt was racking up, and as you got older and started school, we had to pay for all of your supplies, new clothes, extra-curriculars. We never wanted you to feel that we were struggling, so we still signed you up to all the classes, made sure you had new shoes and clothes every season. We wanted you to have a good life." My father exhales deeply, as if he's reliving those hard years.

My knee starts to bounce under Callan's hand and he scoots closer.

"Poker started off good and I made some money. Your mother was ecstatic. After a few weeks, she asked to come with me. I hesitated, but I never hid anything from her. So, one night, we hired a babysitter and went to the club. Your mother was buzzing. I don't know if it was the adrenaline rush of being in a small part of the underground world, or seeing so much money being passed around, but she looked so *alive*. The members of the club ranged from regular folk like me, to high rollers, to bikers."

Callan tenses and a sinking feeling settles in my gut. I'm not well-versed in the motorcycle club world, but if I'm not mistaken, there's really only one gang that controls the streets of Raleigh.

"What bikers?" I ask my *papa*, and he stiffens at the question.

"I'll get to that, *haru-kun*. Your mother started coming with me more often and got involved in taking drugs while she was there. To her, it was just to loosen up and have fun. A small line of coke here, a pill of Molly there. I wasn't too concerned—until it became a problem." My father's face pales.

"Recreational became not-so-recreational, when she started getting high in the middle of the day while I was at work and you were at school."

A vivid memory appears at the forefront of my mind. "I remember one day...I came in from school and mom was acting weird. Her pupils looked dilated, she was all over the place. She couldn't even function to make my dinner. I thought she was sick, so I helped her lie down on the couch. She passed out almost instantly... Turns out, she was high," I murmur the last part.

With time, I understood that my mom was a junkie, but I never realized when it had started. The thought breaks my heart. How could she be high in front of her child and pretend to be sick?

My lips tremble and a small cry escapes. Callan wraps his arm around me and brings me to his chest.

"Yes, she was," my dad confirms. "I came home from work to her passed out on the couch and you sitting right next to her too many times to count. She still didn't think it was a problem, until I forced her to go to rehab. After her first stint, I forbade her from coming back to the poker club with me. At that point, I'd been a member for almost two years. I'd won some, lost some. But it somewhat became my part-time job. Without that income, we would have been broke."

"But this doesn't explain Mom's letters. She said you kept bringing men around. What does that mean, *Papa?*" At this point, I'm desperate to know the truth. Was my mom lying? Is my dad being truthful? The hurt that came with my mother's addiction and death would be amplified if I learn that she also tried to lie to me in her letters.

"Baby," Callan whispers into my ear. "It's okay."

My father notices Callan's attempt to calm me down and a small smile appears on his lips. "How long has this been going on?" He points between us, most likely an attempt to change the subject or delay the inevitable. I want to answer, but my mouth feels like it's filled with cotton balls.

Callan responds on my behalf. "A few weeks, sir."

"You can call me Junpei, please."

"Junpei." Callan nods. "It hasn't been that long, but I feel like I've known your daughter forever. She came into my life at the right moment. I needed a new vet. I didn't know I'd find my life partner, too." The admission makes my heart skip multiple beats. This is the closest he's come to saying, "I love you," and I already can't handle the overwhelming way it makes me feel.

I want to tell him how much he means to me, how much

I've fallen for him. Tears spill down my face and Callan cups it, swiping the streams with both thumbs.

"She's not only been my ranch's saving grace, but mine." He holds my gaze as he addresses my dad, and my heart begins to race. "From what I can tell, it seems like you cared for Naya's mother. And Naya has told me how much you love her and done for her. I hope to make her understand how much I truly care about her."

"My little girl deserves nothing but the best," my *papa* agrees.

"I also know how much Naya loves you and how hard it was for her to confront you about this. She went through a great deal of trauma to get here," Callan continues, and I wince at the thought of that disgusting stranger shoving me into his van, and Mason's harsh words and aggressiveness. Another sob breaks out as my entire body shakes. All of today's events are just crashing in on me now.

My father gets up and kneels in front of me, a struggle in his current physical state. "*Moushi wake gozaimasen*," he says. *There is no excuse.*

"*Iie, Papa*, don't. I'm okay. I'm sorry." I try to get him off the floor, but he refuses to budge.

"Don't be, *haru-kun. I'm* sorry I wasn't able to be there for you. Please tell me what happened."

I shake my head, not able to formulate the words through my whimpers.

Callan speaks up. "I think she needs some time to process, but I can assure you she'll always be safe with me, Junpei. She will never get hurt again. Mark my words." His voice has a dangerous undertone that vibrates through my chest. "Please go on. I'm sure Naya wants to hear the rest of your story."

My dad dips his head and gets back on the sofa. "I understand. As I was saying, I got caught up in the gambling and, one night, I lost a huge amount. One-hundred-thousand dollars."

I wince at the amount.

"I'd been on a winning streak for weeks. I thought I could win the jackpot, but I got too cocky, lost all my money, and owed even more. From then on, things were never the same. The men who owned the poker club, a biker gang, started coming around the house for their money, but I had nothing to offer them other than my time and services. So, I became somewhat of an errand boy for them."

My *papa* exhales, scratching at his forehead as if he could pull off the lines of stress.

I still have so many unanswered questions. *Which biker gang? Who were those men?* The information is going through my ears, but my brain is foggy. How was I so oblivious to all of this?

You were a child. But only for so long. I chose to ignore everything happening around me once I started college. At that point, my mother had been suffering with addiction for years and it was my new normal.

"What does this have to do with Mom using?" I ask, confused.

"Everything. The men—the gang that owned the underground establishment—were the Raleigh Riders."

As soon as the name comes out of my father's mouth, a gasp escapes my lips and Callan swears out loud. "*Cazzo!*" *Fuck!*

If this means what I think it means...

"Mason?" I mutter in disbelief, my eyes burgeoned with tears. I look at my dad and his expression tells me what I need to know. "Mason was giving drugs to mom?"

My father replies, "Not directly, but yes." Bile rises up my throat, I want to throw up. I get off the couch in one swift movement and pace around the living room, shaking my hands out as if it'll help rid me of the complete betrayal I feel from *everyone*.

"Lemme get this straight," Callan says, his voice low and dangerous through my impending panic attack. He lifts himself off the couch and joins me at the window. "You were gamblin' at a poker club run by the Raleigh Riders, you lost *their* money, and ended up becomin' an errand boy for 'em? And you let 'em come to your house, puttin' your wife and daughter in danger?"

My *papa* bows his head. "Yes."

"*Cristo Santo.*" *For God's sake.* "Mason has been runnin' that gang for at least two decades," Callan says to me, and things start to make sense. If Mason was the leader back then... My head whips in my father's direction.

"Did you know Mason at the time?" I ask, my hands now balling into fists.

He doesn't answer right away.

"*PAPA!* Did. You. Know. Mason?" I'm sure there is steam coming out of my ears, but I don't give a shit. My entire life feels like a lie.

"Yes, Naya, I did—"

I don't give him the chance to finish his sentence. "Did you —" I choke on a sob. "Did you tell him about me?" Callan is next to me, seething, maybe even angrier than I am. "Did you set us up?" I'm barely able to get the words out of my mouth. The thought of my father playing matchmaker between Mason and me makes me sick, especially knowing now what he did to my mom.

"No, I didn't. But he saw you at the funeral, and I couldn't do much to stop him," my dad cries out, desperately.

"What do you mean you couldn't stop him?" Callan intervenes. "With all due *respect*, Mr. Ohara, you're her father. You didn't have to give him your *daughter.*"

"He threatened to *kill* us," my father responds, running his fingers through his hair with shaking hands. "I had no choice but to comply with his demands. And once he set his eyes on Naya, there was nothing I could do. He said that if I let him have her, he'd clear all of my debts," he says, avoiding eye contact.

"You *sold* me? I can't believe you, *Papa*! I shout, refusing to accept this is true. "He destroyed our family, and you allowed him to get close to me. How could you?" A wave of sadness passes through me, and my cries turn strangled.

"You hid everything from me all these years. He was Mom's dealer. I met him at her *funeral,* for God's sake! Did you orchestrate that?" Resentment grows inside me like a tumor. I'm devastated, enraged, and suddenly, these four walls I've known my entire life don't feel familiar anymore.

"*Naya chan,* that was not my doing," my father says, shaking his head. "You know Mason. He always gets his way. I tried to fight him on this, but he said he didn't need my blessing to have you. I threatened to tell you the truth about him, but he threatened your life in return. I just couldn't risk you getting hurt." His eyes look haunted, the dark circles underneath making him look almost unrecognizable.

"But I *was* hurt, *Papa*. I was in a controlling and abusive relationship for ten years. And you did *nothing* to protect me."

Tears stream down my face. I can't breathe and everything is moving too quickly around me. Callan wraps his body around mine like a shield.

"How could I ever forgive you for this?"

"Naya, I'm not making excuses, but your mother was a grown woman. A smart woman. When she got clean the first time, she promised she'd never hurt our family again with that disease. But when Mason's men started showing up for their money, she went behind my back for drugs, which they supplied."

"So, why would she say that it was all your fault in her letters?"

"It *was* my fault that the men were around, but *she* made the conscious decision to go back on drugs time and time again. In the end, there's nothing you or I could've done. I did everything possible to help your mother. I loved her deeply. But she sealed her fate when she chose drugs over us."

That reminder stabs me in the heart now as much as it did when my mother died. I was so angry at her for dying. So livid at her for abandoning us. I couldn't believe she chose the high over her daughter and husband. I still miss her everyday, but the choice she made never leaves my mind.

"She didn't want to look like the bad guy, and she was angry at me for repeatedly sending her to rehab. I never wanted to involve you," my *papa* adds quietly.

My entire body is shaking from the sheer amount of rage coursing through my veins. "I want to go back to Springfield," I say to Callan.

"Naya, it's late. At least stay the night," my dad pleads.

Callan agrees. "He's got a point, sweetheart. You're hurt and Springfield is hours away. Let's rest and start over tomorrow." He holds onto my elbow to reassure me and it works.

"Fine. We'll stay. But I'm done for the night, and I need a shower." I retreat from the living room and rush up the stairs, with Callan in tow.

"Are you okay, Princess?" he asks as we enter my childhood room.

It's still decorated the same way I left it. Cream walls, beige carpet, a canopy bed, lavender bed sheets and comforter, and a bunch of random decor and photos laying around the room.

"No," I say as my lips begin to quiver again. This time, I do nothing to stop the flow of tears that stream from my eyes. "I don't know who he is anymore, Callan," I sob.

He walks up to me and softly takes my face in his hand, using his thumb to wipe away the tears.

"You have a lot to process, sweetheart, but you don't have to do it all tonight." The low baritone of his voice combined with his scent soothes my aching heart. I press my cheek against his hand, despite the slight sting of pain from my time under Mason's 'care.' I'm desperate for the feel of him.

I suck in a steadying breath and wipe my other cheek. "I need a bath," I say, wanting to wash this terrible day off.

"I'll run it for you," he responds, placing a kiss on my forehead. "Just point me in the direction of the bathroom."

"Second door on your left." My voice is quiet, even to my own ears. "You really don't have to do that. I can take care of it."

Callan ignores me and walks toward the door. Before he exits, he looks at me over his shoulder. "It's *my* job to take care of you, *principessa.*"

33

Callan

I draw the bath, filling it with hot water and a bit of lavender epsom salt I found in a container off to the side. My mind is still whirring with the information that I just heard. Naya's father's gambling, her mother's addiction, and *Mason*. My blood begins to boil at the thought of Caldwell. He's the root of almost every problem in Naya's life and he's still out there.

I clench my hand into a fist. I've never wanted to kill a man this much. *And I will.* Mason will be begging for the sweet release of death when I get my hands on him. He may have run off tonight, but there's no corner of the earth far enough for him to hide from me. Not only do I despise him for our over a decade-long rivalry, but he's the reason why Naya is suffering.

I send Knox an update, letting him know that Naya and I will be spending the night at the Ohara's. He responds quickly with a thumbs-up and sends the address of a hotel not too far away that he and Grady are staying at.

When I enter Naya's room, I find her curled up on the bed in the fetal position, her eyes closed, breathing slowly. The vision of her so defeated makes my heart swarm with emotions. Anger, sadness, understanding, and...love. I want to blame it on her beauty and grace, but there's something fiery inside her that draws me in. I can't let it go until I've uncovered it.

"Naya," I say quietly, not wanting to startle her. "Your bath is ready, Princess."

Her lids snap open and I see that her cheeks are wet with tears. I follow behind as she silently walks toward the bathroom.

My teeth grind together as I picture the hundreds of ways I'd like to kill Mason for causing her so much pain.

Once inside, she shimmies out of her pants, but her hands tremble as she tries to undo the buttons of her shirt. I place mine over hers and take over until she's fully undressed. I can't help but roam my eyes over her body. Her skin is covered in bruises and abrasions. I need to know exactly what happened to her, but right now isn't the time.

When she gets into the water, I walk away, ready to allow her space in a quiet bath. "Callan." Her voice sounds so weak and frail, and I feel a crack go through my chest. "Stay. Don't go, please."

There's so much anguish in her eyes, both physical and emotional. I close the door. "I'm not goin' anywhere."

Although I would do anything to ease her pain, I'm unsure of what she needs from me right now. I look at the tub of steaming water, it's definitely large enough for two.

"Do you want me to—"

"Please," she interrupts me, as if reading my mind.

Quickly, I remove my clothes and get into the tub, slipping in behind her. She readjusts herself so that she's comfortably seated between my legs. Her head lolls to the side and rests on my shoulder.

We sit like that in comfortable silence for a few minutes before I speak up. "Pass me that," I say gently, pointing to the loofah just within reach of her arm. She hands it to me along with a bottle of body wash. I begin to wash her shoulders, arms, and back, and continue down the rest of her body, ensuring I don't miss an inch of skin. I wish the soap was enough to remove the marks that today left on her soul, but I know only time will heal those wounds, and even that might not be enough.

"Callan," she whispers again. "How do I forgive him? How do I forgive *her*?"

My heart breaks, knowing the torment she must feel in this moment. Neither of her parents are who she thought, and while it may take some time, I'm sure she'll be able to figure things out with her father. Her mother, on the other hand—there's no chance of reconciliation.

I kiss Naya's temple. "I don't have those answers for you, sweetheart. But we'll figure it out together, I promise."

"Thank you for being with me, for *saving* me from Mason. He's been ruining my life even before I knew him." Her tone takes on a hard edge. I clench my fist hard under the water. Just the sound of his name is enough to make me go blind with rage.

"He was supplying my mom with drugs," she continues. "Making my father do his dirty work, and as if that wasn't enough, he had to have *me*, too. He had the entire Ohara family in his palm, and I didn't even realize it." She shakes her head.

"Mason is a snake in the grass, Naya." I do my best to keep my voice calm. "You don't see him 'til he's already sunk his teeth into you. By then, the venom has already spread. I'm not sayin' your father should be forgiven—that decision is yours alone—but if he told the truth, he was just tryin' to provide for his family, whatever way he could. Mason saw a weak spot and lunged for it."

She nods her head. "I never want to see Mason again."

"You won't," I promise, and it's one I intend to keep. Mason will never so much as lay eyes on Naya again.

When I've finished cleaning her up, she turns to straddle me and lets her fingertips gently graze the scar along my chest, up and down, sending shivers all over my body. I place my hands on her hips.

"What happened?" she asks.

I brace myself for the memories of hurt and betrayal. My altercation with Mason is not something I've discussed many times throughout the years. But Naya deserves to know.

"Mason tried to have me killed."

She jolts back, causing the water to ripple and swell against the edge of the tub. "What?"

"Fifteen years ago, I got attacked in the parkin' lot of The Crown, which was called Hamilton's Tavern at the time. It was shortly after I'd started Sinners & Saints. Our crew was small; we didn't have much protection, and I had to trust blindly. A mistake I've never made again," I explain, anger spreading through me.

Naya's eyebrows draw together, making the skin between them wrinkle, and I just want to smooth the worry away with my thumb.

"I knew about the Raleigh Riders, but had always steered clear of them. They had their own turf in Raleigh, and we had ours in Nashville. I thought I could trust the code between gangs. Rhett was one of our newest members. I had no idea he was a Raleigh Rider 'til he attacked me with two others. He managed to shank me in the chest. *'This is from Mason,'* he'd said."

Naya's eyes widen in disbelief.

"They left me to die that night, but Knox found me. And I've been waitin' to get my revenge ever since."

Naya begins to caress my arm, as if to soothe me. I kiss her softly before continuing. "They went into hidin' when they realized I was still alive, but they couldn't hide for long. With the help of the Nashville Devils, my men brought 'em back to the warehouse, barely alive. When I had gained back my strength, I killed 'em. Safe to say, those men aren't a threat anymore. But I've yet to get my hands on Mason, which will change *very* soon," I say through gritted teeth.

"I bought the bar as a final gesture and warnin' to not fuck with me and called it The Crown. Ever since then, my crew has been callin' me *King*."

Naya's hand flies to her chest, goosebumps erupting all over her arms. "Callan, I'm so sorry. How can you even look at me knowing I used to date him, *loved* him," she says with disgust.

"Princess, I'd never judge your character based on who you used to care 'bout. I did question your intentions when I first found out you were linked to him, before I found out you were actually runnin' away from him."

She lets out a huge breath. "I'm so glad he didn't kill you."

"Oh yeah, sweetheart? Why's that?"

Her eyes lock with mine, the gaze both soft and fierce at the same time. I'm entranced, unable to look away as she slowly raises her mouth to mine, wrapping her wet arms around my neck.

The embrace is unhurried as our tongues tangle. It relays the events from the last twenty-four hours, every pent-up emotion that we've had over these past few months, and the words I've yet to say to her.

I nip on her lower lip and she lets out a strained sound, pushing her bare chest against mine. I can feel her hardened nipples rubbing on my skin. With every brush of them, I feel myself getting harder, until I'm no longer able to suppress my own moan.

Naya moves forward until our lower bodies meet and begins to rock against my cock. Even though the water has begun to cool, I can still feel the warmth of her pussy. It takes all of my strength not to slide into her right here and now.

"Not here," I grunt.

Her eyes search mine. "Why?"

"After everythin' you've been through today, you deserve more than a quick fuck in the bathtub. Stand up."

She doesn't hesitate. I stay seated, watching as she rises from the water. Every droplet glistens against her skin.

"Dry yourself off and get into bed. I expect you to be waitin' for me on your back."

A genuine smile plays on her lips and her eyes twinkle with anticipation. "Yes, *King*."

I let out a growl and she giggles, grabbing a towel as she runs out of the bathroom.

34

Naya

I hate Mason. Even more than I did before.

I lie on the bed, quivering with anger. I know all too well the feeling of betrayal by the people you trust.

When Callan comes out of the bathroom, I stare at him, speechless. Callan is a survivor and I've gained even more respect for him.

"Thank you for telling me your story," I say, my voice thick with emotion.

"I want to tell you everythin' about me. And I want to know everythin' about you." He approaches me with ease and my breath hitches when he steps on the bed and places his body on top of mine. "Every time I try to stop my mind from driftin' to thoughts of you, I fail. You might've said you wanted to keep this platonic at first, but I think you're a liar, *amore*." His lips graze mine, sending a jolt of electricity down my spine.

"You might as well quit fightin' now. I'm givin' you one chance to say no. But if I were you, I'd let me rid you of the naggin' ache between your legs. I can smell your arousal from here, *troietta*."

He presses into me a little more and a faint moan escapes my mouth.

"So, what do you say, Princess?"

I'm turned on, emotions swarming my chest. I shouldn't be feeling like this, but I can't stop myself from wanting Callan. The attraction is unstoppable, and my love for him undeniable.

I love him.

I'm *in love* with him. And I don't know if that makes me an idiot for trusting him so soon or getting involved with someone like him again. But Callan has never made me feel anything but cherished, taken care of.

"Fuck me, King. I'm yours." A look of pure lust flashes across his eyes. I'm playing with fire, but I don't mind getting burned if it means I get a taste of him.

Callan backs away slightly, and I feel the absence of his warm body almost right away. He hops off the bed and jerks me forward, bringing my ass to the edge, and he kneels.

The air is stolen from my lungs when he puts his tongue on me, licking my entrance all the way up my clit. I stifle a moan, but it's louder than it should be. *I hope to God my father can't hear this.*

Callan doesn't lick me with slow strokes—he devours me, like I'm his last meal. The act is so dirty, and in my childhood bedroom, that I blush at the thought.

"Oh, fuck, Callan," I whisper-shout as I come with an intensity I've never felt before.

A moment later, he holds onto my neck and shoves his dick inside me, forcing me to take every inch, and I struggle for air as he pounds into me.

"I will fuck you 'til you beg for mercy, *puttanella mia*, and even then, I won't slow down. You've given me permission to own you, and I don't care if it's a bad idea, it's happenin','" he says, his voice strangled by his own moans, the muscles on his arms and legs straining through his tattoos.

Callan works my body so hard, even the slightest move and the gentlest rush of air feel like too much on my clit.

We both come hard as he grunts out, "You're mine, Naya."

Once he pulls out, his cum leaks out of my pussy. "No wastin'. Don't move while I stick my cum back inside you," Callan grunts as he uses his two fingers to push his seed back into me.

Surprise steals the air from my lungs, leaving me breathless.

He collapses against me, his solid, sweaty body stuck to me, and neither of us moves.

Callan looks at me and I know it's written all over my face. The last few years have been difficult, and the past months harder. But I finally found a person that understands me, with whom I don't need to always say what's on my mind.

We haven't said those three words, but I'd be content without them.

There is something between Callan and me that can't be crossed. I was so caught up trying to stay away, I didn't notice the change.

He soon became my savior, and someone I'd miss whenever he would leave. His little quirks became my favorite thing. My mood shifting for the better when he's around. Apart from when he pisses me off, that is. But even then, the push and pull between us exhilarates me, grounds me.

"This was never how I pictured it. So easy, effortless," he says, interrupting my thoughts.

I pause for a moment. "What are you talking about?"

"Fallin' in love."

I freeze, completely stunned. Did I actually hear what I think I heard?

"The day I first met you, I was walkin' through an ordinary week. Survivin'. And when I saw you—this small, feisty woman with the most gorgeous eyes and lips—and after the ridiculous way you charged at me for bein' a dick to you, I felt...*alive*. For the first time in years, I could relax. You felt like a horse ride through a late summer field. Freein'; a breath of fresh air."

I crinkle my nose, trying to stop tears from forming in my eyes.

"I couldn't spend a minute without you in my mind. I tried to brush it off, not one to believe in love at first sight. But your face haunted my memories every time I closed my eyes. I was in denial for so long."

My heart rate increases as I listen to Callan declare his feelings for me. I don't have any words, shocked that he feels the same way I do.

"My relationship with Alison taught me what I didn't want, but you showed me what I deserve. I vowed to never open my heart again to another woman. But when you came into my life, I couldn't get rid of you, as hard as I tried," he says with a little wink.

I shove his chest and let out a choked laugh, the tears now freely flowing from my eyes.

He wipes the tears off my face. "Fallin' in love with you was easy, Princess. Admittin' it to myself was the hardest part. I love you, Naya. Always will."

I close my eyes, feeling an intense wave of happiness travel through me. I place my palm on his chest and lean forward.

"Callan, you anchored yourself to my soul the moment I first saw you, even if I didn't know it. An indestructible tether was created between us that day, and I was foolish for ever denying my feelings. I fell in love with you when I realized I had a protector, savior, a man who worshiped me out of pure love. A man who could also get on every one of my last nerves." We grin at each other.

"And for that, I will forever be yours, King."

35

Callan

Naya's words are still ringing in my head when I lean forward to press my lips against hers, warmth pooling in my chest.

"I love you and all that you are," Naya adds softly, her eyes searching mine.

"Say it again."

"I love you. I love you. I love you."

I grab her face and smother it with kisses, leaving her gasping for air and laughing out loud. The sound is gentle and feminine, unfettered, and it takes over my entire body. I've rarely seen Naya smile this much around me these past months. But her walls seem to have broken, and she's finally letting me in.

And it's all because of me. I made her smile. She's in love with *me,* and I can't help but be proud that I'm the one to make her come apart. I want to hear her say *I love you* over and over again until she's out of breath.

"My *papà* treated my *mamma* and me like gold. He gave us a good life. He was our protector, savior, leader. I want to be that person for you, Naya. I want to be strong when you need me to be, funny when you're down, and adventurous when you're bored. And I want to be able to lean on you in return. I want to be your forever, Princess."

She smiles, her eyes glittering with so much emotion. "You're stuck with me now, grump."

"I'm a damn lucky guy, then."

We spend the rest of the night in each other's arms, talking about life and our future plans. Eventually drifting off to a peaceful sleep.

When I wake up, my cock is hard and my mind is assaulted with images of Naya from last night. Watching her come apart at my mercy felt like a religious experience. One that I intend to partake in regularly from here on out, especially now that we've admitted our feelings.

I bring my hands up to my face to rub the tiredness out of my eyes and catch a whiff of her scent still lingering on my fingers. I groan at the smell. I can't fucking wait to put my mouth on Naya's pussy and taste her again. I reach for the elastic band on my wrist and tie my hair up as I lift myself out of bed, careful not to wake her.

After what happened yesterday, and our admissions, I'm even more eager to find Mason and make him pay for the pain and suffering he put both Naya and me through.

I'm a patient man. I've waited fifteen years to avenge my attempted murder, but once you threaten and hurt what's mine, there's no stopping the lengths I'll go to keep them safe. Naya is mine to protect, and I can't have her psycho ex-boyfriend roaming the streets anymore, plotting to take us down any chance he gets.

He's tried to kill me once, and hurt Naya twice. He'll never touch either of us again.

It's early and the house is quiet as I walk down the stairs. Naya's father is nowhere to be found. I sit at the kitchen table and call Knox to pick me up. Where I'm planning to go is no place I want Naya to be. So, I'd rather get a head start so we can both head back to Springfield later today in peace.

Before leaving, I shoot Naya a quick text for her to see when she wakes up.

> Me: I'm runnin errands with Knox and Grady. I'll be back soon. Don't leave the house without me.

I don't want her to worry about me, but I'll tell her the truth when I'm back in her arms.

When I hop into the truck twenty minutes later, Knox grumbles, "Couldn't let us sleep in for one day, could you?" Grady is in the backseat, still half asleep. Knox looks up at the house. "Where's shorty?"

"Still asleep. Hopin' we'll be back before she wakes."

He glances at me, a gleam in his eye. "Where we headed, King?"

I look at the message Jackson sent me with the address to Caldwell's second home. That place is meant to be a secret—a safe house for when the little bitch needs to hide. After what he pulled, I'm sure that's exactly where he is now.

Unfortunately for him, there's no hiding from Jax. I just never bothered having him search for Mason's hiding holes before. I'd never planned on bringing the war to Mason's doorstep, but by going after Naya, he made this even more personal.

"We're goin' to pay Mason a visit," I reply.

Knox lets out a holler. "Hell yeah!"

As we drive, the three of us begin to formulate our plan of attack. It's unlikely that Mason will be in the house alone, but I doubt that his whole crew will be there. Maybe a few extra men for protection, but nothing we can't handle.

Knox and I will enter the home together, and Grady will stay in the car so that we have a quick getaway if needed. Jackson was already on his way to Raleigh hours ago, probably anticipating I'd want to finish the job today—that Brit has some sixth sense, I swear—in case we need back up.

We pull up to the house at a snail's pace, not wanting to alert anyone of our presence. It's an older style home in a deserted area on the outskirts of town. The front porch looks as if it's about to fall apart. Mason's green F-150 is parked out front. *Bingo.*

There's no security. I chuckle to myself at the man's arrogance. He's almost made this too easy. Did he really think I wouldn't come looking for him after all he's done?

I feel the rage that has been simmering inside of me for the last fifteen years begin to boil over.

I raise the tonneau cover to the truck and we pick out our weapons. I've got my knife on me, but I'll be saving that for last. The same way Mason tried to have my life ended, is the way his will end at my hands.

Though, unlike him, I don't need someone else to do my dirty work.

I'll kill him myself.

The weight of the gun in my hand as we approach the front step sends a rush of energy down my spine. I look over at Knox and see him wide-eyed, quivering with anticipation, no sign of the exhaustion from when he first picked me up.

I give him a nod and he removes a lockpick from his pocket. The door unlocks after a few seconds, and we enter.

The house is quiet and in complete darkness, but I know

Mason is here. Silently, we check each room on the main floor. The first two are empty, but in the third room, we find one of Mason's men passed out in a chair, facing the window to the driveway, an empty bottle of bourbon on the floor next to him. Clearly, he was meant to be keeping watch, but his ineptitude worked to our advantage.

Knox creeps up behind him, glock in hand, and whispers into his ear. "Time to wake up, buddy."

The man startles, disoriented. He doesn't get the chance to utter a word or figure out what's happening before Dav knocks him out with a forceful blow to the head with the side of his gun. He won't be waking up again anytime soon.

"Pathetic. He barely even made it fun," Knox mutters as he stares at his victim's limp body on the ground.

I chuckle before looking up to the second floor, where I'm sure Mason's room is. "Let's go."

"Do you think there are more men up there?"

I shake my head. "I doubt it."

I'd expect him to have all of his guards downstairs, so they could alert him to intruders. He felt secure enough here that one sorry excuse of a guard was all he thought he needed. We walk up the steps and I curse internally when one of the steps creaks beneath our feet. Knox and I pause, listening for any indication that our target may have heard us, but the house remains quiet.

I glance down the hall once we make it to the top of the steps. Every room has a single door, except for the one at the very end, which has large double doors. *Mason.* My body tingles with anticipation at the thought of finally removing this fucker from my life. *Our* lives.

We keep walking, Knox growing more and more disappointed with each empty room we find.

"Stay here," I command when we reach Mason's door. "Only come in if you hear me shout, got it?"

Knox looks as if he's about to argue, and I shake my head. "He tried to have me killed and has hurt Naya in more ways than I care to count. This is between me and him. When he dies, I want the last thing he sees to be my face."

Dav's eyes grow dark and he takes a step back. "Alright. Holler if you need me, King."

I nod, raise my gun, and open the door to the bedroom. It's darker than the rest of the house, but the second I cross the threshold, the bedside light turns on, casting the room in a warm orange glow.

Mason is sitting on the bed, holding his own gun.

"I was wondering how much longer it would take you to get up here," he drawls, his face smug. "I almost came and got you myself."

I grind my teeth. I've waited years for the opportunity to be this close to him and the urge to kill him is damn near overwhelming.

We keep our weapons pointed at each other. I know I'm a better shot than Mason, and with quicker reflexes, too, but chances are, I may still get hurt.

"I should've killed you years ago, you son of a bitch," I seethe.

"Uh-uh," he says as he rises from the bed, waving the gun at me. "It's too bad you didn't die that night. Thanks for getting rid of Rhett for me, by the way. I would've killed him myself for failing at the job."

"Why didn't you come for me yourself? Are you that much of a pussy that you had your men do your dirty work?

Mason flares his nostrils. "I couldn't be bothered to waste my time on a worthless, little club. You are just a kid, threatening my plan to take over in Tennessee."

I scoff. "You're a fuckin' joke, Mason. You've had fifteen years to step foot on our territory. Why now?" I ask him, inching closer to him.

"I was waiting for the perfect moment. And now seems like a great time, with recent *developments*." He grins, as if he knows something I don't.

I draw my eyes together. *Is he referring to Naya?*

"I suppose there's no chance that you brought my girl with you?" Mason adds, a complacent grin appearing on his face.

My eyes burn with rage. Hearing him refer to Naya as *his* has me considering whether I should end this now with one quick shot to the head. But I refuse. That would be too gracious of an end for a man like Mason. He deserves to be slaughtered like the brute that he is.

When I say nothing, he continues. "I must say, I was surprised that Naya was so willin' to jump into bed with you." He lets out a dark chuckle. "That wasn't the girl I knew, but I suppose people change. If she wants to be a whore, then I guess I'll let you have my sloppy seconds."

Anger courses through my veins and my grip on the gun tightens. "Don't you *dare* talk about her like that."

His eyebrows raise. "Oh, come on now, Hudson. Don't tell me you've fallen for her. She doesn't have the stomach for this sort of life, no matter how good the pussy is."

Fury vibrates through me as I charge at him. "Shut the fuck up," I spit.

"One more step and she's dead." Mason quickly reaches in his back pocket and presses on something.

I halt, an immediate tightness in my chest. "What the fuck do you mean, Mason?"

"Do you really think I wasn't expecting you? I've got men stationed at her father's house, ready to barge in at a moment's notice," he responds, darkness in his tone. "If you get any closer, they'll open fire and your precious girl will *die*."

A cold, tight knot forms in my gut as I recognize the risk, but I see red and all logical thought leaves me. I hope my hotheadedness won't backfire.

Before he even has the chance to realize what's happening, I shoot him in the wrist holding the object, the left knee cap, and once more in the stomach, all in quick succession. He crumples to the floor, releasing his gun and object in his hand. I walk up to him and kick them in the corner of the room, ignoring his pained moans.

I shout for Knox and he enters the room. "What's goin' on?"

"Call Jax and tell him to send backup to Naya's house. Now! Then, call her and instruct her to safety. Mason has men stationed around her father's property," I explain, panicked.

I drop to my knees in front of Mason, tucking my own weapon away, and grab him by his throat. "You just don't know when the fuck to shut up, do you, Caldwell." I squeeze and watch his skin turn purple, eyes bulging as he sputters. I release his throat only to punch him square in the face. He whimpers in pain, and I hear the satisfying crunch of his nose breaking. "She might've been yours at some point in time, but you fucked up. You will never see her again."

I punch him again, more of his blood seeping onto the floor. It's not enough, but I have to end this quickly and hurry back to the house in case Naya is hurt.

"You tried to ruin *my* girl's life. You had her father under your command, her mother hooked on your shit, and you still think you deserve her?" He lets out a low, gurgled laugh, causing blood to drip from his lips, and I punch him again. "There isn't a universe where she'll ever be yours. She's part of the Sinners & Saints now. And you..." I look down at him in disgust, "are *nothin'*," I spit, as I whip out my knife.

He tries to wriggle away from me when he catches the glint of the steel, but his injuries make his attempt futile.

At that same moment, Knox runs back in. "I alerted Jax and the guys rushed over to the house and intercepted all piece of shit Raleigh Riders before they were able to get in. She's safe."

I let out a huge sigh of relief. "Thanks, Dav."

I turn back toward Mason and press the tip of the blade against his neck, watching as a droplet of blood forms.

"I've been waitin' for this moment for fifteen years, ever since you had Rhett jump me." Rage rolls through me as I recall that night. I push the knife harder into his neck as my muscles coil with rage. "I was young then, just gettin' my start, but I knew one day, *I* would be the one to end you."

I'm exhilarated, knowing that Mason has fully lost, and I can finally kill him with no ounce of regret. Keeping the weapon against his neck, I continue with a laugh. "Any last words you'd like to say?"

"Fu—" I silence him as I drag the blade across his throat. Blood spurts from his body, and I get up to leave, pocketing my knife, not giving his body a second glance.

We rush back to the Ohara residence. Outside, I see my men roaming the front yard, which confirms that Mason's men never made it in the house. My heart hammers against my ribcage when I step through the door. Naya is pacing in the foyer, visibly shaking.

I scan her body. She's not hurt. *She's fine.*

She jumps when she sees me. "Where'd you go?" she asks, a tremble in her voice. Tears start spilling from her eyes, a crash of worry and adrenaline. "Knox called and told us to steer clear from all windows and doors. And there were men outside. I didn't know where you were, and Knox wouldn't say anything," she says all in one breath, her voice stuttering between her sobs.

"Everythin' is okay. I just had to take care of some business." I close the distance between us and cup her jaw with my palm.

She pauses, her gaze focused on me. "Sinners & Saints business?"

"Somethin' like that," I reply, thinking back at Mason's pathetic body bleeding out in his room.

Naya sees right through me. "You went after him, didn't you?"

I hesitate, but keep my eyes trained on hers, watching for any indication that she would be upset if I told her the truth. I know she hates Mason and said she never wanted to see him again, but I'm unsure if she would agree with the *permanency* of what I've done.

"Is he..." Her words trail off.

"He won't be an issue anymore, Princess."

I see a flicker of understanding cross her face before she exhales and wraps her arms around me, tightly. Her body slumps against mine, losing its stiff posture. "I'm just happy you're alive, Callan."

I press a kiss to the top of her head. "Your safety is all that matters, darlin'."

"I love you," she murmurs against my chest, the words like a drug to my system. Suddenly, any worries or concerns I had about what the Raleigh Riders might do when they realize their president is dead, are gone.

Until a cough interrupts our moment.

Standing in the kitchen watching us is Junpei, his face a mixture of worry and desperation.

I feel Naya tense in my arms.

"Don't mean to interrupt, but can I speak with you, Naya?"

"Anything you want to say to me, you can say in front of Callan, as well," she responds.

Her father swipes a palm over his face and sighs. "I never meant to cause you pain. If I had known that Mason would hurt you, I would have found a way to—"

"But you *did* know, *Papa*," Naya says, her voice cold. "You knew exactly who he was. And you didn't do anything. You were aware of the role he played with Mom, and you still stood by and watched as I dated him for years!"

Junpei lowers his eyes to the ground, and I take her hand, giving it a gentle squeeze.

"I'm sorry, Naya. If I could go back in time and change things, I would."

"Sorry isn't enough, *Papa*. I feel like I don't even know you." Her voice cracks at the last bit. "We're going back to Springfield. I'll let you know when we've made it."

Junpei's face falls, but he doesn't try to convince his daughter to stay. Naya keeps a firm grasp on my hand as she leads me back to her bedroom to gather her stuff.

Once we're ready to go, she turns to face me. "I don't know what to do, Callan. I'm lost. I can't even trust the one family member I have left. I've never felt this alone in my life."

I tilt her chin up so that she's looking directly at me. "Sweetheart, I promise that I'll be beside you through it all, and I'll always be here for you to lean on. You will never have to feel alone again. I'll be your family for as long as you'll have me."

"Is forever too long?" she asks with a laugh, as tears brim in her eyes.

"It's not long enough," I respond with ease, knowing there's no chance that I'd ever let this woman slip from my grasp. "Now, where do we go from here, Princess? You mentioned goin' back to Springfield, but we can go anywhere you want."

She shakes her head, then reaches up to kiss me. "I want to go home."

EPILOGUE
Naya

Six months later

"**A**ll those boxes can go upstairs. The rest can stay on the main floor," I tell the men who are carrying my belongings into the house. They all have Sinners & Saints jackets on.

I look in the mirror at the entryway and admire the matching leather one I have on, made specifically for me. Callan was so excited to gift me my own S&S jacket on my thirtieth birthday a few weeks ago, he could barely keep it a secret. If it weren't for me almost begging him to keep my gift a surprise, he would've given it to me the second he received it.

I stare at my reflection, chin high, shoulders back, and standing tall, proud to officially be part of the Sinners & Saints. Never would I have imagined I'd join a Motorcycle Club, but it's been six months of Heaven by Callan's side, and I can't wait to stand with him forever.

Since leaving my father back in Raleigh, it's been a lot of highs and lows. Our relationship is getting better by the day as I'm slowly learning to forgive his mistakes, but I still struggle. Callan has been my rock along the way, and I couldn't be more thankful.

Now that Mason is no longer a problem, we can finally move on with our lives, not worried about him interfering. The thought of never seeing Mason again gives me relief. Callan didn't hesitate to *eliminate* him for me. I still cringe at the idea of Callan being involved in so much violence and gore, but I wouldn't change a thing about him.

When he asked me to become a member, it was almost as if he were asking for my hand in marriage. My chest exploded with happiness. I was honored and thrilled for this new adventure.

I can't wait to marry Callan, and I know he's impatient, too. But I keep insisting on taking one step at a time. And six months after admitting our feelings to each other, I'm finally moving in with him at All Saints.

If it were up to him, I would've moved in the day after we'd come back. But he respected my wishes to go at a slower pace, despite his displeasure. To soften the blow, I slept at the ranch almost every night, but kept all my belongings at my place. A compromise to convince myself we weren't rushing into anything. Though it feels like I have barely seen him these past few months—between my late nights at the clinic's office, busy, non-stop days with new clients, and trying to spend time with my dad. I've missed him *a lot*.

All that changes today.

Callan walks into the house, a huge grin plastered on his face, and lifts me up, twirling me around until we're both dizzy with excitement. "Today's the day," he says, wild with joy.

"Today's the day," I confirm, matching his smile. Callan's happiness is contagious.

"How's the move goin', darlin? Are the guys doin' a good job?" he asks, already glaring at the crew as they walk in and out of the house. Some of them scatter away.

"It's going great! Thank you for getting them to help," I

reply, kissing him softly on the lips, and he immediately softens again, my heart throbbing with glee.

"It's not like they had a choice."

I scoff. "Callan! You better be paying them for this."

He laughs and grabs me by the hips, lifting me up to wrap my legs around his waist. "*Si, cuore mio.* I'll compensate 'em for their time."

My heart does that thing it always does when he speaks to me in Italian, and the feeling sends a flutter down my core. I wrap my arms around his neck, his hot skin against mine giving me goosebumps. "Thank you, *amore mio*," I say, and Callan freezes, a sudden catch in his breath. I've never spoken to him in his language, but if this is how he reacts, I should do it more often.

He squeezes my ass and walks us right out the door. "Where are you taking me?" I ask him, giggling.

"I want to show you somethin'." This man is always full of surprises.

Callan carries me all the way through both stables, and when we come out on the other side, he sets me down in front of a small house-like building I've never seen before. *How?* "Callan, what is this?"

"Go inside." He hands me a set of keys, and I unlock the door.

When I walk into the space, I'm filled with an overwhelming feeling of awe. It's an office equipped with everything from a desk and chair, to a little kitchenette. "How–how did you pull this off?"

"I've been workin' on it since we got back from Raleigh. I knew you'd move in one day and figured you'd need your own space to work in the evenin's and weekends. I teamed up with Laura to design it and get some of your favorite things."

I walk farther in and see copies of my veterinary diplomas

on the wall. My lungs expand to their fullest through deep, satisfied breaths. I'm proud of how far I've come in my career and the clinic. The past few months have been very prosperous for us and we're on the right path to success. We're getting busier, our clientele has expanded, and Laura has decided to continue her studies to become a vet.

On the desk sits a large vase of fresh white lilies. A knot forms in my throat as I reach for the flowers and bring them to my nose.

"I want to continue this tradition with you," Callan explains. "Lilies represent love and devotion, but most importantly, rebirth. And you, sweetheart, have turned into the strongest, most resilient woman I've ever met." Tears swell in my eyes.

Callan smiles and looks around the room. "I hope you like it?" he asks, a hint of nervousness in his voice.

I run toward him, almost tackling him to the floor. "Are you kidding? I love it, Callan! It's perfect."

"I'm glad you do, sweetheart. There's another door back there to a bathroom. I almost didn't put one, thinkin' I'd never see you if this place was fully equipped, but Knox and Laura talked some sense into me," he says, and I laugh.

"You're one crazy man."

"Crazy for you, Princess," he retorts with a wink.

"I wouldn't have it any other way."

Callan

I hate surprises, but seeing the look on Naya's face any time I surprise her makes my heart jolt.

I'd been working on this little project ever since we got back six months ago, and it was hard as shit to hide from her. How do you conceal a fucking building?

Thankfully, Naya has been so busy at the clinic and spending some time with her father that she hasn't really been gallivanting around the ranch much. She'd come home to my bed exhausted, and then have to do it all over again the next morning. I've missed her. Not even the ranch and S&S business could distract me fully, and I'm so fucking happy that she's finally moving in.

And this new office will mean she'll be able to have less late nights and finish things up closer to the ranch, without having to drive home in the dark after a busy day.

She's been adamant on taking things slow—whatever that means—and I've been fucking patient. But enough is enough. I gave her six months to get her shit together. And here we are.

I have one last surprise up my sleeve.

"Before we head back to the house, I want to pass by the barn. You comin'?"

Naya takes one last look around her new office. "Yes! One

quick stop, then I have to head back. The guys are probably just leaving my stuff everywhere," she says, already anxious about the amount of unpacking she'll have to do.

"Don't worry, it'll be worth it."

We walk through the stables again, then out to the barn on the other side of the property. When we get to the door, Naya halts her steps, noticing the floral arch made out of white lilies and greenery.

"Callan..." she mutters.

I grab her hand and lead her through the entrance. Once inside, we step onto a white carpet that ends with another arch, this one with white draping. Tealights hang from the ceiling, illuminating the space just enough. On each side of the little walkway are bales of hay decorated with more flowers.

Naya looks like she's seen a ghost, tears slowly making their way down her cheeks. "Callan..." she repeats.

"Walk with me, *amore mio*." She wipes her cheeks and puts her hand in mine. We walk the short distance to the archway, and I stand facing her. Suddenly, I become nervous about what I'm going to do. My palms are sweaty, and my heart pounds a hundred miles an hour. But when I look down at Naya, her soft eyes and beautiful smile give me the push I need.

"Naya, *sei l'amore della mia vita*." *You are the love of my life*. Emotion swells in my throat. "Before you, I was simply a man with no plans for the future, livin' day to day with a closed heart. But you've given me hope, meanin', and I wake up everyday excited for what's to come."

Naya sniffles, and I grab her hands, palms up, and softly rub my thumbs over them. A little trick I came up with to calm her racing mind when her feelings are too much to bear.

Right away, she loosens her shoulders and releases a pent-up breath.

"I want to spend the rest of my days lovin' you, takin' care of you. I want to share my life with you."

Naya lets out a little gasp, finally realizing what I'm planning. "Oh my God, Callan!"

On cue, the barn doors open and Knox ushers Bert and Ernie in, both wearing little bowties. They strut over to us, and Naya bends over to greet them. When they reach us, Knox grins at us and leaves.

She's now freely crying and laughing out of happiness, and seeing her this elated makes me want to give her the world. She holds Bert up, and I kneel on the ground, taking the little box that was attached to Ernie's collar.

I stare up at the most beautiful woman and ask, "Naya Jun Ohara, will you marry me?"

Without hesitation, Naya meets me on the ground and grabs my face with both palms. "Yes! Yes, of course I'll marry you!" she yells, giving me kisses all over my face. The warmth of her touch penetrates my skin, and I feel intoxicated with love.

I stand, lifting Naya up with me, and take her to one of the bales covered with fabric, where I lay her on her back. I kiss her lips, paying close attention to every noise she makes, while my hands roam her body. Her tongue meets mine, and I suck on it gently. She arches her back, lets out a moan, and I pull her closer to my body. I can feel her getting more turned on by the second.

My cock strains against my jeans, aching to be let out and shoved in the depths of Naya's pussy. But I want to please her first, show her how much it means to me that she's agreed to marry me.

I kiss my way down her jaw, neck, chest, making sure to stop at her tits, licking and nibbling her perfect nipples. She cries out in pleasure. I love that I can get her aroused so quickly.

"Callan, please," she begs, and I know exactly what she needs.

I lift up her dress, thanking the Heavens she decided not to wear pants, and shove her panties to the side. "Mine," I growl, my own arousal growing by the second as I relish her scent. My cock needs to be freed *now*.

I unbuckle my belt, unzip my jeans, and release my throbbing length as I get on my knees in front of Naya. Without a second to spare, I rip her panties off, eliciting a gasp out of her, and put my mouth right on her center. She screams, her hips moving in rhythm with the strokes of my tongue. Her wetness coats my chin as I dip it in and out of her pussy, and her taste makes me shudder.

"So fuckin' good. You taste like my future wife."

The harshness of my tone and the sincerity of my words make Naya gush all over my face. I tug on my cock as I ride the wave to her orgasm and she chants, "Oh my God, oh my God, oh my God."

"*La mia brava piccola puttanella.*" *My good little slut.* "Come for me so I can shove my dick far down your throat," I say with a grunt, my balls tingling with anticipation. I have to calm myself down before I come all over my fucking hand.

Naya lets go and comes with a fierce intensity, her clit pulsing on my tongue. "Yes, Callan. Yes!"

I keep sucking on her clit until she is writhing under me. "It's too much, please," she complains with a hysterical giggle. I love when she's in a euphoric state, it makes me want to eat her alive.

"I'm only stoppin' 'cause I have other plans in mind," I say with a smirk. Naya's eyes narrow.

I reach behind the stack of hay and pull out a small bottle of lube.

"What's that?" she asks, but I ignore the question.

"Stay on your back and keep your legs open for me, darlin'," I order as I open the bottle and let some of the clear liquid drop on her pussy. She hisses from the coldness and tenses a little. "Relax, baby."

She loosens up at my words, but still eyes me skeptically. "What are you planning with that?"

"To take what I own," I reply, dragging my lube-slicked fingers down to her asshole. She jolts on contact. "Every part of you is mine, *principessa*, includin' this tight little hole." I let my thumb slide in and she sucks in a breath. "I'll be gentle, I promise. And when you're stretched out and ready for me, I'm gonna fuck your sweet ass 'til it's filled with my cum. Okay, sweetheart?"

Naya's mouth parts, chest expanding. "Yes, King," she says, licking her lips.

I bring my thumb in and out of her hole, paying attention to her body's reactions. After a short while, Naya lets out soft moans, a clear telltale that she's starting to enjoy the feeling of having something in her ass. I add more lube to my hand and push another finger in.

"You're such a good girl, baby. Are you ready for my cock?"

She nods, and I slather lube all over my length, putting the tip right at the entrance of the tight hole. I'm so hard, it's almost painful. The need to explode inside her is unbearable.

Slowly, I inch my dick inside her and the tightness is almost enough for me to come on the spot. My eyes roll back as my entire body shudders, skin erupting with goosebumps.

"Fuck, *amore*, you're so goddamn tight."

"More," Naya says, her tone husky.

"My greedy little slut," I respond, backing in and out a few times, before shoving myself deeper into her. She gasps, but doesn't slow me down. When I'm buried to the hilt, she seems to have adjusted to my girth.

I fuck her asshole at a slow and steady pace. It feels too fucking good, it's almost illegal.

"Fuck, Callan. You're so big."

"You can take it, Princess," I grunt, my orgasm already building, sensation growing in my balls. "Reach down and touch yourself. I want you to come for me again," I demand, and she obliges, moving her small fingers to her clit and rubbing it with urgency.

I bring my head down to her chest and suck a nipple into my mouth. "Oh, God," Naya moans. Her breaths become hurried, her chest rising rapidly. She's close.

And so am I.

"Come with me, baby," I murmur in her ear.

Just like that, Naya cries out, the sound is music to my ears.

Moments later, I explode inside her, letting my cum fill her up to the brim. "Fuuuuuck!"

We take a moment to calm our breathing, our gazes holding. My heart palpitates.

Her big brown eyes burn a mark on my skin that I would wear proudly. I don't see her beauty. I *feel* it.

Naya bites on her bottom lip and speaks up. "I love you, future husband."

I grin. "I love you, future wife."

I'll never get over how much I love Naya. I don't think there could ever be a point where I'd feel close enough to her. I want her pressed against me, on top of me, below me, and not a second goes by where I don't want to be *in* her.

Naya can fight me all she wants—I'll spend eternity bickering with her—but she's mine now, and I don't intend to ever let her go.

Acknowledgments

If you've made it this far, thank you for reading!

The idea for this book was born from our mutual love of cowboys, unhinged criminals, and men with filthy mouths that call us cute nicknames like "Darlin'." What started as a joke turned into a whole novel and we couldn't be more excited to share our Sinners & Saints world with you! Being on our own separate writing journeys brought us together, and we've grown even closer while writing King of Sinners. We put so much time, effort, and love into this book, so we hope you enjoyed it!

We couldn't have done this without the excitement that so many of you showed us throughout our journey. And without the support of the people who made it possible.

To our beloved editor, Jennifer. Not only did you bend over backwards to finish editing this book on our super short time-frame, you made sure that our story got the TLC that it deserved. We will forever be haunted by your 'Physical reactions' comments, but you make us better writers in every sense. We're extremely thankful for all the hard work you put in to make our book the best that it could be. We can't wait to keep you busy with book two and more! We love you.

A big thanks to our proofreader, Stevi, for stepping in at the last moment and polishing up our baby. You have such a keen eye that we couldn't do without! We appreciate how much love you showed us during your read-through. We got the Stevi stamp of approval!

Pia, our cover designer, thank you! You brought our visions to life. From the Sinners & Saints emblem to the book cover, we couldn't have chosen a better person to work with for this project. You are a talent!

To our formatter, Melissa, thank you for your quick work and attention to detail. We're thankful for your expertise and can't wait to work with you again in the future!

Jessica and Nikki, our beta readers, the two first persons to read our story, thank you so much for taking the time to be our last pair of eyes before finalizing the book! Your comments and feedback were much appreciated. We love you both!

To Nicola from Dark Desires Book Box, thank you for collaborating with us on the most exciting part of our release! You are a gem and the merch that you created is the perfect way to celebrate our series.

Last but not least, our Street Team! Thank you so much for being a part of our journey! Your contribution to our release has not gone unnoticed. Your support, shares, and excitement motivated us to deliver the best version of our story! We hope we made you proud.

Again, thank you to everyone who gave King of Sinners a chance.